This volume contains
RANMA 1/2 PART EIGHT #8 through
#13 in their entirety.

Story & Art by Rumiko Takahashi

English Adaptation by Gerard Jones & Toshifumi Yoshida

*

Touch-Up Art & Lettering/Wayne Truman
Cover Design/Hidemi Sahara
Graphics &Layout/Sean Lee
Assistant Editor/Bill Flanagan
Editor/Julie Davis

*

Managing Editor/Annette Roman
Director of Sales & Marketing/Dallas Middaugh
Editor-in-Chief/Hyoe Narita
Publisher/Seiji Horibuchi

*

First published in Japan by SHOGAKUKAN, INC.

*

For the purposes of publication in English,
the artwork in this publication
is in reverse from the original Japanese version.

Printed in Canada

*

Published by Viz Communications, Inc.
P.O. Box 77010
San Francisco, CA 94107

*

10 9 8 7 6 5 4 3
First printing, November 2000
Third printing, November 2001

VIZ GRAPHIC NOVEL

RANMA 1/2™

STORY & ART BY
RUMIKO TAKAHASHI

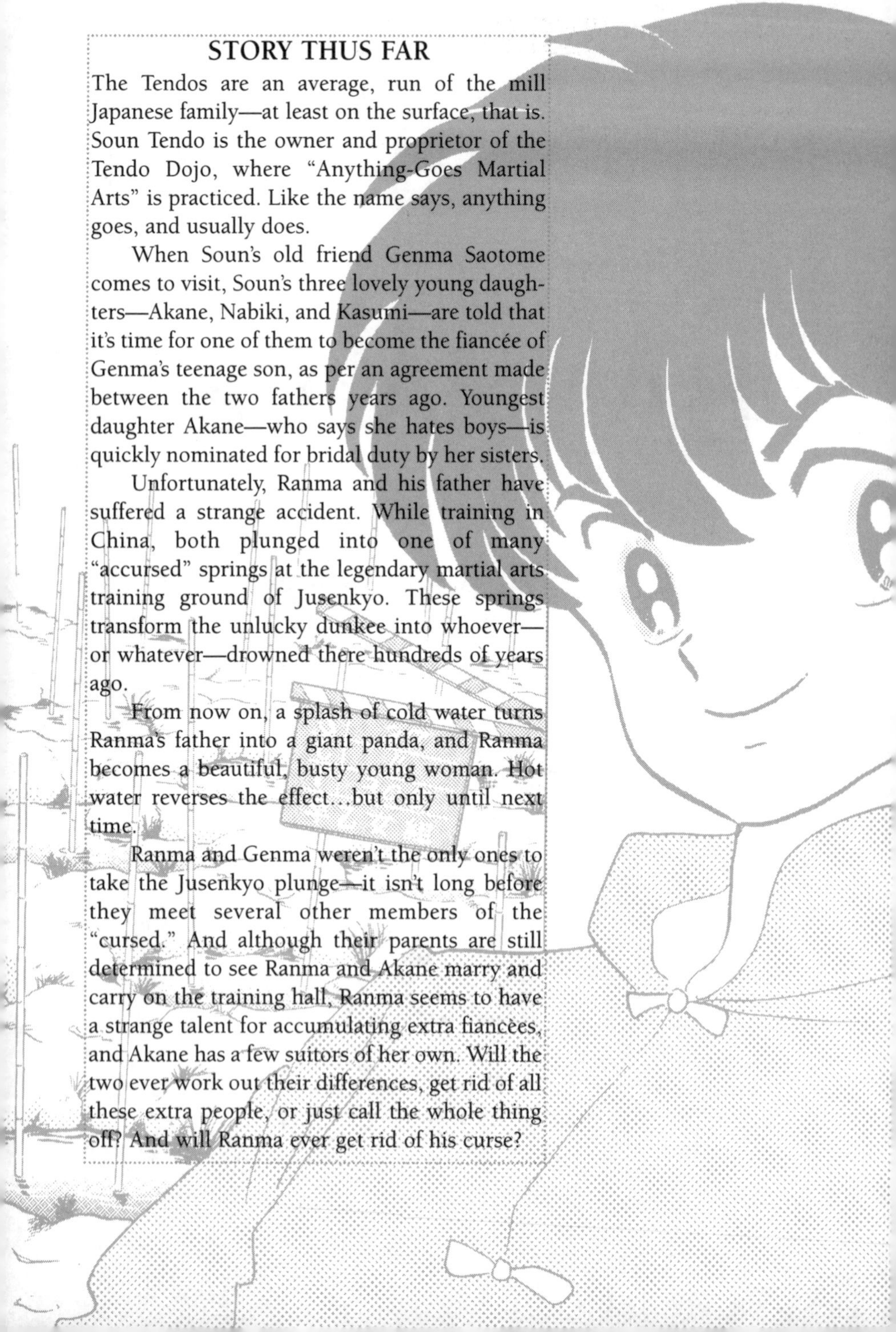

STORY THUS FAR

The Tendos are an average, run of the mill Japanese family—at least on the surface, that is. Soun Tendo is the owner and proprietor of the Tendo Dojo, where "Anything-Goes Martial Arts" is practiced. Like the name says, anything goes, and usually does.

When Soun's old friend Genma Saotome comes to visit, Soun's three lovely young daughters—Akane, Nabiki, and Kasumi—are told that it's time for one of them to become the fiancée of Genma's teenage son, as per an agreement made between the two fathers years ago. Youngest daughter Akane—who says she hates boys—is quickly nominated for bridal duty by her sisters.

Unfortunately, Ranma and his father have suffered a strange accident. While training in China, both plunged into one of many "accursed" springs at the legendary martial arts training ground of Jusenkyo. These springs transform the unlucky dunkee into whoever—or whatever—drowned there hundreds of years ago.

From now on, a splash of cold water turns Ranma's father into a giant panda, and Ranma becomes a beautiful, busty young woman. Hot water reverses the effect...but only until next time.

Ranma and Genma weren't the only ones to take the Jusenkyo plunge—it isn't long before they meet several other members of the "cursed." And although their parents are still determined to see Ranma and Akane marry and carry on the training hall, Ranma seems to have a strange talent for accumulating extra fiancées, and Akane has a few suitors of her own. Will the two ever work out their differences, get rid of all these extra people, or just call the whole thing off? And will Ranma ever get rid of his curse?

CAST OF CHARACTERS

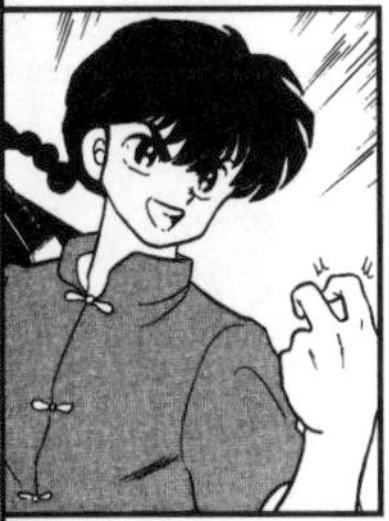

Ranma
A young martial artist with far too many fiancées. He changes into a girl when splashed with cold water.

Ryoga
A martial artist with no sense of direction, a crush on Akane, and a grudge against Ranma. He changes into a small, black pig.

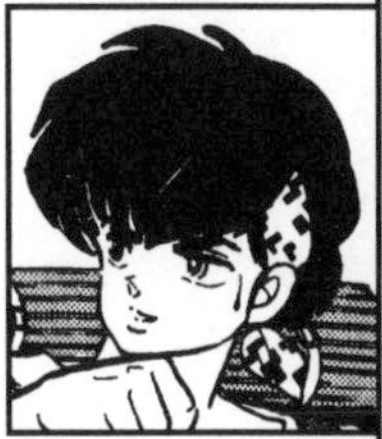

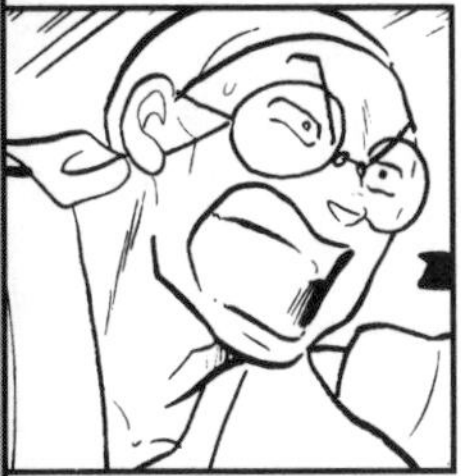

Genma Saotome
Ranma's lazy father who changes into a panda.

Jusenkyo Guide
The tour guide to the legendary training ground and cursed Chinese springs of Jusenkyo.

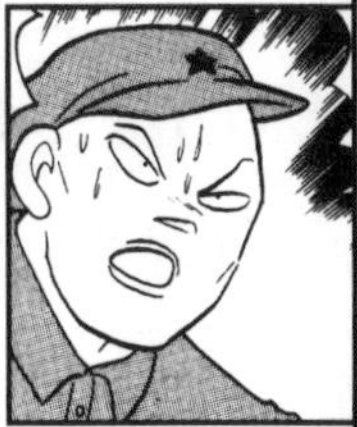

The Tendo Family

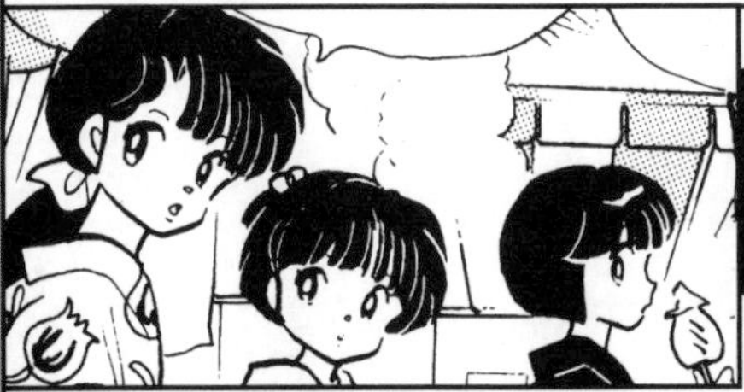

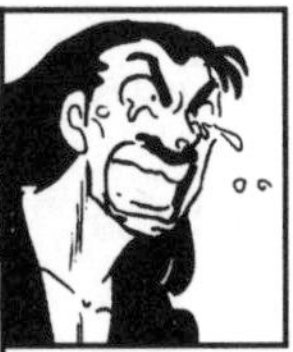

Soun Tendo
The easily excitable head of the Tendo martial arts dojo.

Kasumi Tendo
The oldest, a gentle home-maker.

Akane Tendo
The youngest daughter, a tomboy, and Ranma's fiancée.

Nabiki Tendo
The middle daughter, always out to make a few yen.

Mousse
The boy who's been in love with Shampoo since their childhood together in China. He changes into a duck.

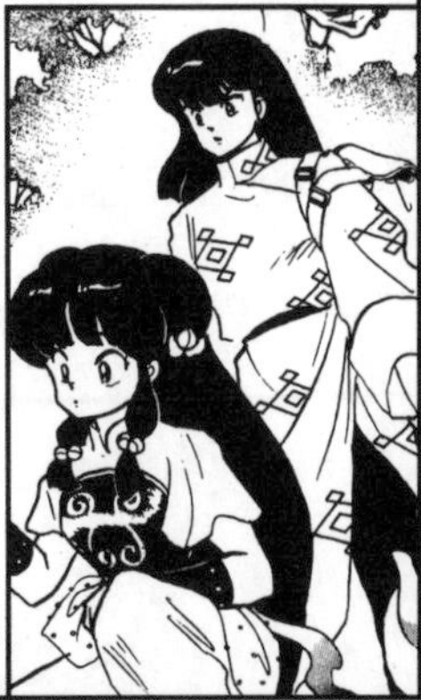

Shampoo
A girl from a tribe of Chinese amazons who is determined to marry Ranma. She changes into a cat.

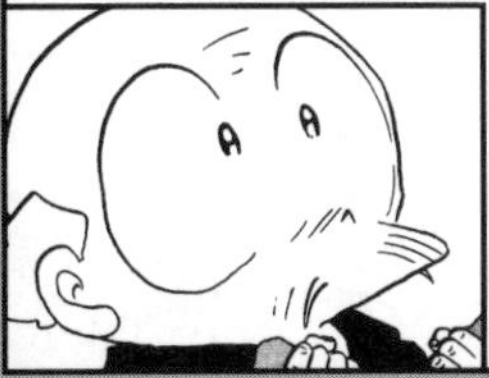

Happosai
Perverted martial-arts master who taught Soun and Genma.

CONTENTS

Part 1

THE CURSE OF THE SCROLL!

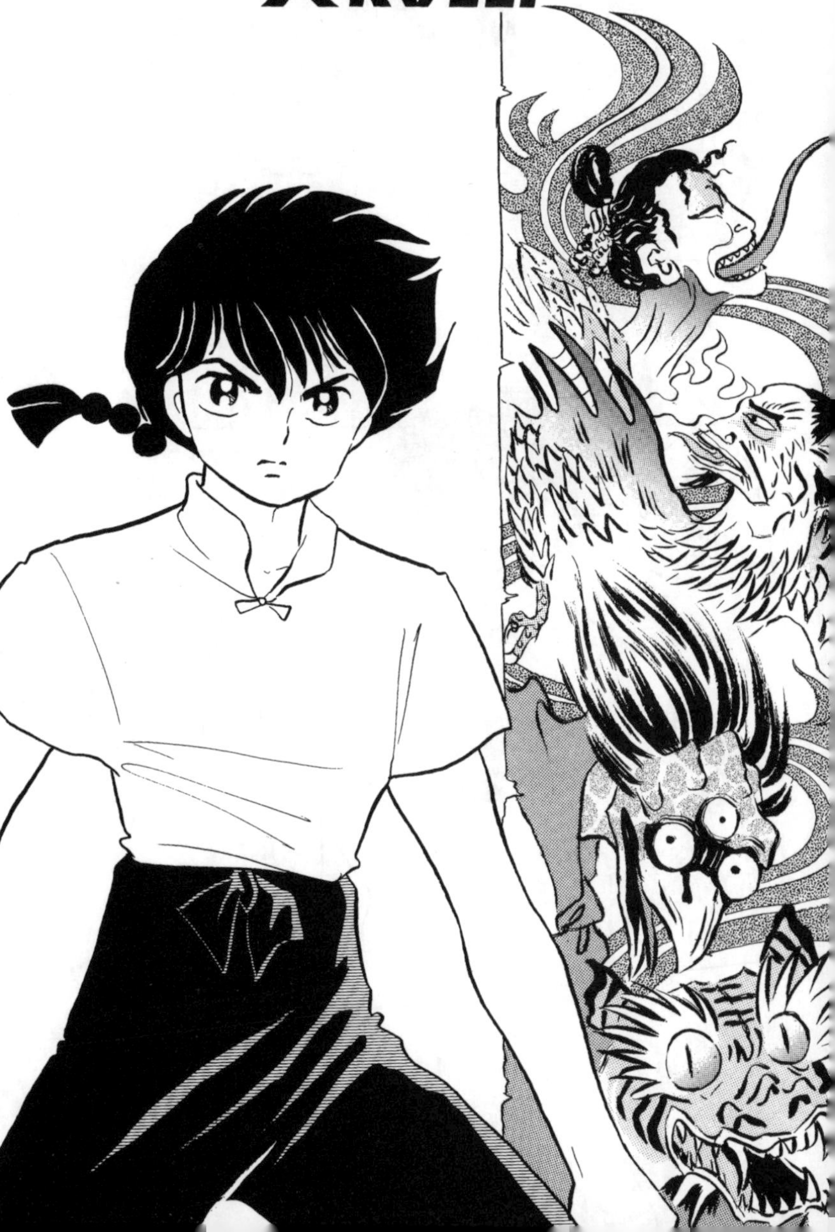

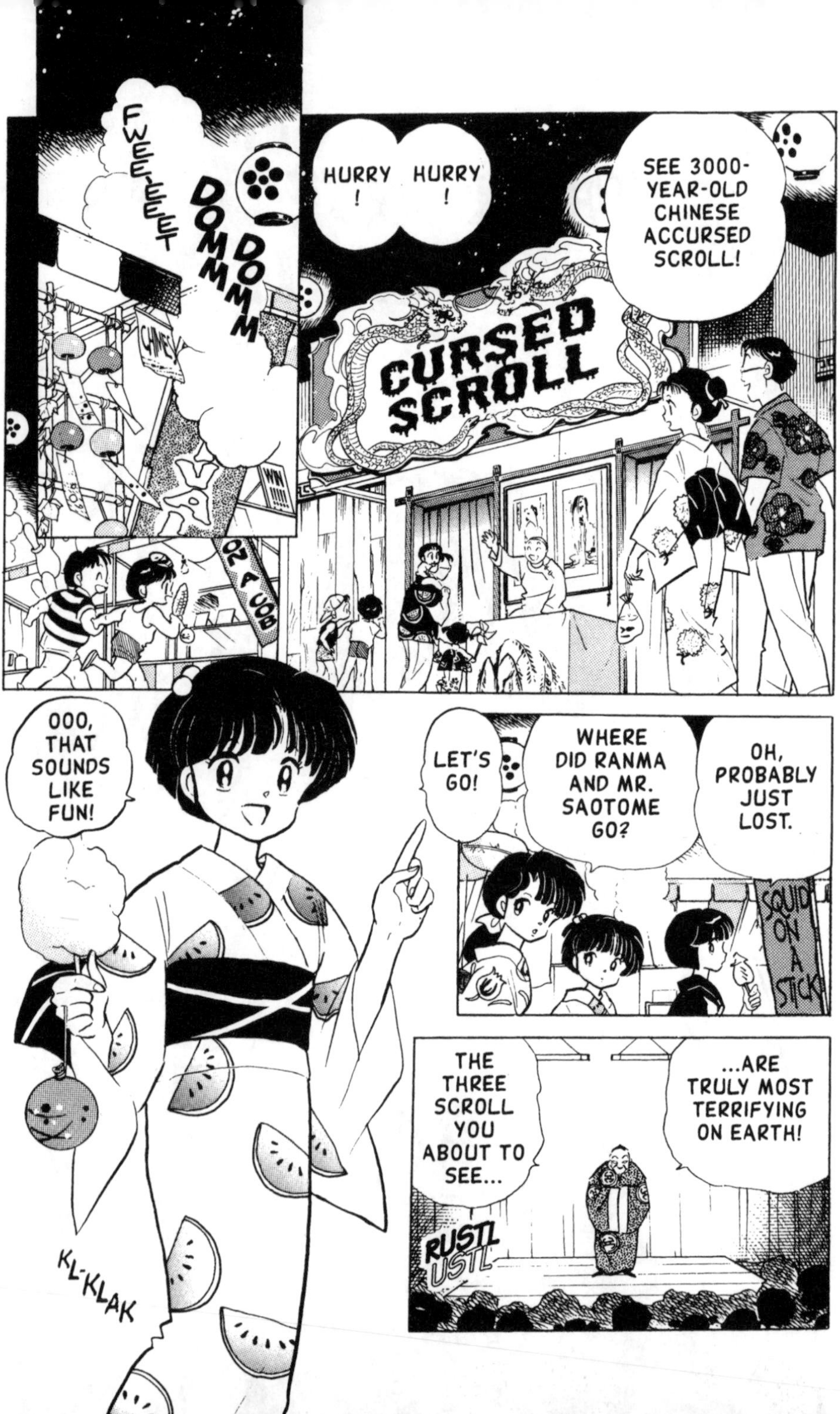
FWEE-EEET
DOMMM
DOMMM
CHINES
WIN!!!!!
ON A COB
HURRY!
HURRY!
SEE 3000-YEAR-OLD CHINESE ACCURSED SCROLL!
CURSED SCROLL
OOO, THAT SOUNDS LIKE FUN!
KL-KLAK
LET'S GO!
WHERE DID RANMA AND MR. SAOTOME GO?
OH, PROBABLY JUST LOST.
SQUID ON A STICK
THE THREE SCROLL YOU ABOUT TO SEE...
...ARE TRULY MOST TERRIFYING ON EARTH!
RUSTL
USTL

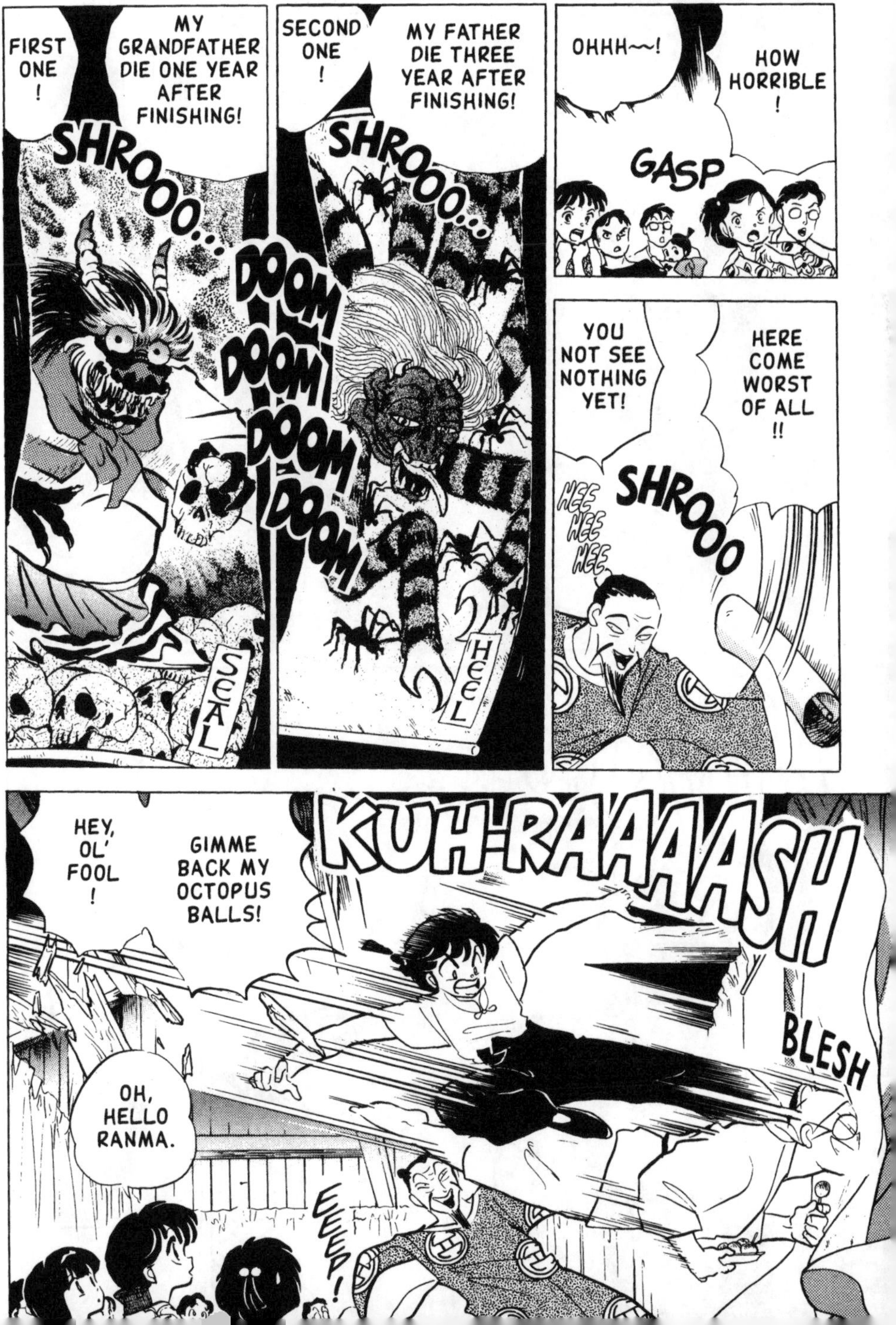
FIRST ONE !
MY GRANDFATHER DIE ONE YEAR AFTER FINISHING!
SHROOO...
DOOM DOOM DOOM DOOM
SEAL
SECOND ONE !
MY FATHER DIE THREE YEAR AFTER FINISHING!
SHROOO...
HEEL
OHHH~~!
HOW HORRIBLE !
GASP
YOU NOT SEE NOTHING YET!
HERE COME WORST OF ALL !!
HEE HEE HEE
SHROOO
HEY, OL' FOOL !
GIMME BACK MY OCTOPUS BALLS!
KUH-RAAAAASH
BLESH
OH, HELLO RANMA.
EEEP!

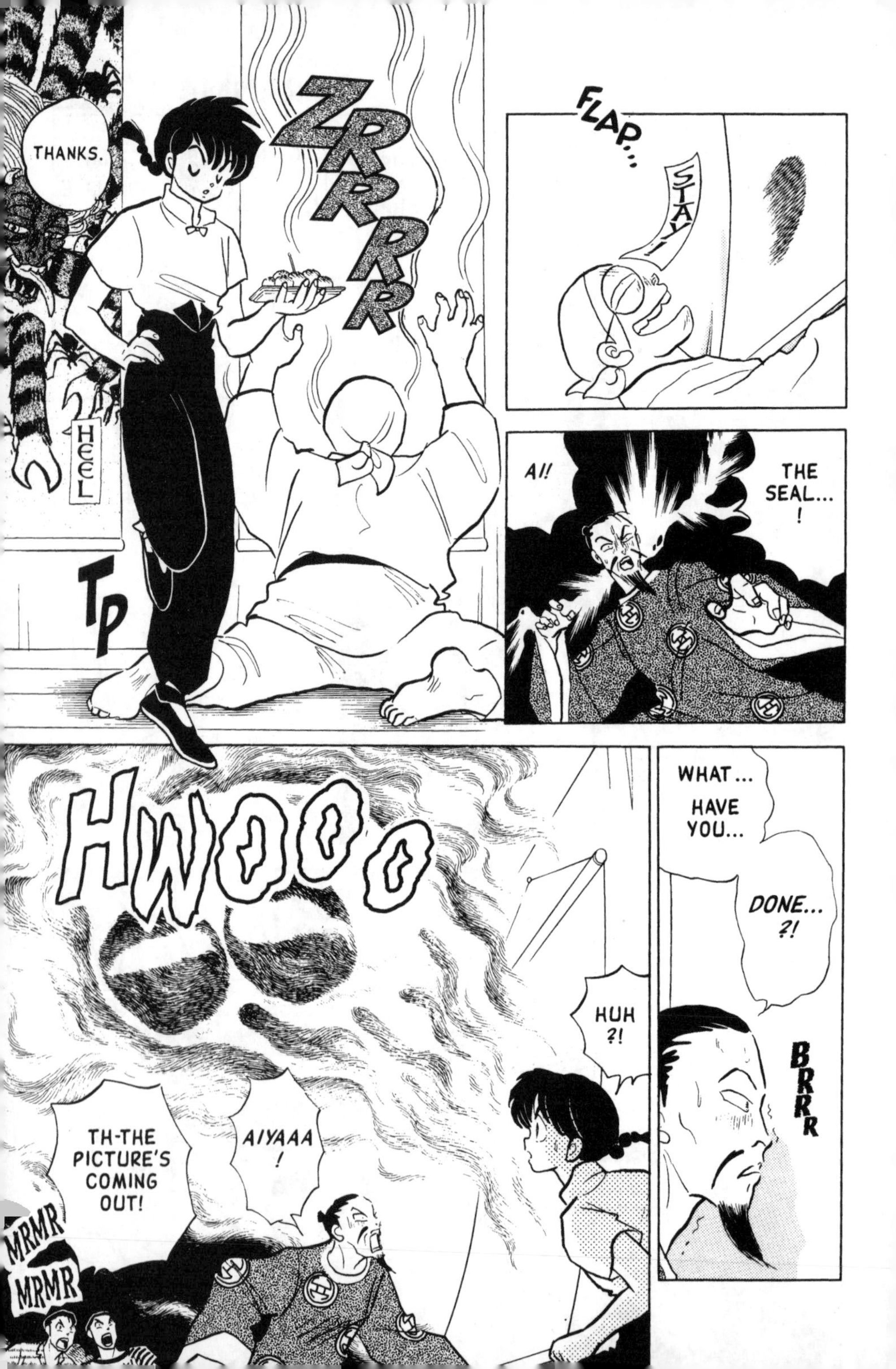
THANKS.
HEEL
ZRRRR
TP
FLAP...
STAY
AI!
THE SEAL... !
HWOOO
TH-THE PICTURE'S COMING OUT!
AIYAAA !
MRMR MRMR
HUH ?!
WHAT... HAVE YOU...
DONE... ?!
BRRR

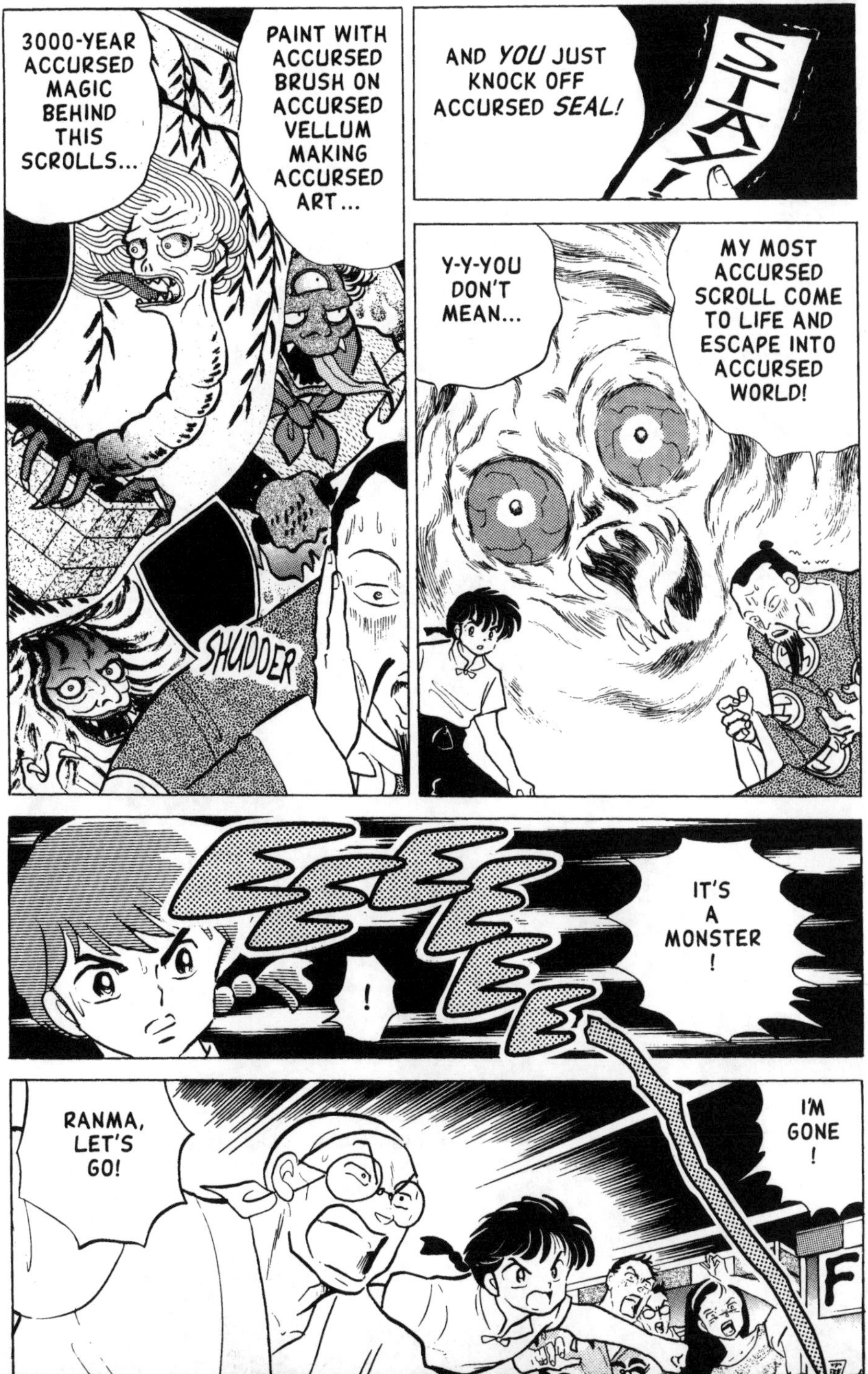
3000-YEAR ACCURSED MAGIC BEHIND THIS SCROLLS...
PAINT WITH ACCURSED BRUSH ON ACCURSED VELLUM MAKING ACCURSED ART...
SHUDDER
AND *YOU* JUST KNOCK OFF ACCURSED *SEAL!*
STAY!
Y-Y-YOU DON'T MEAN...
MY MOST ACCURSED SCROLL COME TO LIFE AND ESCAPE INTO ACCURSED WORLD!
EEEEEEE
!
IT'S A MONSTER!
RANMA, LET'S GO!
I'M GONE!
F

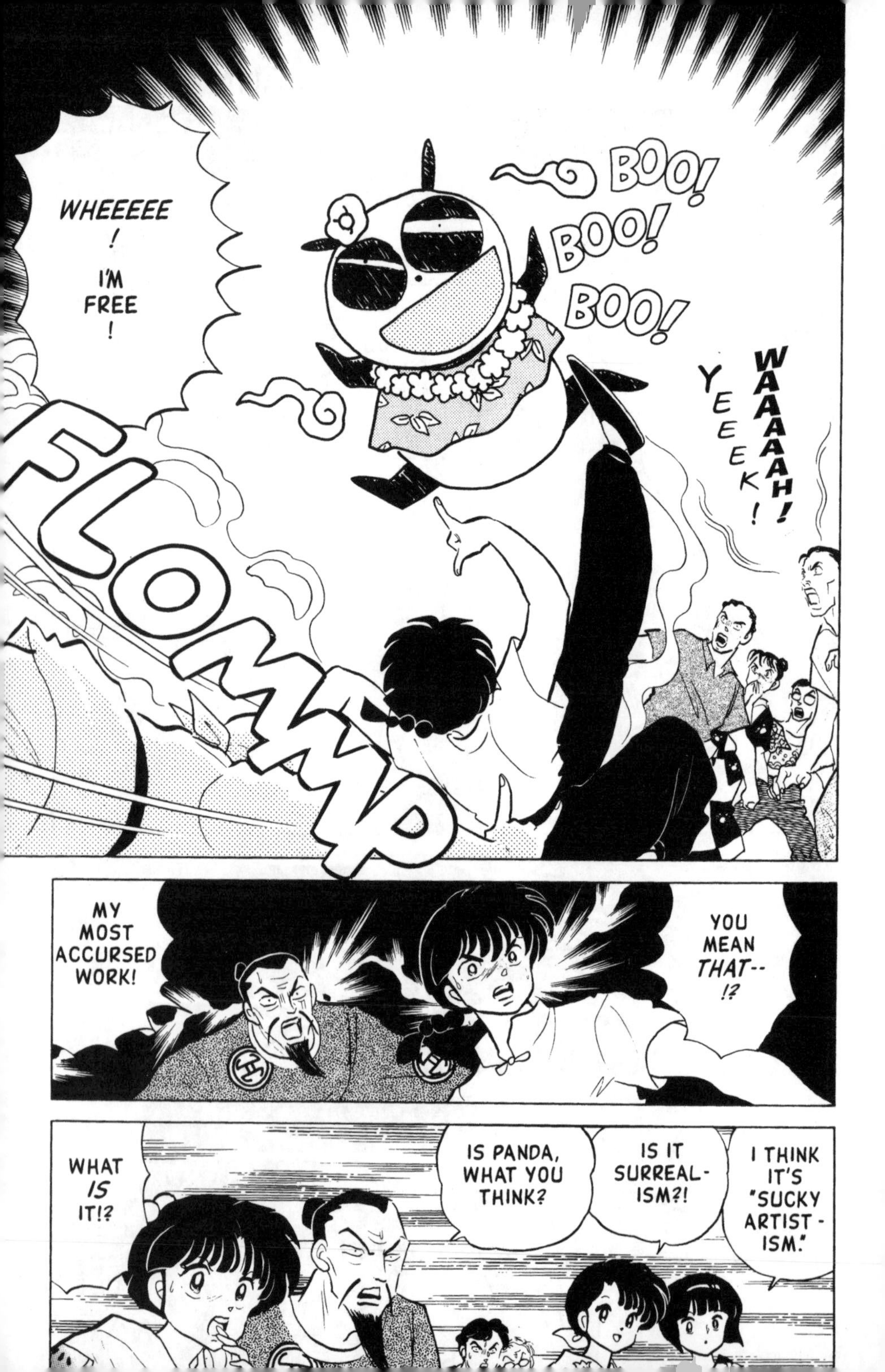
WHEEEEE! I'M FREE!
BOO! BOO! BOO!
YEEEEK!
WAAAAAAH!
FLOMMP
MY MOST ACCURSED WORK!
YOU MEAN THAT--!?
WHAT *IS* IT!?
IS PANDA, WHAT YOU THINK?
IS IT SURREAL-ISM?!
I THINK IT'S "SUCKY ARTIST-ISM."

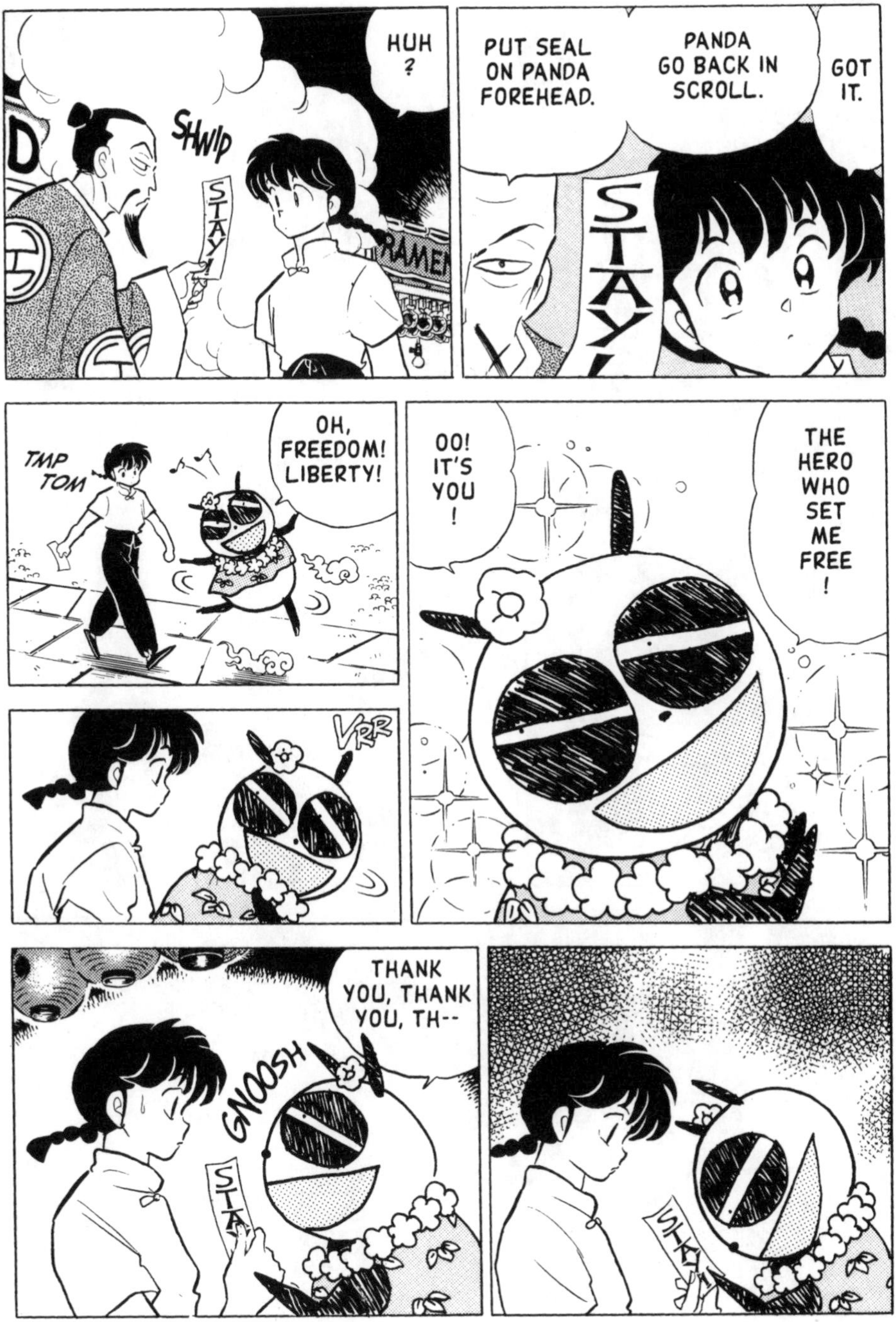
HUH ?
SHWIP
STAY!
RAMEN
PUT SEAL ON PANDA FOREHEAD.
PANDA GO BACK IN SCROLL.
GOT IT.
STAY!
TMP TOM
OH, FREEDOM! LIBERTY!
OO! IT'S YOU !
THE HERO WHO SET ME FREE !
VRR
THANK YOU, THANK YOU, TH--
GNOOSH
STAY
STAY

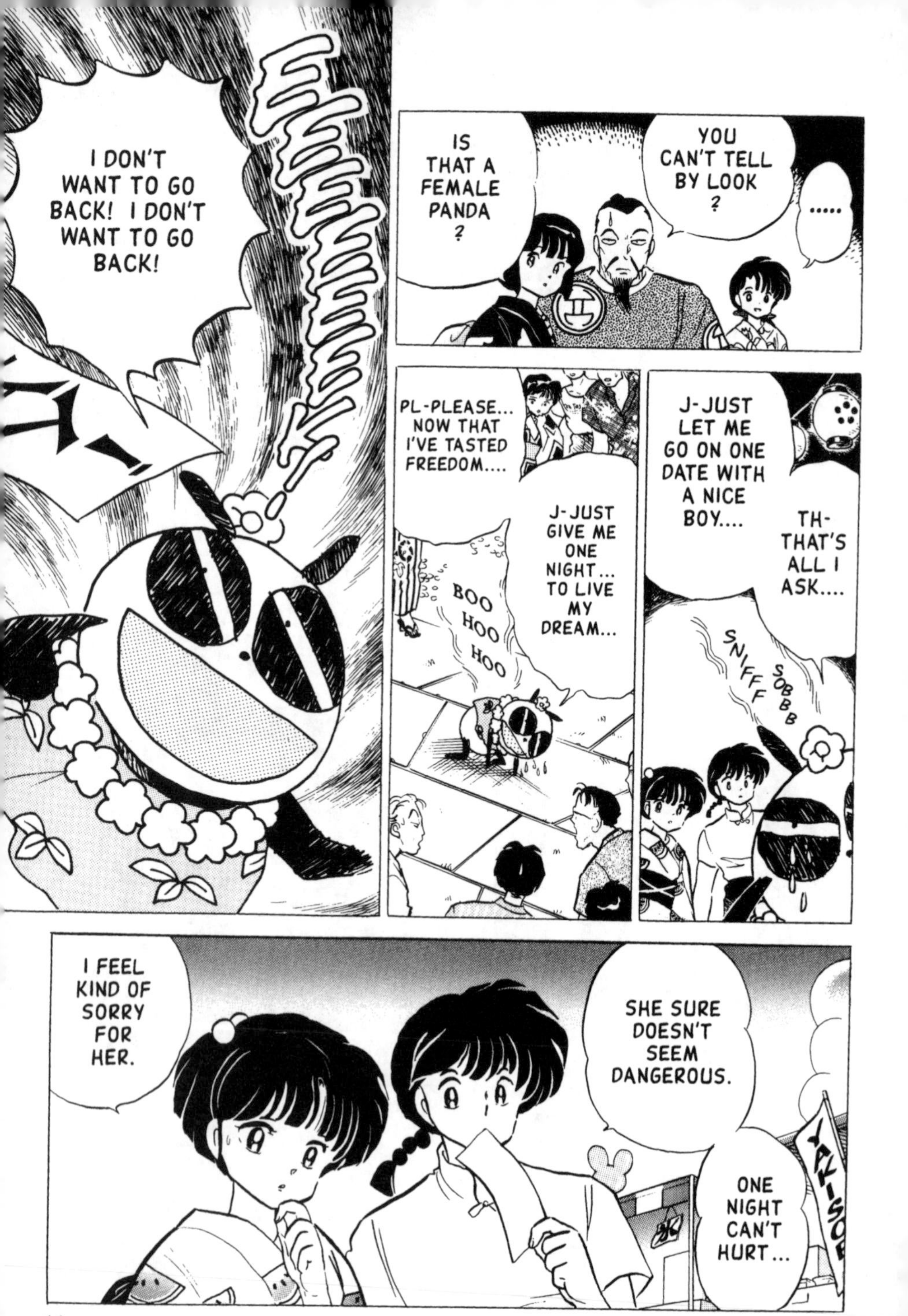
I DON'T WANT TO GO BACK! I DON'T WANT TO GO BACK!
IS THAT A FEMALE PANDA ?
YOU CAN'T TELL BY LOOK ?
.....
PL-PLEASE... NOW THAT I'VE TASTED FREEDOM....
J-JUST GIVE ME ONE NIGHT... TO LIVE MY DREAM...
BOO HOO HOO
J-JUST LET ME GO ON ONE DATE WITH A NICE BOY....
TH-THAT'S ALL I ASK....
SNIFFF SOBBB
I FEEL KIND OF SORRY FOR HER.
SHE SURE DOESN'T SEEM DANGEROUS.
ONE NIGHT CAN'T HURT...
YAKISO

GLUP

YOU'LL GO BACK WILLINGLY IF YOU GET YOUR WISH?

UH-HUH

BLUSH

WHAT DO YOU THINK YOU'RE DOING?

DON'T YOU FEEL SORRY FOR HER, POP?

HERE YOU GO--ONE BOYFRIEND!

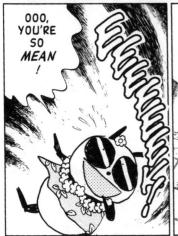

OOO, YOU'RE SO MEAN!

ONLY ONE NIGHT TO LIVE MY DREAM...

AND THEY BRING ME SUCH AN UGLY PANDA...

SOBB SNIFF

GR

TEE, HEE!

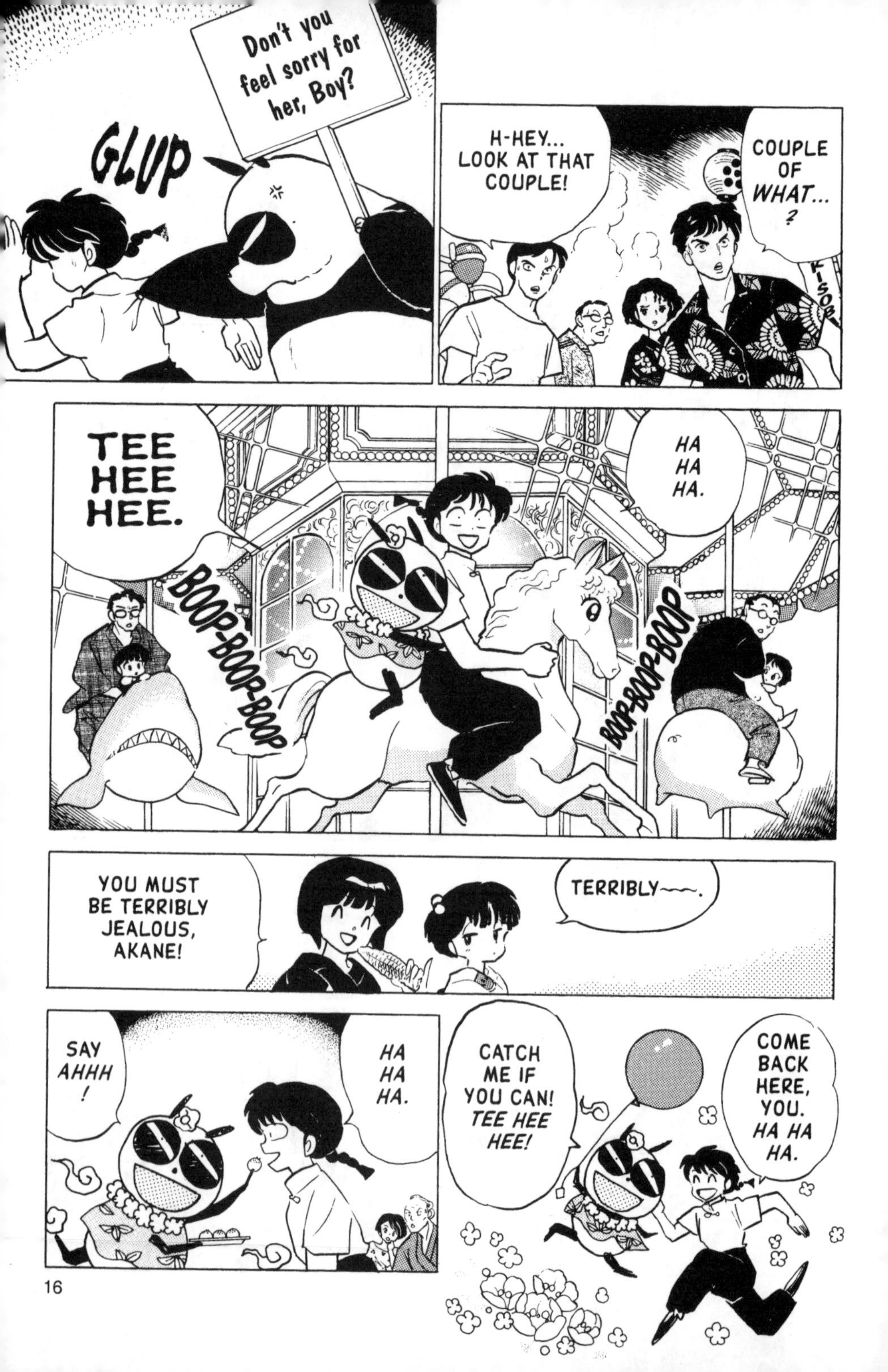
Don't you feel sorry for her, Boy?
GLUP
H-HEY... LOOK AT THAT COUPLE!
COUPLE OF WHAT...?
TEE HEE HEE.
BOOP-BOOP-BOOP
BOOP-BOOP-BOOP
HA HA HA.
YOU MUST BE TERRIBLY JEALOUS, AKANE!
TERRIBLY~~~.
SAY AHHH!
HA HA HA.
CATCH ME IF YOU CAN! TEE HEE HEE!
COME BACK HERE, YOU. HA HA HA.

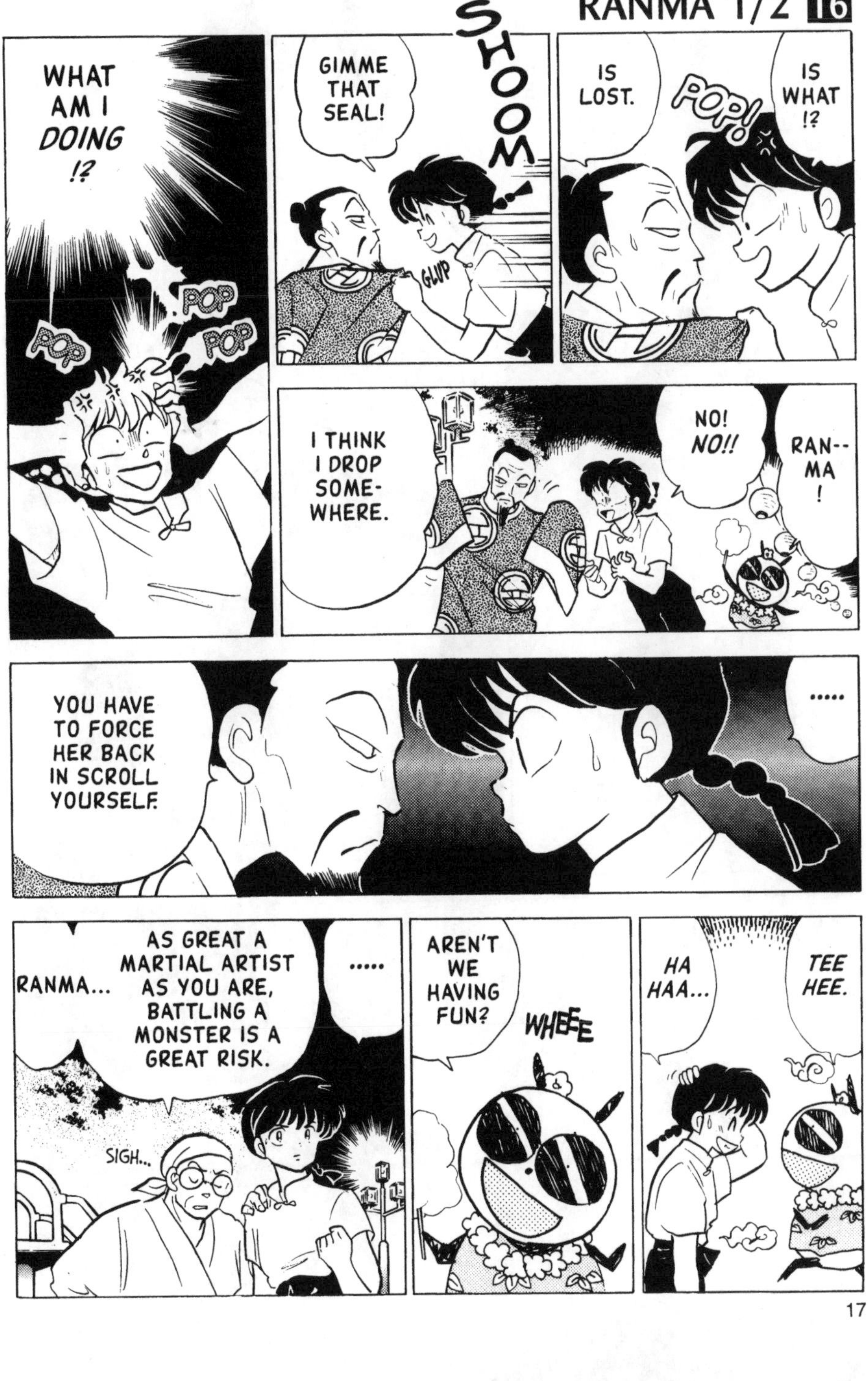
WHAT AM I *DOING* !?
POP
POP
POP
GIMME THAT SEAL!
SHOOM
GLUP
IS LOST.
POP!
IS WHAT !?
I THINK I DROP SOME-WHERE.
NO! *NO!!*
RAN--MA !
YOU HAVE TO FORCE HER BACK IN SCROLL YOURSELF.
.....
RANMA...
AS GREAT A MARTIAL ARTIST AS YOU ARE, BATTLING A MONSTER IS A GREAT RISK.
.....
SIGH...
AREN'T WE HAVING FUN?
WHEEE
HA HAA...
TEE HEE.

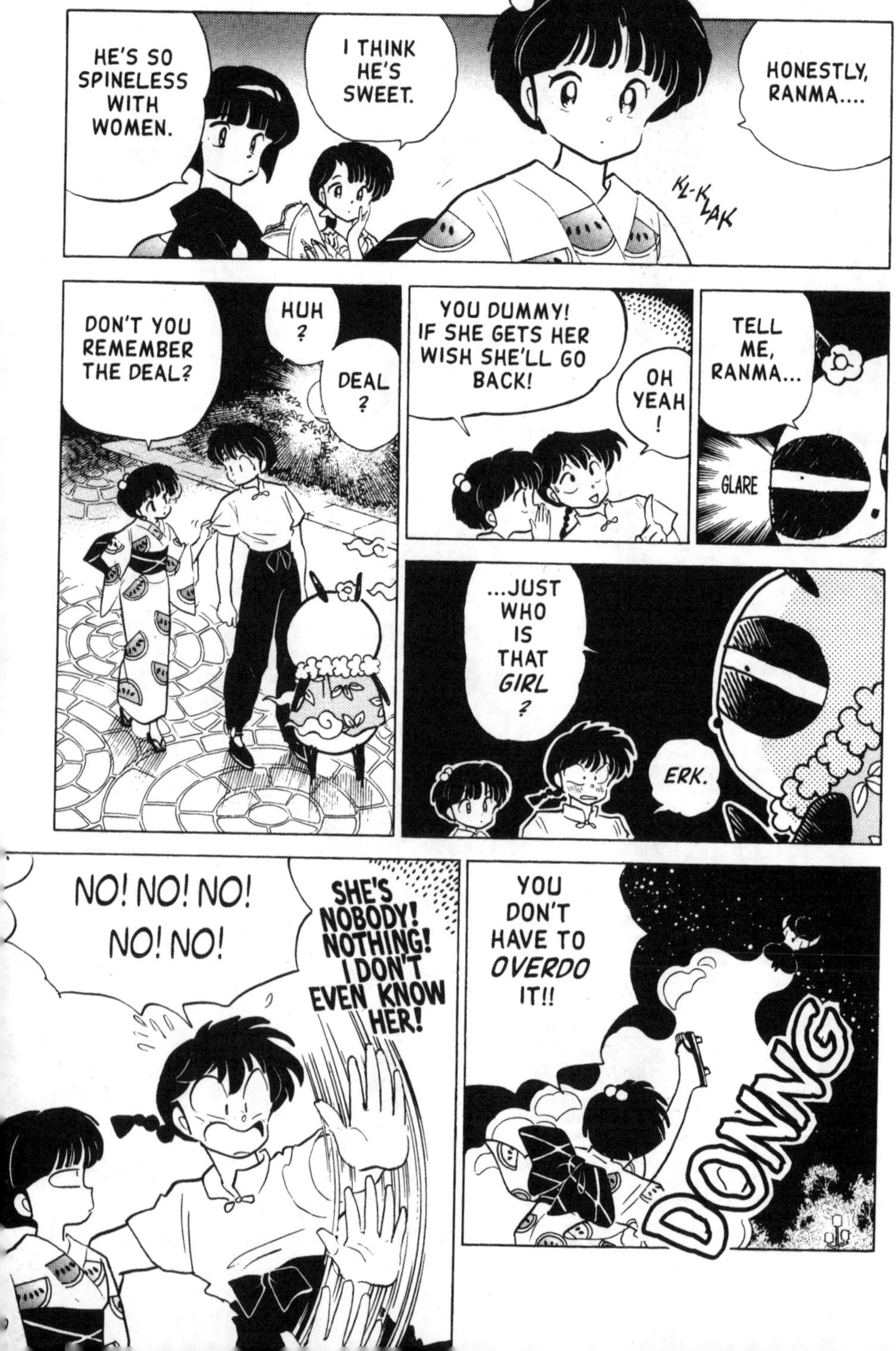
HE'S SO SPINELESS WITH WOMEN.
I THINK HE'S SWEET.
HONESTLY, RANMA....
KL-KLAK
DON'T YOU REMEMBER THE DEAL?
HUH?
DEAL?
YOU DUMMY! IF SHE GETS HER WISH SHE'LL GO BACK!
OH YEAH!
TELL ME, RANMA...
GLARE
...JUST WHO IS THAT GIRL?
ERK.
NO! NO! NO! NO! NO!
SHE'S NOBODY! NOTHING! I DON'T EVEN KNOW HER!
YOU DON'T HAVE TO OVERDO IT!!
DONNG

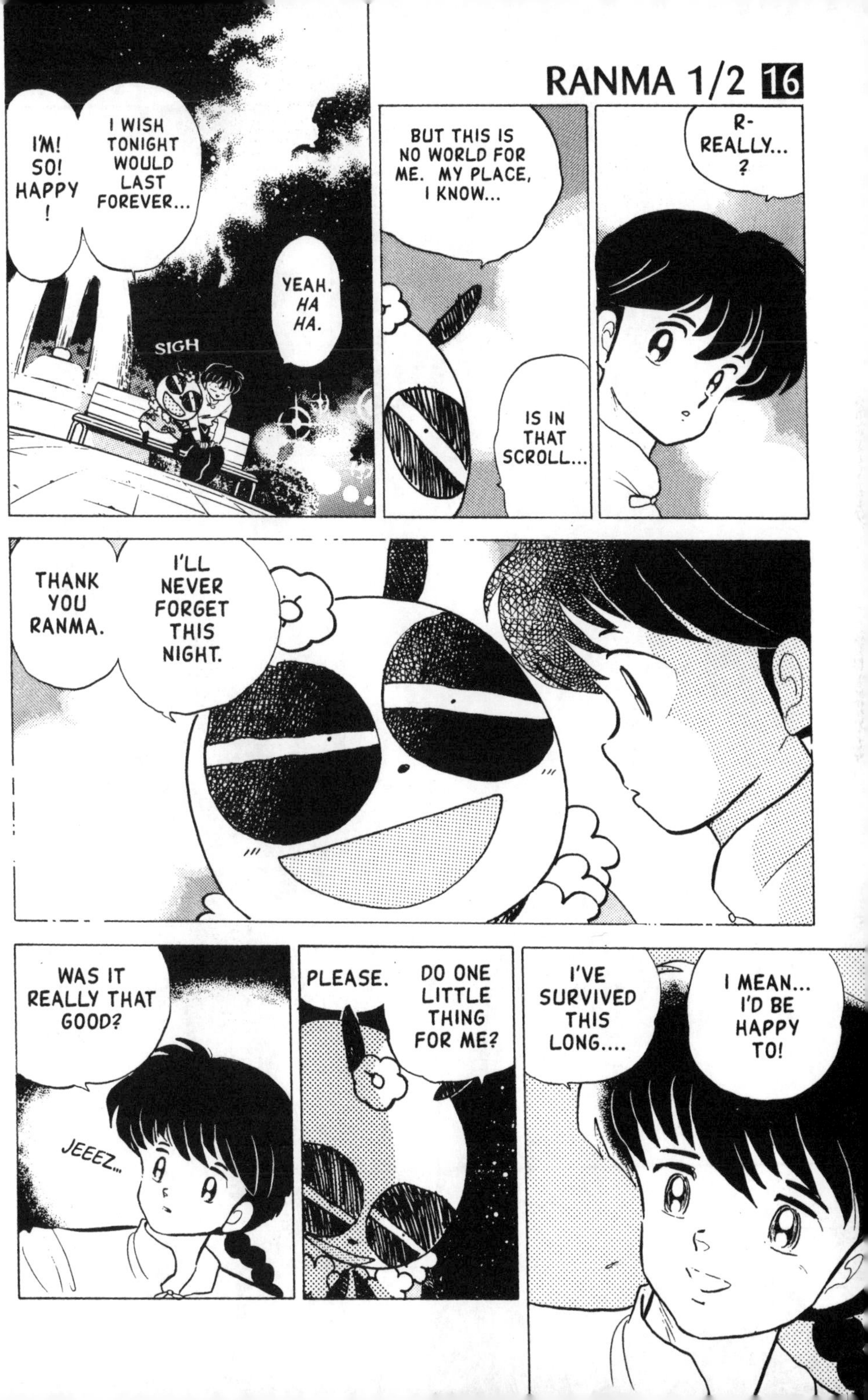
I'M! SO! HAPPY!
I WISH TONIGHT WOULD LAST FOREVER...
YEAH. HA HA.
SIGH
BUT THIS IS NO WORLD FOR ME. MY PLACE, I KNOW...
IS IN THAT SCROLL...
R-REALLY...?
THANK YOU RANMA.
I'LL NEVER FORGET THIS NIGHT.
WAS IT REALLY THAT GOOD?
JEEEZ...
PLEASE.
DO ONE LITTLE THING FOR ME?
I'VE SURVIVED THIS LONG....
I MEAN... I'D BE HAPPY TO!

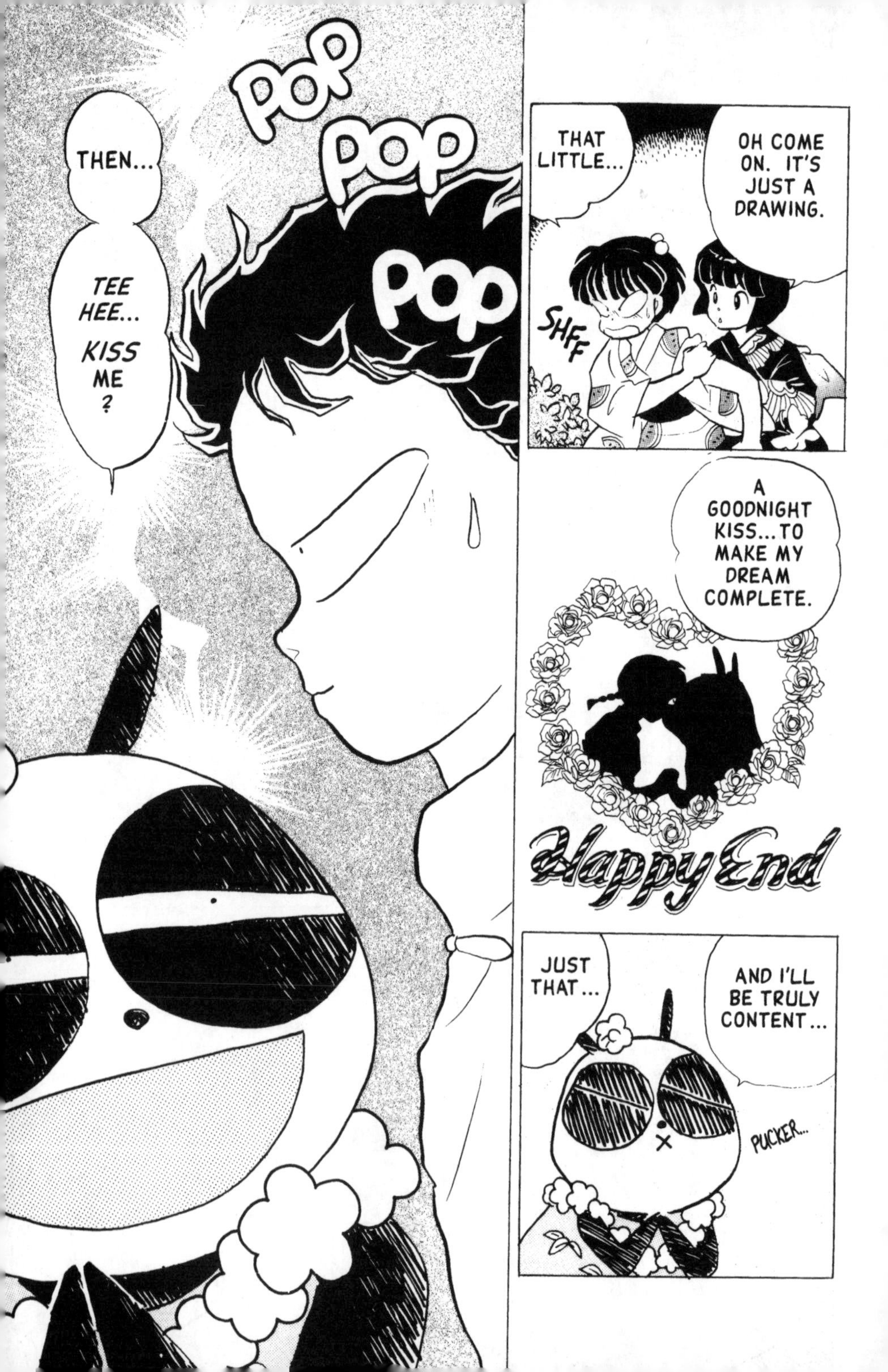
THEN...
POP
POP
TEE HEE... KISS ME?
POP
THAT LITTLE...
OH COME ON. IT'S JUST A DRAWING.
SHFF
A GOODNIGHT KISS...TO MAKE MY DREAM COMPLETE.
Happy End
JUST THAT...
AND I'LL BE TRULY CONTENT...
PUCKER...

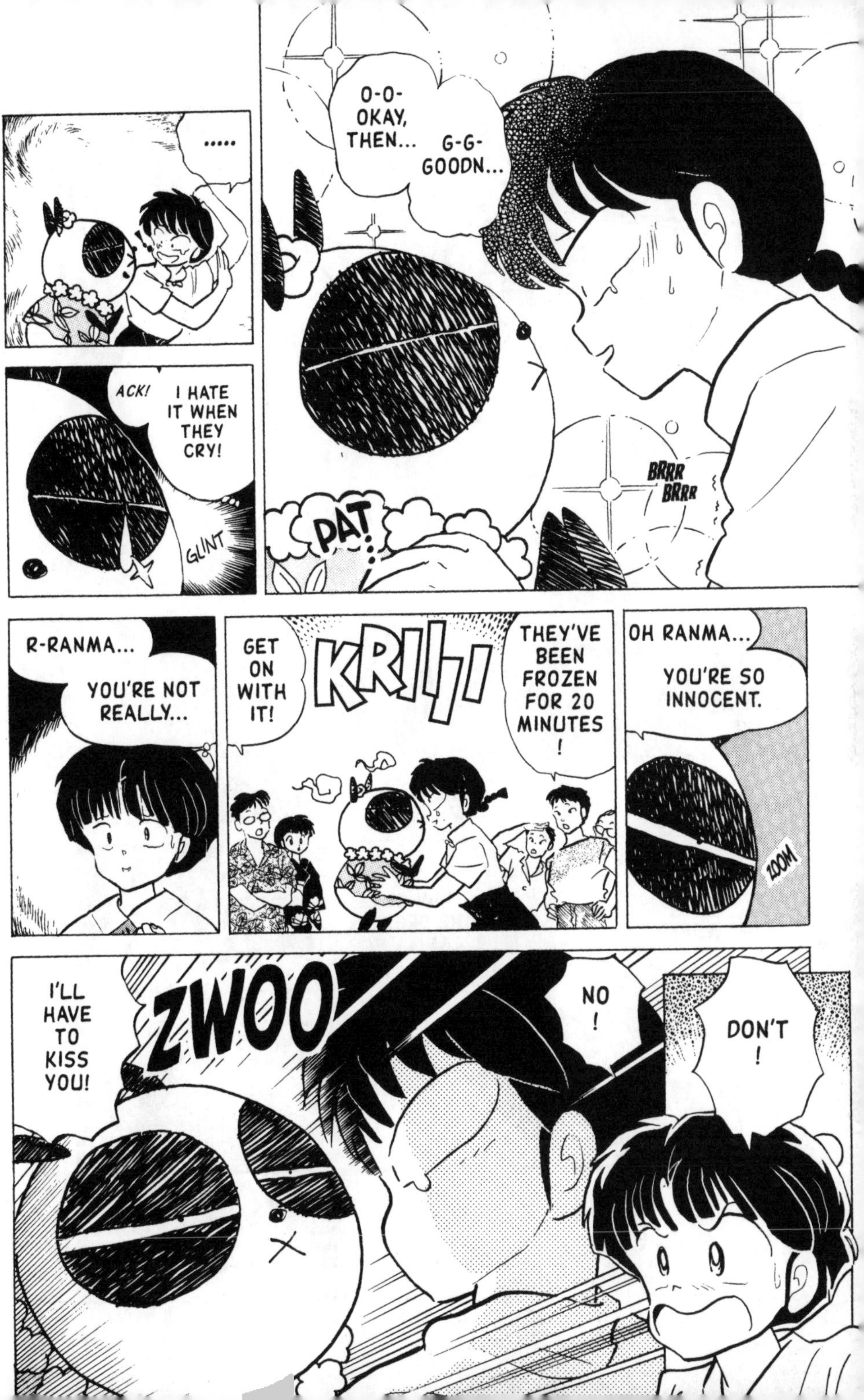
.....
ACK!
I HATE IT WHEN THEY CRY!
GLINT
O-O-OKAY, THEN...
G-G-GOODN...
BRRR BRRR
PAT
R-RANMA...
YOU'RE NOT REALLY...
GET ON WITH IT!
KRIIII
THEY'VE BEEN FROZEN FOR 20 MINUTES!
OH RANMA...
YOU'RE SO INNOCENT.
ZOOM
I'LL HAVE TO KISS YOU!
ZWOO
NO!
DON'T!

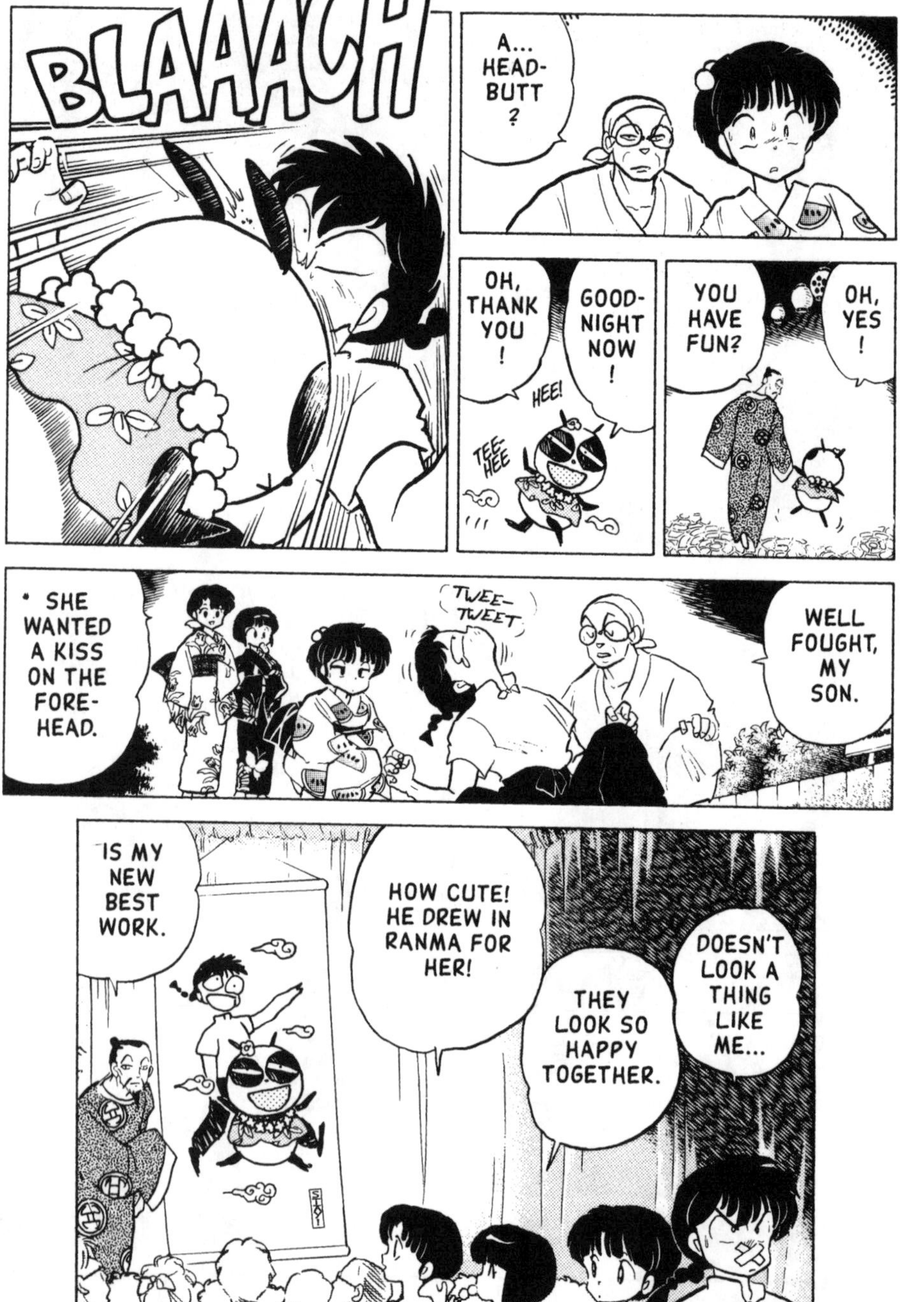
BLAAACH
A... HEAD-BUTT?
OH, THANK YOU!
GOOD-NIGHT NOW!
HEE!
TEE-HEE
YOU HAVE FUN?
OH, YES!
* SHE WANTED A KISS ON THE FOREHEAD.
(TWEE-TWEET)
WELL FOUGHT, MY SON.
IS MY NEW BEST WORK.
HOW CUTE! HE DREW IN RANMA FOR HER!
THEY LOOK SO HAPPY TOGETHER.
DOESN'T LOOK A THING LIKE ME...

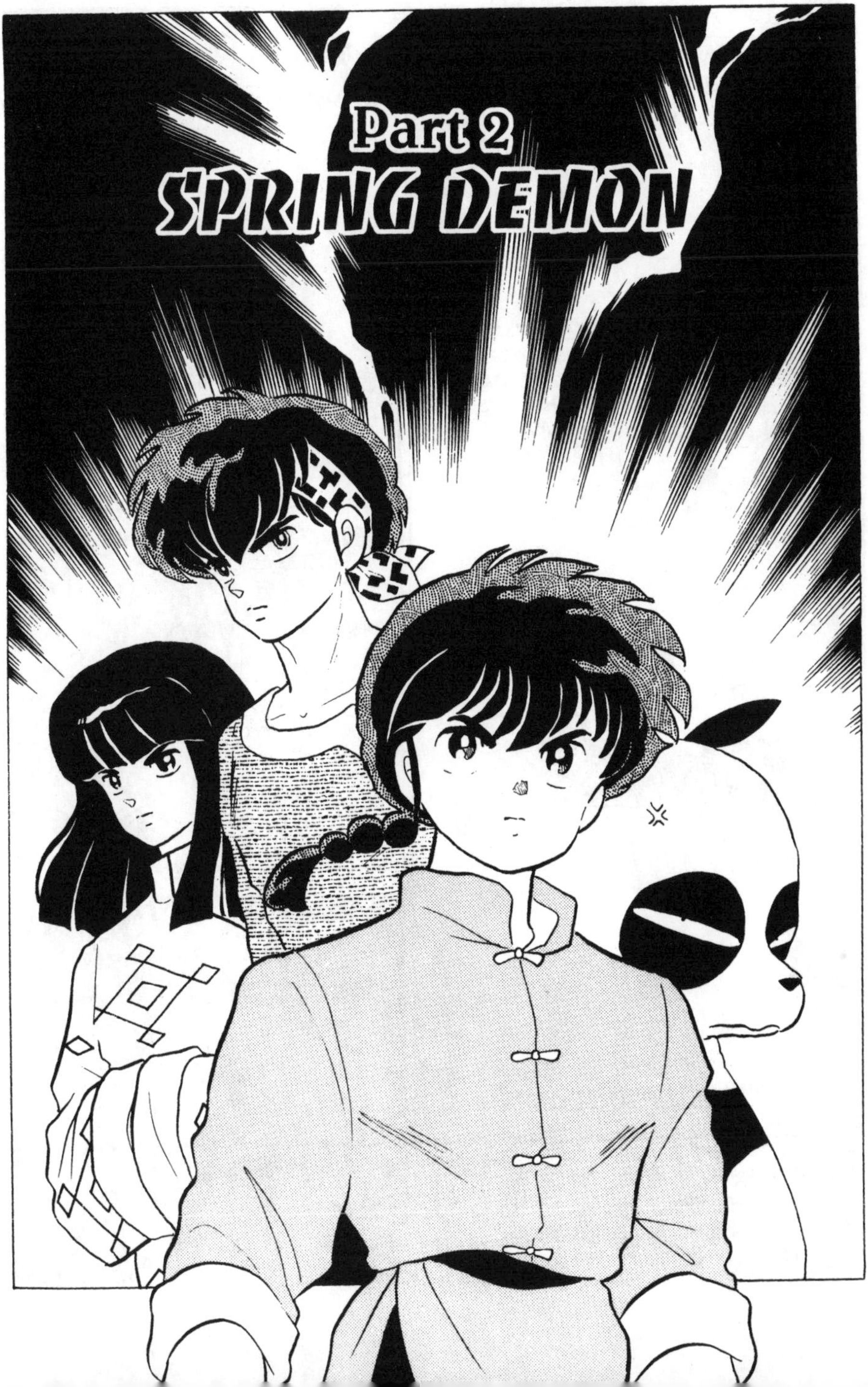
Part 2
SPRING DEMON

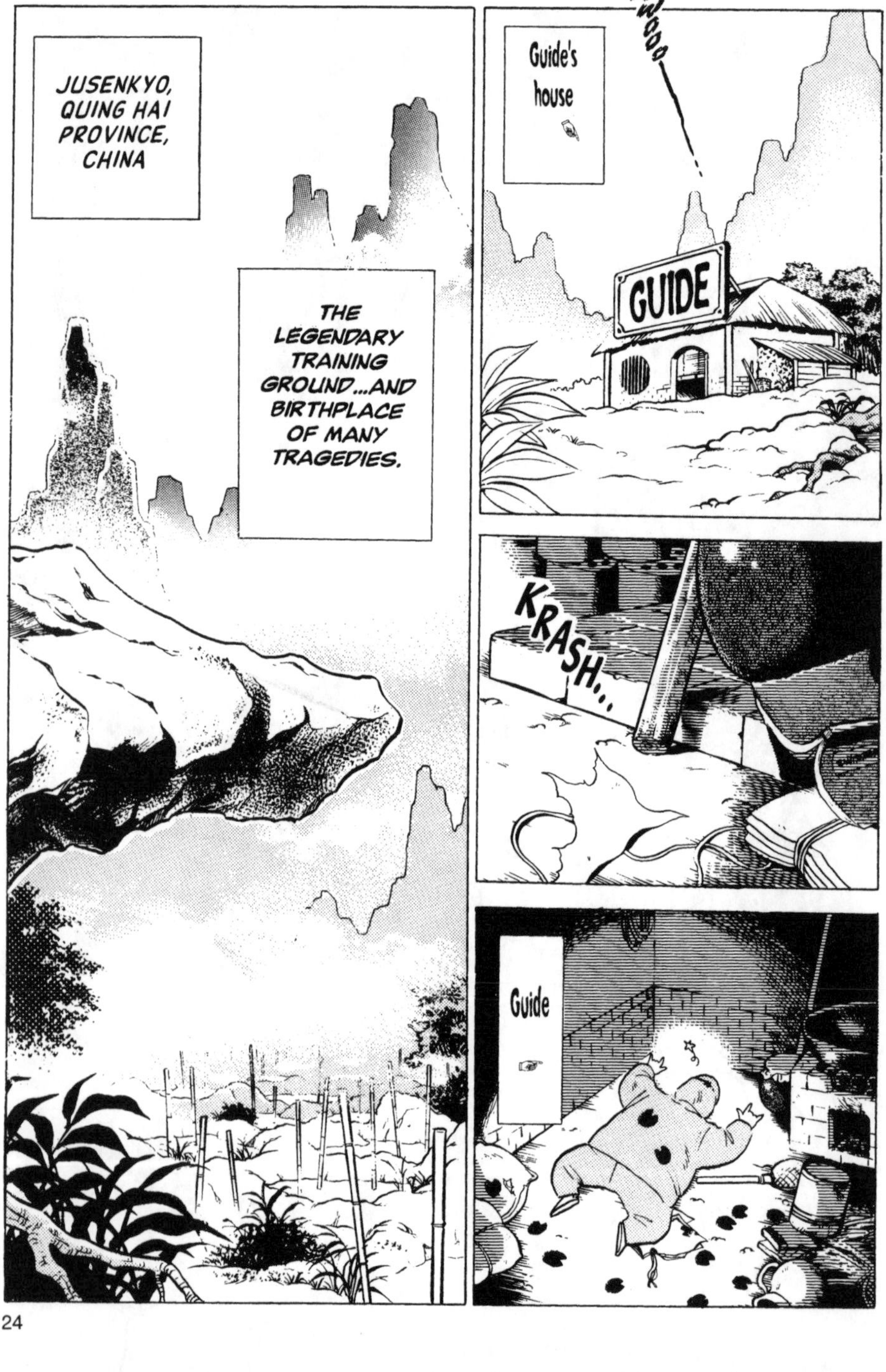
JUSENKYO, QUING HAI PROVINCE, CHINA
THE LEGENDARY TRAINING GROUND...AND BIRTHPLACE OF MANY TRAGEDIES.
HWOOO
Guide's house
GUIDE
KRASH...
Guide

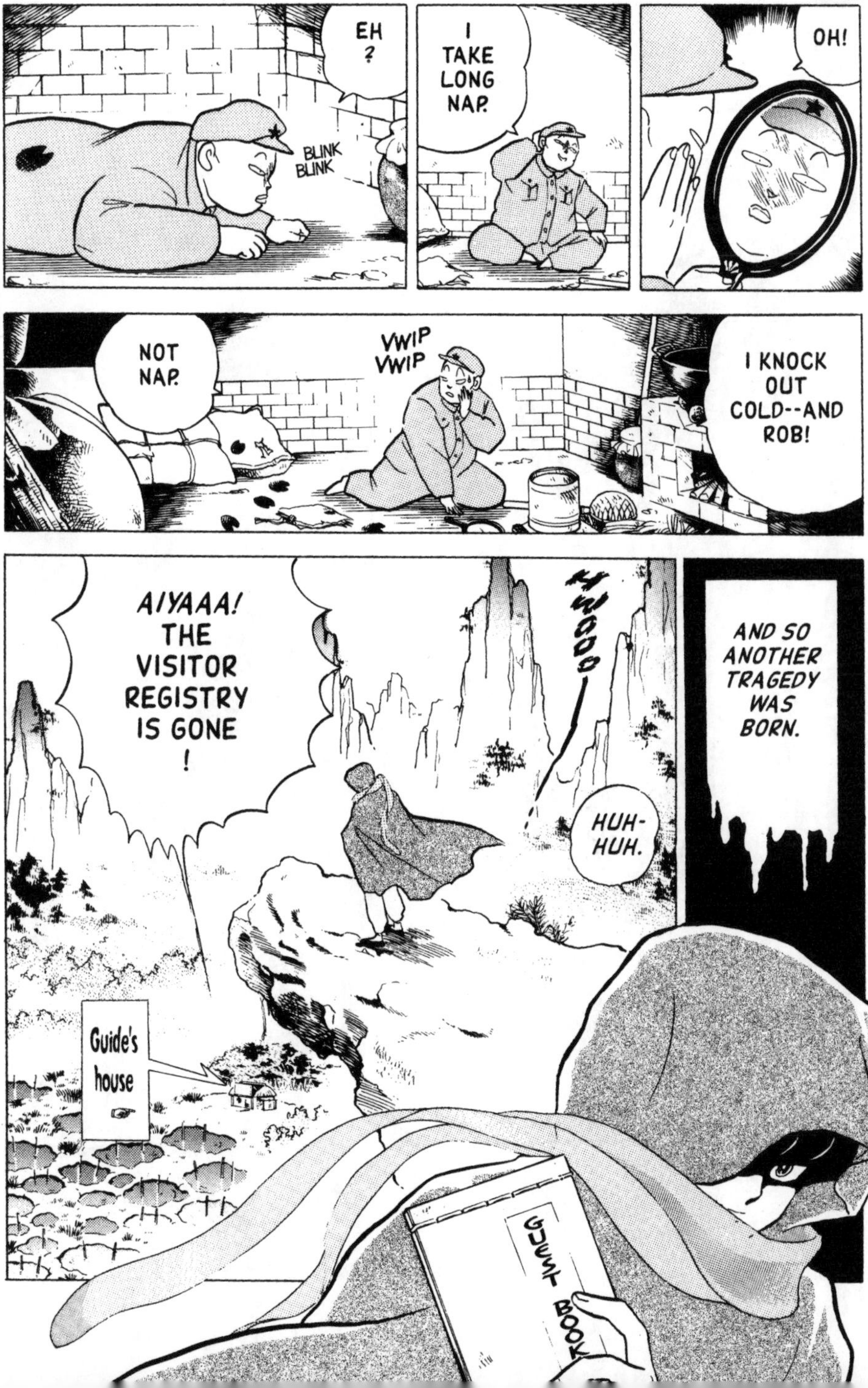
EH ?
BLINK BLINK
I TAKE LONG NAP.
OH!
NOT NAP.
VWIP VWIP
I KNOCK OUT COLD--AND ROB!
AIYAAA! THE VISITOR REGISTRY IS GONE !
HWOOO
HUH-HUH.
AND SO ANOTHER TRAGEDY WAS BORN.
Guide's house
GUEST BOOK

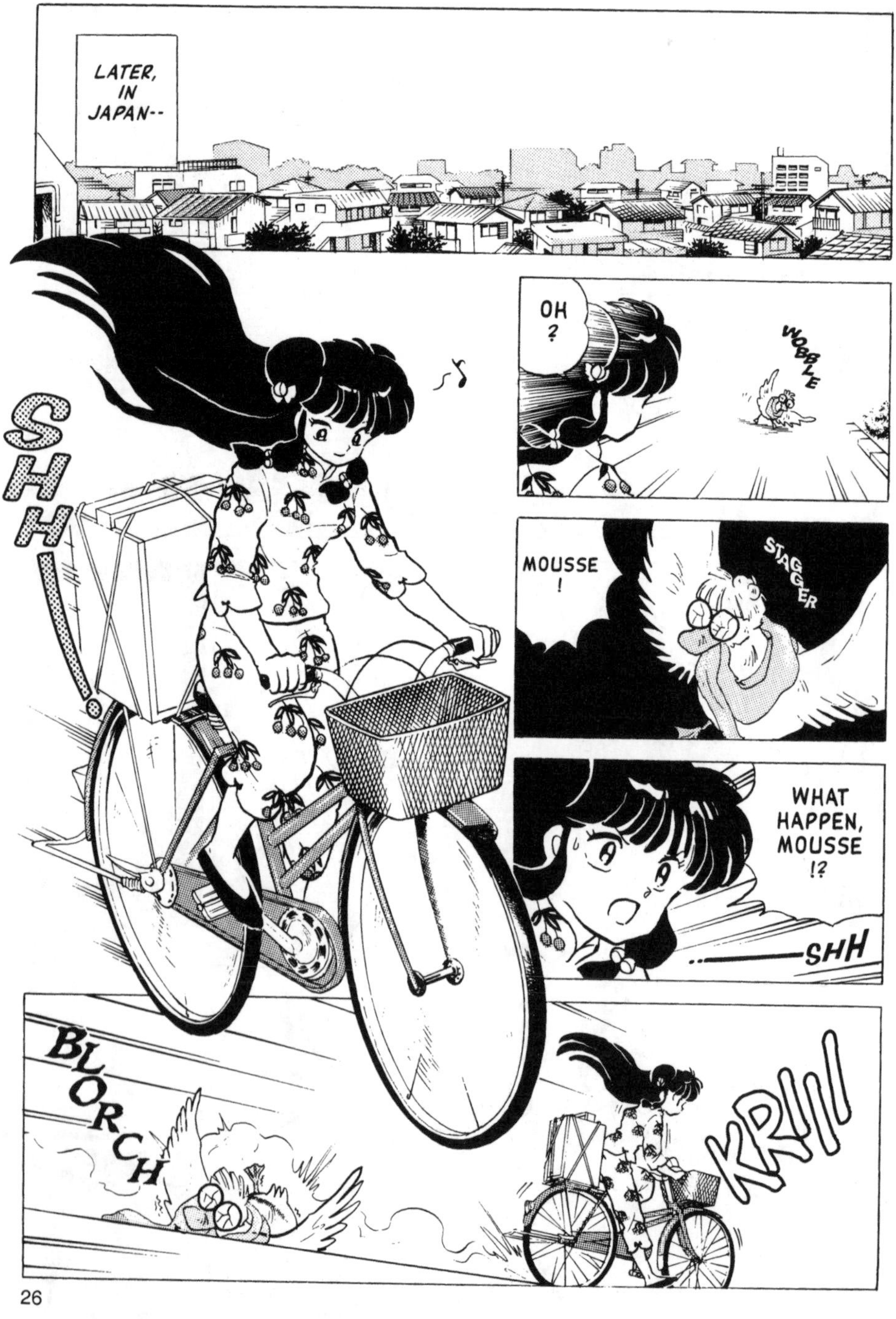
LATER, IN JAPAN--
SHH!!
OH ?
WOBBLE
MOUSSE !
STAGGER
WHAT HAPPEN, MOUSSE !?
SHH
BLORCH
KRIII

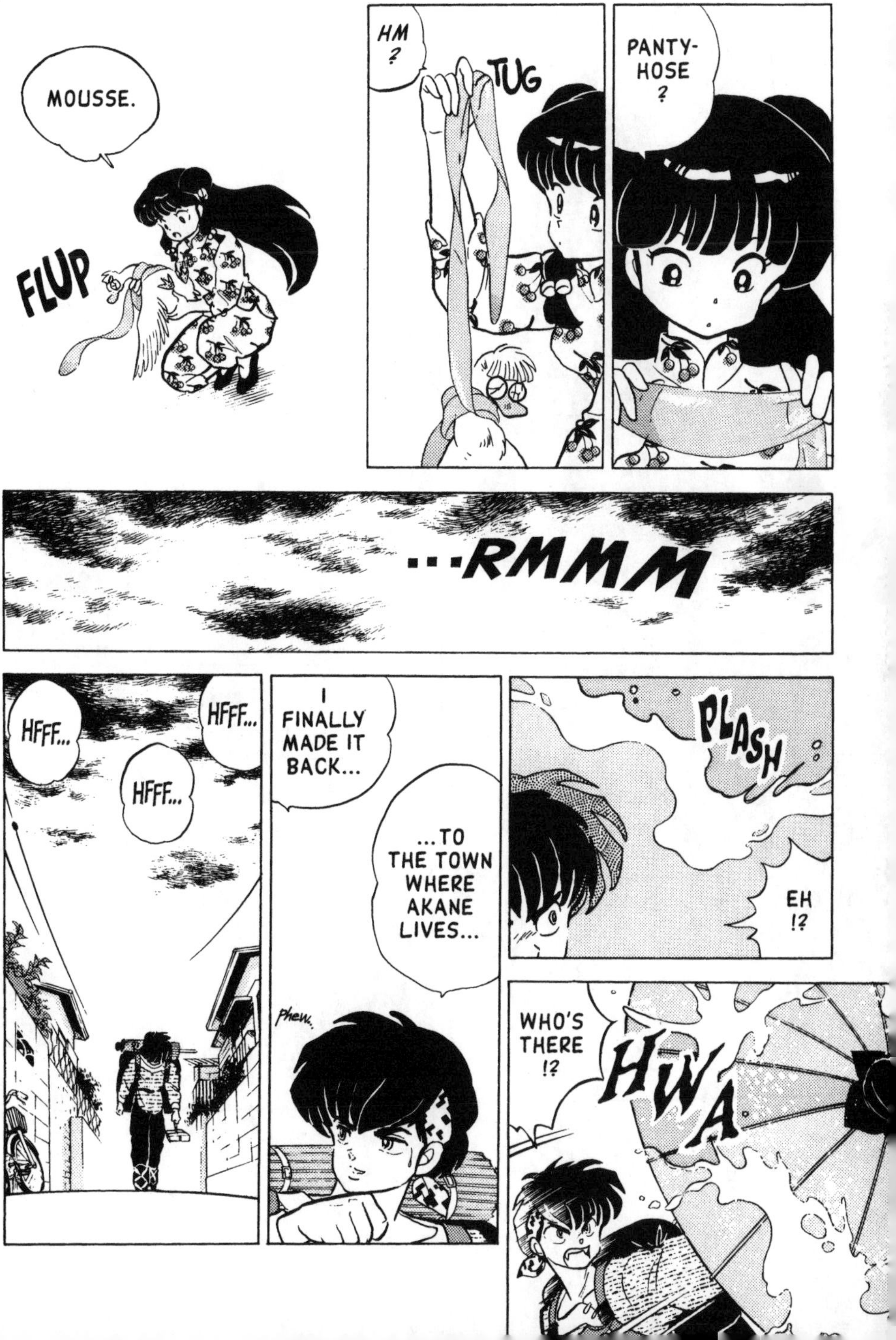
MOUSSE.
FLUP
HM ?
TUG
PANTY-HOSE ?
...RMMM
HFFF...
HFFF...
HFFF...
I FINALLY MADE IT BACK...
...TO THE TOWN WHERE AKANE LIVES...
phew.
PLASH
EH !?
WHO'S THERE !?
HWA

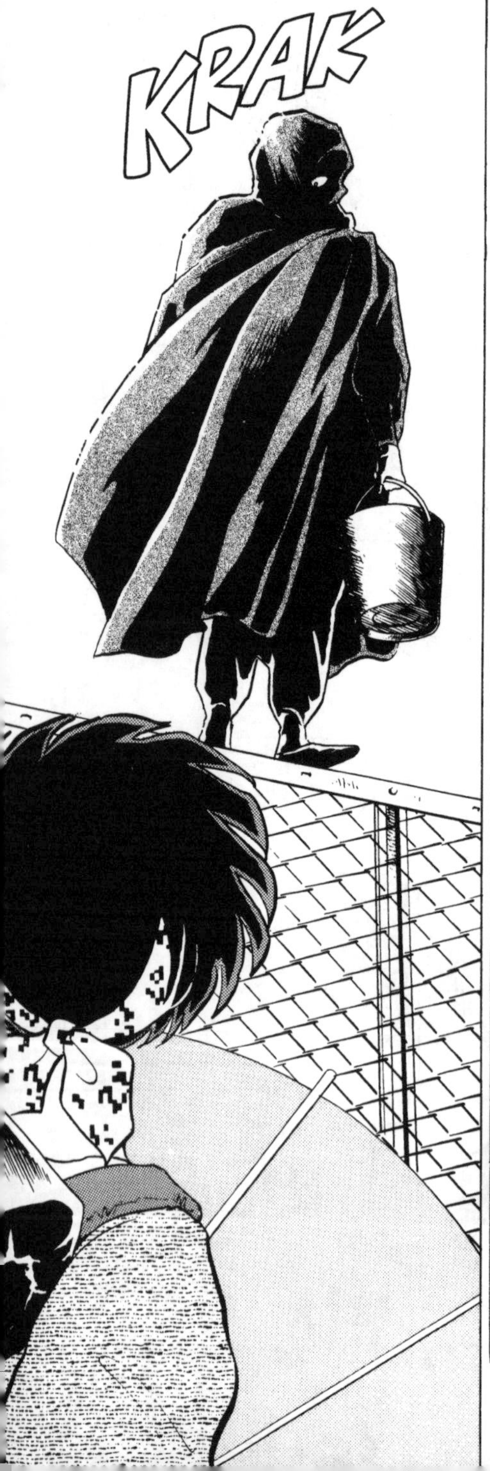
KRAK

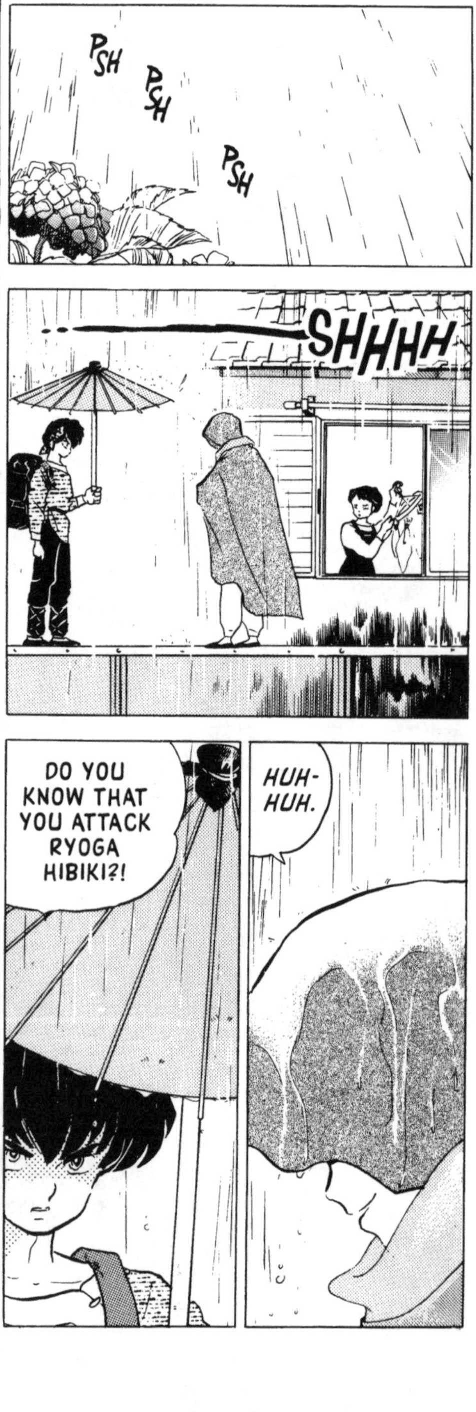
PSH
PSH
PSH
SHHHH
DO YOU KNOW THAT YOU ATTACK RYOGA HIBIKI?!
HUH-HUH.

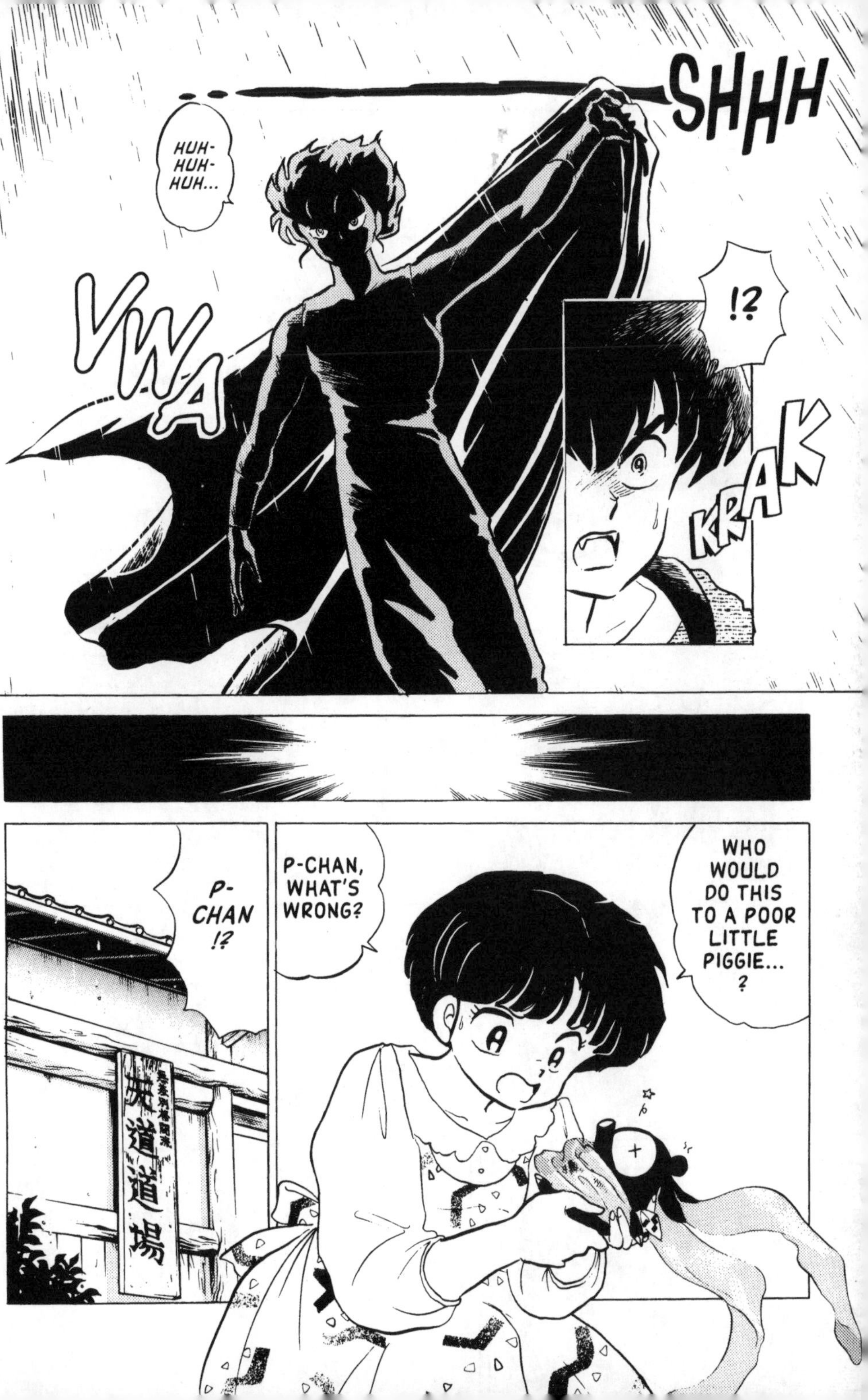
HUH-HUH-HUH...
SHHH
VWA
!?
KRAK
P-CHAN !?
P-CHAN, WHAT'S WRONG?
WHO WOULD DO THIS TO A POOR LITTLE PIGGIE...?

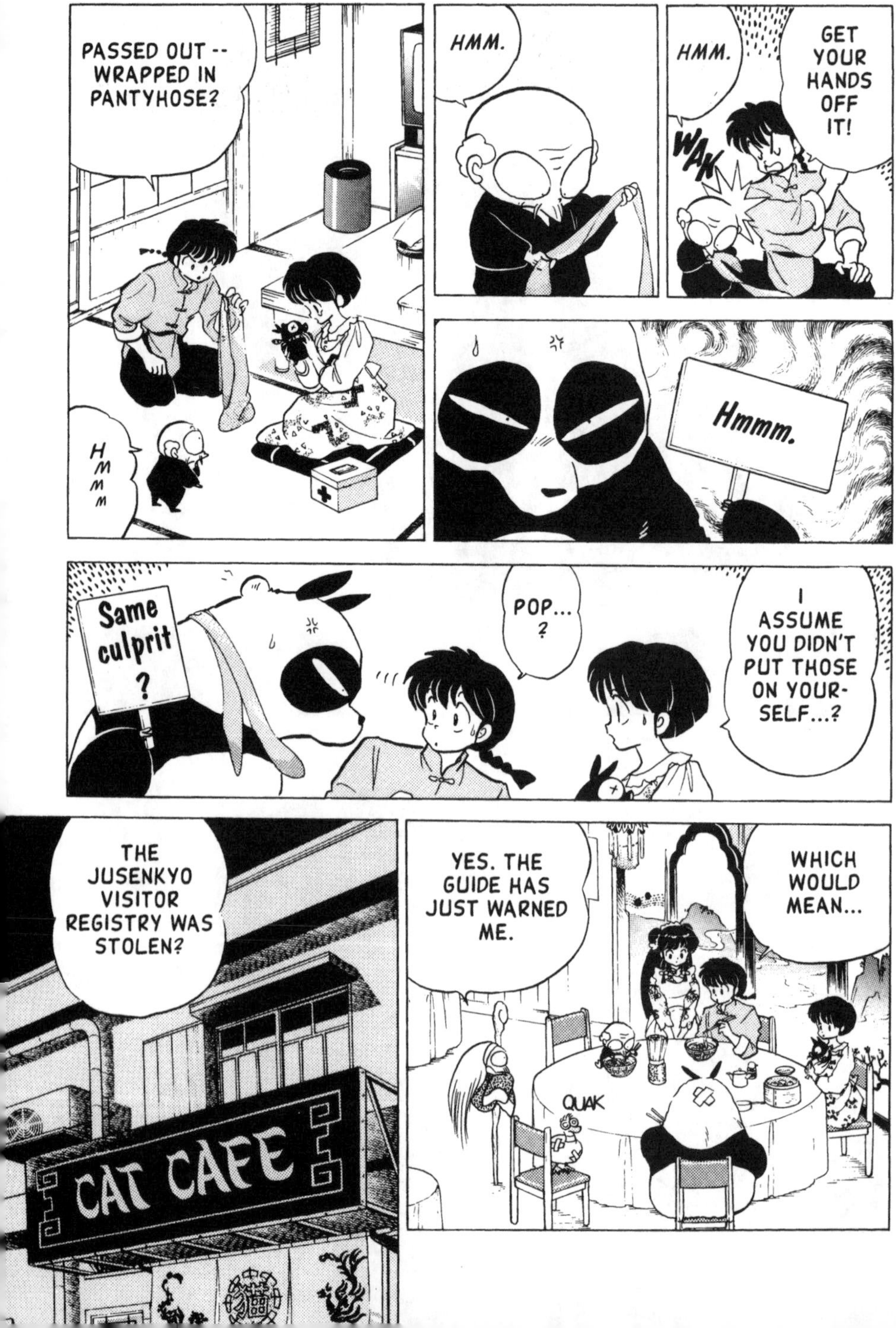
PASSED OUT -- WRAPPED IN PANTYHOSE?
H M M M
HMM.
HMM.
GET YOUR HANDS OFF IT!
WAK
Hmmm.
Same culprit ?
POP... ?
I ASSUME YOU DIDN'T PUT THOSE ON YOUR-SELF...?
THE JUSENKYO VISITOR REGISTRY WAS STOLEN?
CAT CAFE
YES. THE GUIDE HAS JUST WARNED ME.
WHICH WOULD MEAN...
QUAK

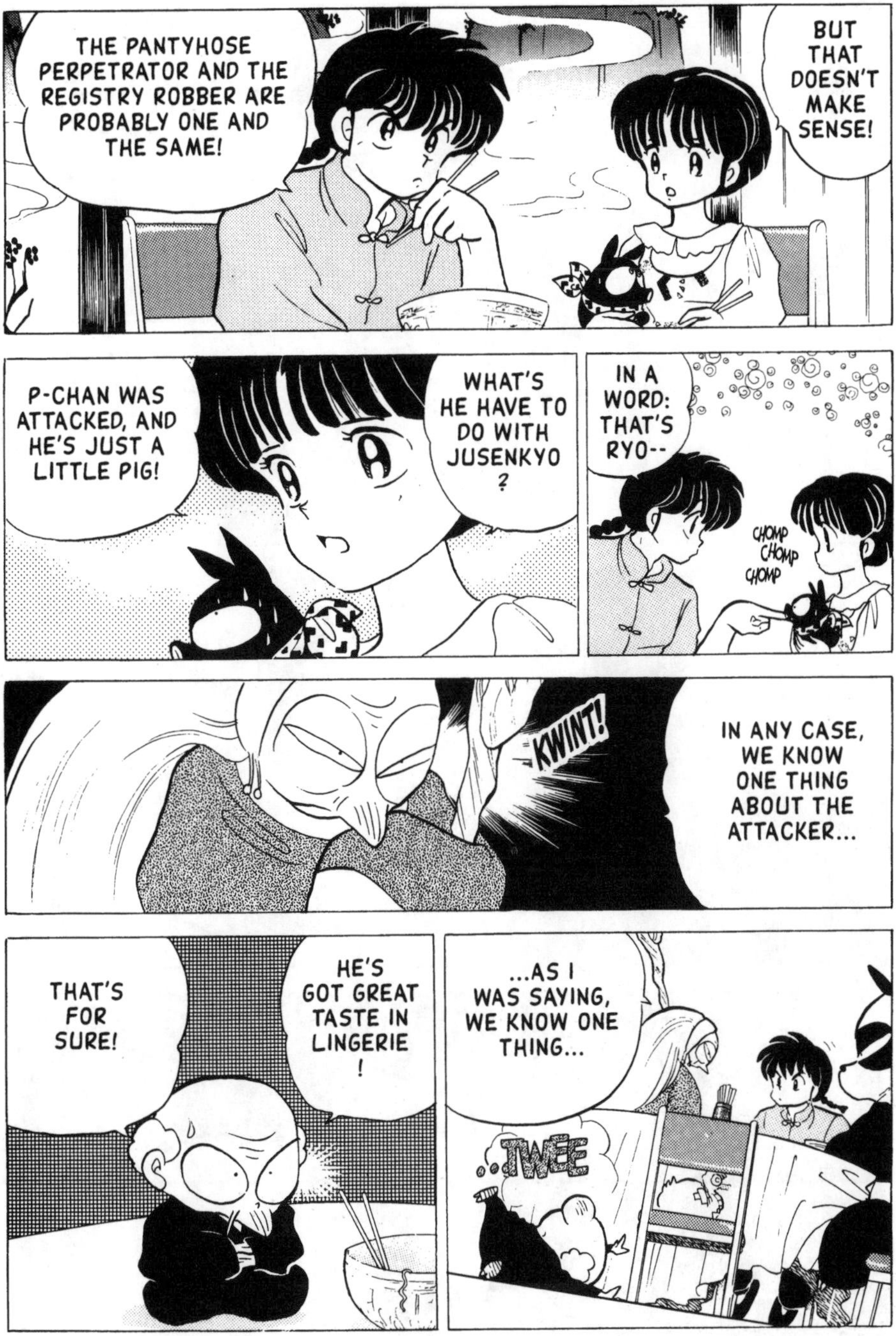
THE PANTYHOSE PERPETRATOR AND THE REGISTRY ROBBER ARE PROBABLY ONE AND THE SAME!
BUT THAT DOESN'T MAKE SENSE!
P-CHAN WAS ATTACKED, AND HE'S JUST A LITTLE PIG!
WHAT'S HE HAVE TO DO WITH JUSENKYO?
IN A WORD: THAT'S RYO--
CHOMP CHOMP CHOMP
KWINT!
IN ANY CASE, WE KNOW ONE THING ABOUT THE ATTACKER...
THAT'S FOR SURE!
HE'S GOT GREAT TASTE IN LINGERIE!
...AS I WAS SAYING, WE KNOW ONE THING...
TWEE

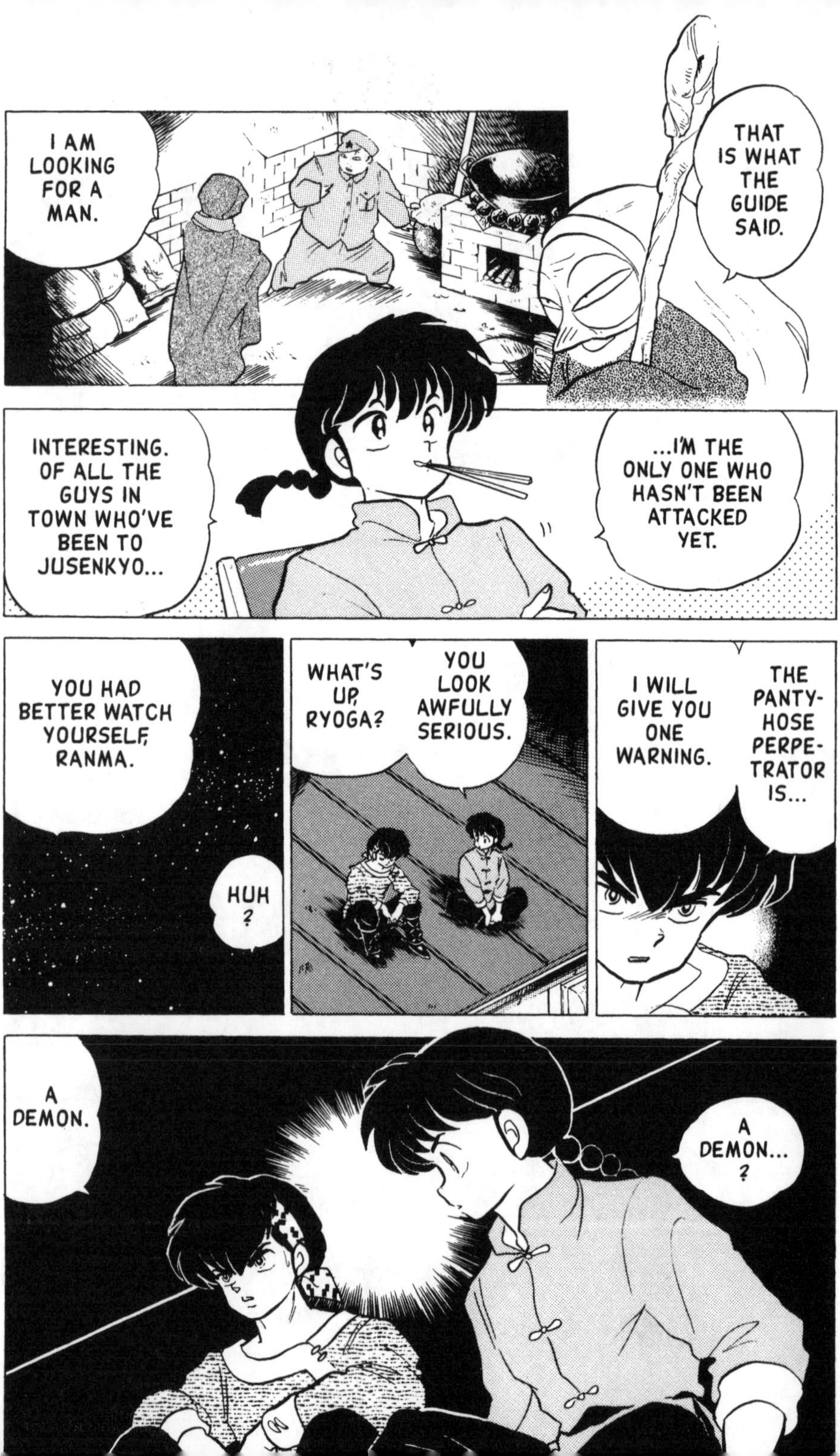
I AM LOOKING FOR A MAN.
THAT IS WHAT THE GUIDE SAID.
INTERESTING. OF ALL THE GUYS IN TOWN WHO'VE BEEN TO JUSENKYO...
...I'M THE ONLY ONE WHO HASN'T BEEN ATTACKED YET.
YOU HAD BETTER WATCH YOURSELF, RANMA.
HUH?
WHAT'S UP, RYOGA?
YOU LOOK AWFULLY SERIOUS.
I WILL GIVE YOU ONE WARNING.
THE PANTY-HOSE PERPETRATOR IS...
A DEMON.
A DEMON...?

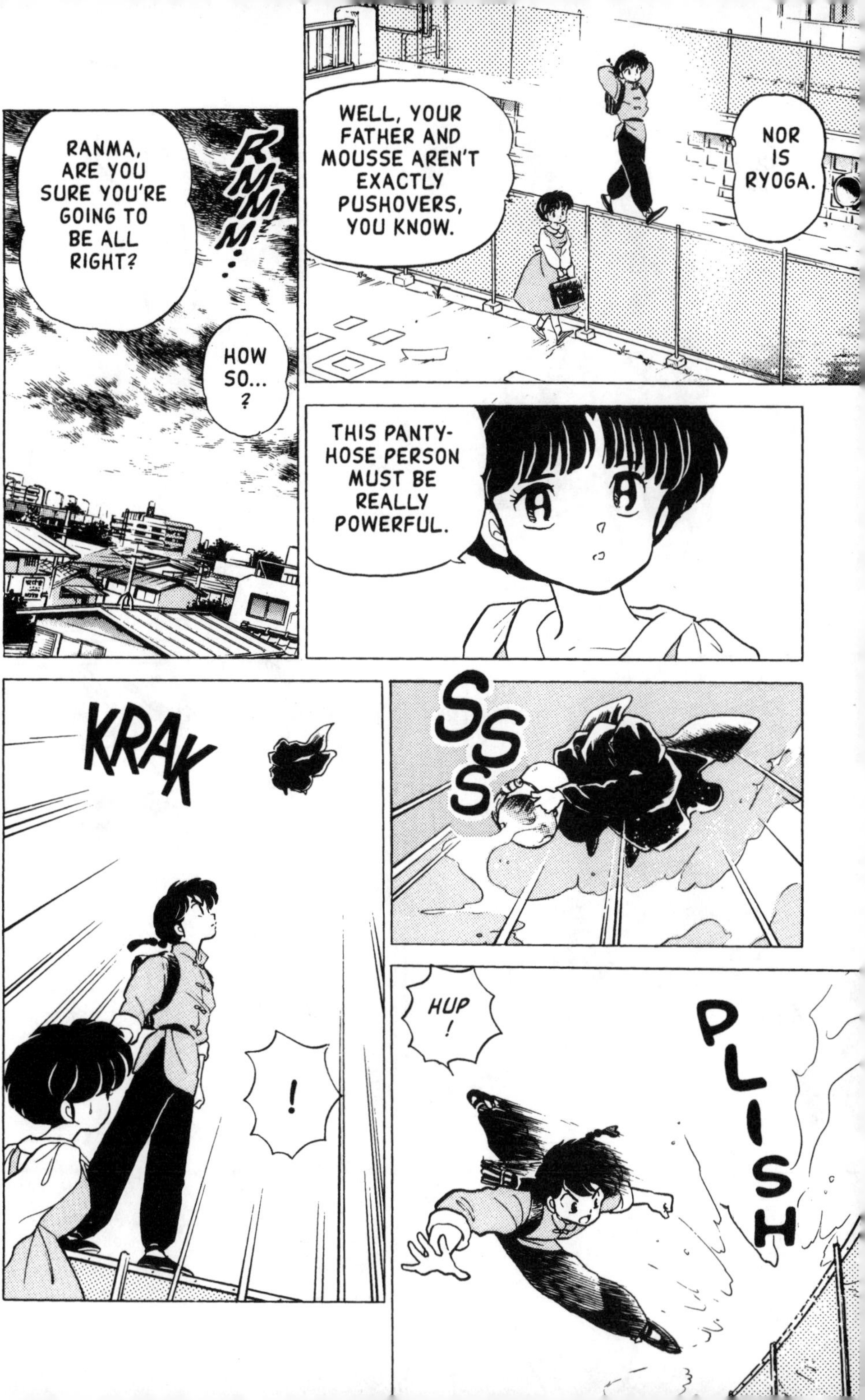
RANMA, ARE YOU SURE YOU'RE GOING TO BE ALL RIGHT?
RMMM...
HOW SO...?
WELL, YOUR FATHER AND MOUSSE AREN'T EXACTLY PUSHOVERS, YOU KNOW.
NOR IS RYOGA.
THIS PANTY-HOSE PERSON MUST BE REALLY POWERFUL.
KRAK
!
SSS
HUP!
PLISH

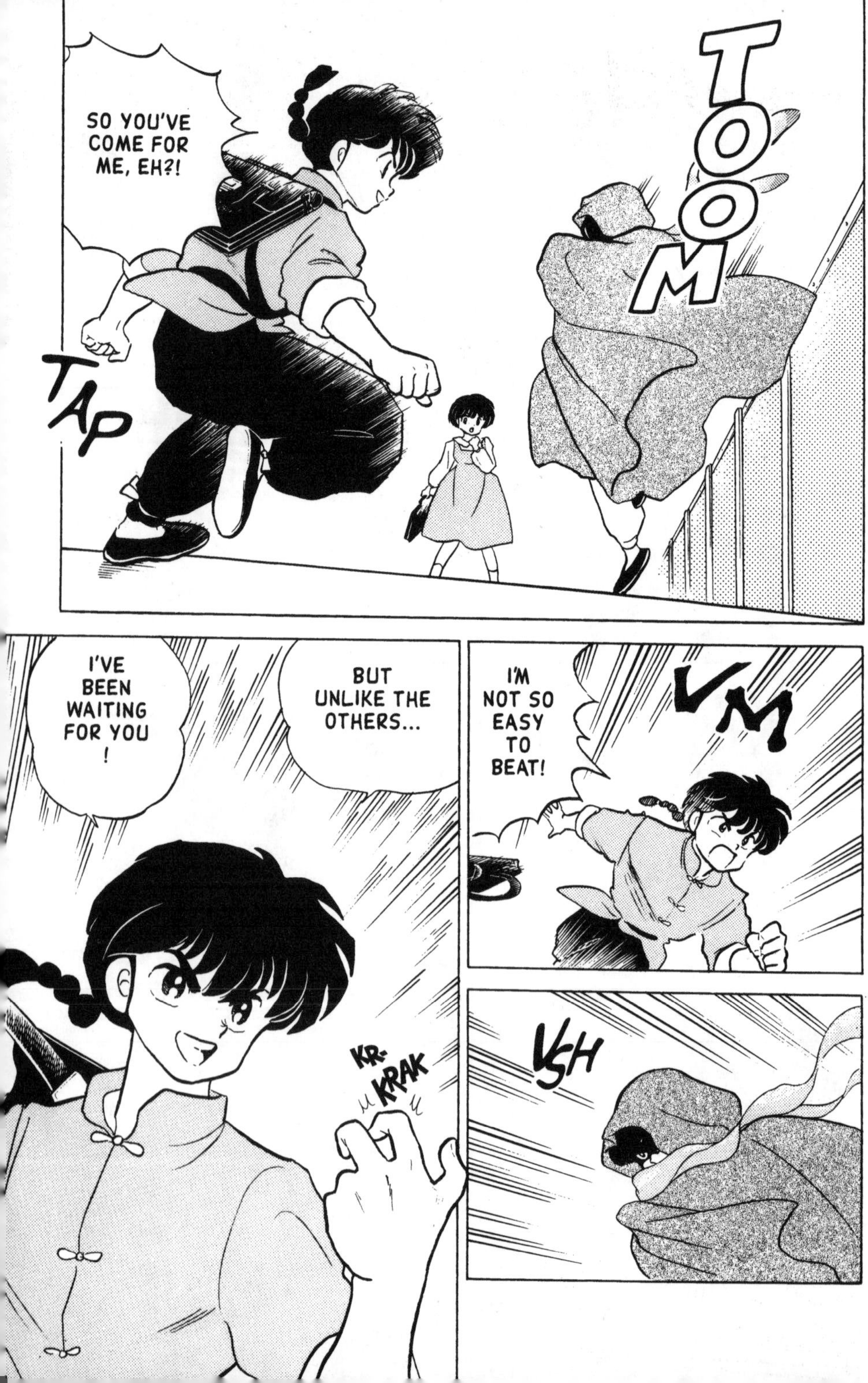
SO YOU'VE COME FOR ME, EH?!
TAP
TOOOM
I'VE BEEN WAITING FOR YOU!
BUT UNLIKE THE OTHERS...
KR-KRAK
I'M NOT SO EASY TO BEAT!
VM
VSH

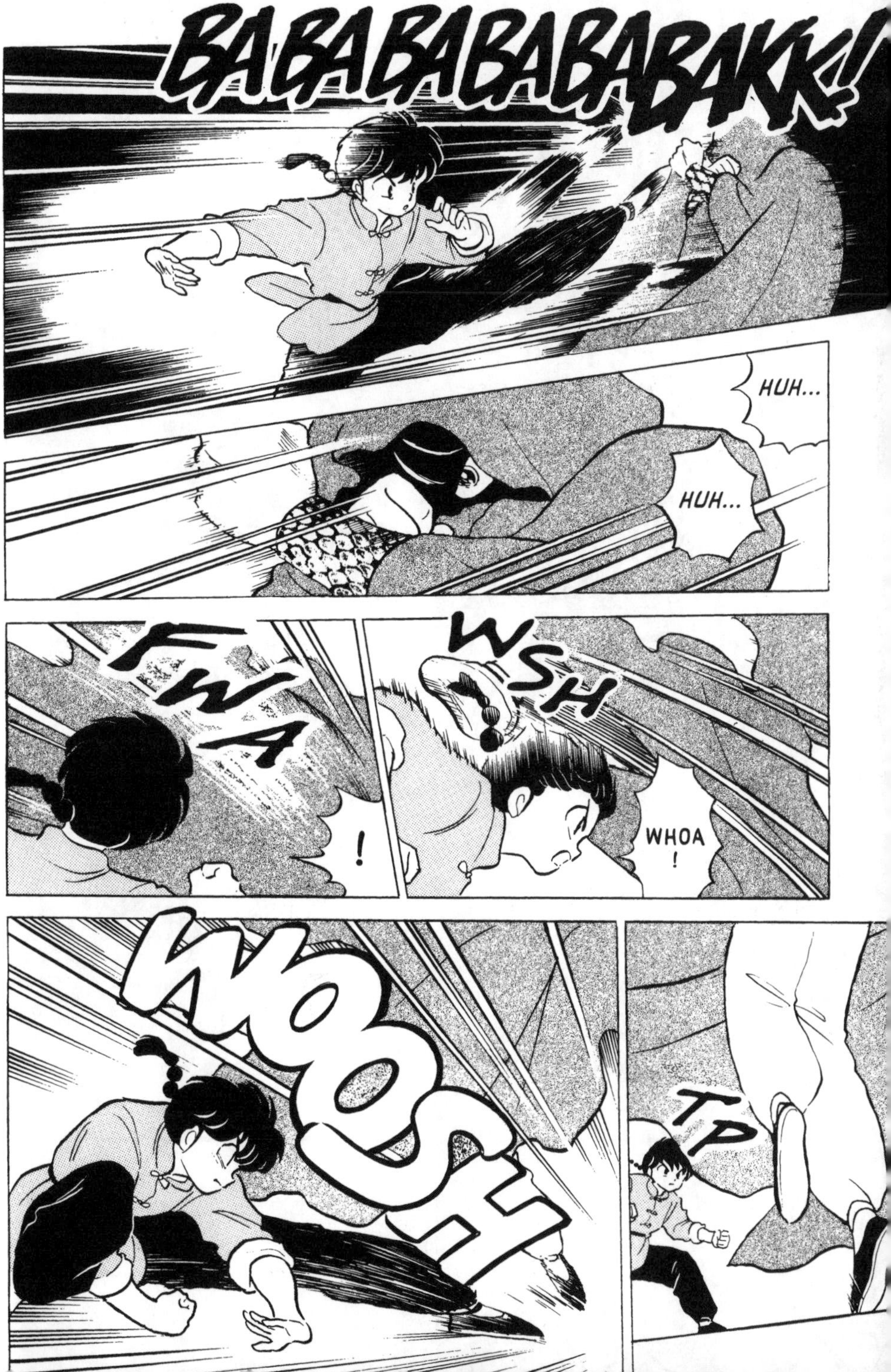
BABABABABABABAKK!
HUH...
HUH...
FWA
!
WSH
WHOA
!
WOOSH
TP

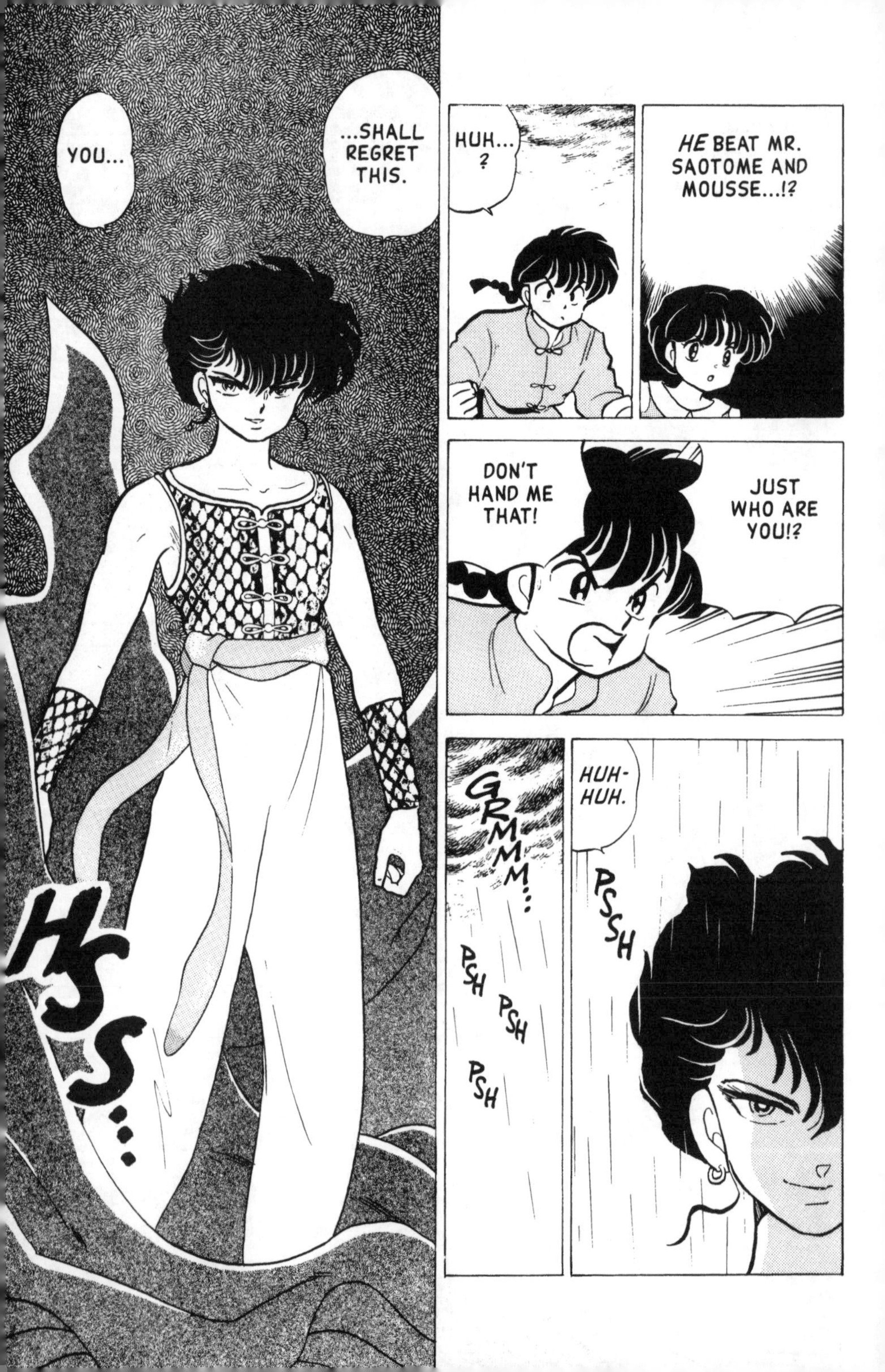
YOU...
...SHALL REGRET THIS.
HSS...
HUH...?
HE BEAT MR. SAOTOME AND MOUSSE...!?
DON'T HAND ME THAT!
JUST WHO ARE YOU!?
GRMMM...
PSH
PSH
PSH
HUH-HUH.
PSSSH

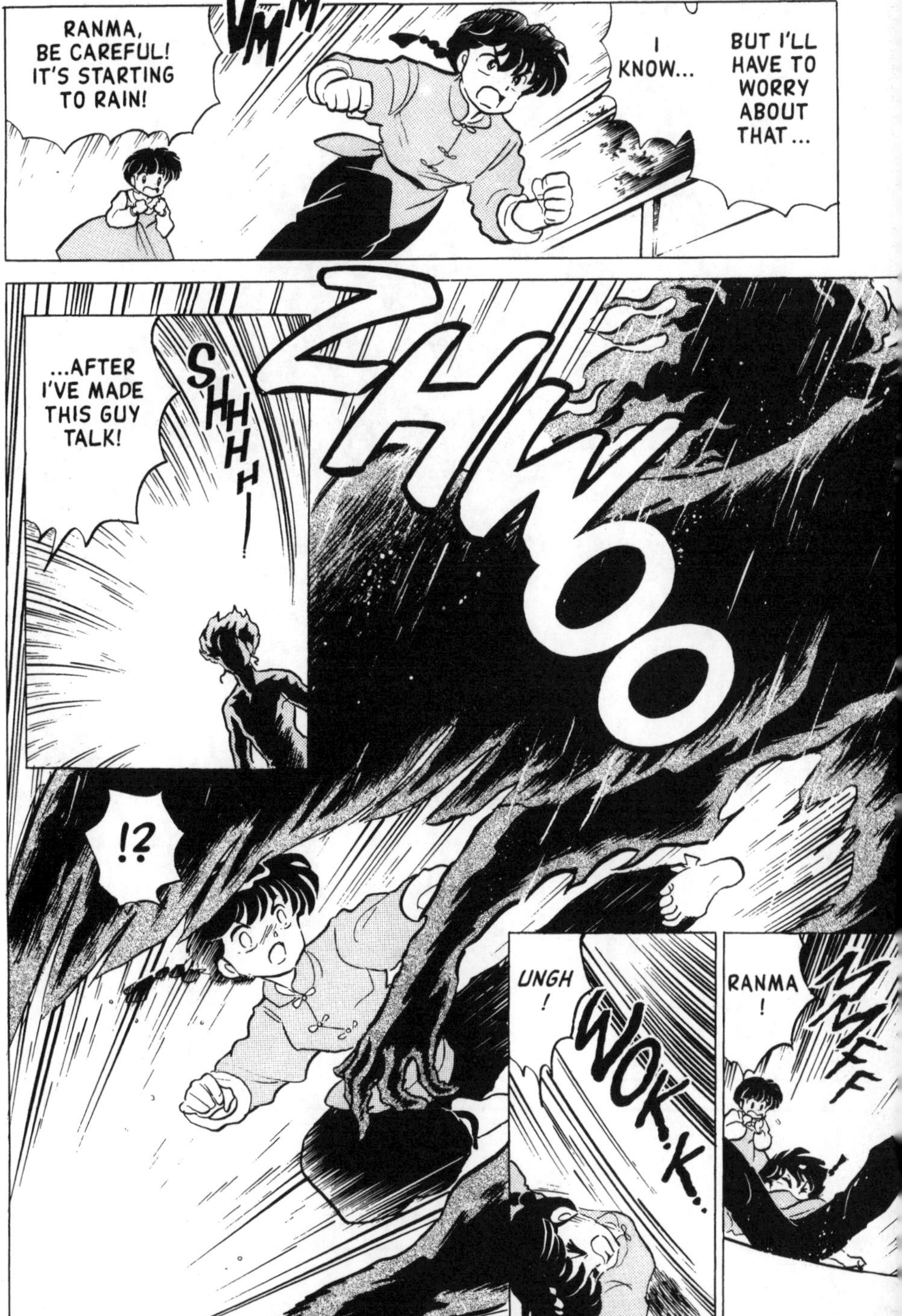
RANMA, BE CAREFUL! IT'S STARTING TO RAIN!
VMMM
I KNOW...
BUT I'LL HAVE TO WORRY ABOUT THAT...
...AFTER I'VE MADE THIS GUY TALK!
SHHHH!
ZHWOO
!?
UNGH!
WOK..K..
RANMA!
MMFF!

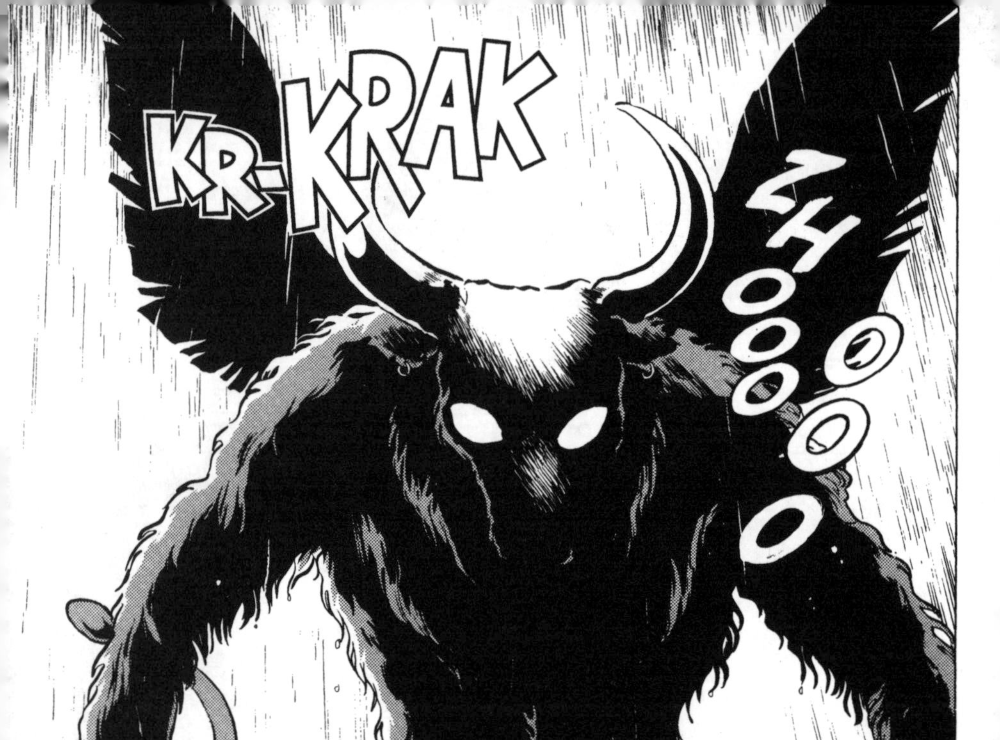
KR-KRAK
ZHOOOOOO
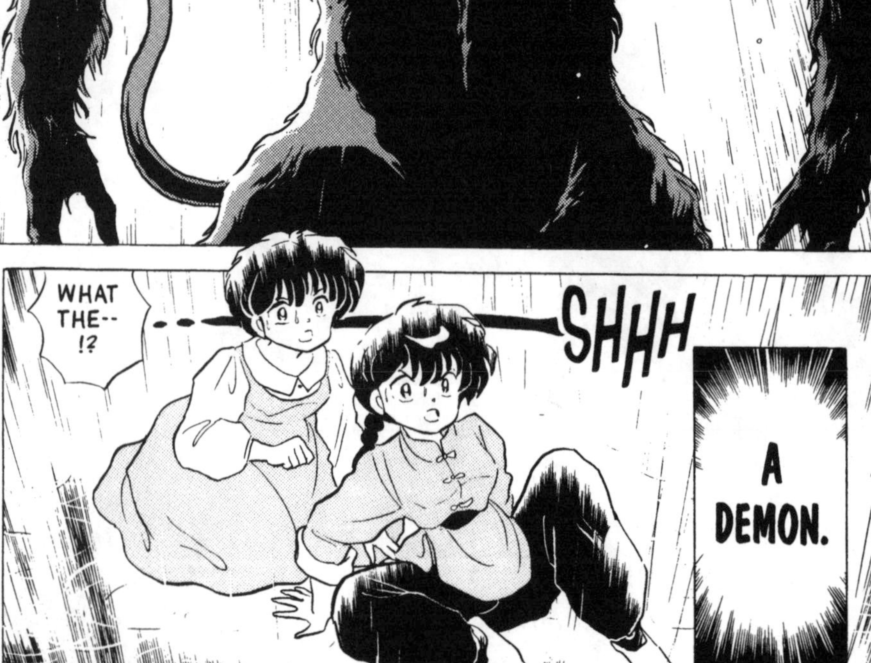
WHAT THE-- !?
SHHH
A DEMON.

Part 3
THE DEMON'S TALE

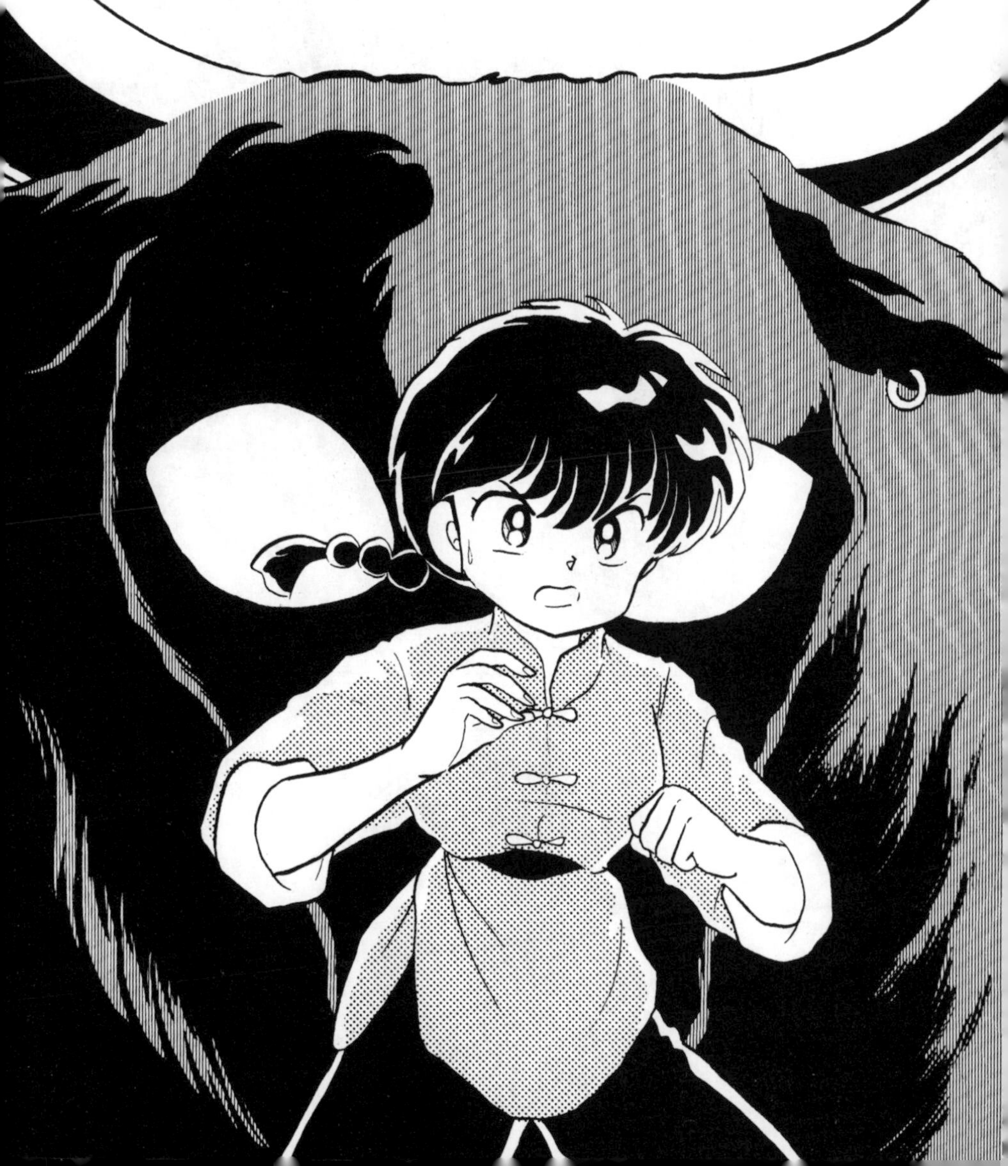

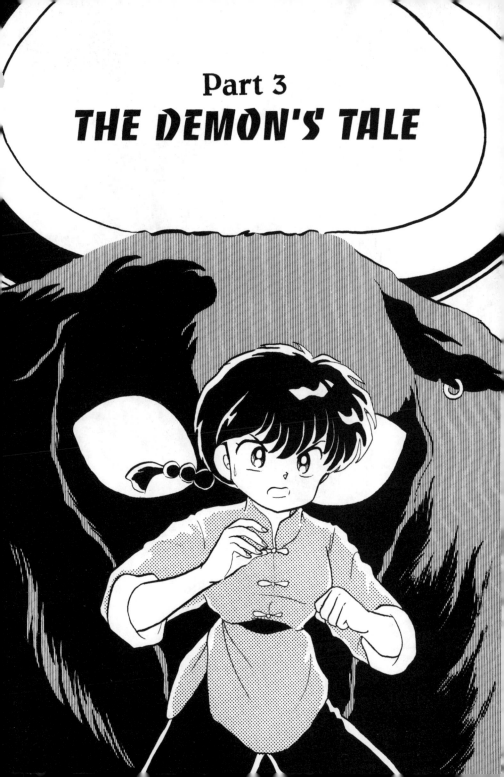

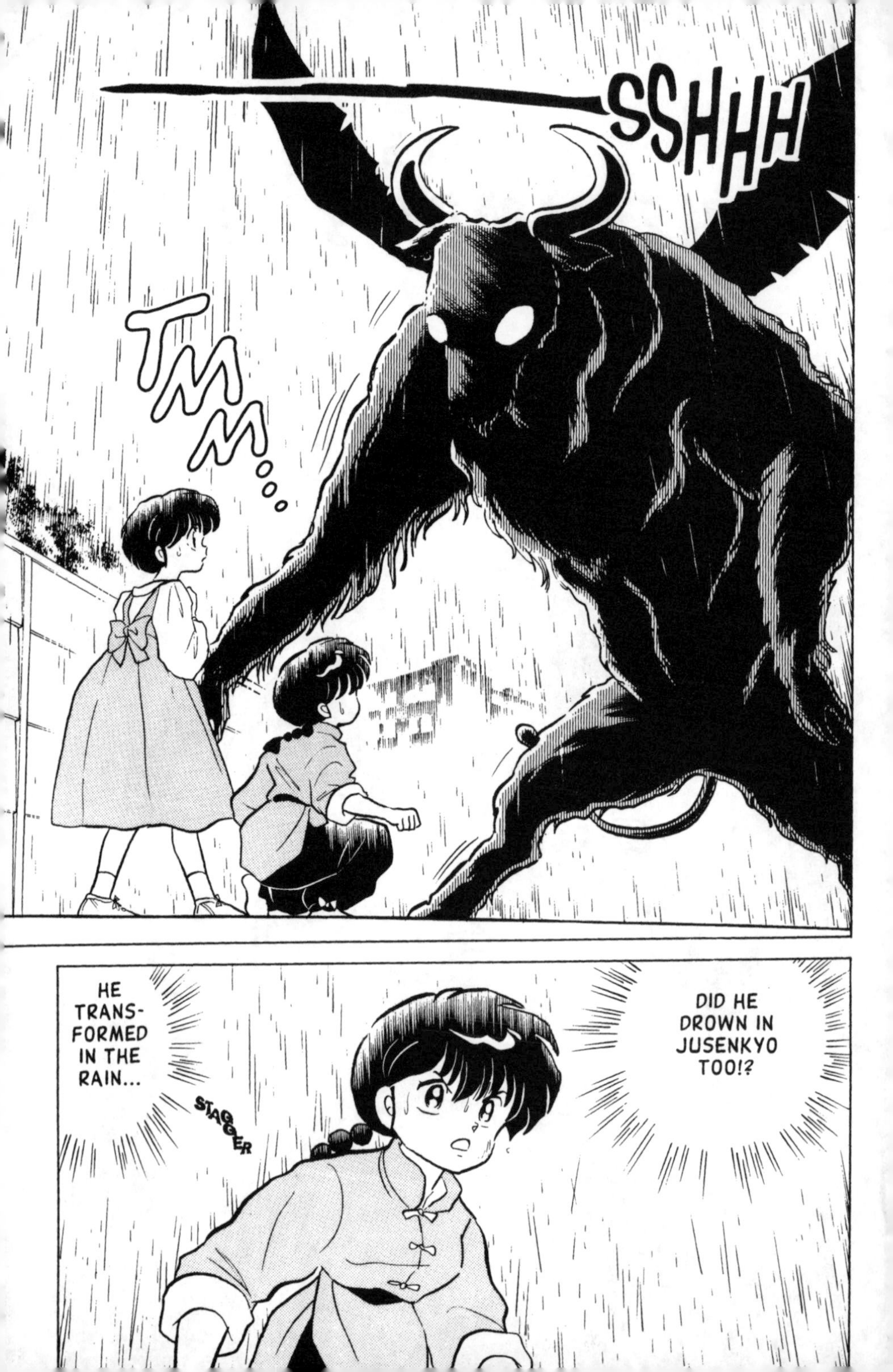
SSHHH
TMMooo
HE TRANS-FORMED IN THE RAIN...
STAGGER
DID HE DROWN IN JUSENKYO TOO!?

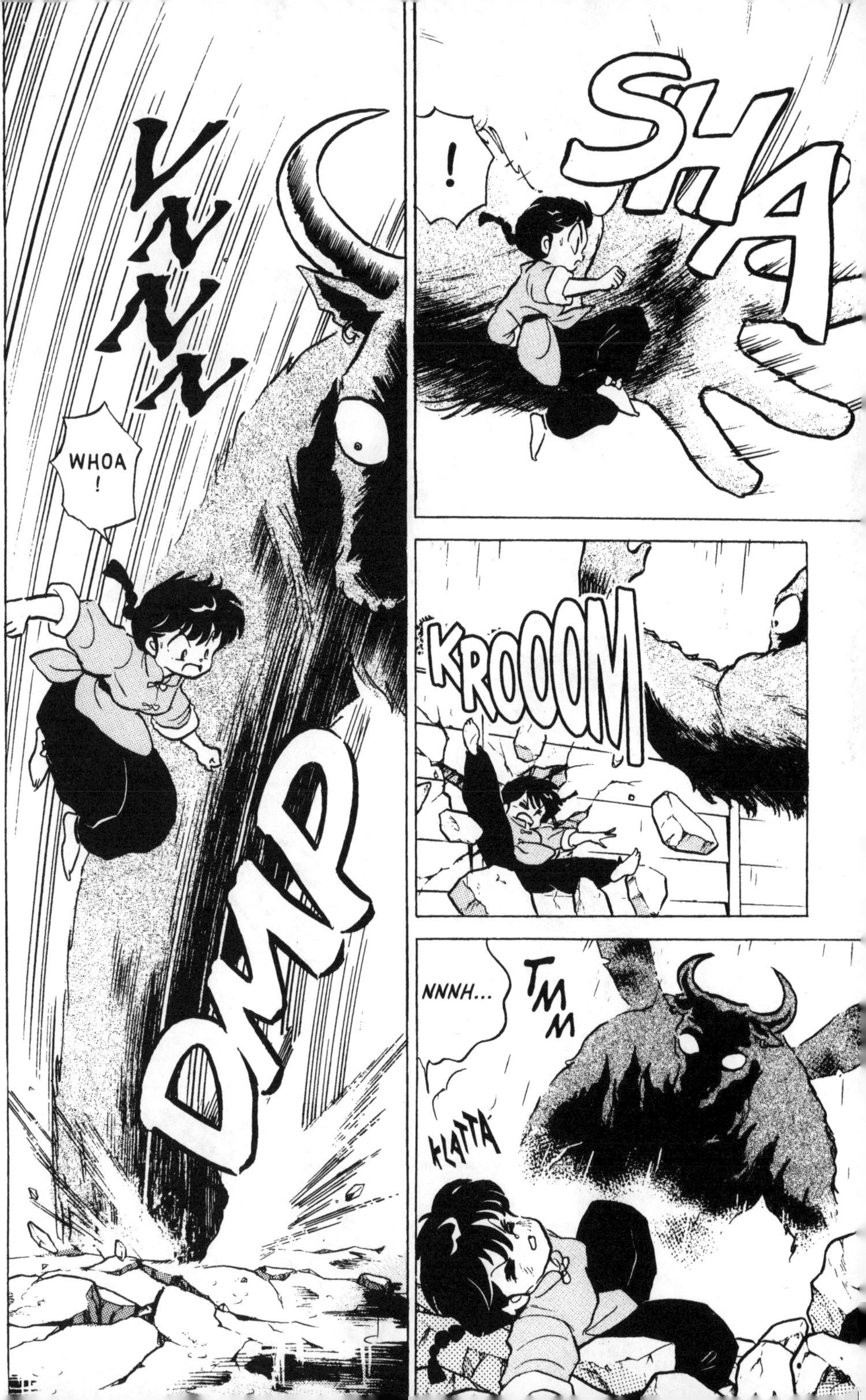
VNNNN
WHOA!
DMP
!
SHA
KROOOM
NNNH...
TMM
KLATTA

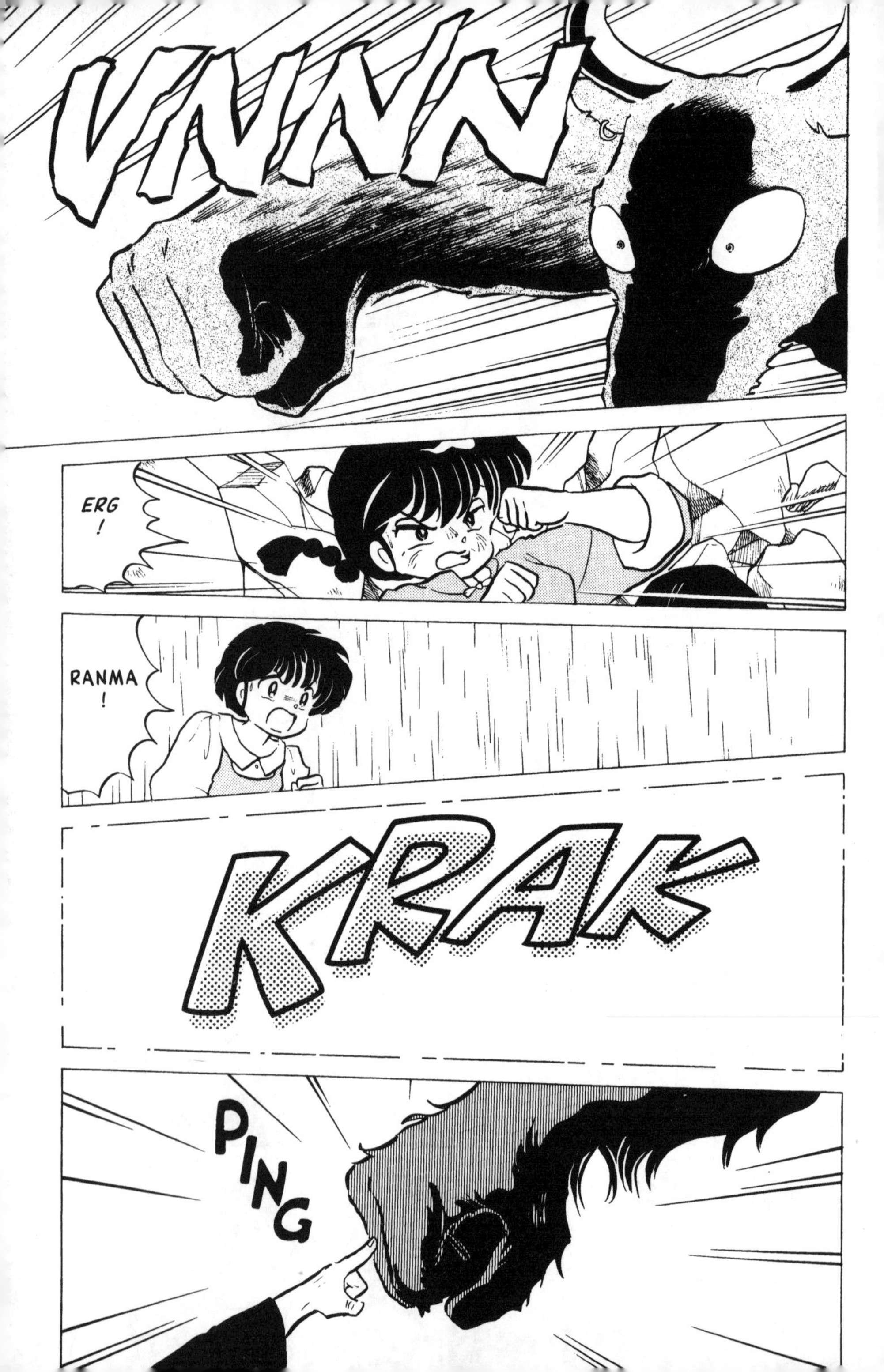
VNNN
ERG!
RANMA!
KRAK
PING

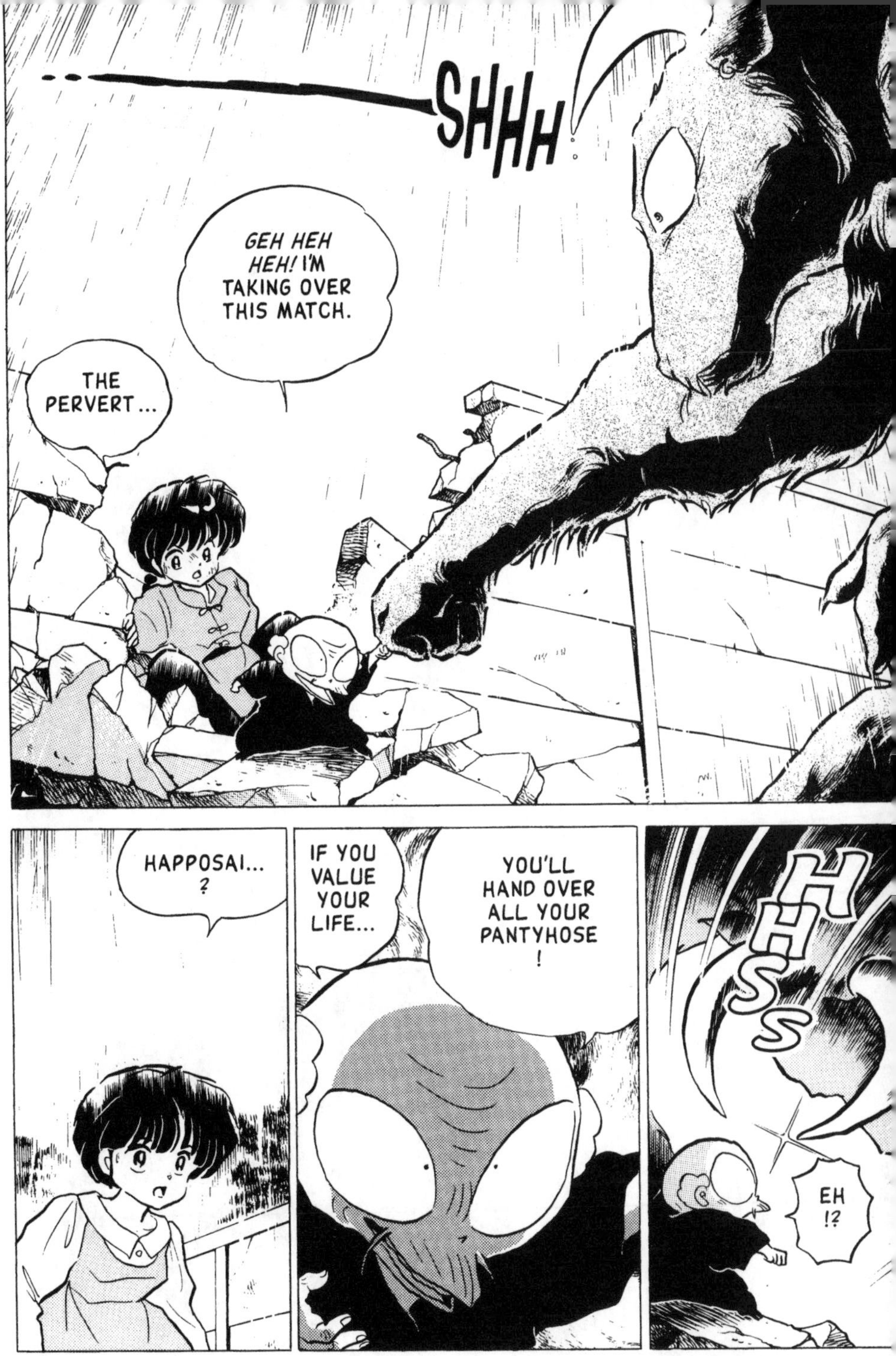

SHHH
GEH HEH HEH! I'M TAKING OVER THIS MATCH.
THE PERVERT...
HAPPOSAI...?
IF YOU VALUE YOUR LIFE...
YOU'LL HAND OVER ALL YOUR PANTYHOSE!
HHSS
EH!?

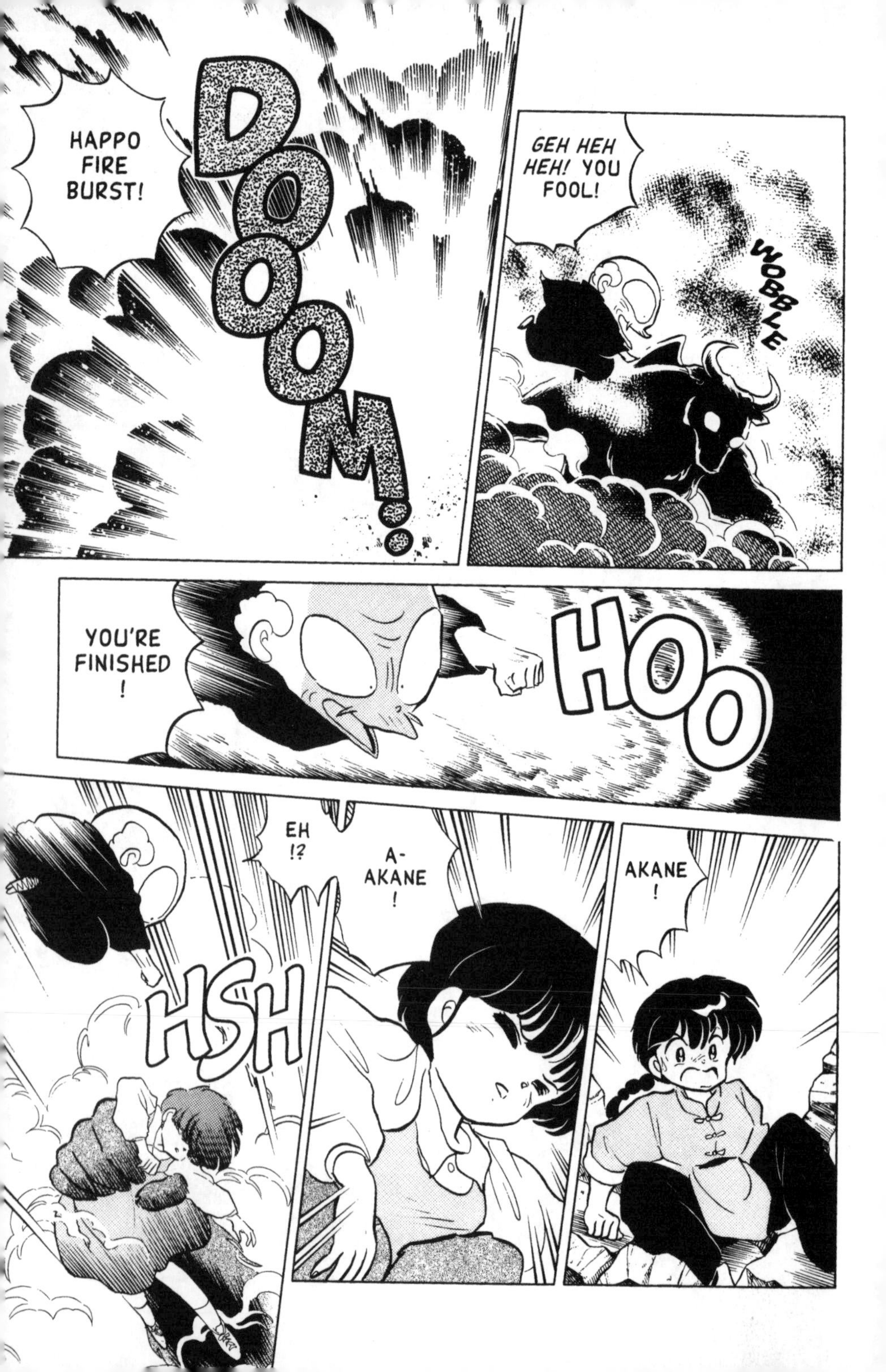
HAPPO FIRE BURST!
DOOOOM!
GEH HEH HEH! YOU FOOL!
WOBBLE
YOU'RE FINISHED !
HOO
HSH
EH !?
A-AKANE !
AKANE !

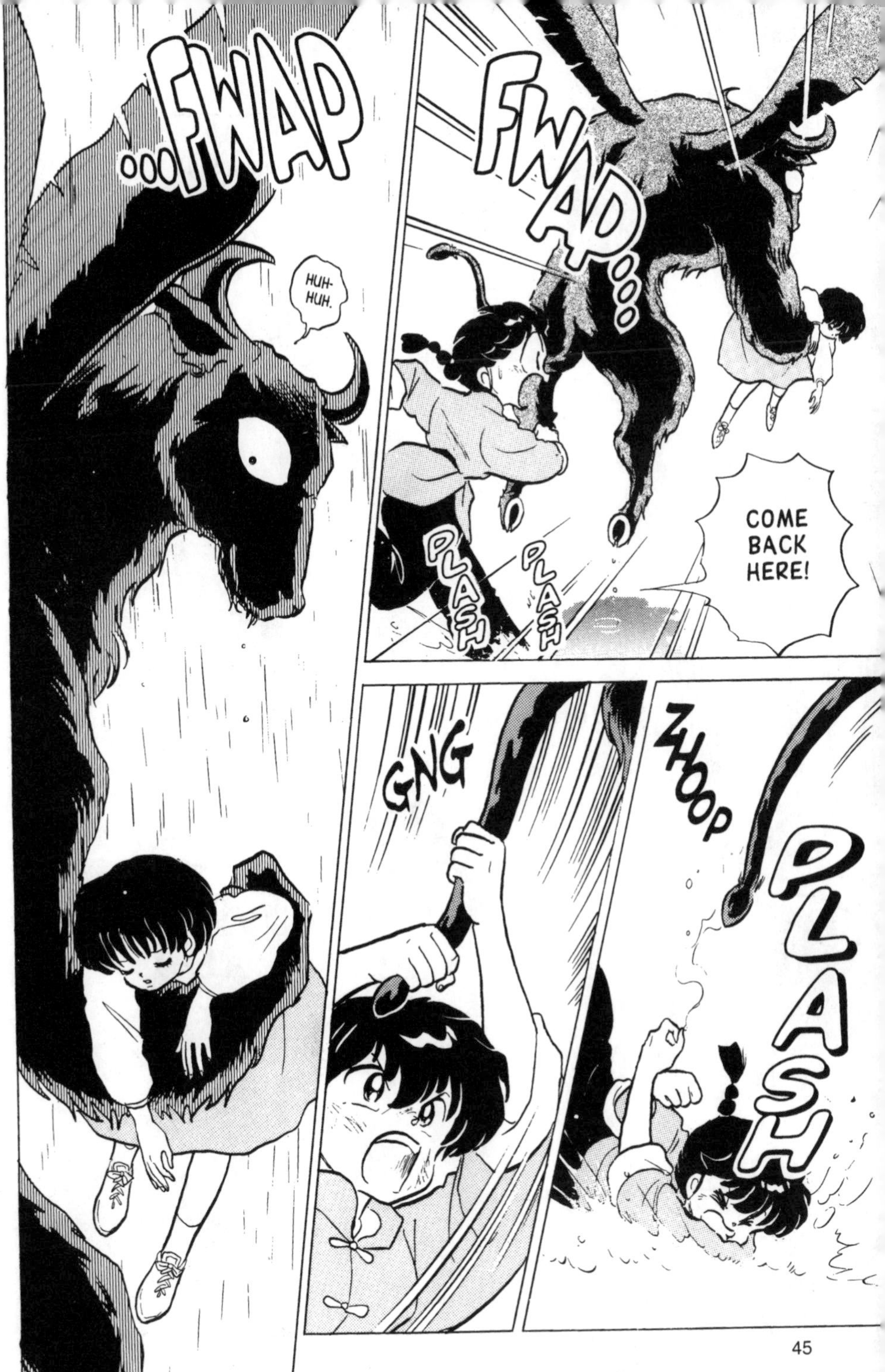
...FWAP
HUH-HUH.
FWAP...
PLASH
PLASH
COME BACK HERE!
GNG
ZHOOP
PLASH

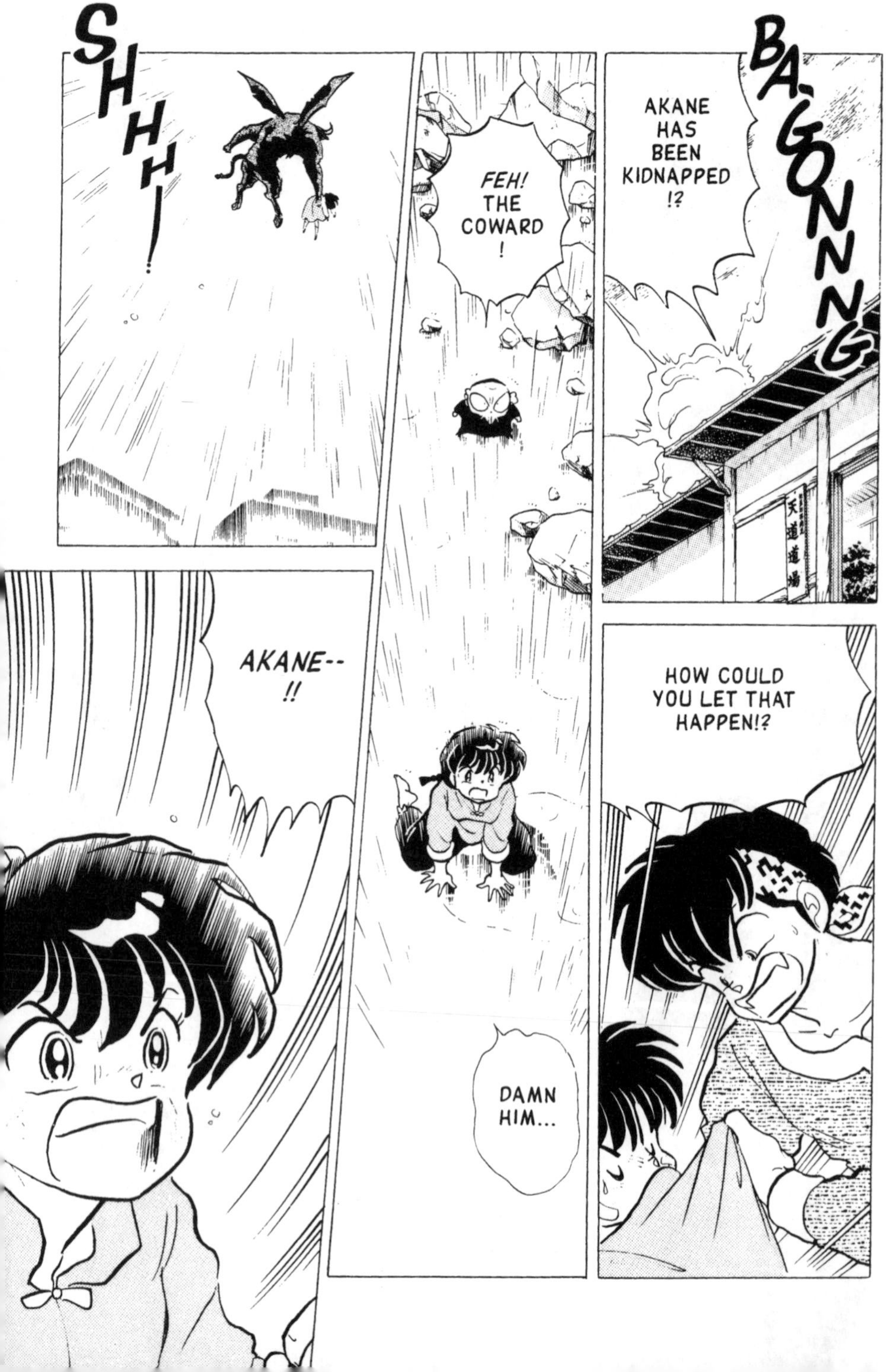
SHHHH!
AKANE-- !!
FEH! THE COWARD!
DAMN HIM...
BAGONNNG
AKANE HAS BEEN KIDNAPPED!?
HOW COULD YOU LET THAT HAPPEN!?

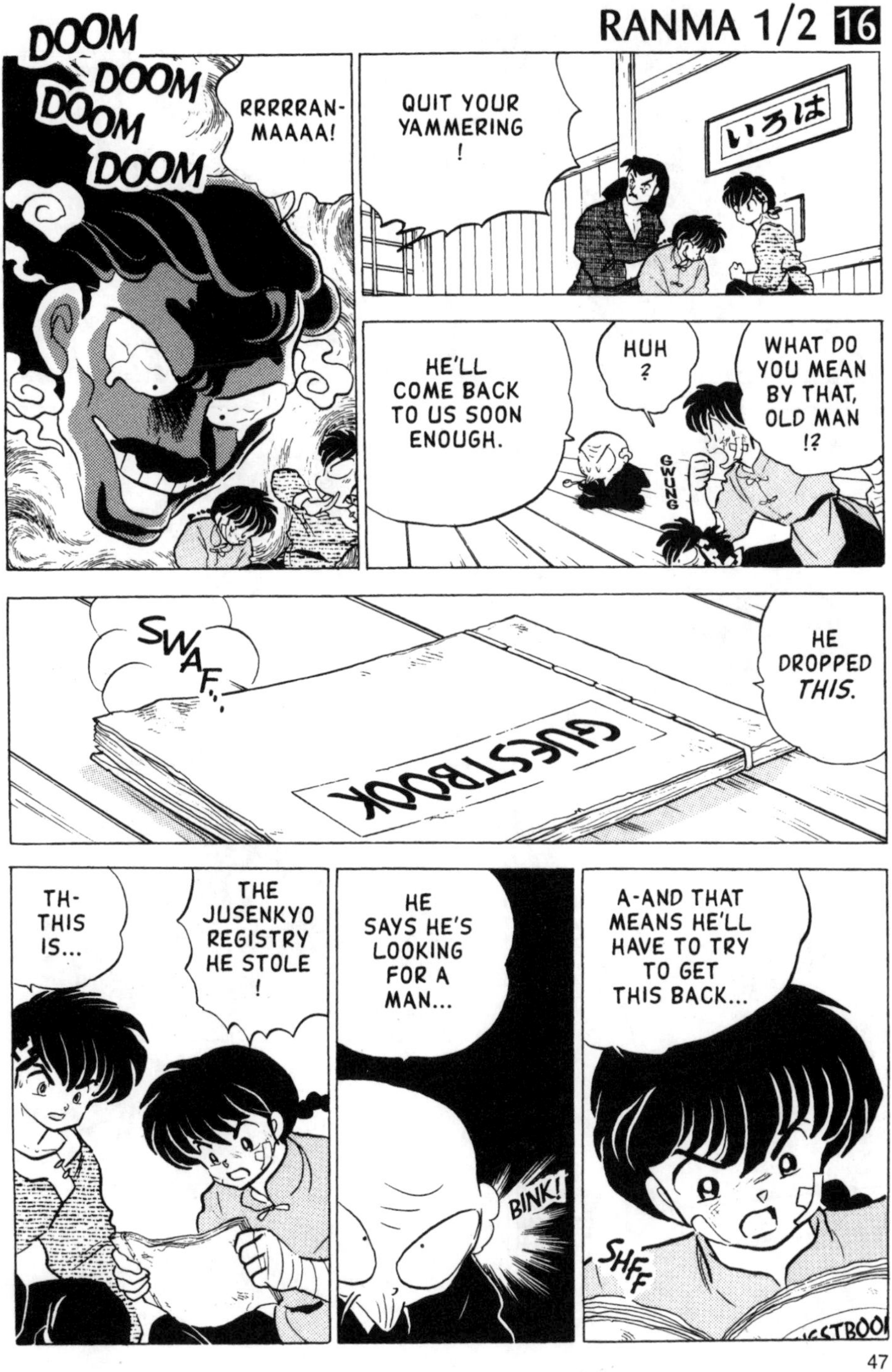
DOOM DOOM DOOM DOOM
RRRRRAN-MAAAA!
QUIT YOUR YAMMERING!
いろは
HE'LL COME BACK TO US SOON ENOUGH.
HUH?
WHAT DO YOU MEAN BY THAT, OLD MAN!?
GWUNG
SWAF...
GUESTBOOK
HE DROPPED *THIS.*
TH-THIS IS...
THE JUSENKYO REGISTRY HE STOLE!
HE SAYS HE'S LOOKING FOR A MAN...
BINK!
A-AND THAT MEANS HE'LL HAVE TO TRY TO GET THIS BACK...
SHFF

FWIP

HMM....

HE'S ATTACKED MANY PEOPLE.

HM?

THERE'S ONE NAME THAT'S NOT CROSSED OUT...

THE ONE HE'S LOOKING FOR!?

GUESTBOOK

BECAUSE OF THIS MAN MY DAUGHTER'S BEEN KIDNAPPED!

SOBB SOBB

B-BUT...

IS IT A CODE?

IT LOOKS LIKE A DRAWING.

OR MAYBE IT'S...

AMATEURS!

LEMME SEE IT...

VIP

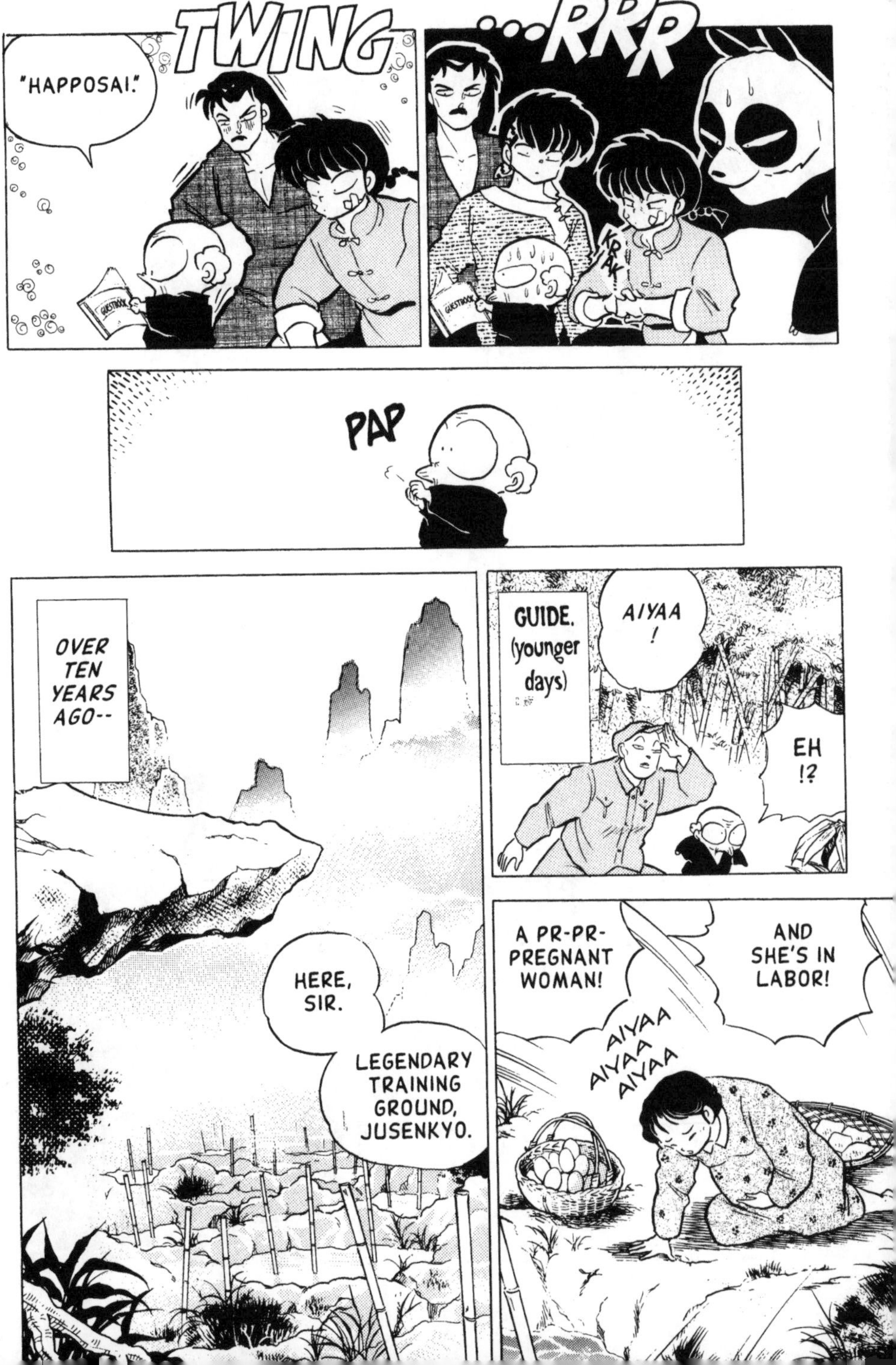
TWING
"HAPPOSAI."
...RRR
KRAK
PAP
OVER TEN YEARS AGO--
HERE, SIR.
LEGENDARY TRAINING GROUND, JUSENKYO.
GUIDE. (younger days)
AIYAA!
EH!?
A PR-PR-PREGNANT WOMAN!
AND SHE'S IN LABOR!
AIYAA AIYAA AIYAA

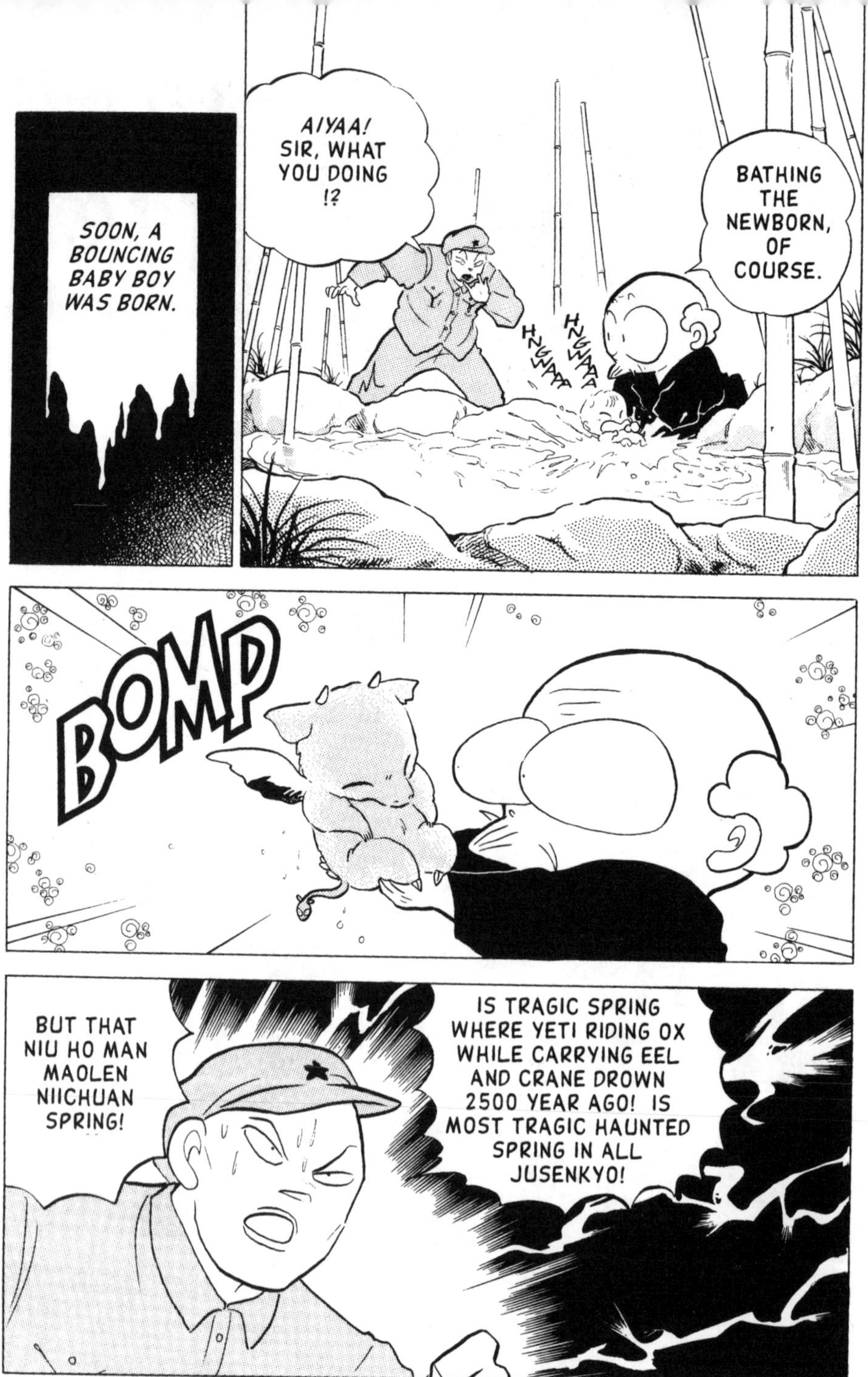
SOON, A BOUNCING BABY BOY WAS BORN.
AIYAA! SIR, WHAT YOU DOING !?
HNGWAAA
HNGWAAA
BATHING THE NEWBORN, OF COURSE.
BOMP
BUT THAT NIU HO MAN MAOLEN NIICHUAN SPRING!
IS TRAGIC SPRING WHERE YETI RIDING OX WHILE CARRYING EEL AND CRANE DROWN 2500 YEAR AGO! IS MOST TRAGIC HAUNTED SPRING IN ALL JUSENKYO!

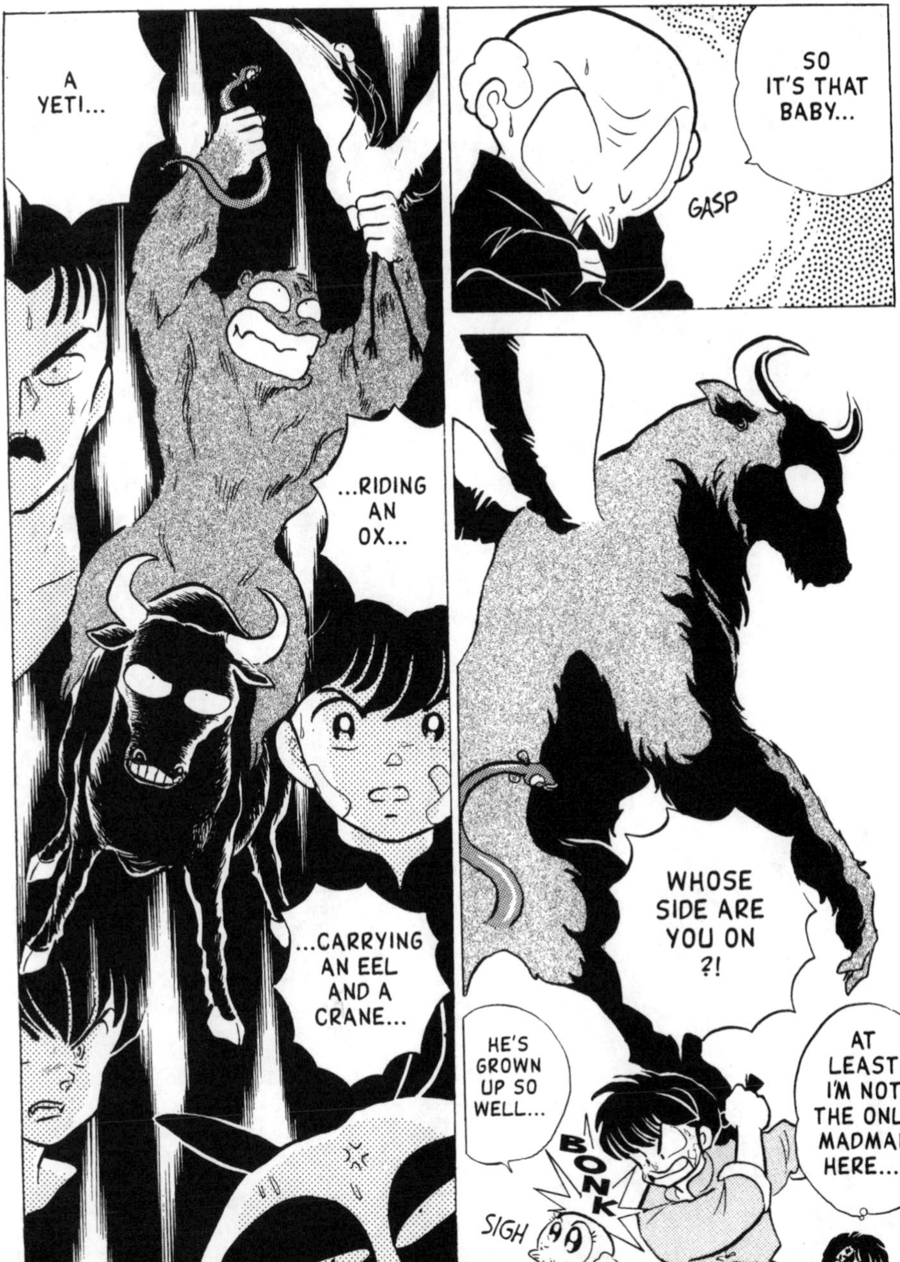
A YETI...
...RIDING AN OX...
...CARRYING AN EEL AND A CRANE...
SO IT'S THAT BABY...
GASP
WHOSE SIDE ARE YOU ON ?!
HE'S GROWN UP SO WELL...
BONK
SIGH
AT LEAST I'M NOT THE ONLY MADMAN HERE....

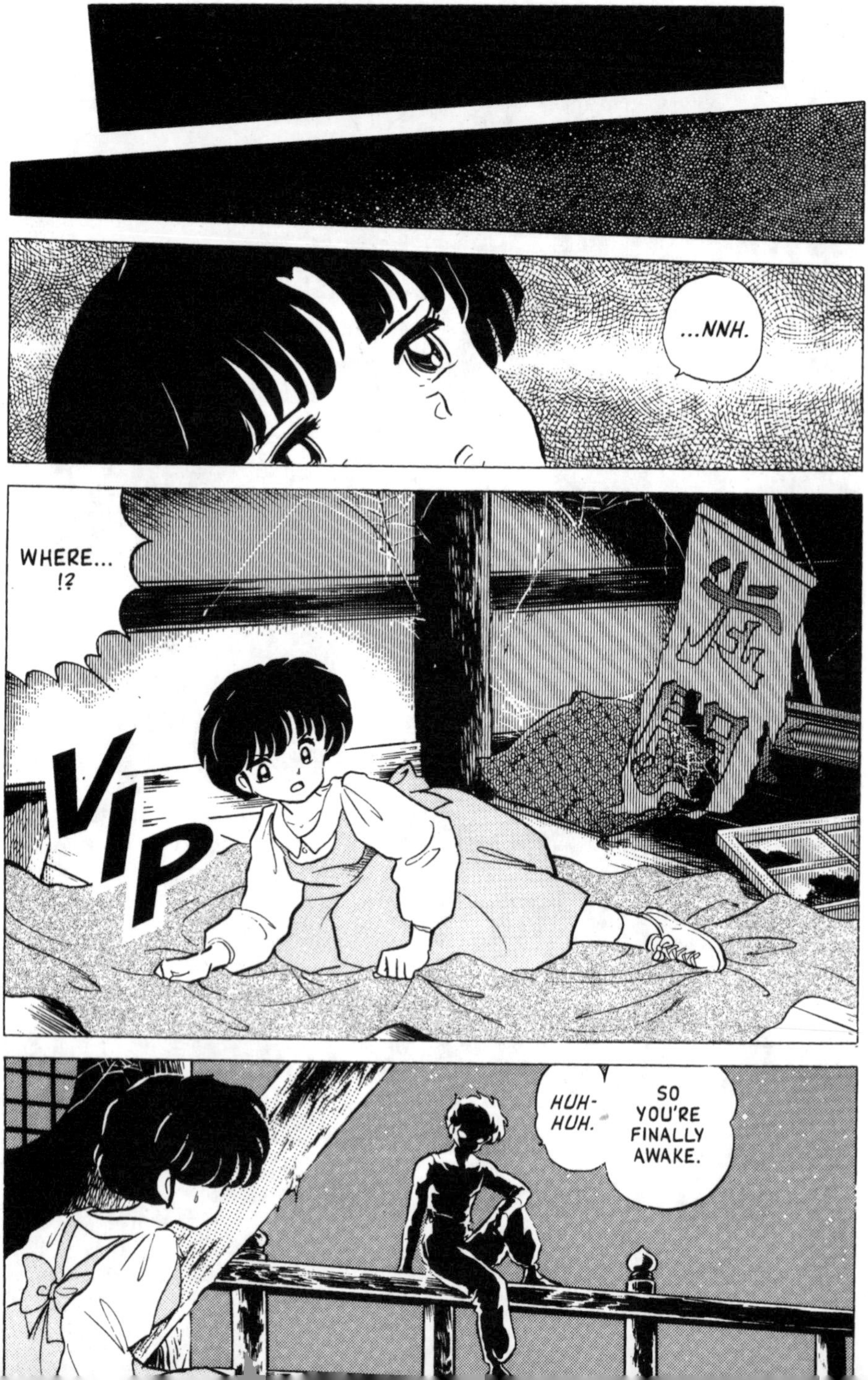
...NNH.
WHERE... !?
VIP
HUH-HUH.
SO YOU'RE FINALLY AWAKE.

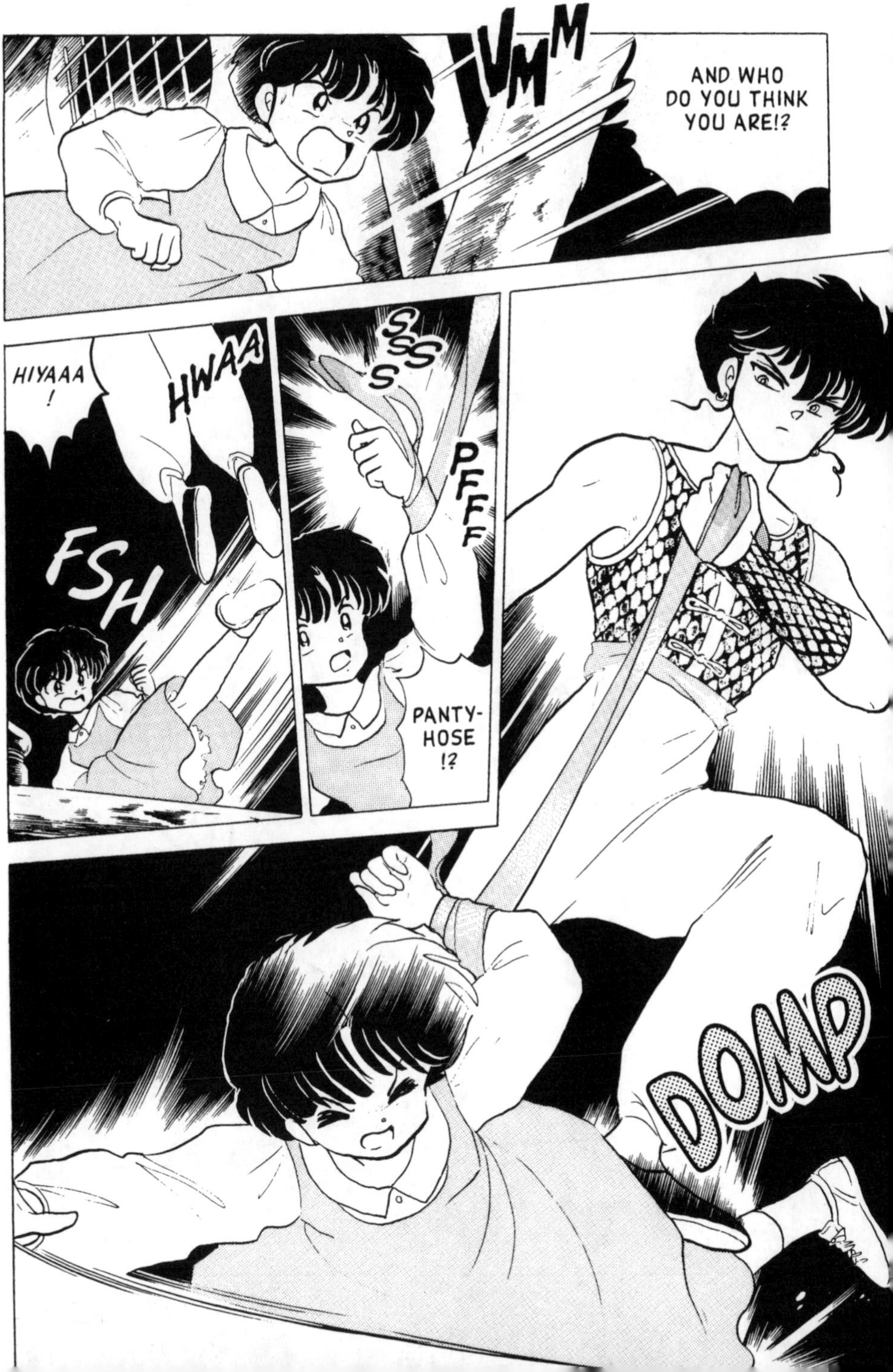
VMMM
AND WHO DO YOU THINK YOU ARE!?
HIYAAA!
HWAA
FSH
SSSS
PFFF
PANTY-HOSE!?
DOMP

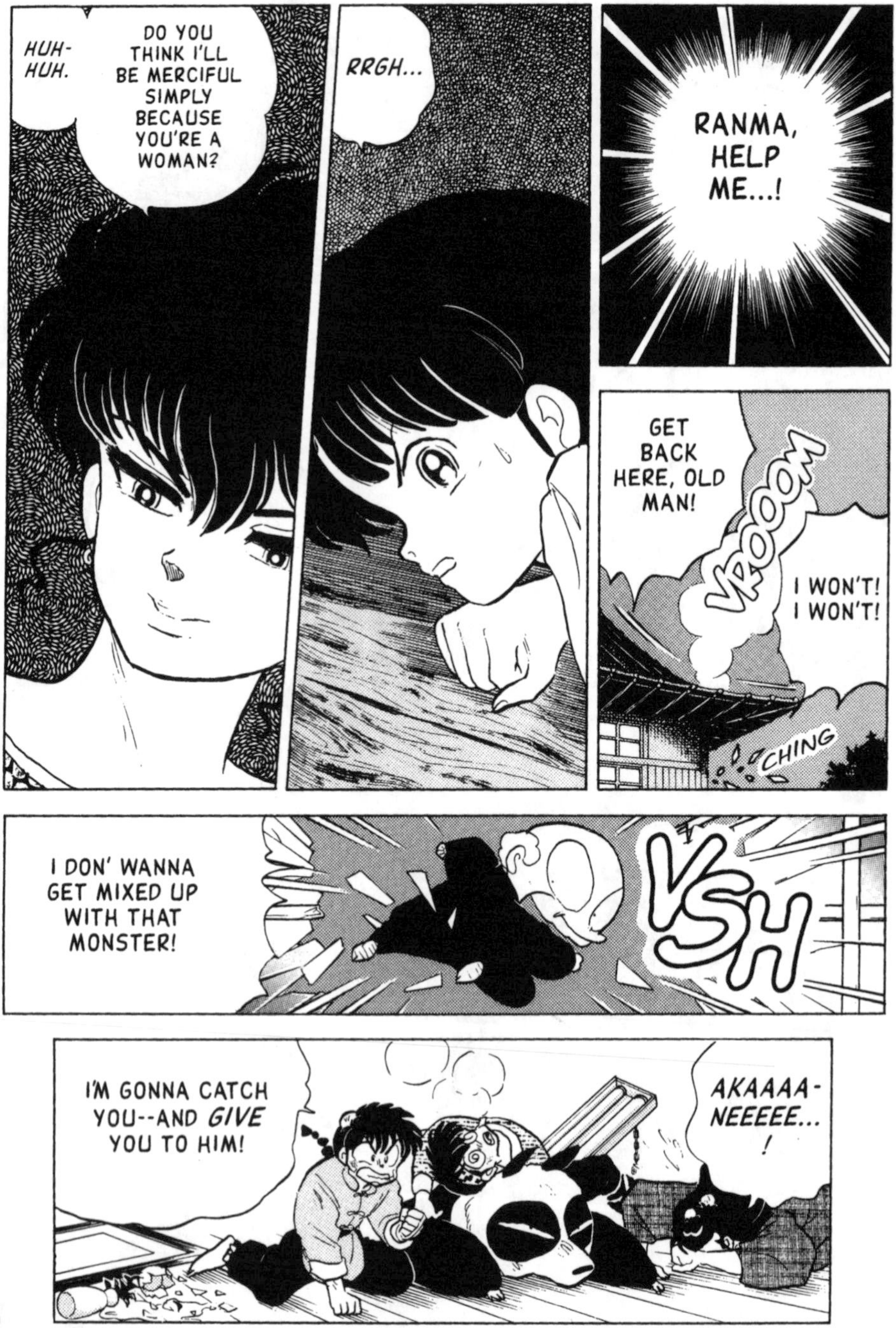
HUH-HUH.
DO YOU THINK I'LL BE MERCIFUL SIMPLY BECAUSE YOU'RE A WOMAN?
RRGH...
RANMA, HELP ME...!
GET BACK HERE, OLD MAN!
VROOOM
I WON'T! I WON'T!
CHING
I DON' WANNA GET MIXED UP WITH THAT MONSTER!
VSH
I'M GONNA CATCH YOU--AND *GIVE* YOU TO HIM!
AKAAAA-NEEEEE...!

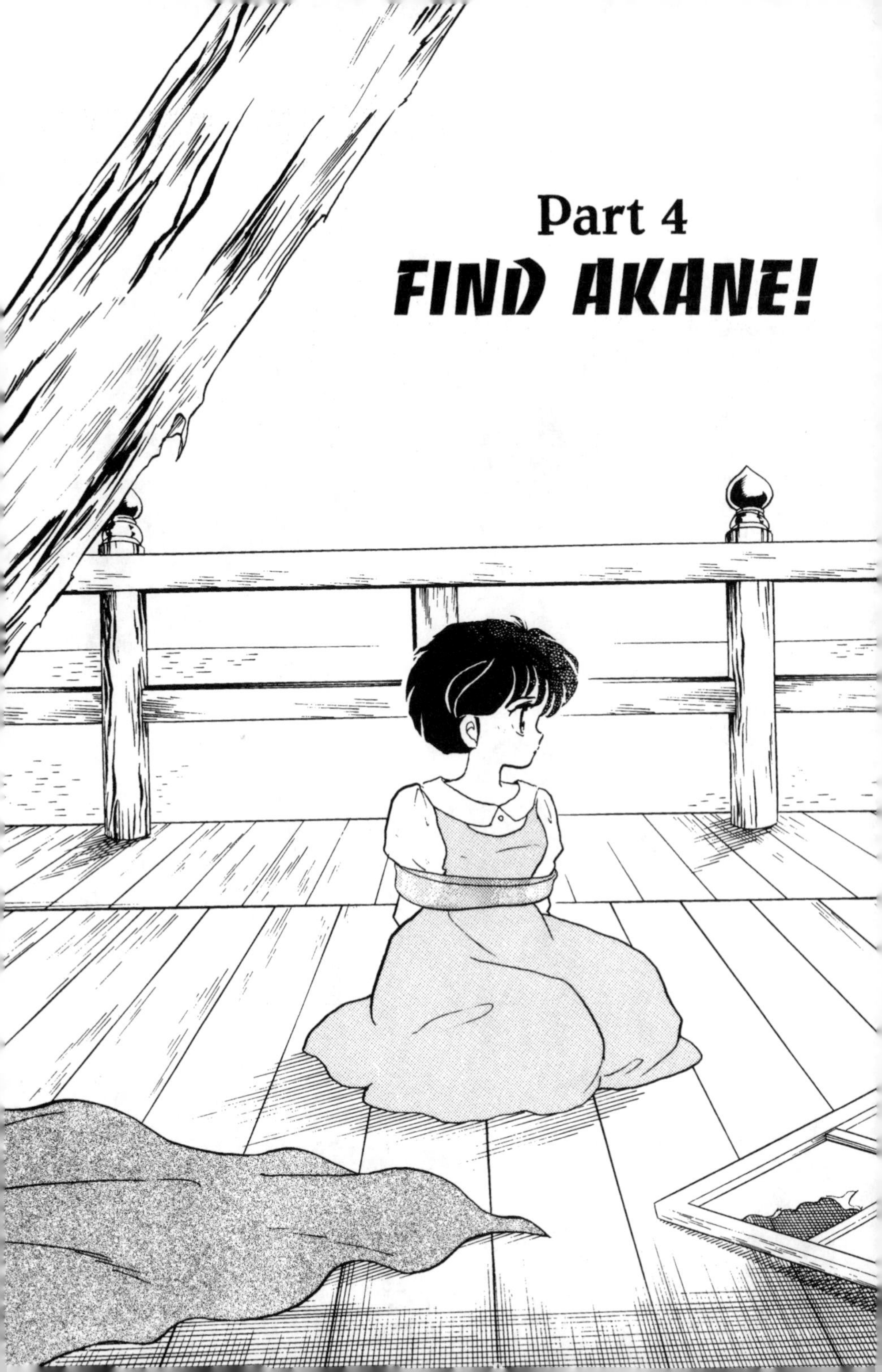
Part 4
FIND AKANE!

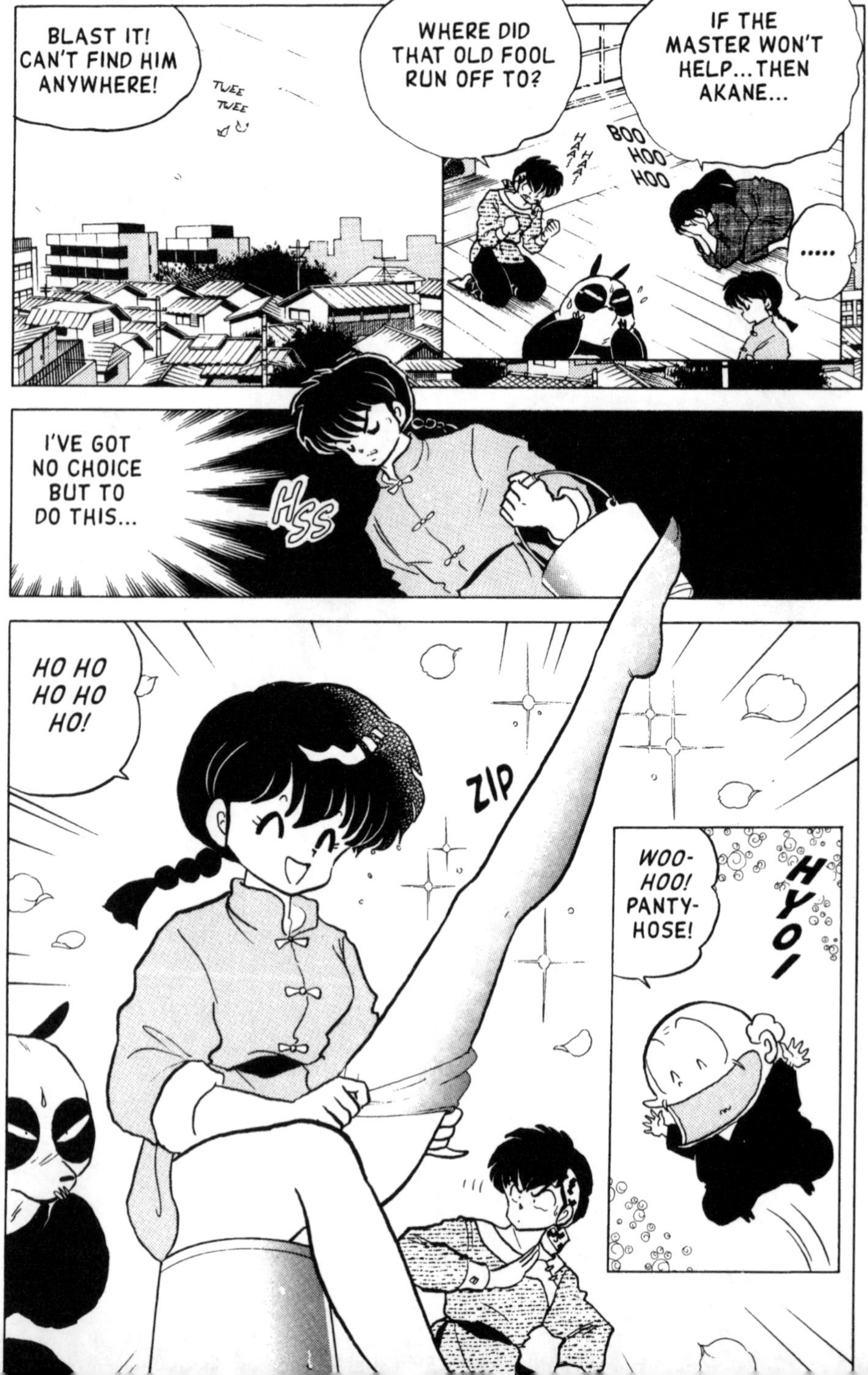
BLAST IT! CAN'T FIND HIM ANYWHERE!
TWEE TWEE
WHERE DID THAT OLD FOOL RUN OFF TO?
IF THE MASTER WON'T HELP...THEN AKANE...
HA! HA!
BOO HOO HOO
.....
I'VE GOT NO CHOICE BUT TO DO THIS...
HSS
HO HO HO HO HO!
ZIP
WOO-HOO! PANTY-HOSE!
HYOI

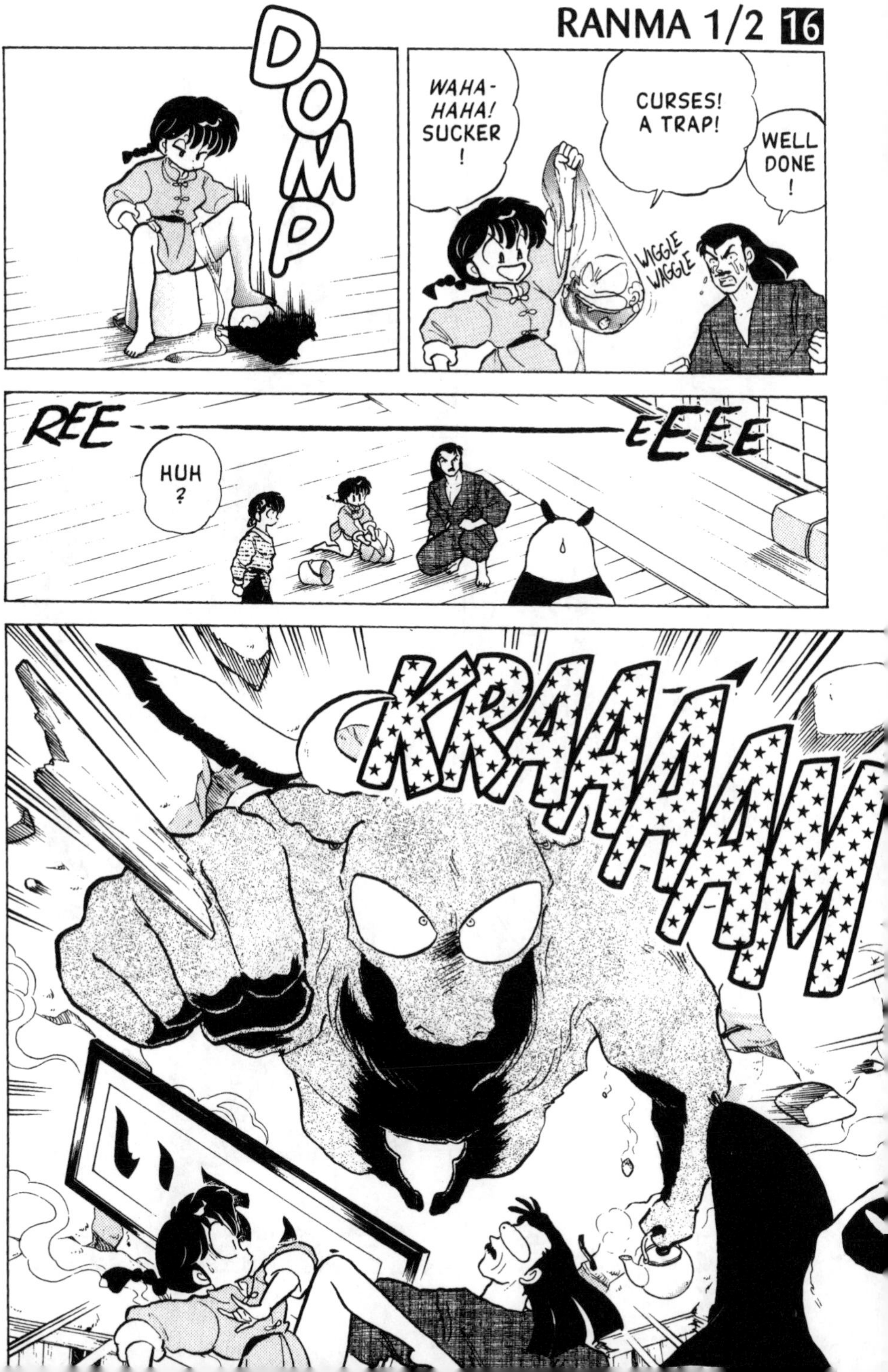
DOMP
WAHA-HAHA! SUCKER!
CURSES! A TRAP!
WELL DONE!
WIGGLE WAGGLE
REE-----EEEE
HUH?
KRAAAAM

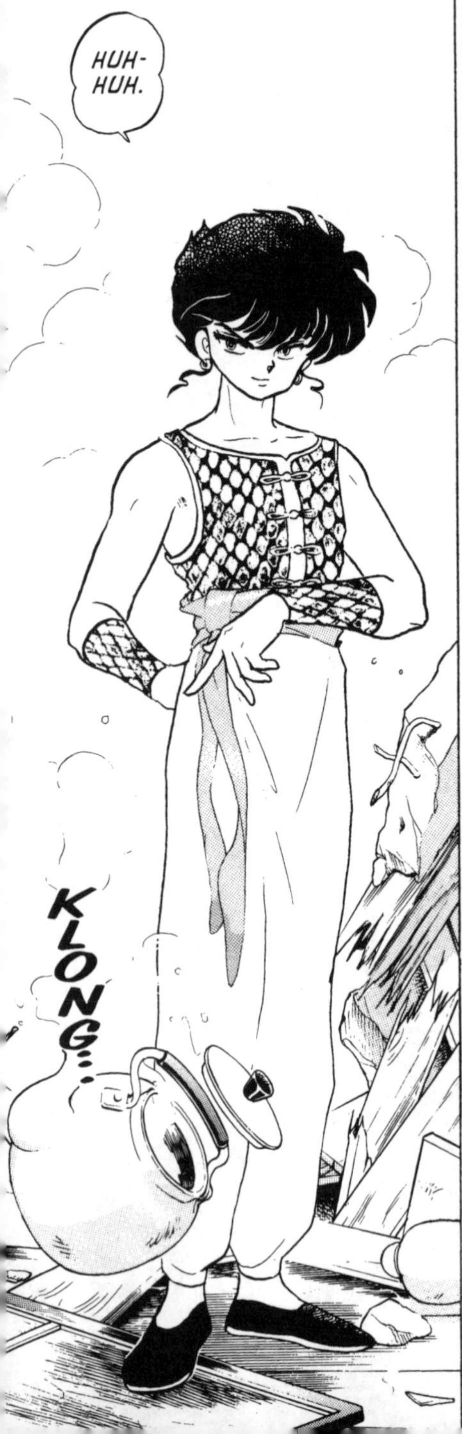
HUH-HUH.
KLONG...

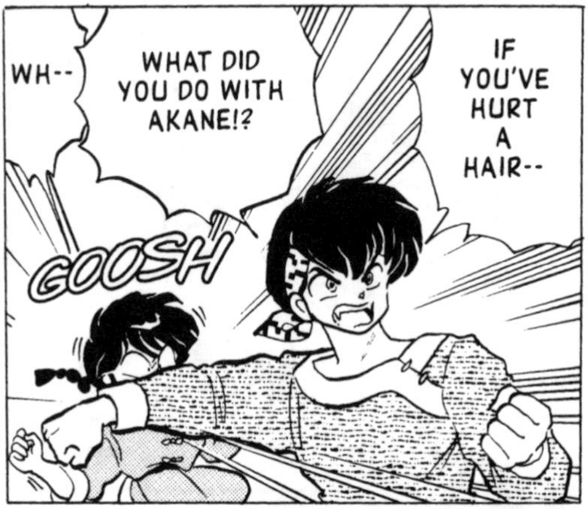
WH--
WHAT DID YOU DO WITH AKANE!?
IF YOU'VE HURT A HAIR--
GOOSH

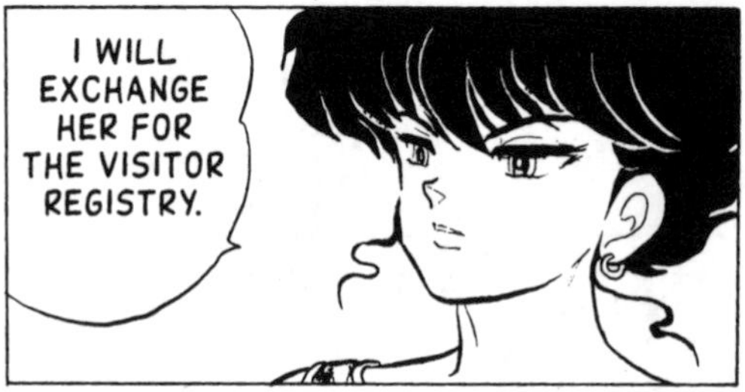
I WILL EXCHANGE HER FOR THE VISITOR REGISTRY.

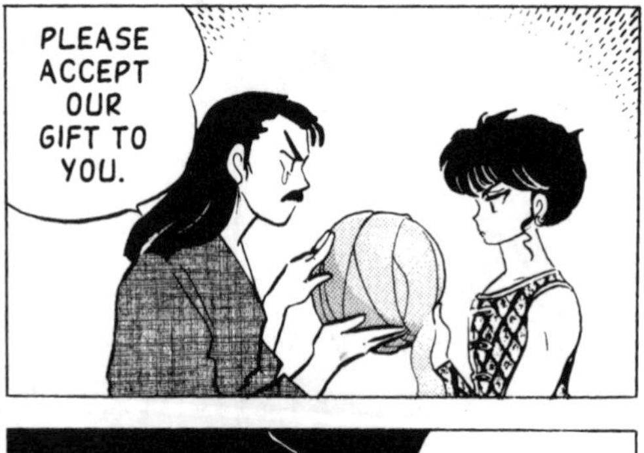
PLEASE ACCEPT OUR GIFT TO YOU.

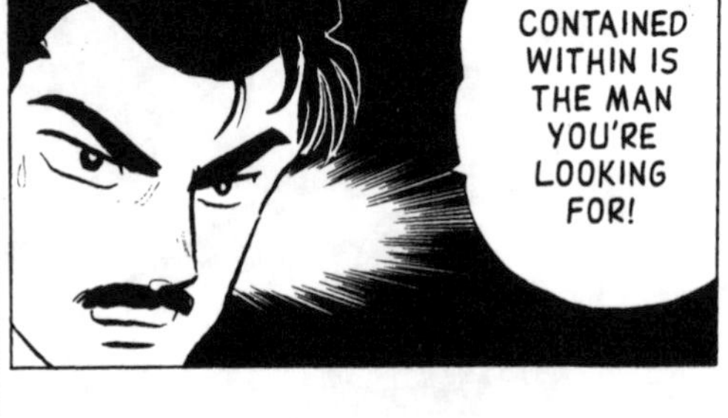
CONTAINED WITHIN IS THE MAN YOU'RE LOOKING FOR!

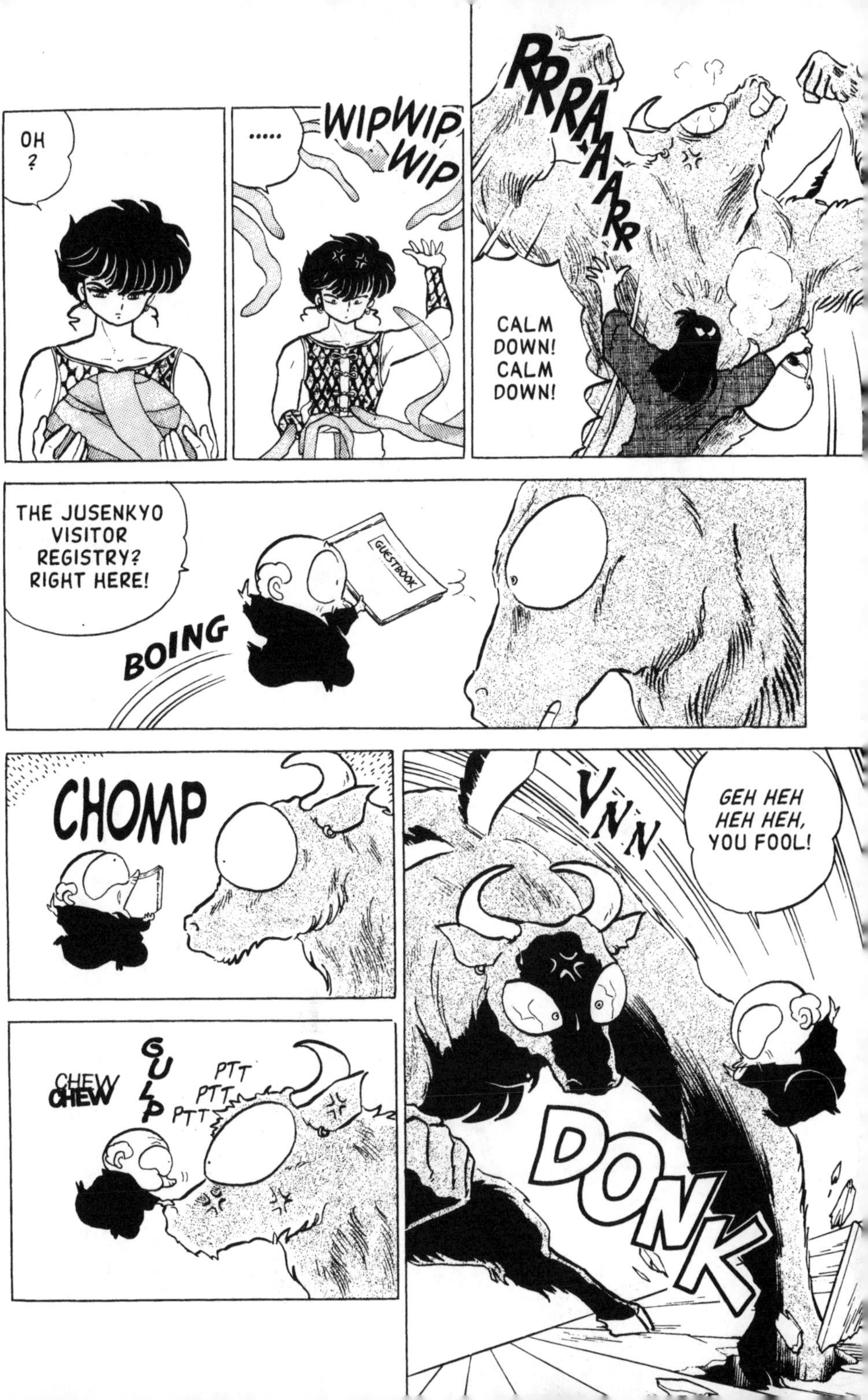
OH ?
.....
WIPWIP WIP
RRRAAAARR
CALM DOWN! CALM DOWN!
THE JUSENKYO VISITOR REGISTRY? RIGHT HERE!
GUESTBOOK
BOING
CHOMP
CHEW CHEW
GULP
PTT PTT PTT
VNN
GEH HEH HEH HEH, YOU FOOL!
DONK

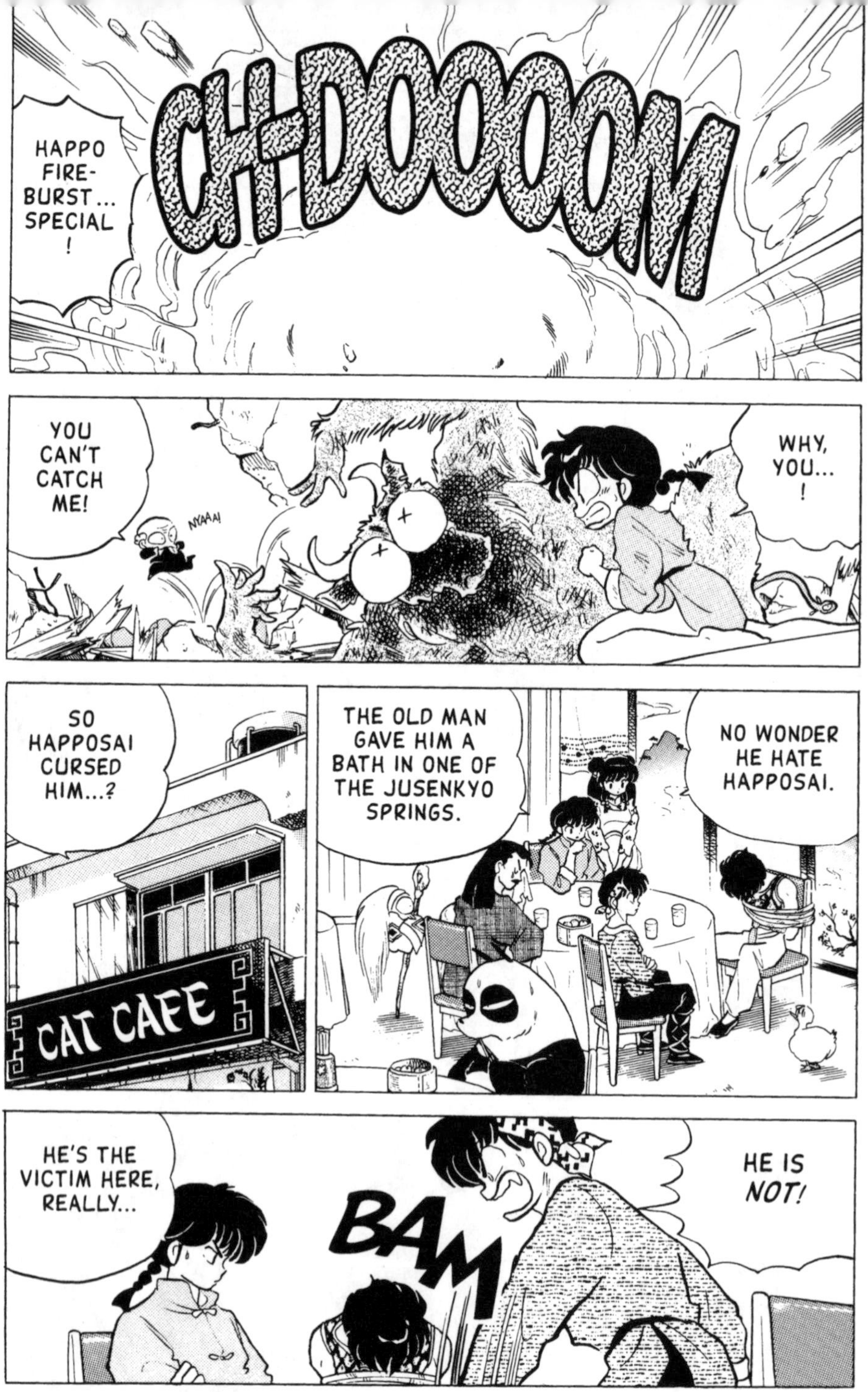
HAPPO FIRE-BURST... SPECIAL!
CH-DOOOOM
YOU CAN'T CATCH ME!
NYAAA!
WHY, YOU...!
SO HAPPOSAI CURSED HIM...?
CAT CAFE
THE OLD MAN GAVE HIM A BATH IN ONE OF THE JUSENKYO SPRINGS.
NO WONDER HE HATE HAPPOSAI.
HE'S THE VICTIM HERE, REALLY...
BAM
HE IS *NOT!*

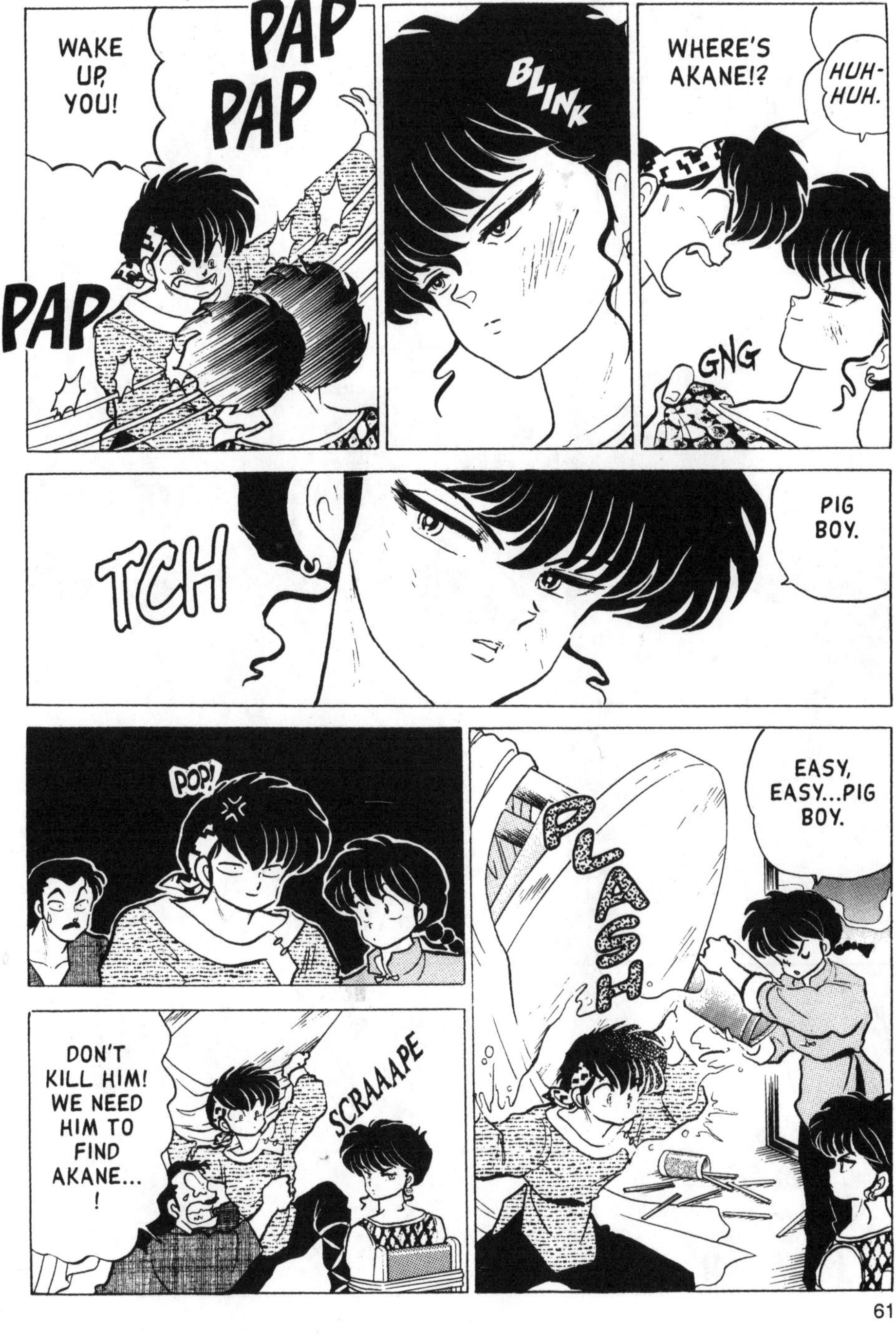
WAKE UP, YOU!
PAP PAP
PAP
PAP
BLINK
WHERE'S AKANE!?
HUH-HUH.
GNG
TCH
PIG BOY.
POP!
DON'T KILL HIM! WE NEED HIM TO FIND AKANE... !
SCRAAAPE
EASY, EASY...PIG BOY.
PLASH

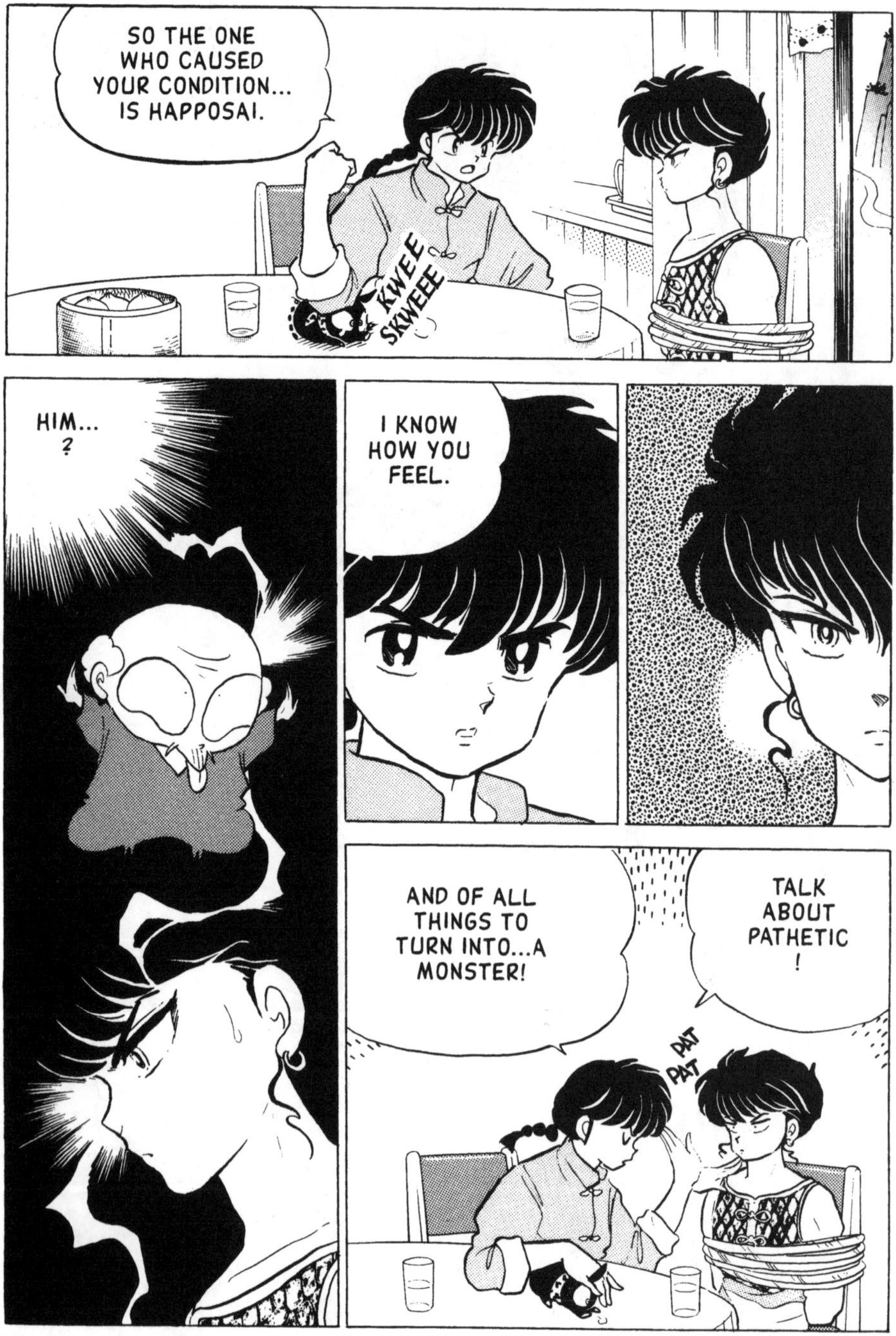
SO THE ONE WHO CAUSED YOUR CONDITION... IS HAPPOSAI.
KWEE SKWEEE
HIM... ?
I KNOW HOW YOU FEEL.
AND OF ALL THINGS TO TURN INTO...A MONSTER!
TALK ABOUT PATHETIC !
PAT PAT

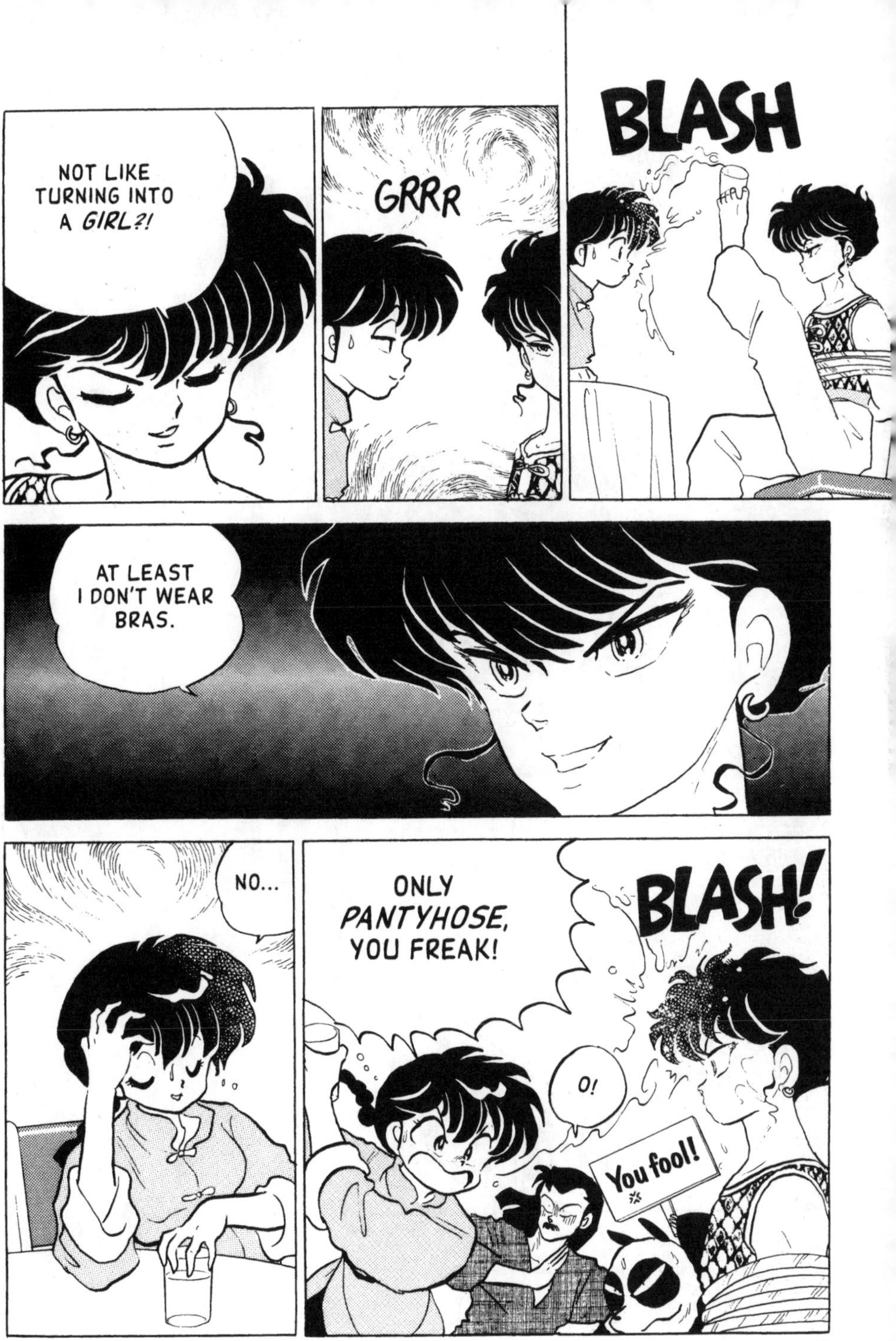
NOT LIKE TURNING INTO A GIRL?!
GRRR
BLASH
AT LEAST I DON'T WEAR BRAS.
NO...
ONLY PANTYHOSE, YOU FREAK!
BLASH!
O!
You fool!

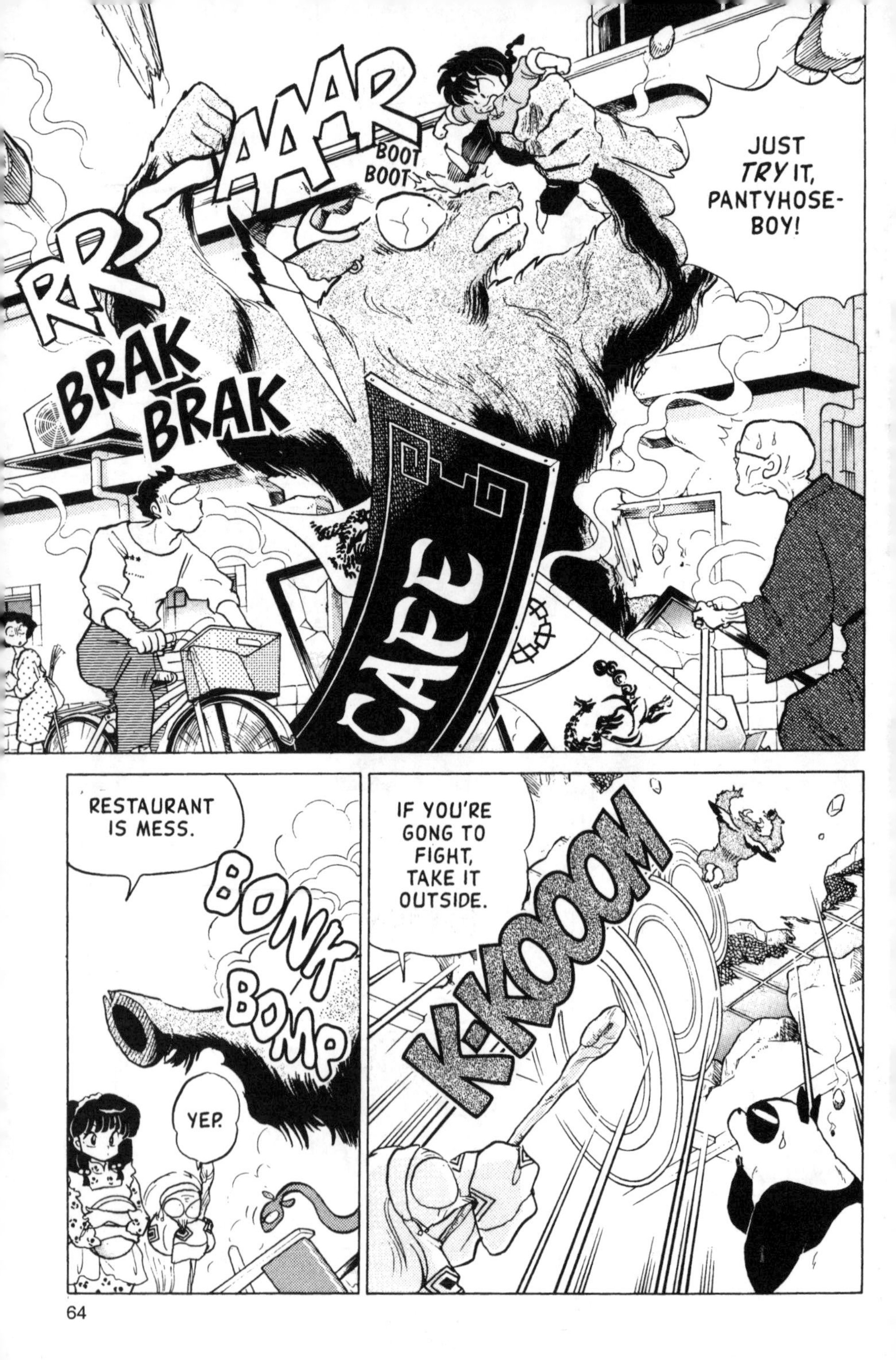
RRSTAAAR
BOOT BOOT
JUST TRY IT, PANTYHOSE-BOY!
BRAK BRAK
CAFE
RESTAURANT IS MESS.
BONK BOMP
YEP.
IF YOU'RE GONG TO FIGHT, TAKE IT OUTSIDE.
K-KOOOM

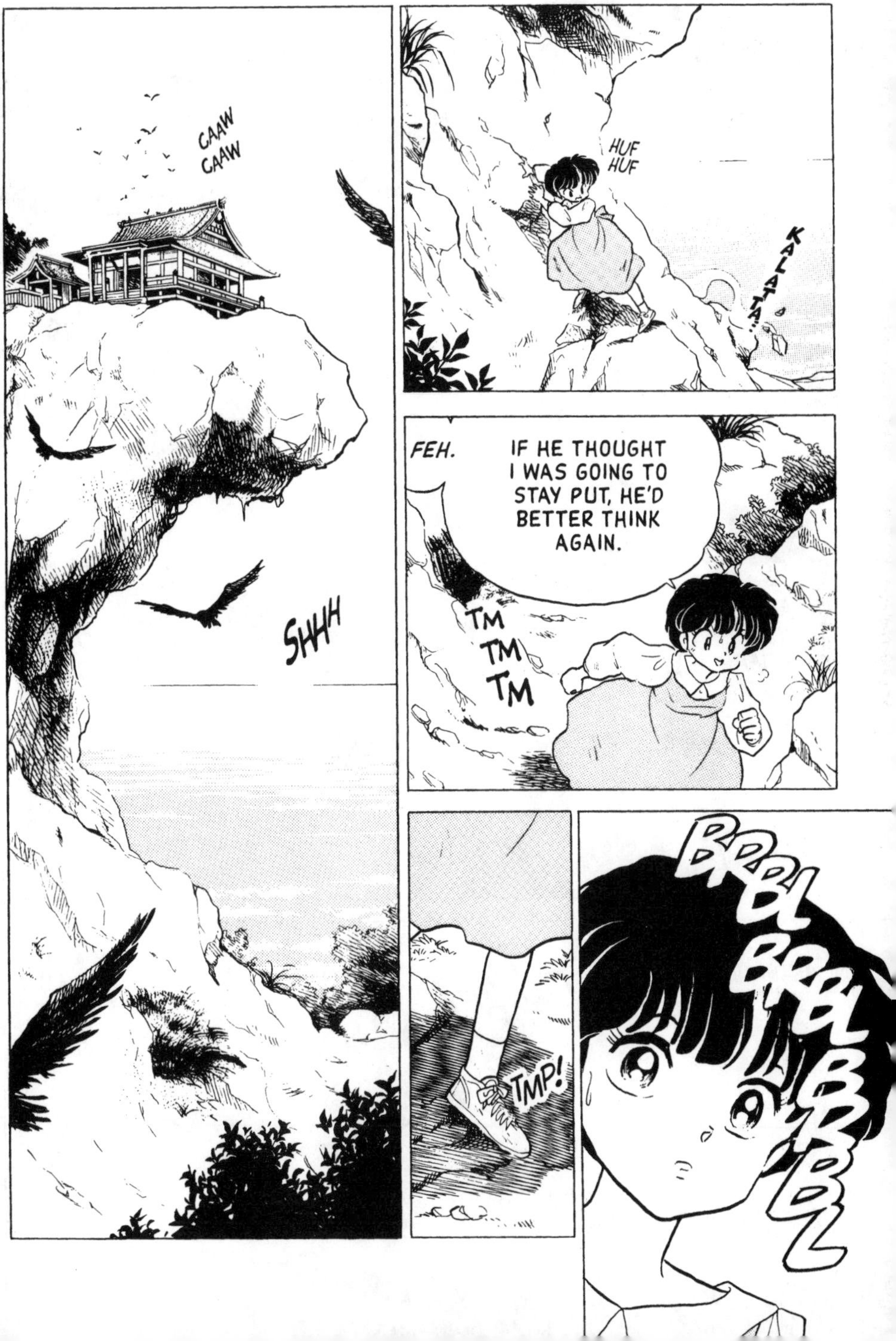
CAAW
CAAW
SHHH
HUF
HUF
KALATTA...
FEH.
IF HE THOUGHT I WAS GOING TO STAY PUT, HE'D BETTER THINK AGAIN.
TM
TM
TM
TMP!
BRBL
BRBL
BRBL

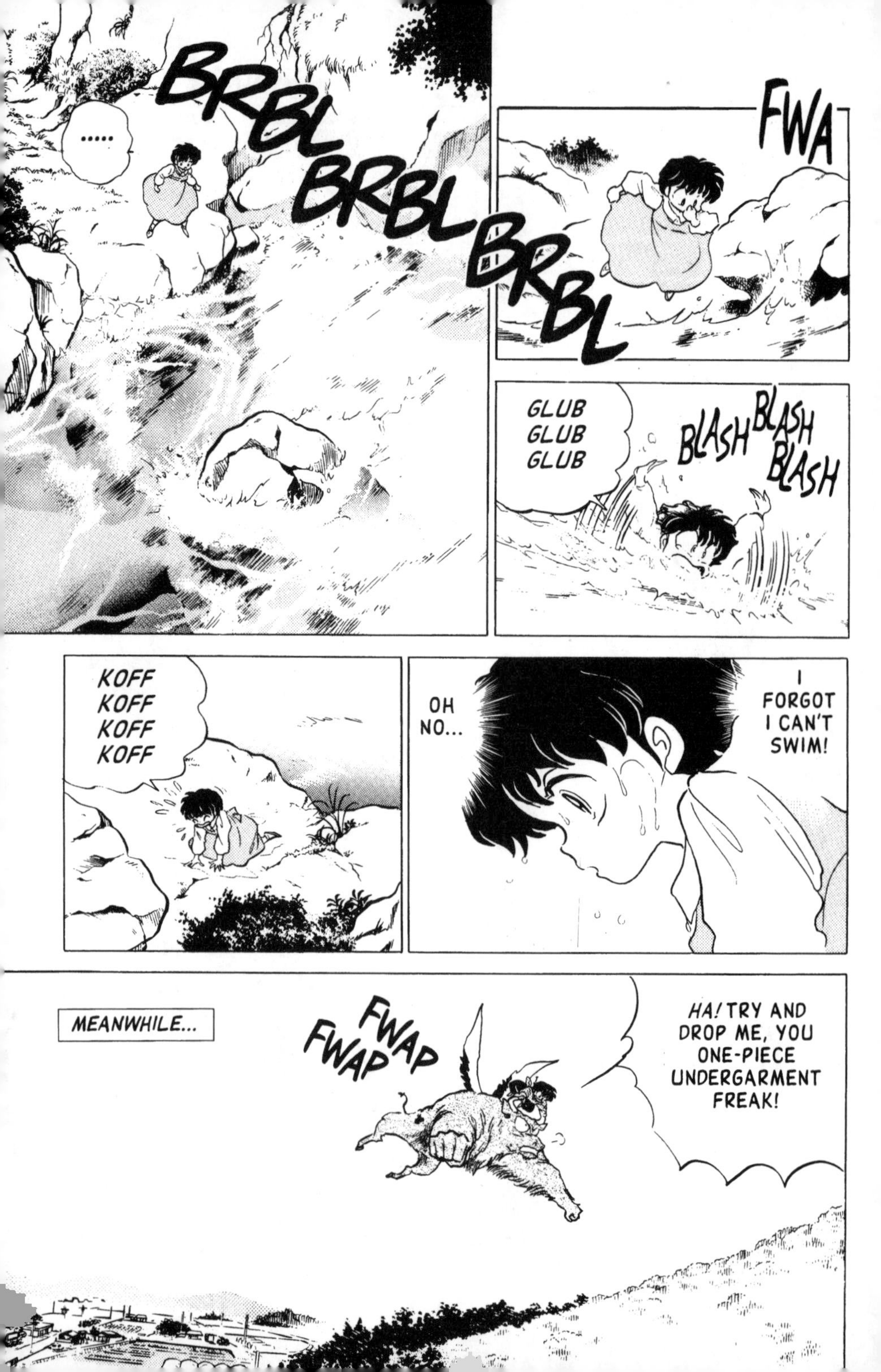
......
BRBL BRBL BRBL
FWA
GLUB GLUB GLUB
BLASH BLASH BLASH
KOFF KOFF KOFF KOFF
OH NO...
I FORGOT I CAN'T SWIM!
MEANWHILE...
FWAP FWAP
HA! TRY AND DROP ME, YOU ONE-PIECE UNDERGARMENT FREAK!

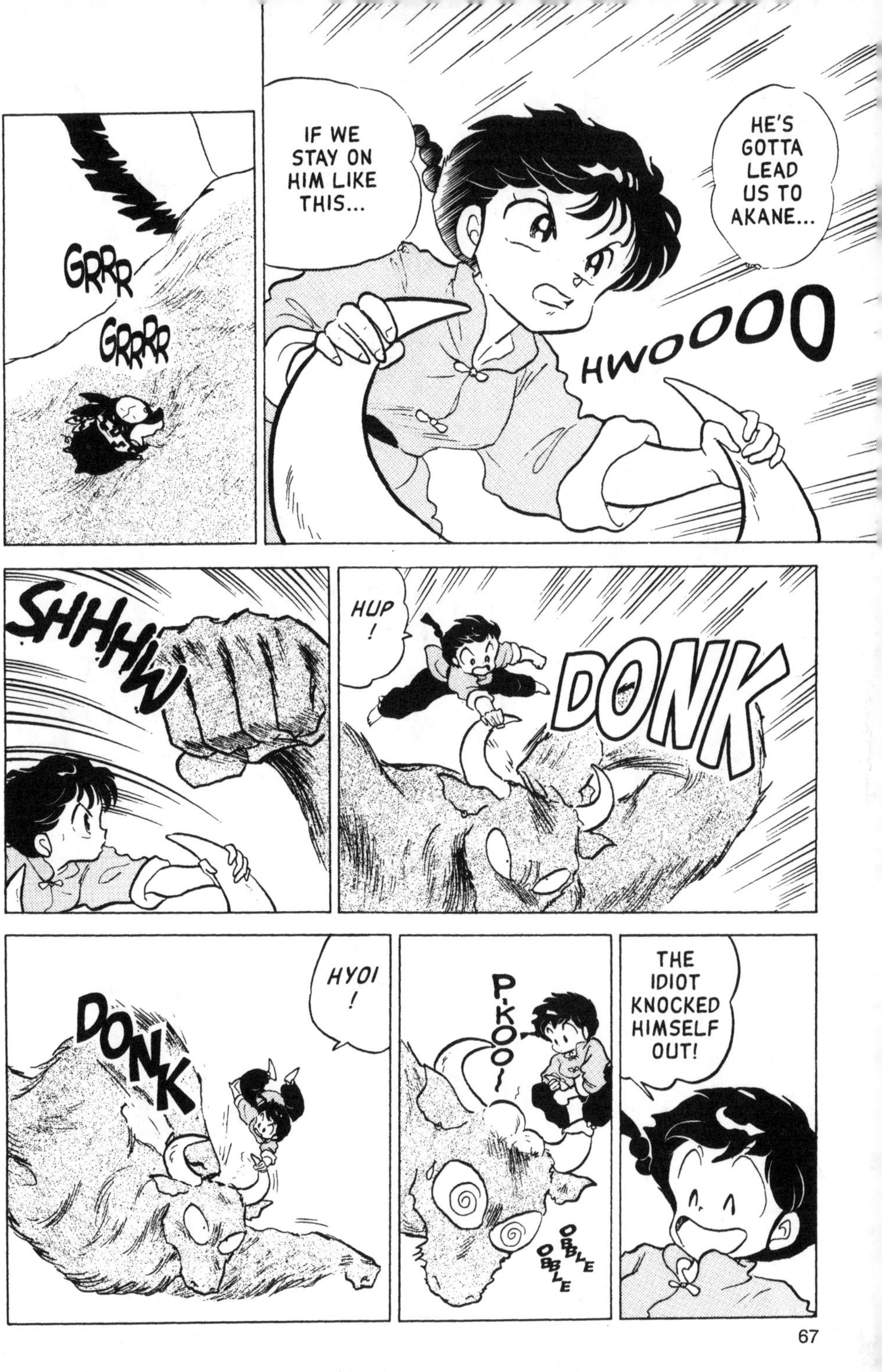
GRRR
GRRRR
IF WE STAY ON HIM LIKE THIS...
HE'S GOTTA LEAD US TO AKANE...
HWOOOOO
SHHHW
HUP!
DONK
DONK
HYOI!
P-KOO~
OBBLE OBBLE
THE IDIOT KNOCKED HIMSELF OUT!

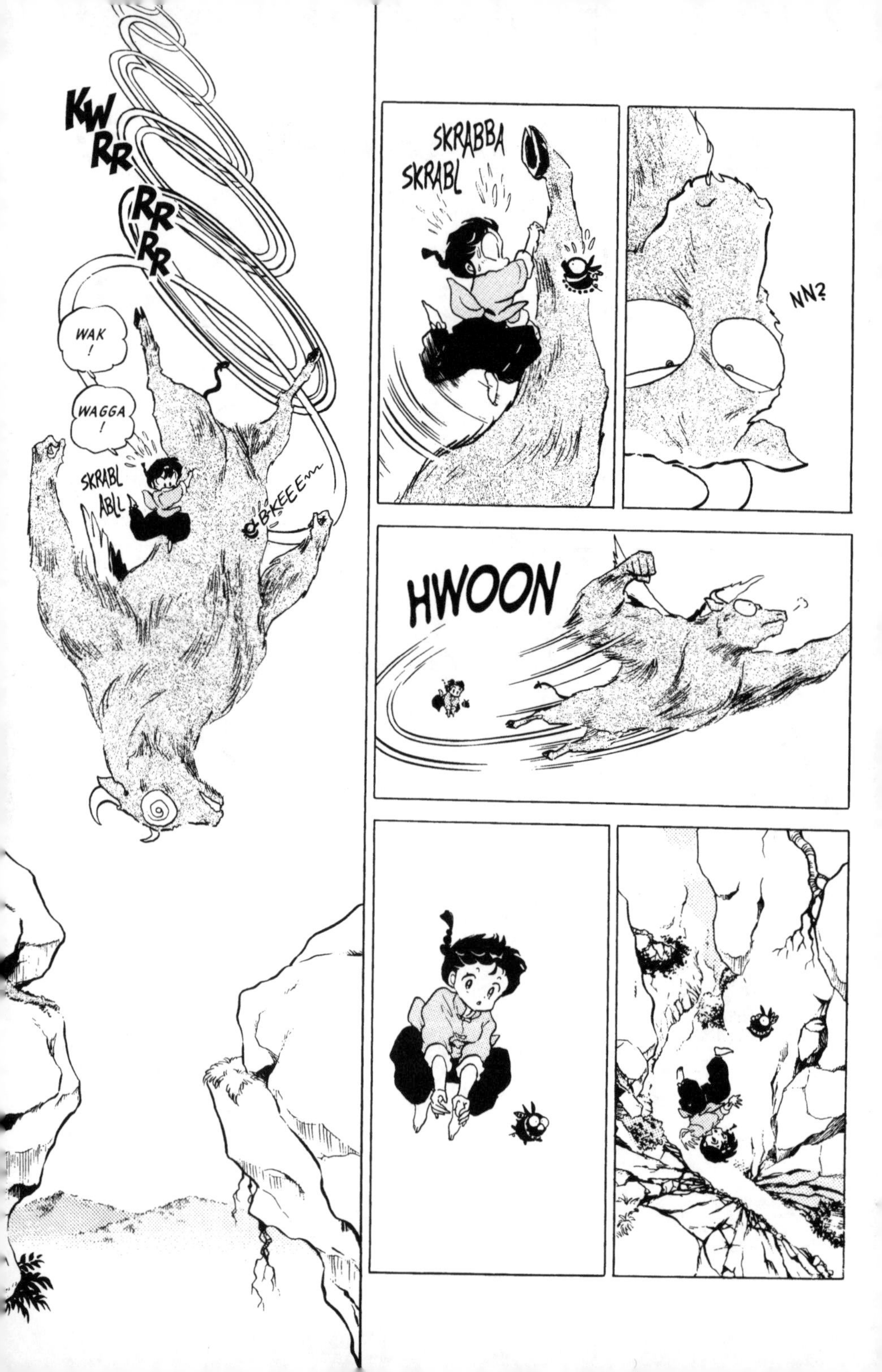
KWRRRRRR
WAK!
WAGGA!
SKRABL ABLL
B-KEEE~~
SKRABBA
SKRABL
NN?
HWOON

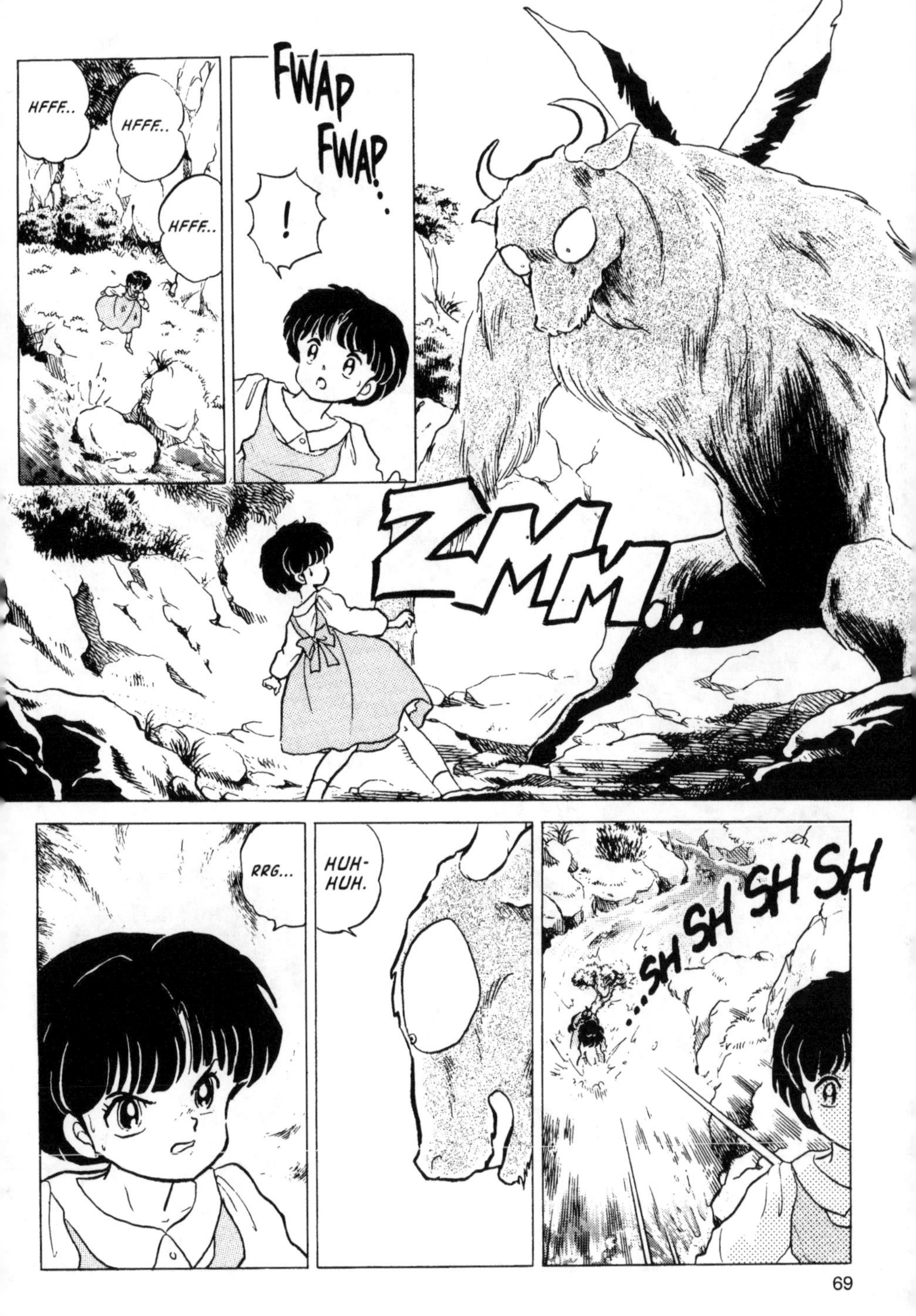

HFFF...
HFFF...
HFFF...
FWAP FWAP...
!
ZMM...
RRG...
HUH-HUH.
...SH SH SH SH SH

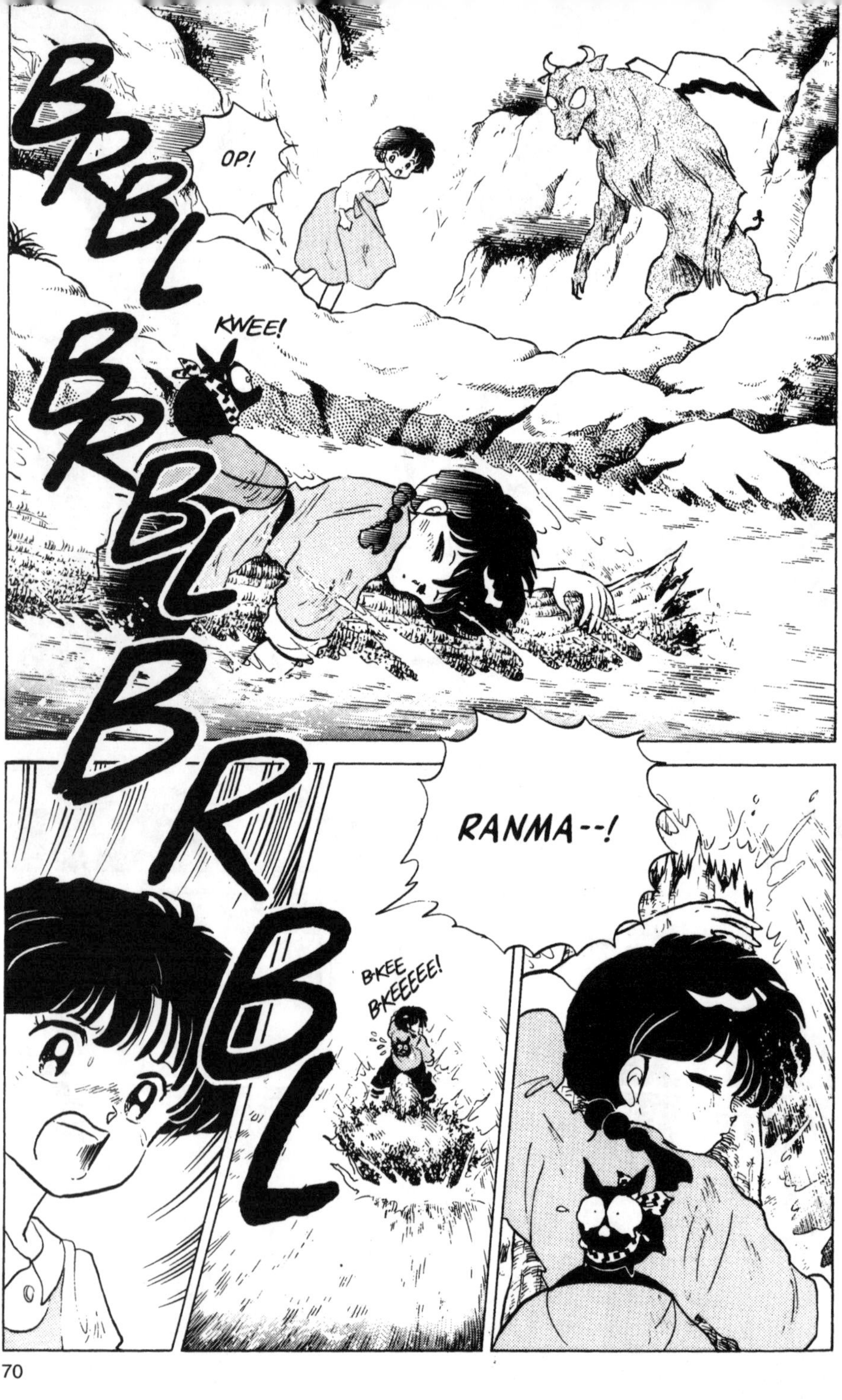
BRBL BRBL BRBL
OP!
KWEE!
RANMA--!
B-KEE B-KEEEEE!

Part 5
S.W.A.T
(Save Widdle Akane Team)

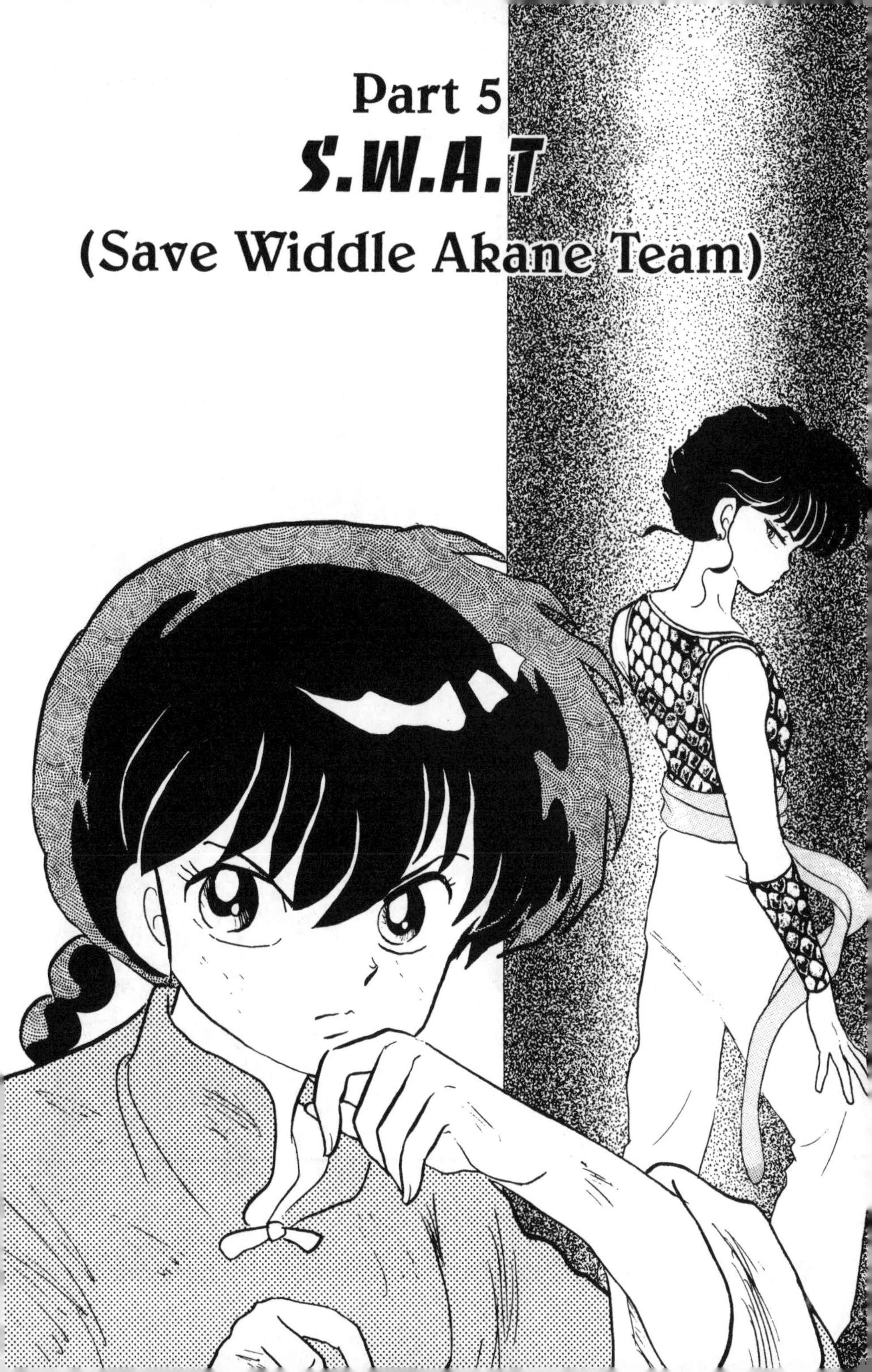

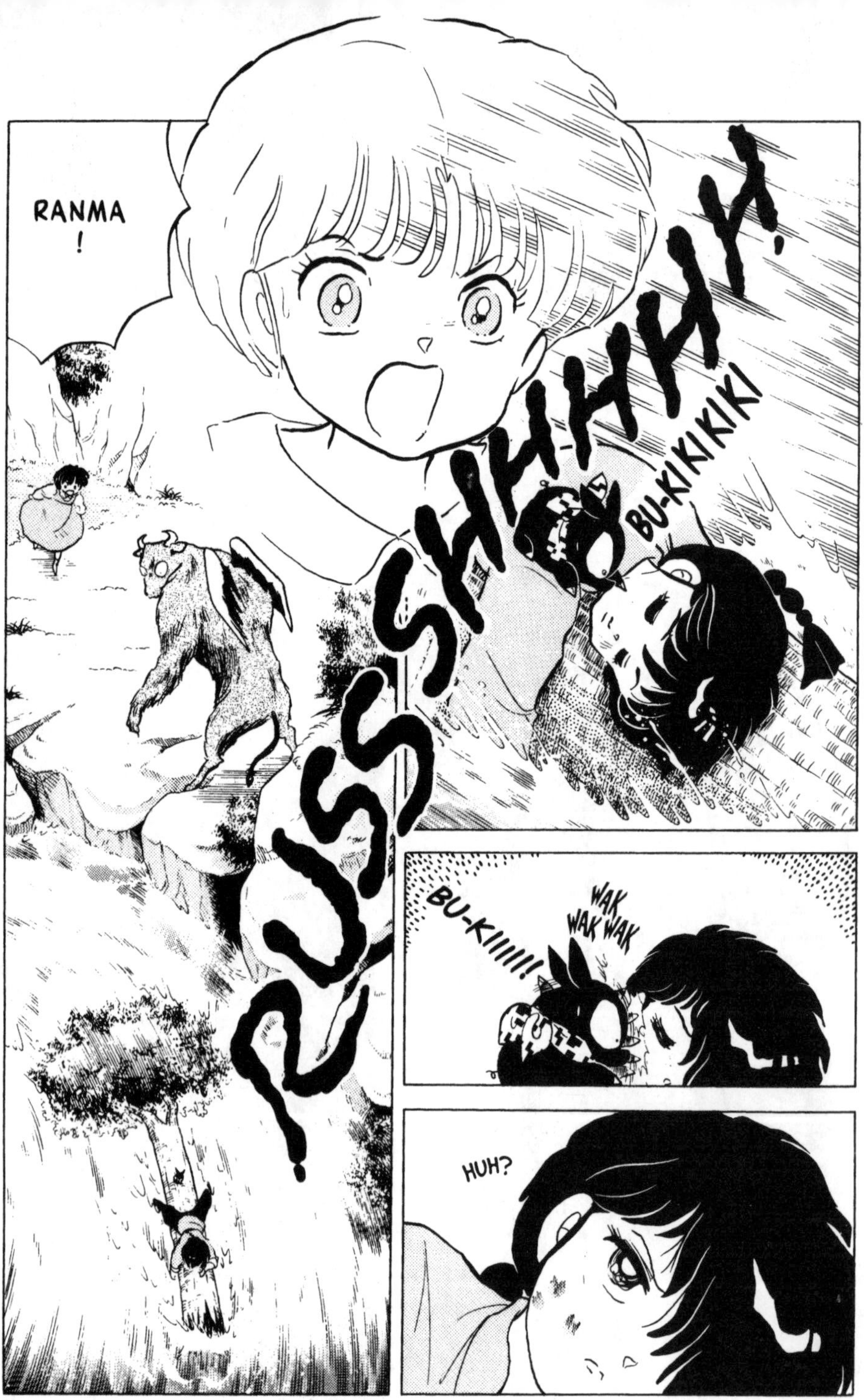
RANMA
!
RUSSHHHH!
BU-KIKIKIKI
BU-KIIIIII!
WAK
WAK WAK
HUH?

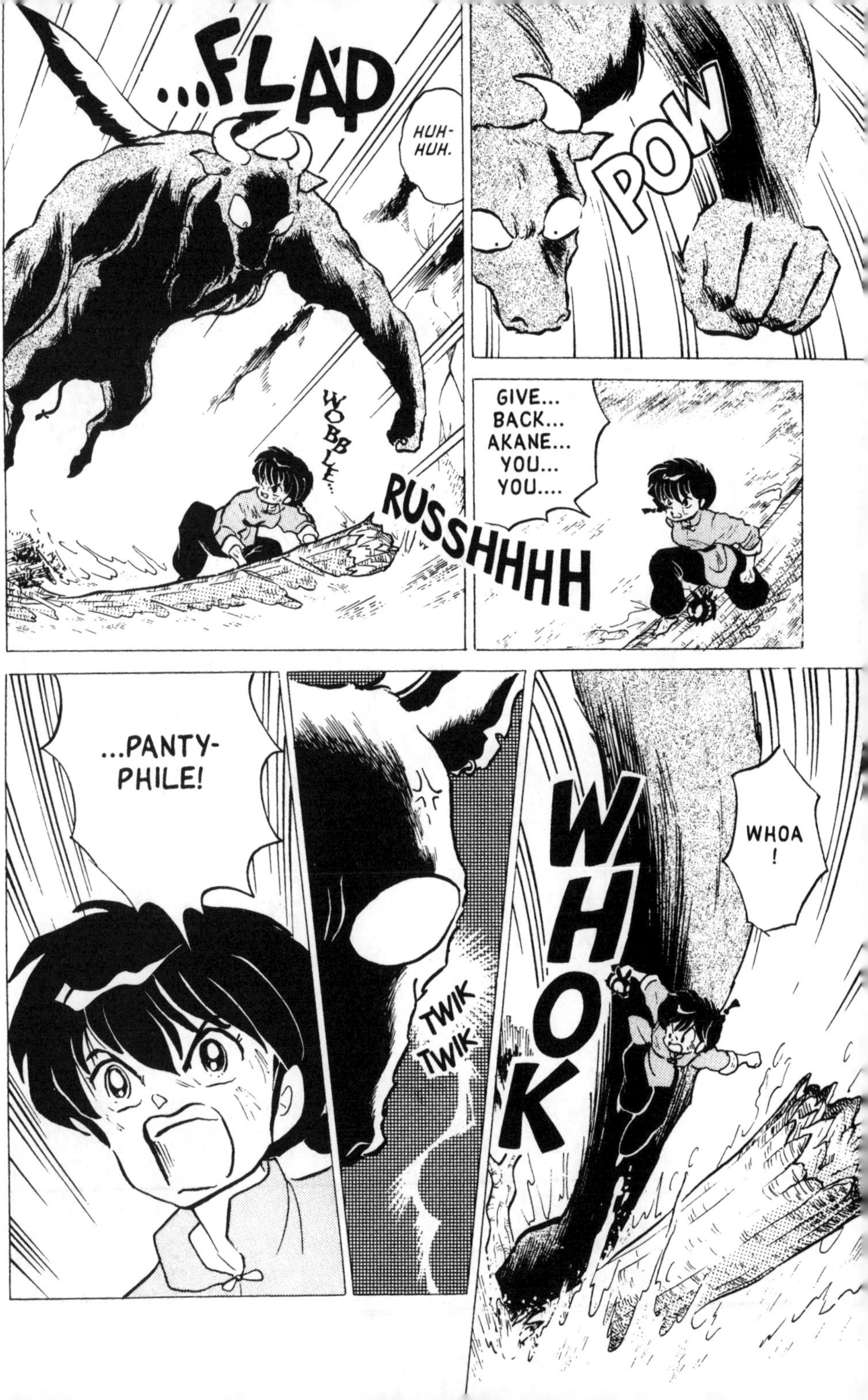
...FLAP
HUH-HUH.
WOBBLE...
RUSSHHHH
POW
GIVE... BACK... AKANE... YOU... YOU....
...PANTY-PHILE!
TWIK TWIK
WHOA!
WHOK

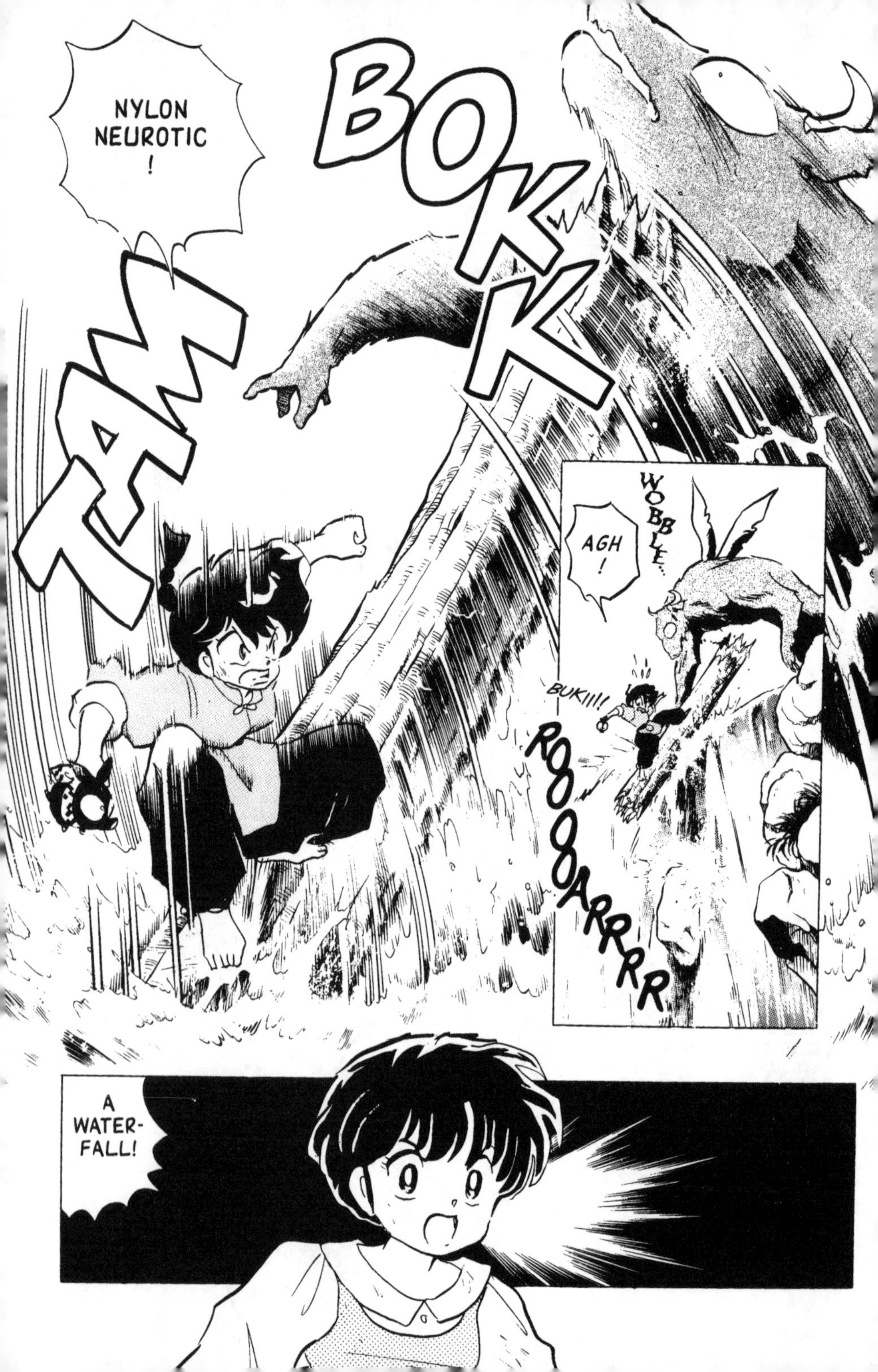
NYLON NEUROTIC !
TAM
BOKKK
AGH !
WOBBLE...
BUKIII!
ROOOOARRRRR
A WATER-FALL!

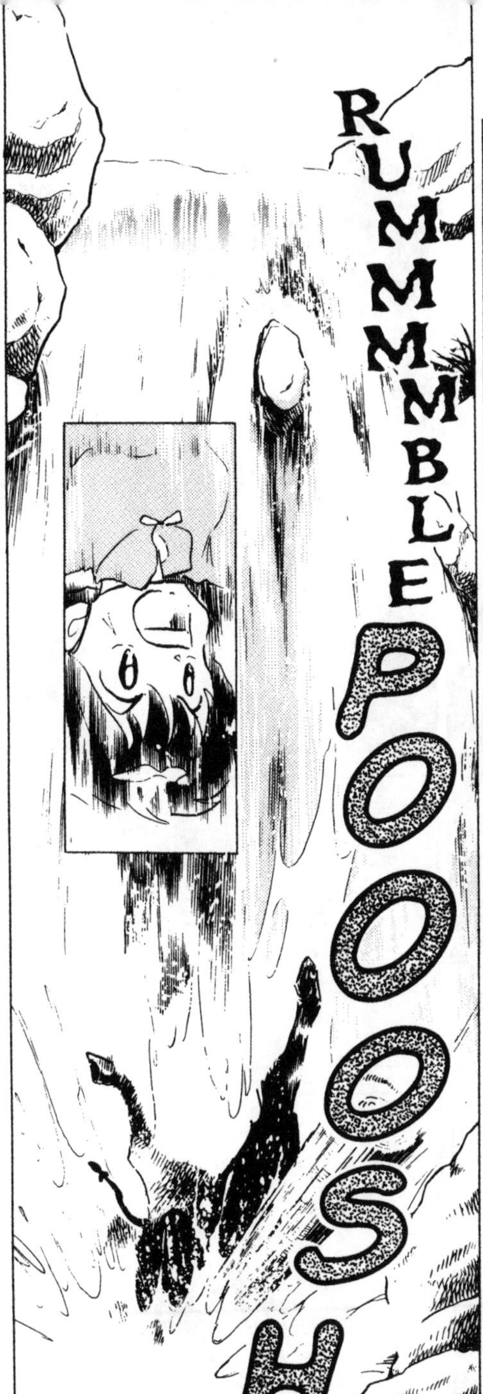
RUMMMMBLE
POOOSH

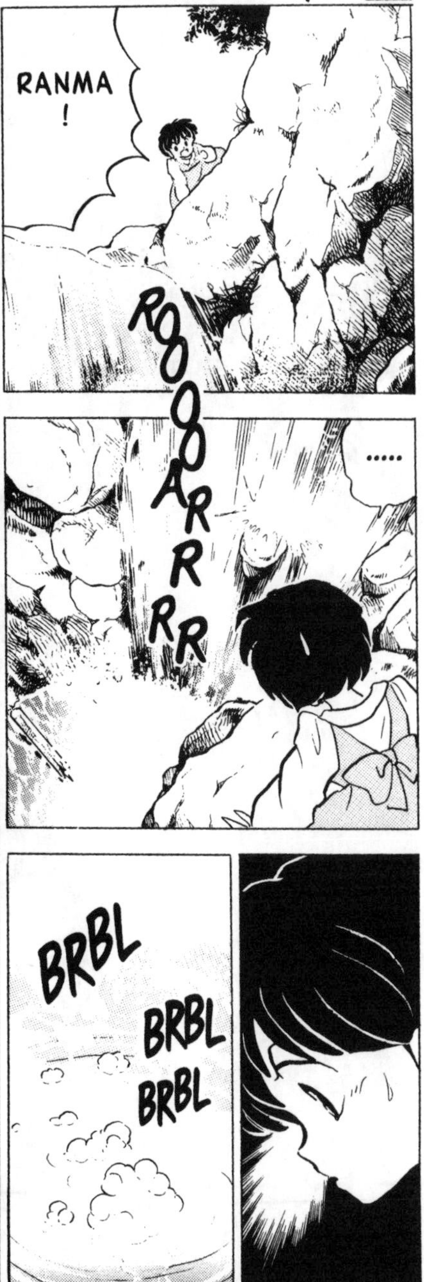
RANMA !
ROOOOARRRR
.....
BRBL
BRBL
BRBL

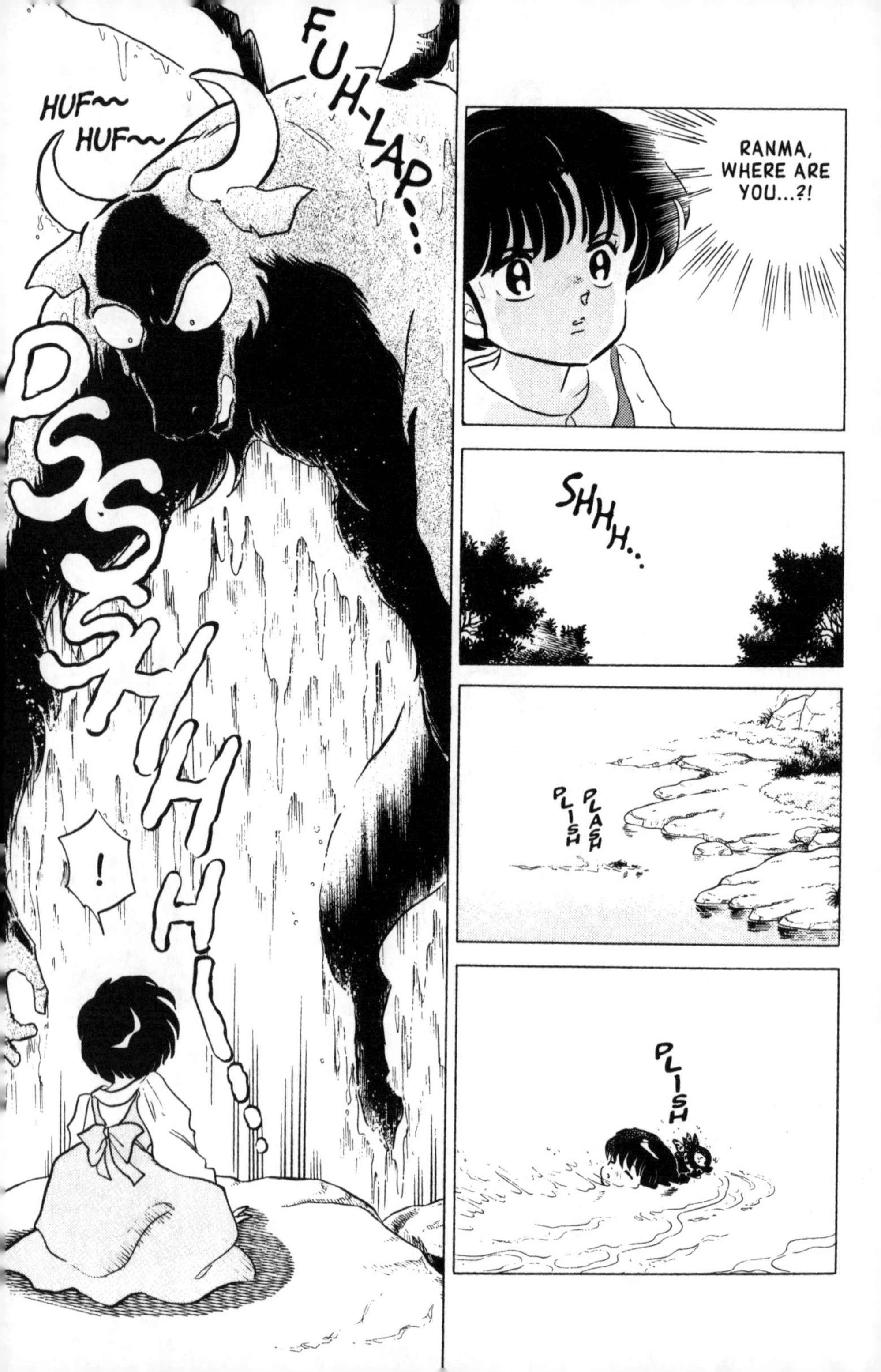
HUF~~ HUF~~
FUH-LAP...
DSSSHHH
!
RANMA, WHERE ARE YOU...?!
SHHH...
PLISH PLASH
PLISH

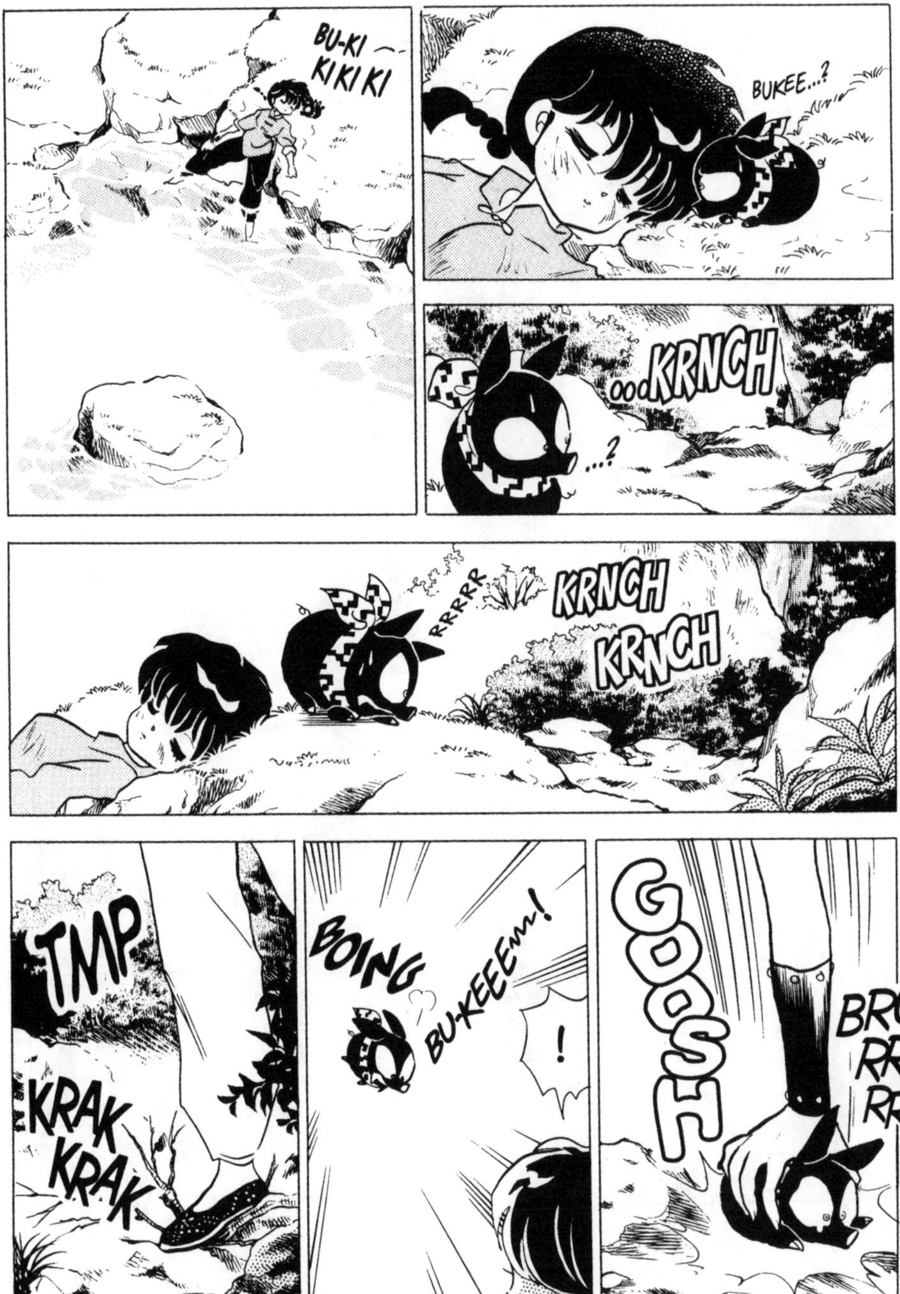
BU-KI
KI KI KI
BUKEE...?
...KRNCH
...?
RRRRR
KRNCH
KRNCH
TMP
KRAK
KRAK
KRAK
BOING
BU-KEEE...!
!
GOOSH
BRG
RRG
RRG

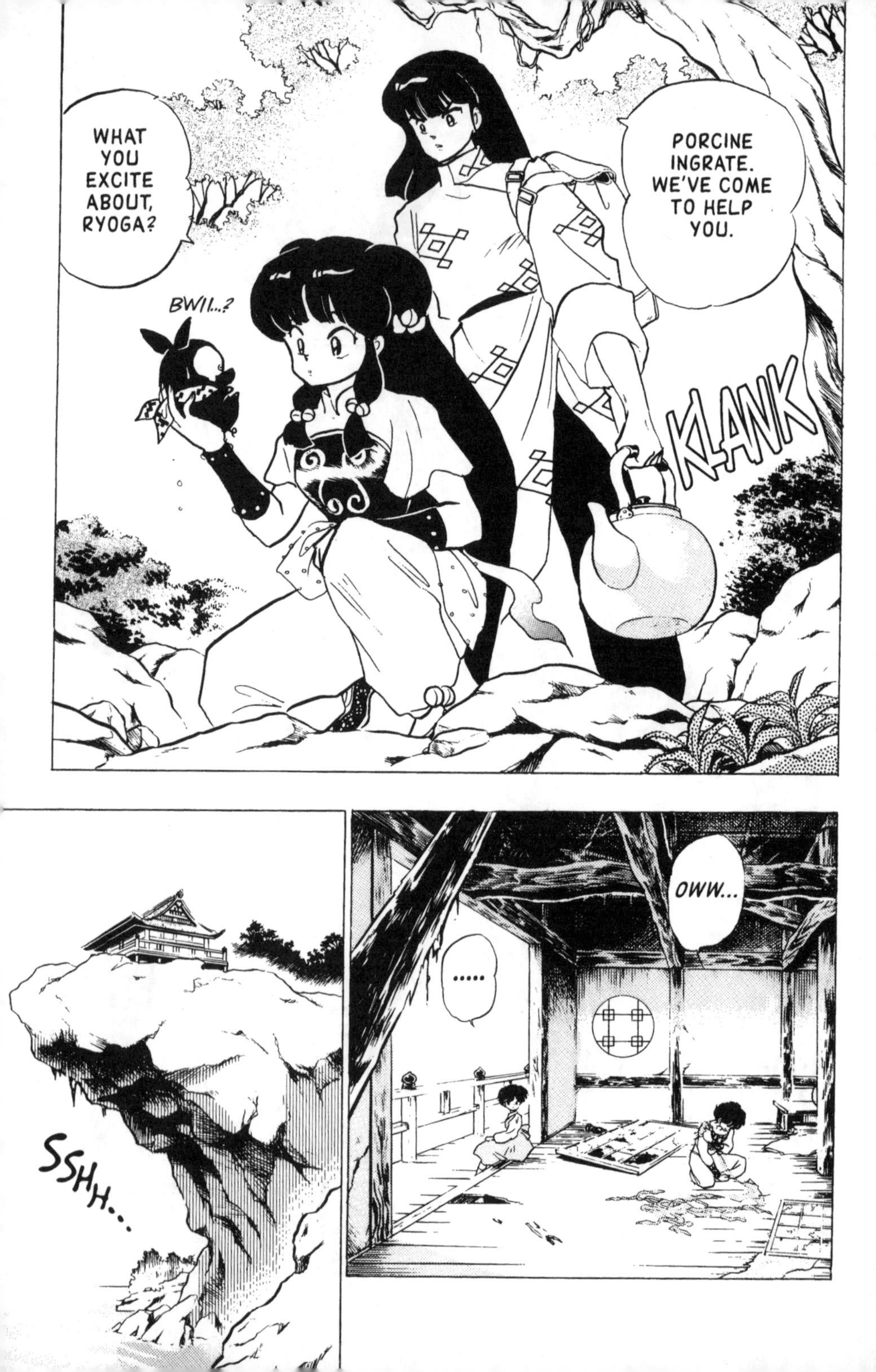
WHAT YOU EXCITE ABOUT, RYOGA?
BWII...?
PORCINE INGRATE. WE'VE COME TO HELP YOU.
KLANK
SSHH...
OWW...
......

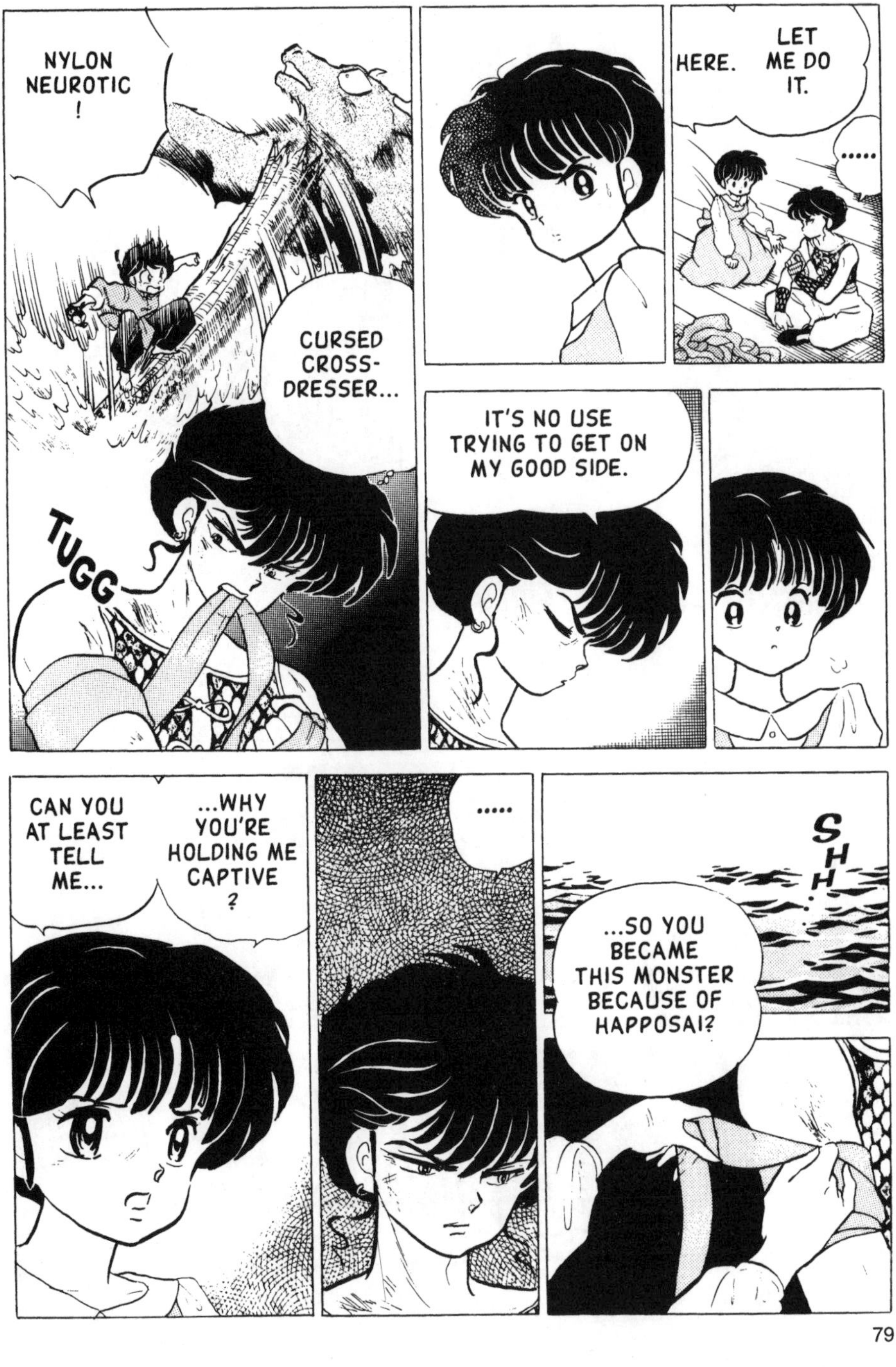
NYLON NEUROTIC !
CURSED CROSS-DRESSER...
TUGG
HERE.
LET ME DO IT.
.....
IT'S NO USE TRYING TO GET ON MY GOOD SIDE.
CAN YOU AT LEAST TELL ME...
...WHY YOU'RE HOLDING ME CAPTIVE ?
.....
SHH...
...SO YOU BECAME THIS MONSTER BECAUSE OF HAPPOSAI?

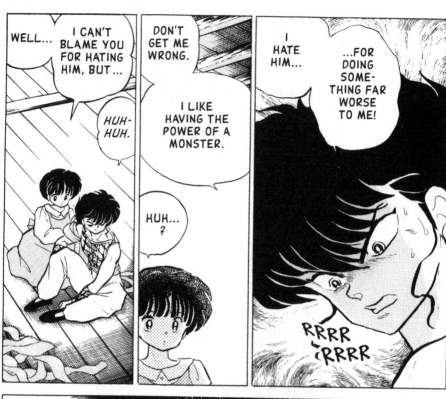

WELL... I CAN'T BLAME YOU FOR HATING HIM, BUT...

HUH-HUH.

DON'T GET ME WRONG.

I LIKE HAVING THE POWER OF A MONSTER.

HUH...?

I HATE HIM...

...FOR DOING SOMETHING FAR WORSE TO ME!

RRRR RRRR

WORSE THAN BECOMING A MONSTER...?

WHAT COULD HAPPOSAI HAVE DONE...?

HUH-HUH...

ANYWAY...

BEFORE I GET THAT OLD MAN...

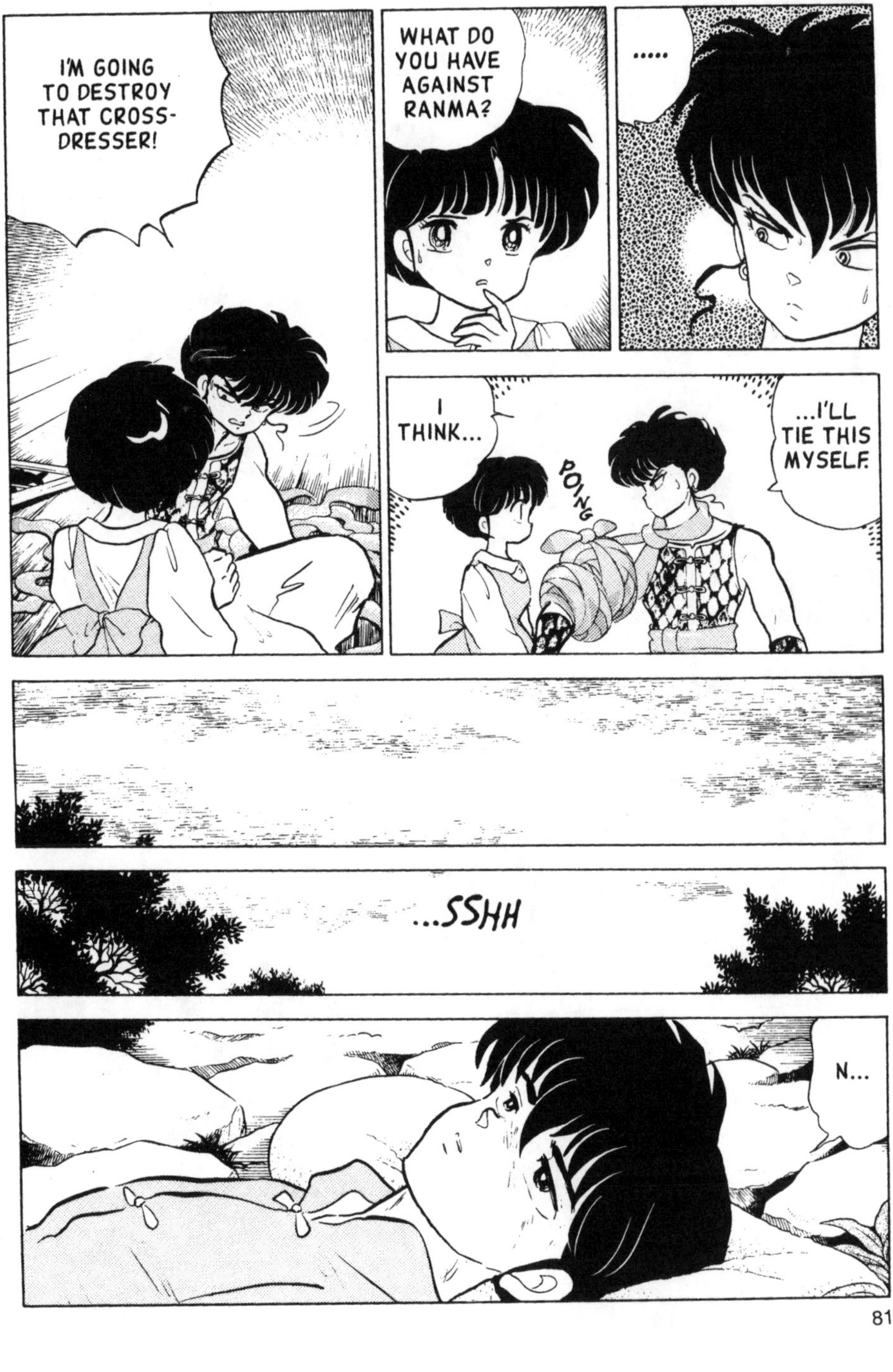
I'M GOING TO DESTROY THAT CROSS-DRESSER!
WHAT DO YOU HAVE AGAINST RANMA?
.....
I THINK...
POING
...I'LL TIE THIS MYSELF.
...SSHH
N...

AH!
RANMA
AWAKE!

HUH
?

SHAMPOO...

MOUSSE...

WH-
WHAT
IN...
?

IT WOULD BE
SMARTER TO FIGHT
THAT MONSTER AS
A GROUP.

WE
HELP
RESCUE
AKANE!

I DON'T
BUY IT.
WHAT ARE
YOU UP
TO?

FEH...

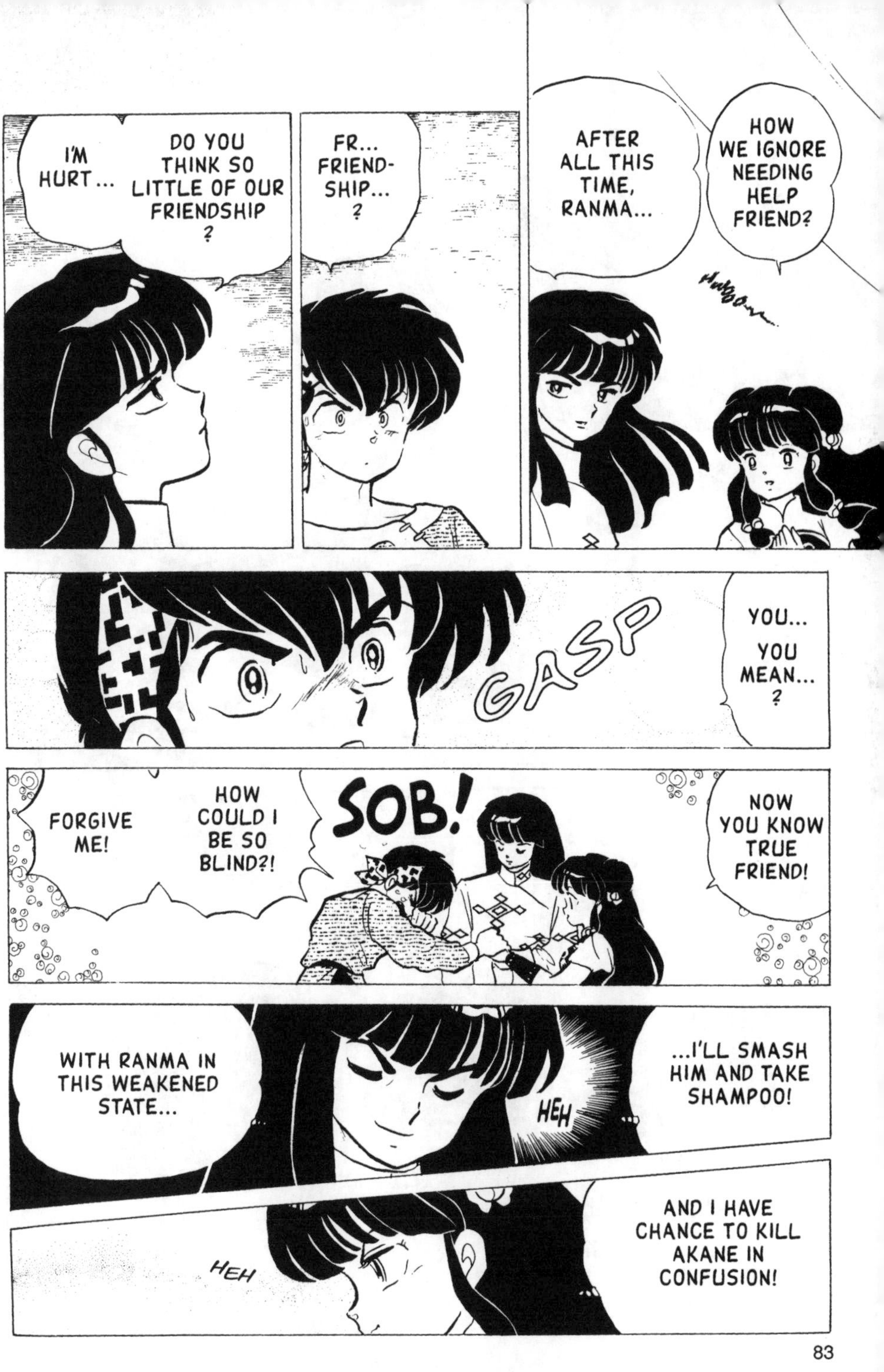
I'M HURT...
DO YOU THINK SO LITTLE OF OUR FRIENDSHIP?
FR... FRIEND-SHIP...?
AFTER ALL THIS TIME, RANMA...
HOW WE IGNORE NEEDING HELP FRIEND?
GASP
YOU... YOU MEAN...?
FORGIVE ME!
HOW COULD I BE SO BLIND?!
SOB!
NOW YOU KNOW TRUE FRIEND!
WITH RANMA IN THIS WEAKENED STATE...
HEH
...I'LL SMASH HIM AND TAKE SHAMPOO!
HEH
AND I HAVE CHANCE TO KILL AKANE IN CONFUSION!

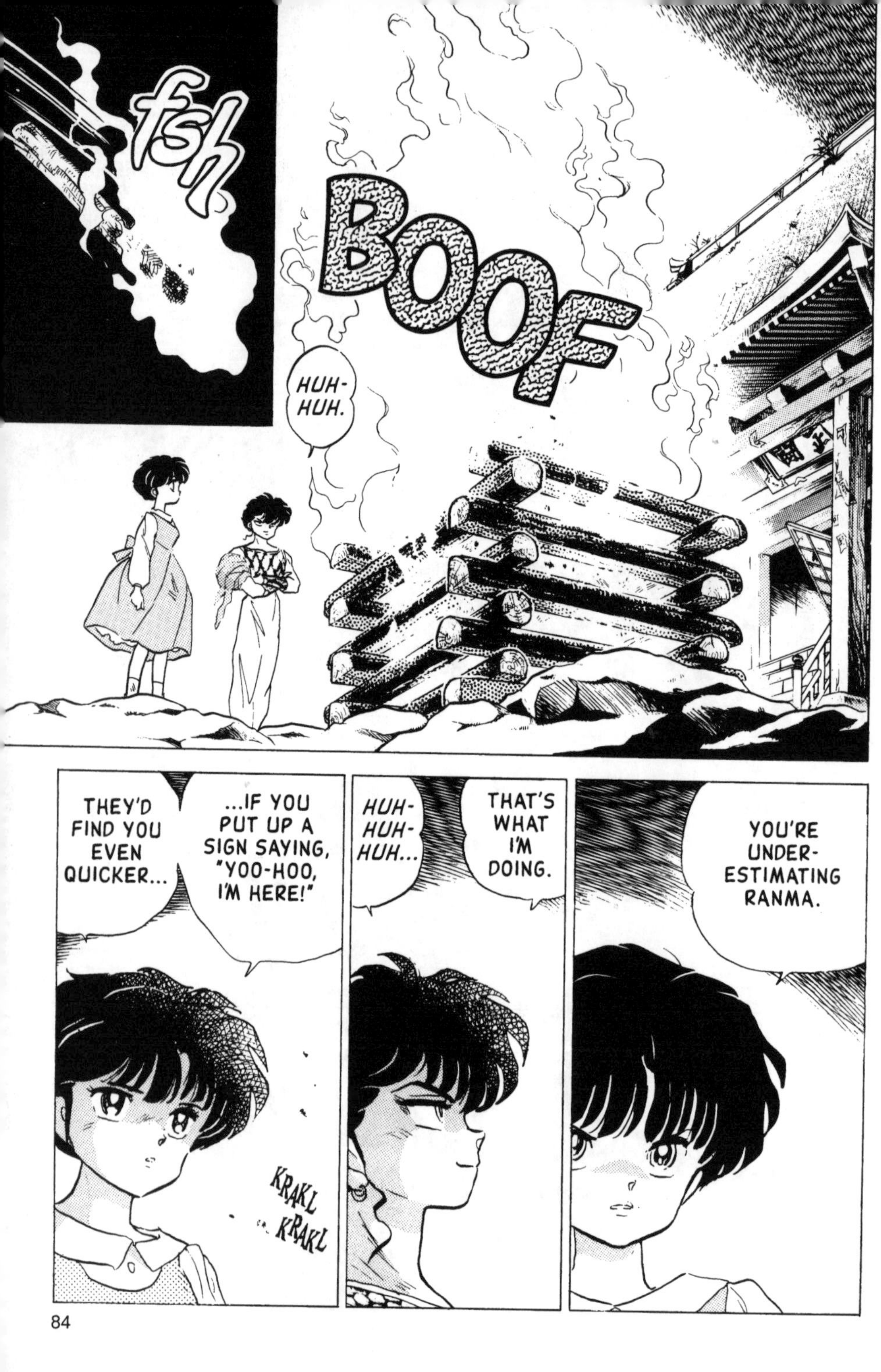
fsh
BOOF
HUH-HUH.
THEY'D FIND YOU EVEN QUICKER...
...IF YOU PUT UP A SIGN SAYING, "YOO-HOO, I'M HERE!"
KRAKL KRAKL
HUH-HUH-HUH...
THAT'S WHAT I'M DOING.
YOU'RE UNDER-ESTIMATING RANMA.

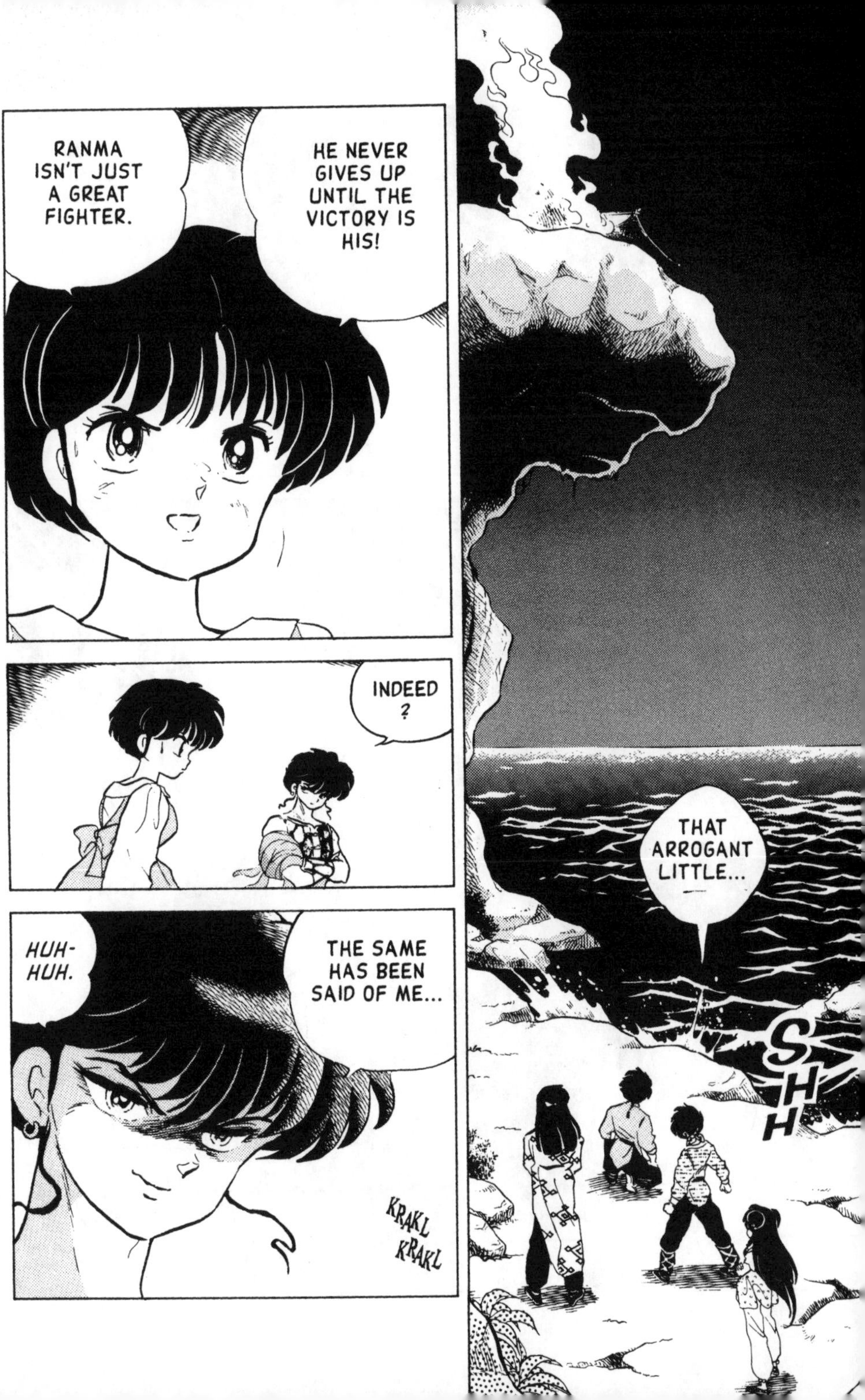
RANMA ISN'T JUST A GREAT FIGHTER.
HE NEVER GIVES UP UNTIL THE VICTORY IS HIS!
INDEED?
HUH-HUH.
THE SAME HAS BEEN SAID OF ME...
KRAKL KRAKL
THAT ARROGANT LITTLE...
SHH

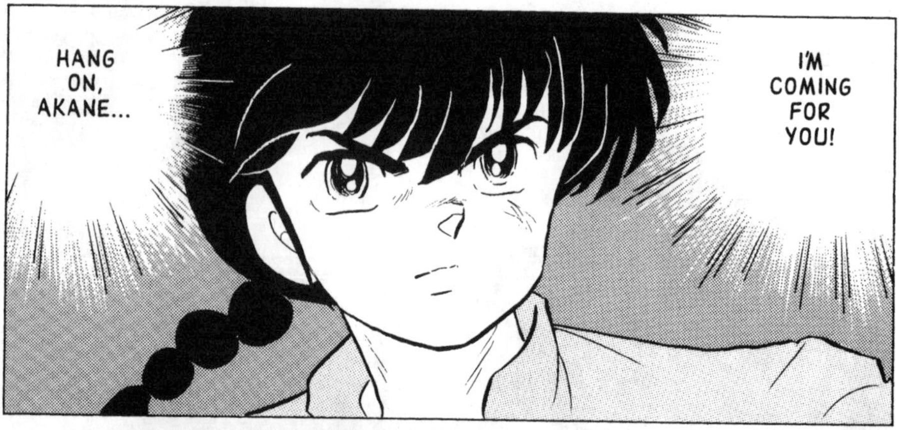
HANG ON, AKANE...
I'M COMING FOR YOU!

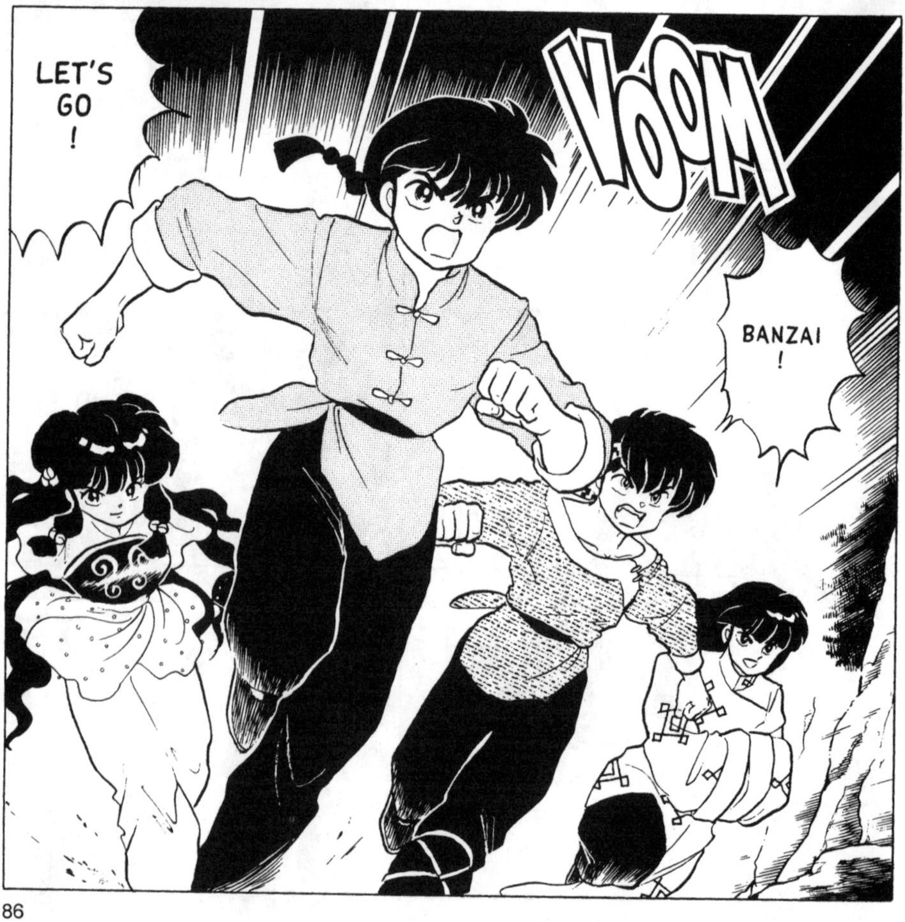
LET'S GO !
VOOM
BANZAI !

Part 6
THE WATERY GRAVE

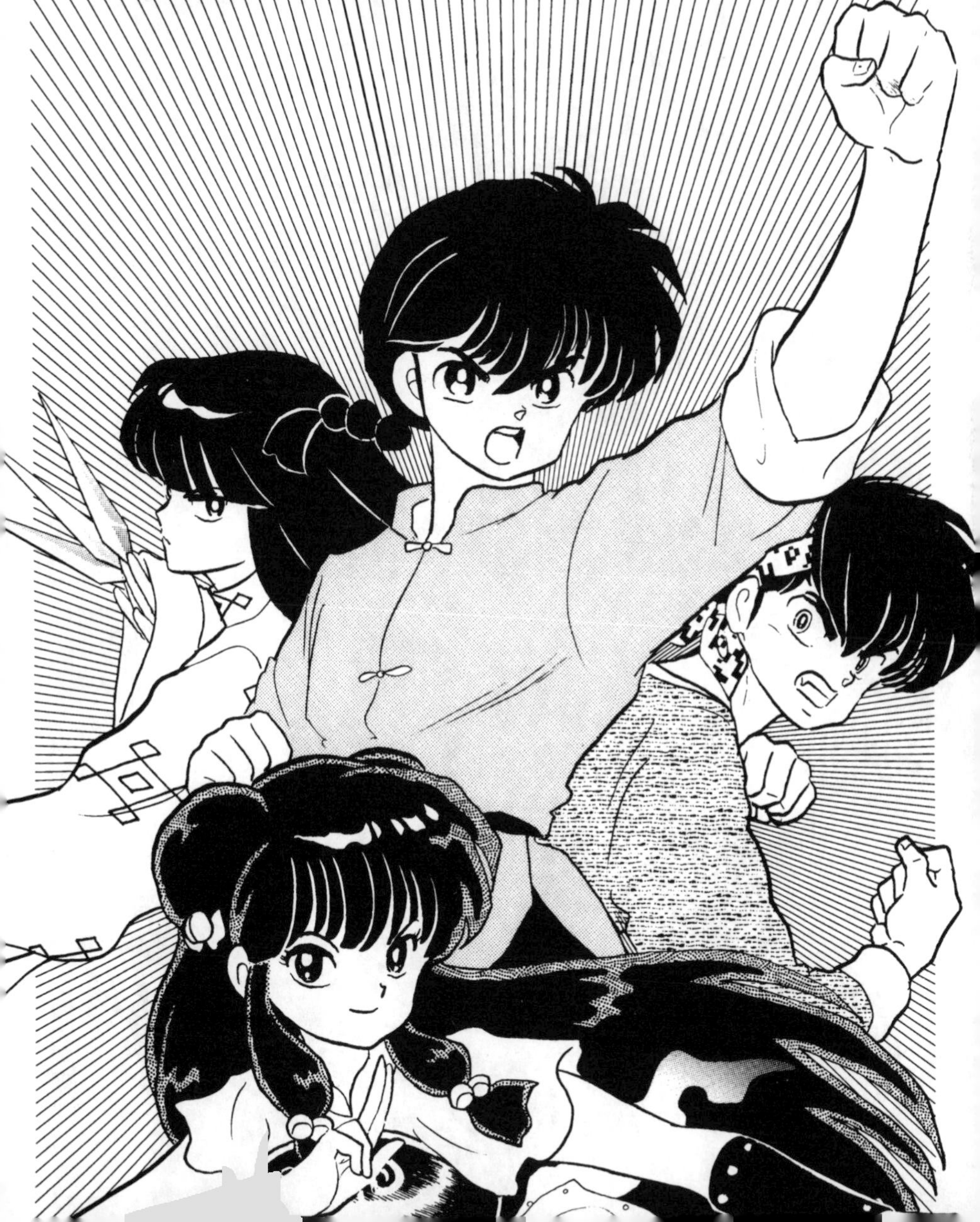

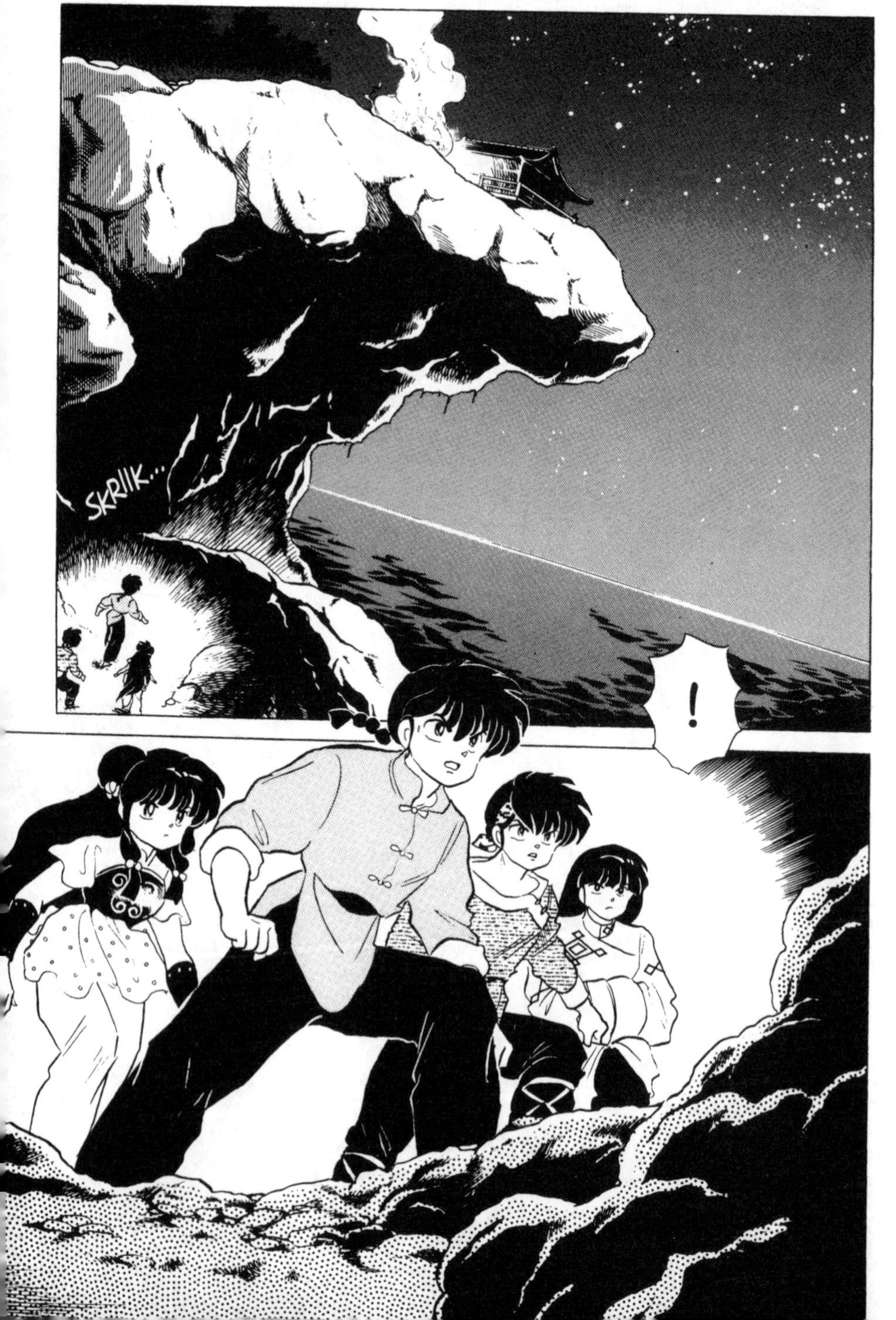
SKRIIK...
!

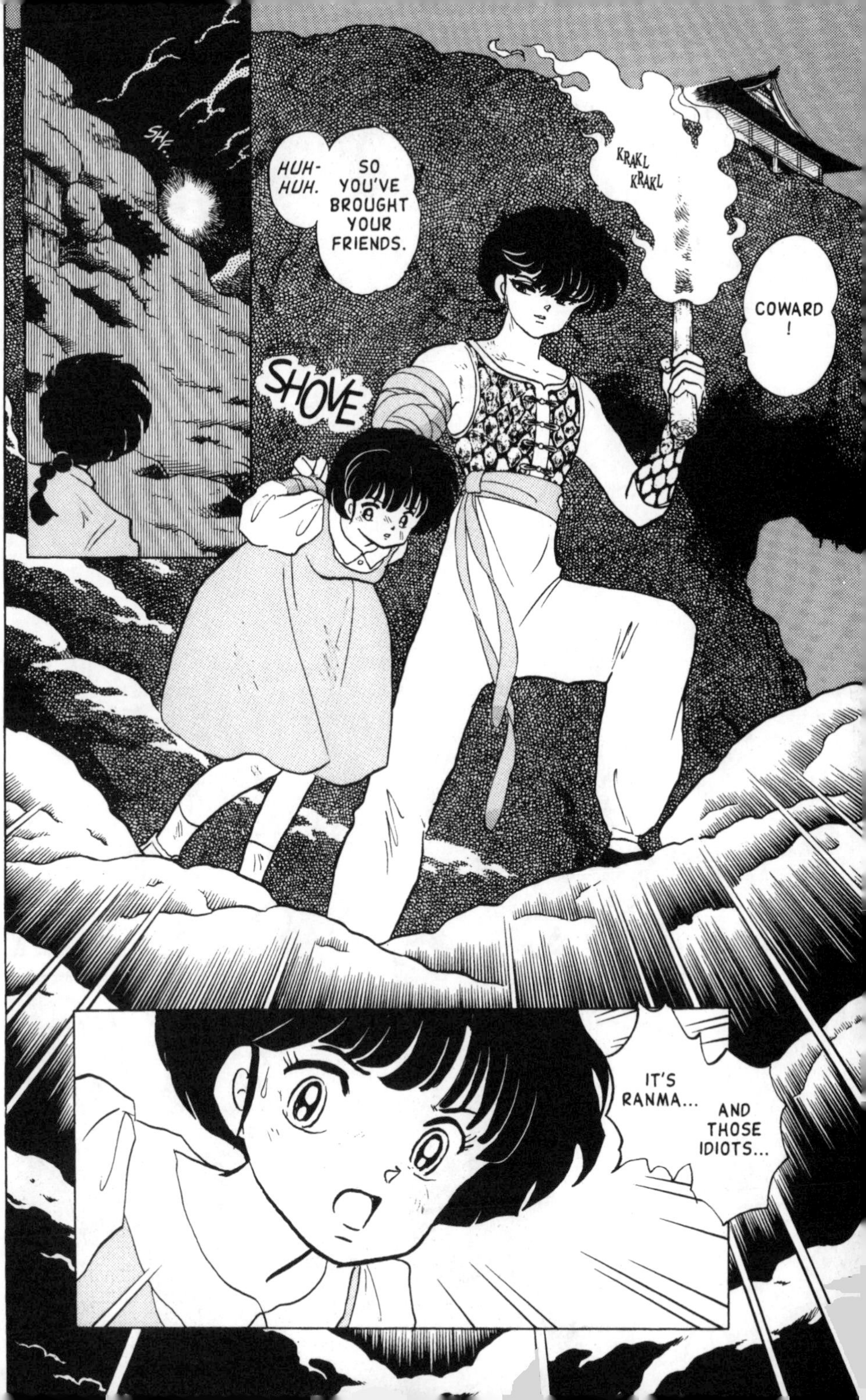
SHF...
HUH-HUH.
SO YOU'VE BROUGHT YOUR FRIENDS.
KRAKL KRAKL
COWARD!
SHOVE
IT'S RANMA...
AND THOSE IDIOTS...

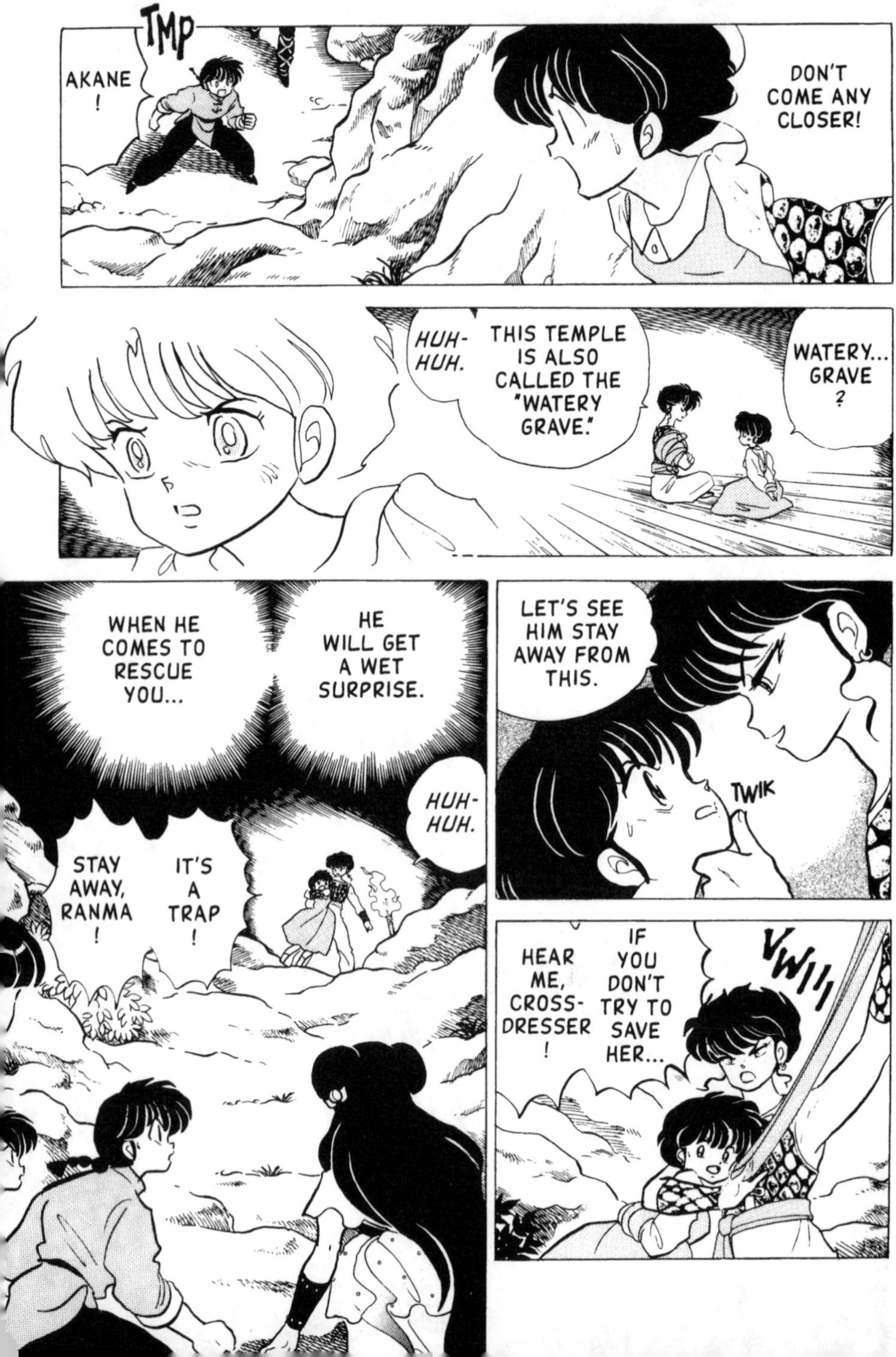
TMP
AKANE!
DON'T COME ANY CLOSER!
HUH-HUH.
THIS TEMPLE IS ALSO CALLED THE "WATERY GRAVE."
WATERY... GRAVE?
WHEN HE COMES TO RESCUE YOU...
HE WILL GET A WET SURPRISE.
HUH-HUH.
STAY AWAY, RANMA!
IT'S A TRAP!
LET'S SEE HIM STAY AWAY FROM THIS.
TWIK
HEAR ME, CROSS-DRESSER!
IF YOU DON'T TRY TO SAVE HER...
VWIII

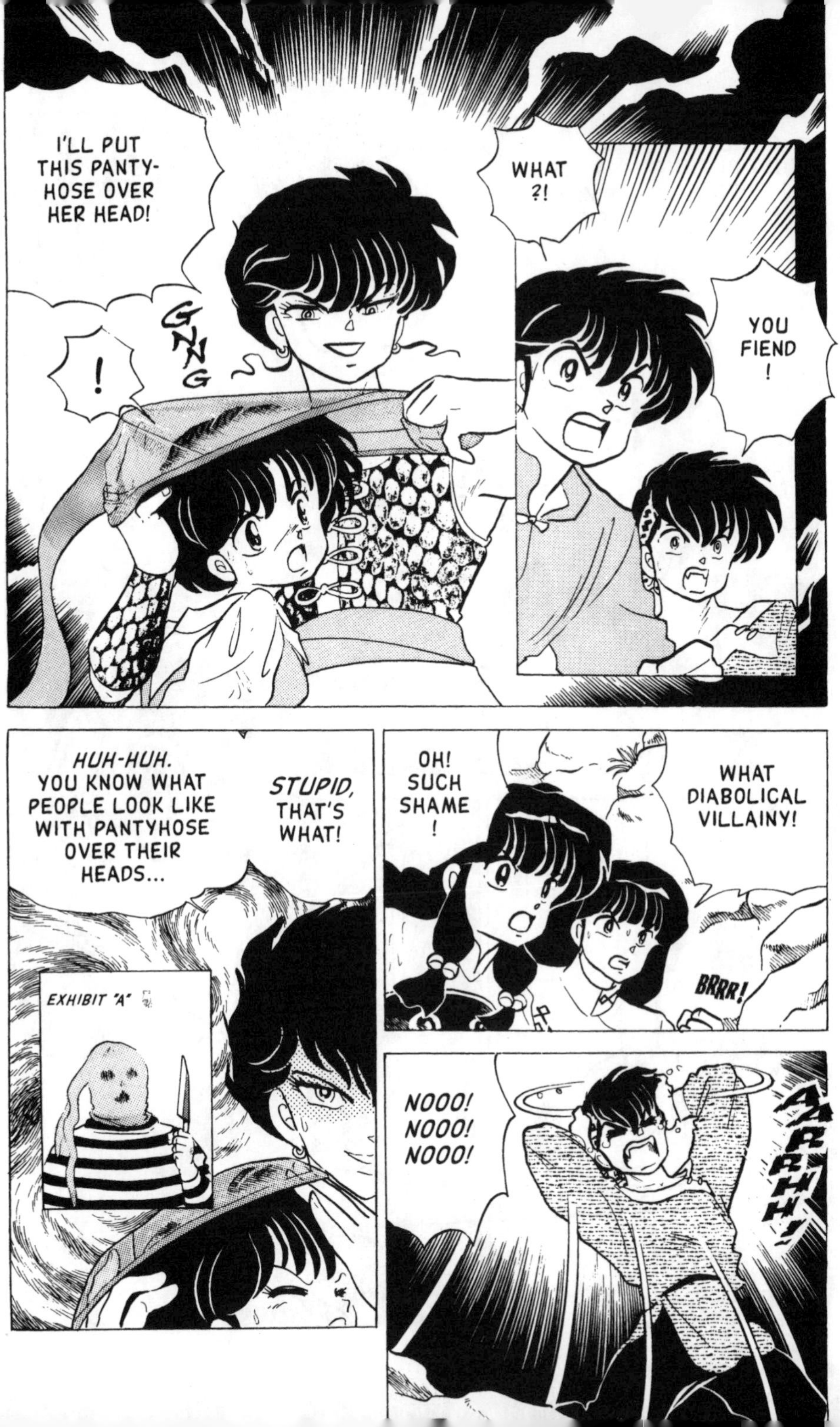
I'LL PUT THIS PANTY-HOSE OVER HER HEAD!
GNNG
!
WHAT ?!
YOU FIEND !
HUH-HUH. YOU KNOW WHAT PEOPLE LOOK LIKE WITH PANTYHOSE OVER THEIR HEADS...
STUPID, THAT'S WHAT!
EXHIBIT "A"
OH! SUCH SHAME !
WHAT DIABOLICAL VILLAINY!
BRRR!
NOOO! NOOO! NOOO!
AARHH!

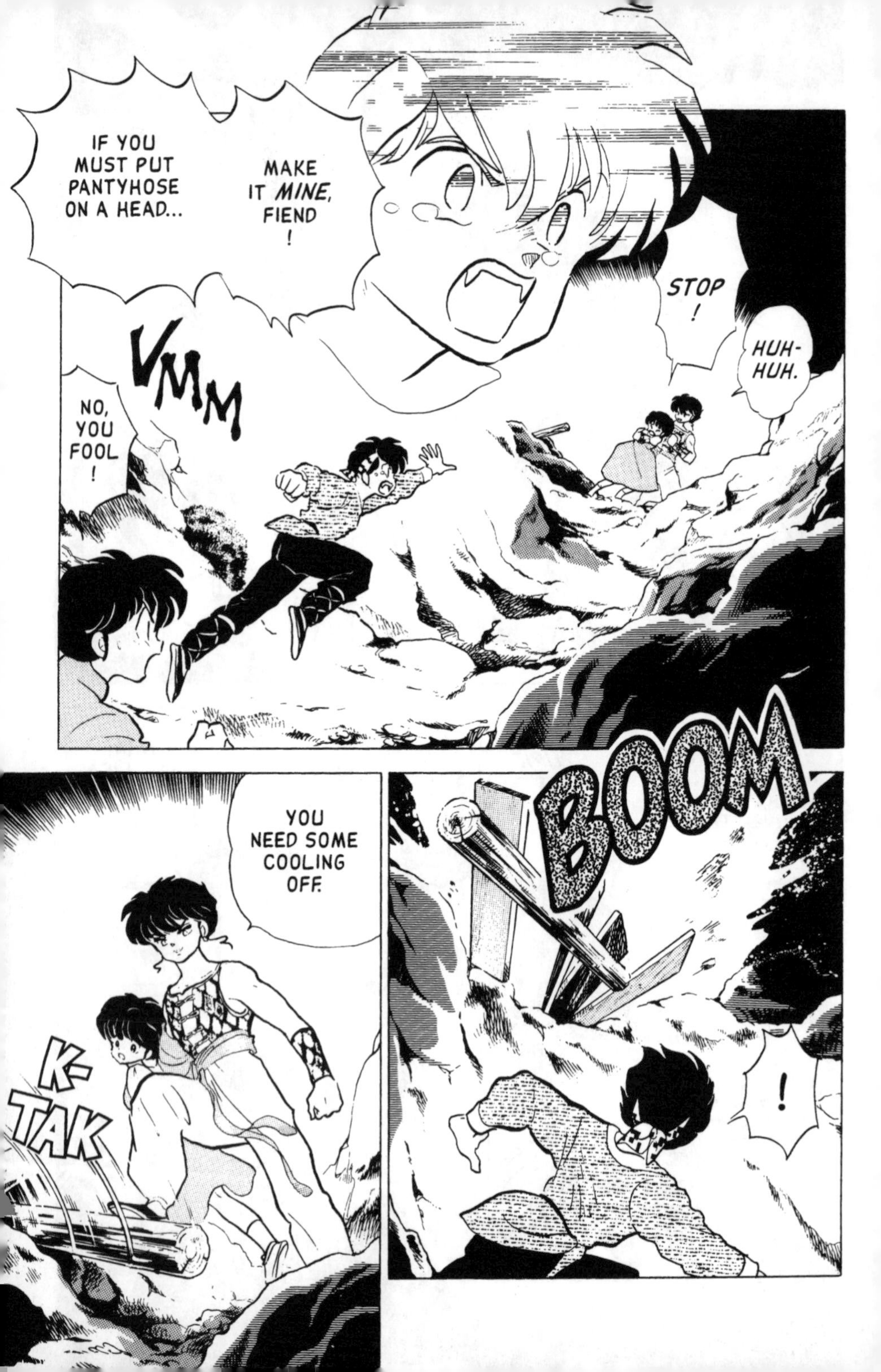

IF YOU MUST PUT PANTYHOSE ON A HEAD...
MAKE IT MINE, FIEND !
STOP !
HUH-HUH.
VMM
NO, YOU FOOL !
YOU NEED SOME COOLING OFF.
K-TAK
BOOM
!

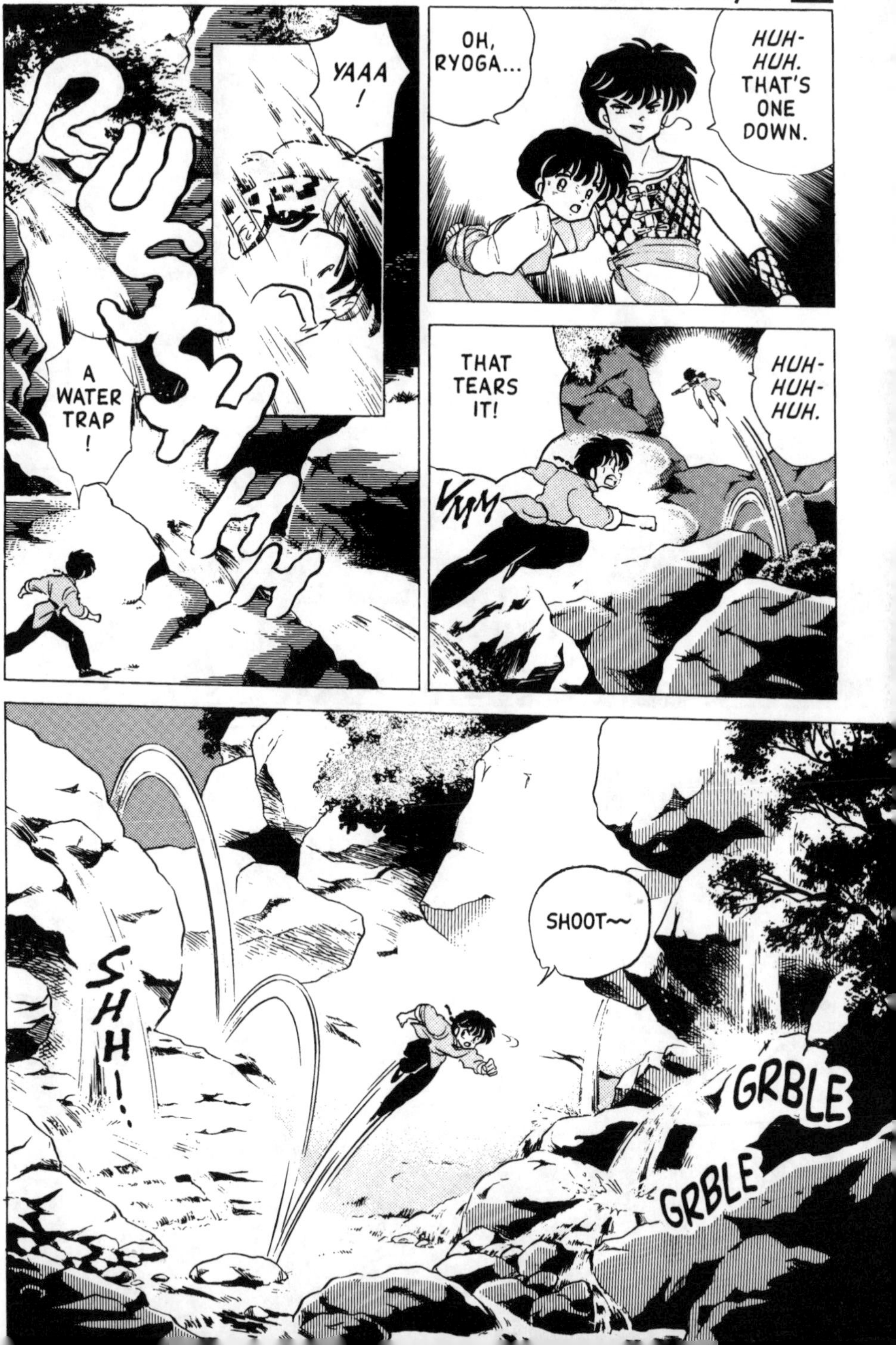
YAAA!
A WATER TRAP!
OH, RYOGA...
HUH-HUH. THAT'S ONE DOWN.
THAT TEARS IT!
VMM
HUH-HUH-HUH.
SHH!!
SHOOT~~
GRBLE
GRBLE

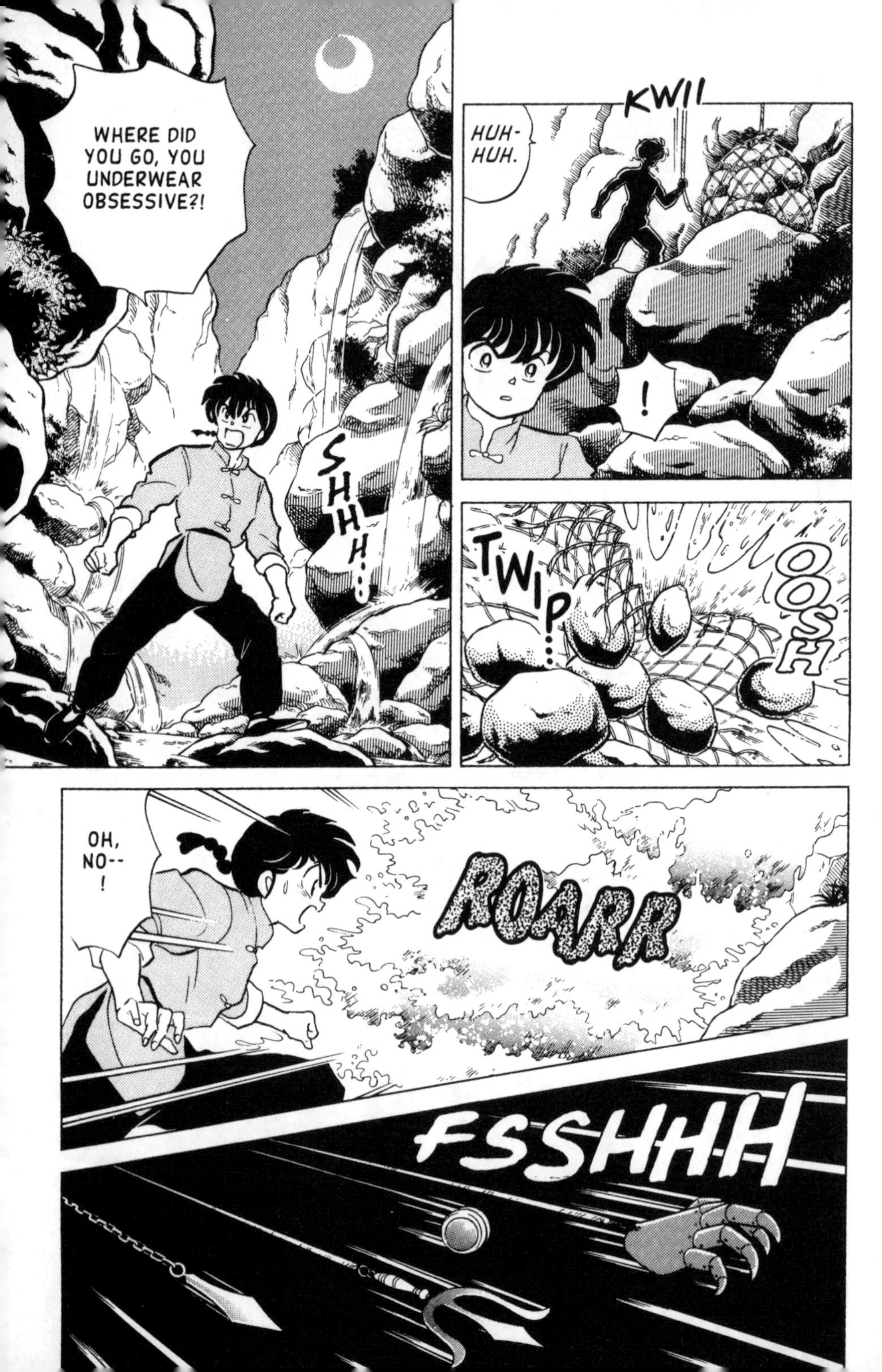
WHERE DID YOU GO, YOU UNDERWEAR OBSESSIVE?!
SHHH...
KWII
HUH-HUH.
!
TWIP...
OOSH
OH, NO--!
ROARR
FSSHHH

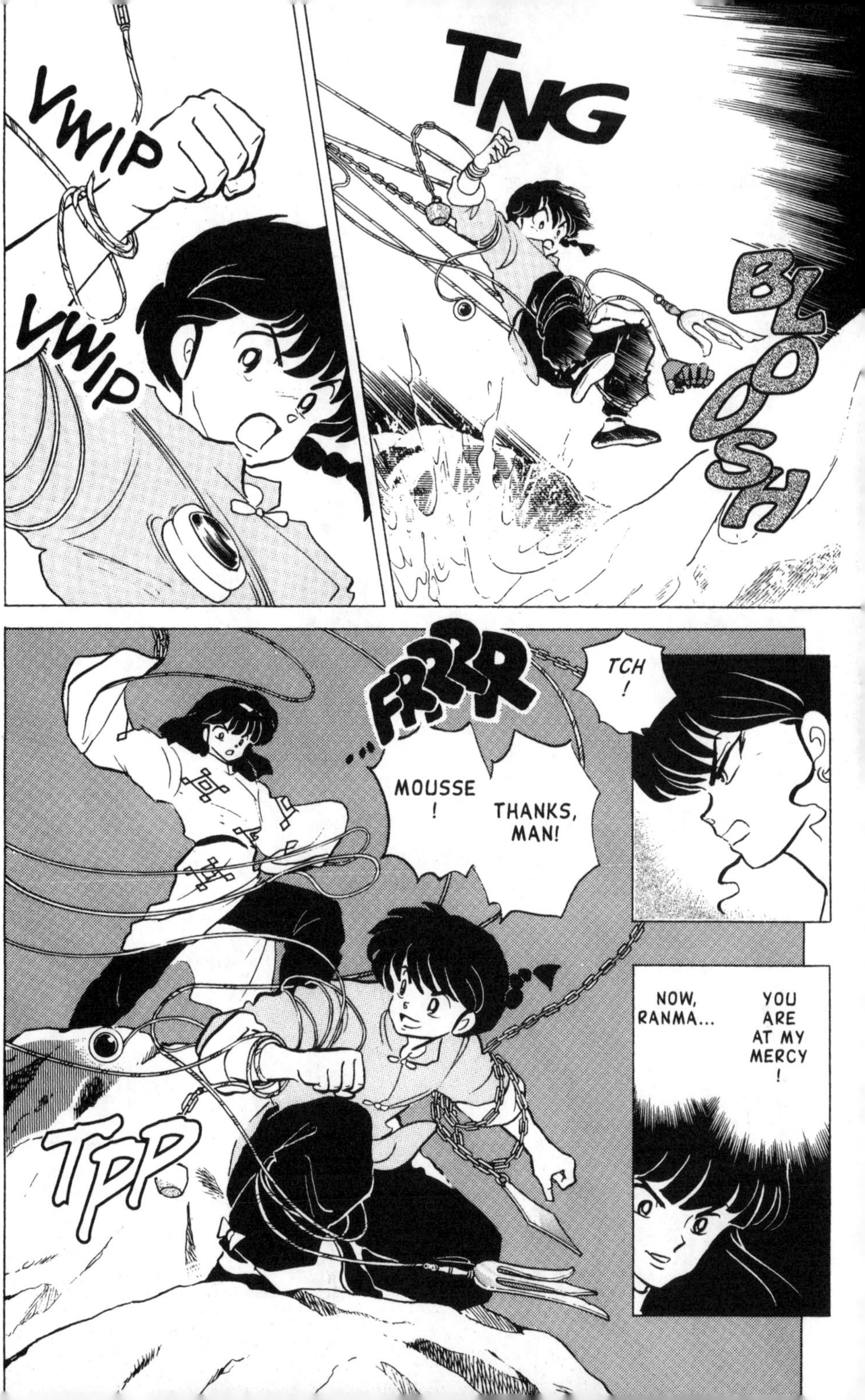
VWIP
VWIP
TNG
BLOOOSH
FRRRR
...
MOUSSE!
THANKS, MAN!
TCH!
TDP
NOW, RANMA...
YOU ARE AT MY MERCY!

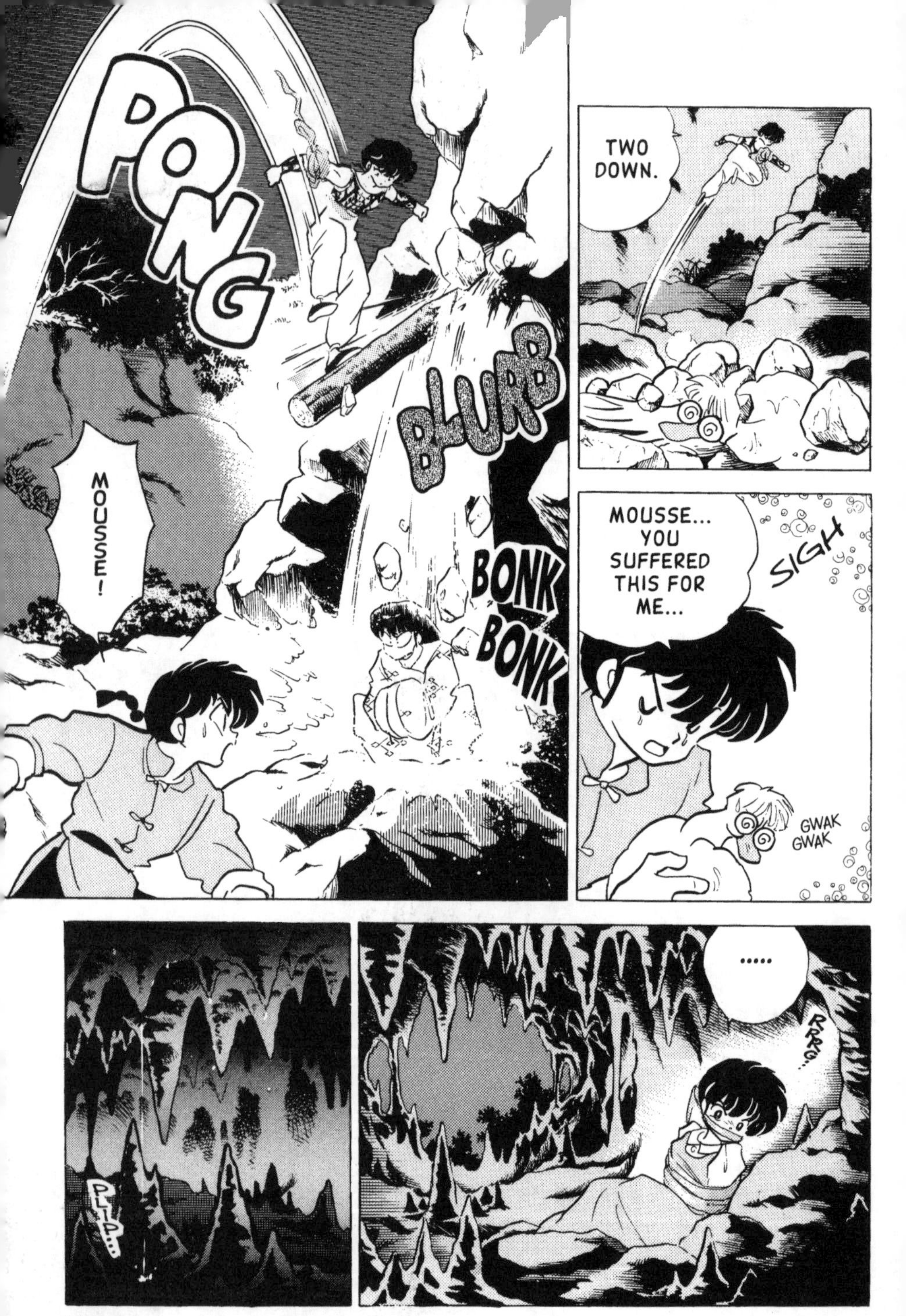
PONG
BLURB
MOUSSE!
BONK
BONK
TWO DOWN.
MOUSSE... YOU SUFFERED THIS FOR ME...
SIGH
GWAK GWAK
PLIP...
......
RRRG...

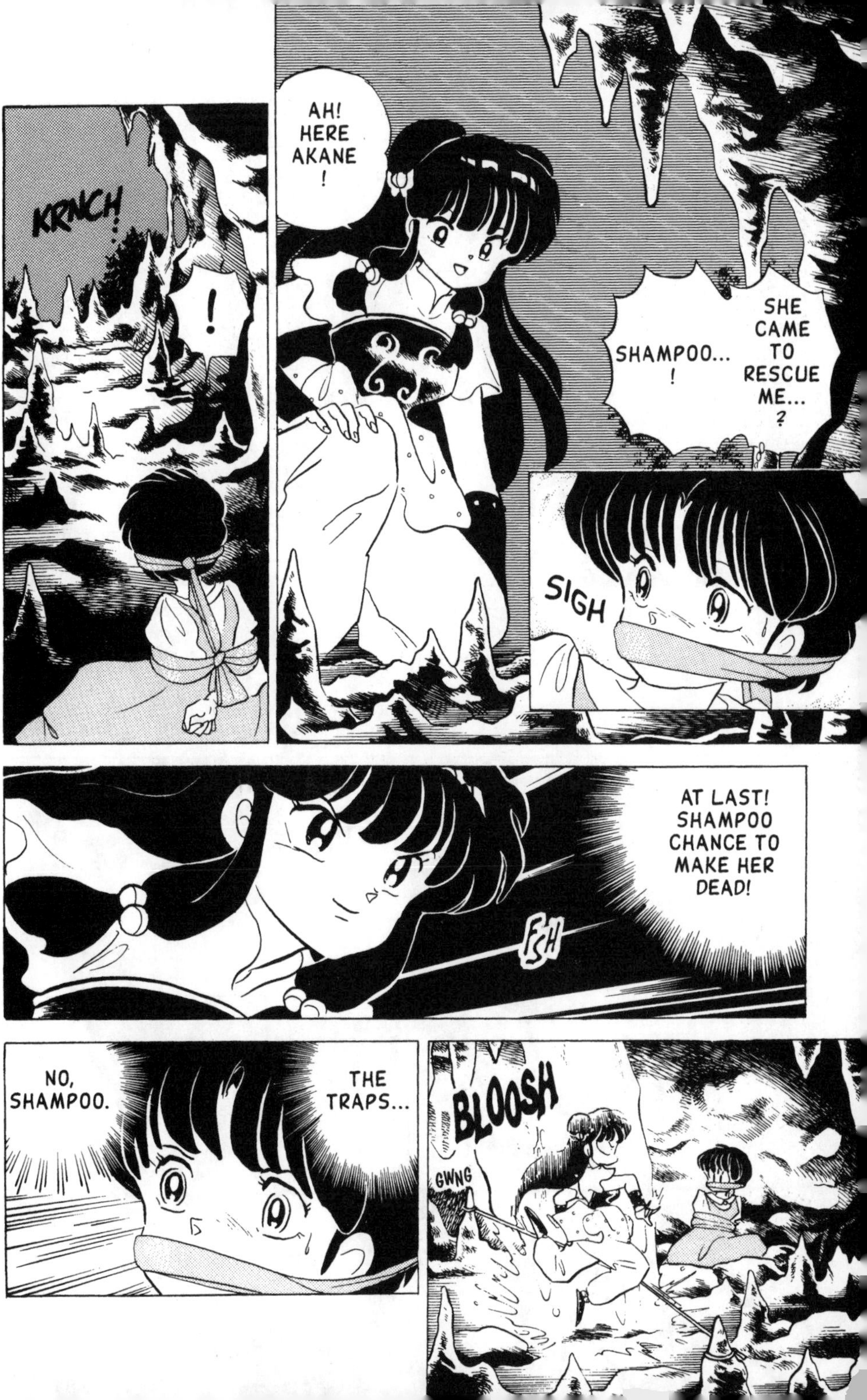
KRNCH
!
AH! HERE AKANE !
SHAMPOO... !
SHE CAME TO RESCUE ME... ?
SIGH
AT LAST! SHAMPOO CHANCE TO MAKE HER DEAD!
FSH
NO, SHAMPOO.
THE TRAPS...
BLOOSH
GWNG

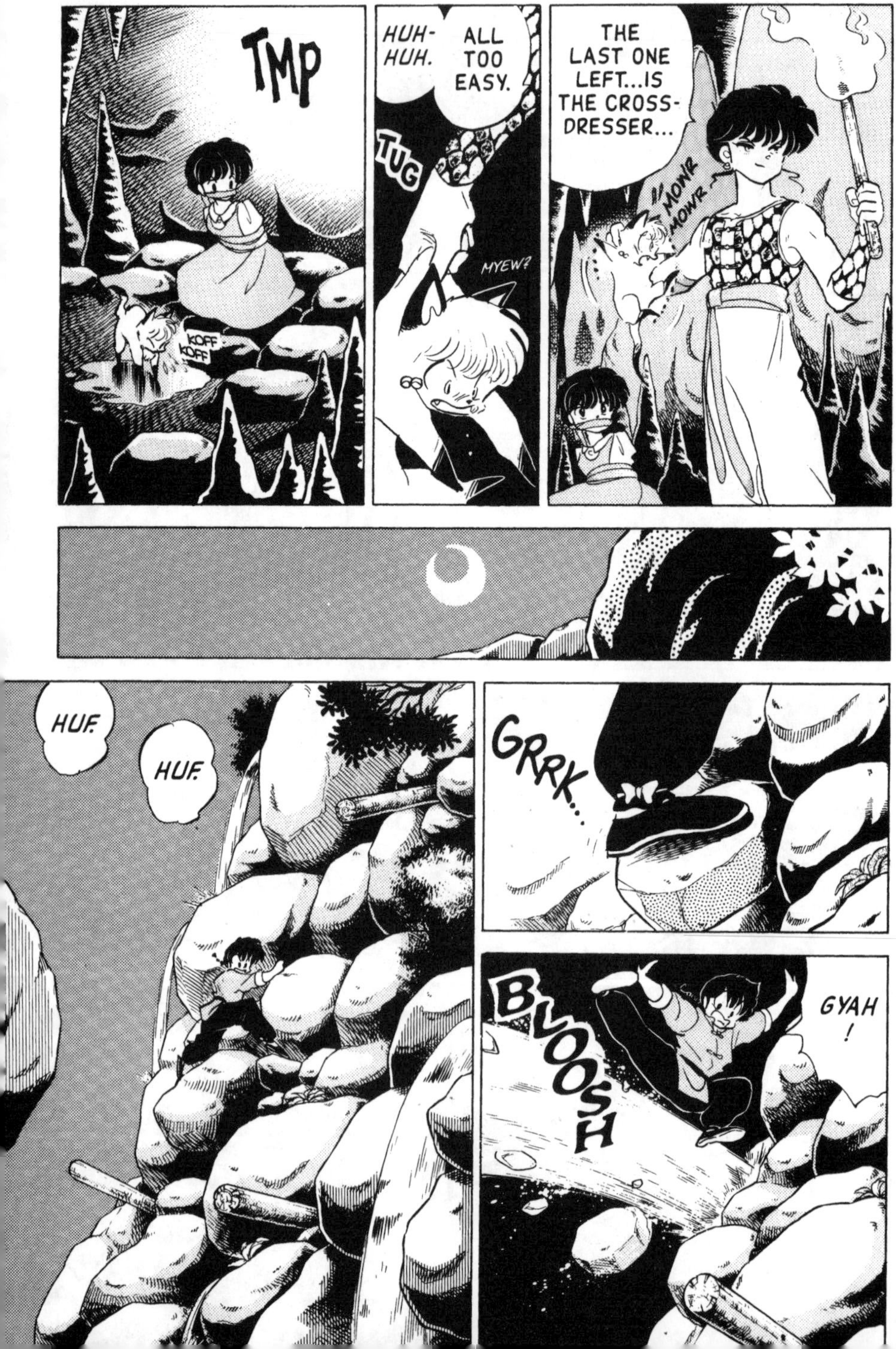
TMP
KOFF KOFF
HUH-HUH.
ALL TOO EASY.
TUG
MYEW?
THE LAST ONE LEFT...IS THE CROSS-DRESSER...
MOWR MOWR
HUF.
HUF.
GRRK...
BLOOSH
GYAH!

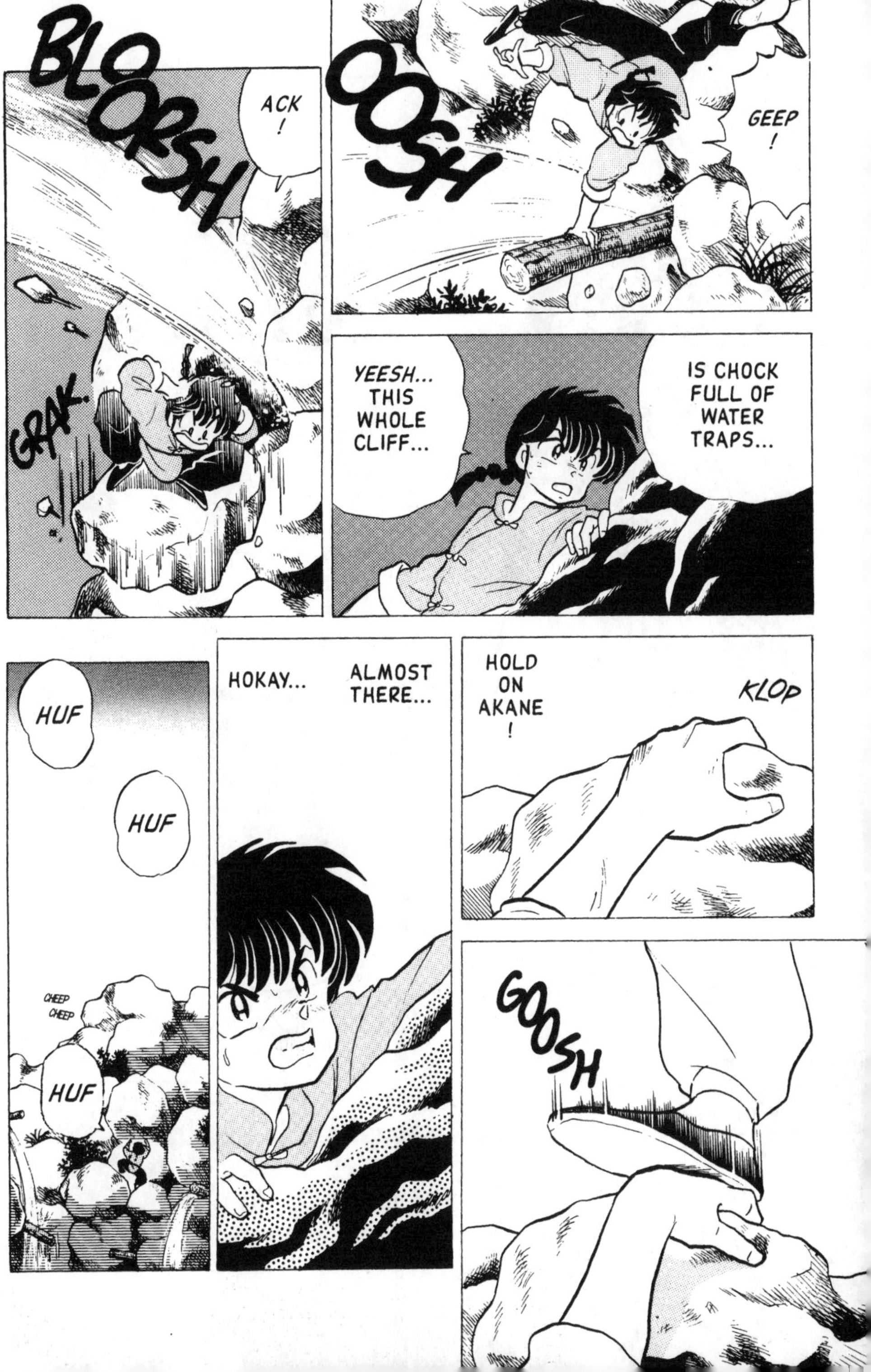
BLOORSH
ACK!
GRAK
OOSH
GEEP!
YEESH... THIS WHOLE CLIFF...
IS CHOCK FULL OF WATER TRAPS...
HUF
HUF
CHEEP CHEEP
HUF
HOKAY...
ALMOST THERE...
HOLD ON AKANE!
KLOP
GOOSH

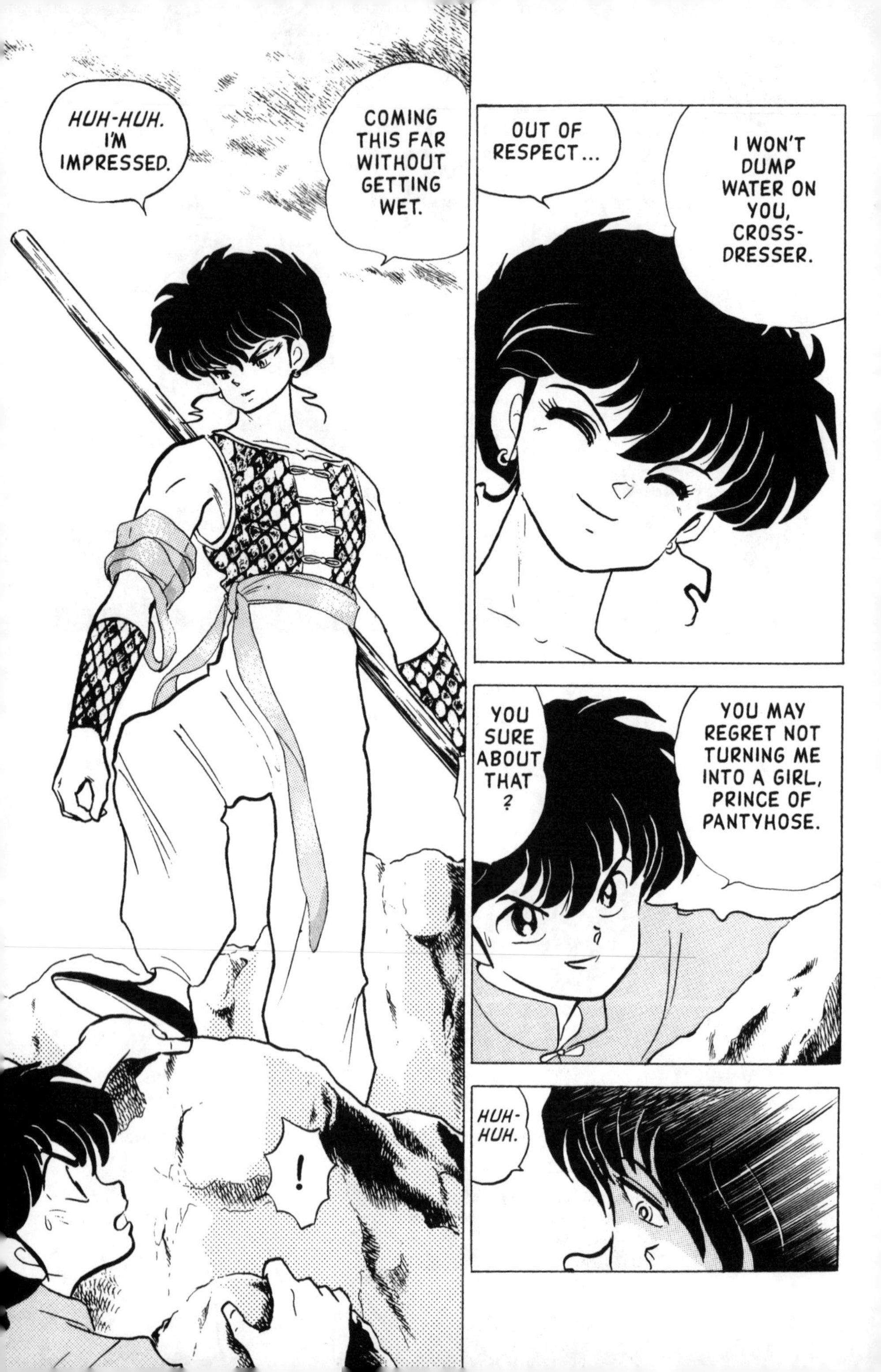
HUH-HUH. I'M IMPRESSED.
COMING THIS FAR WITHOUT GETTING WET.
!
OUT OF RESPECT...
I WON'T DUMP WATER ON YOU, CROSS-DRESSER.
YOU SURE ABOUT THAT?
YOU MAY REGRET NOT TURNING ME INTO A GIRL, PRINCE OF PANTYHOSE.
HUH-HUH.

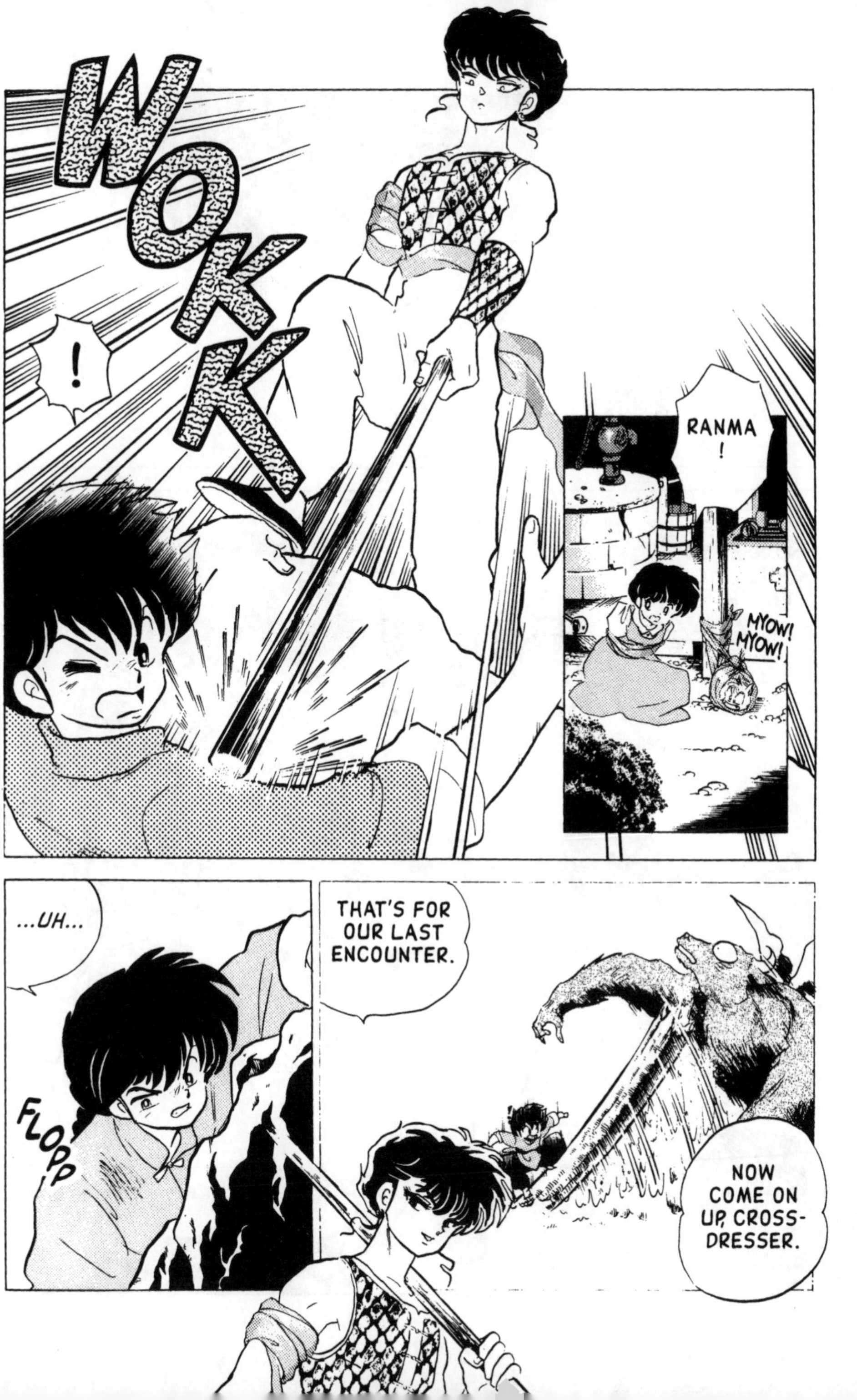
WOKK
!
RANMA !
MYOW! MYOW!
...UH...
FLOPP
THAT'S FOR OUR LAST ENCOUNTER.
NOW COME ON UP, CROSS-DRESSER.

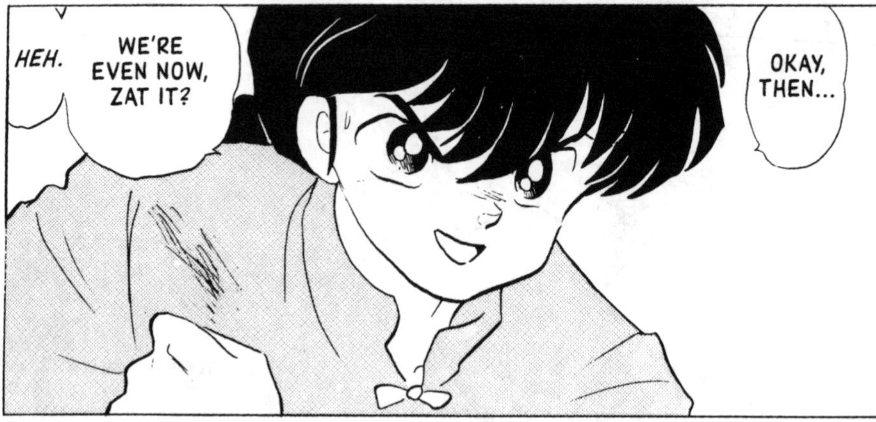
HEH.
WE'RE EVEN NOW, ZAT IT?
OKAY, THEN...

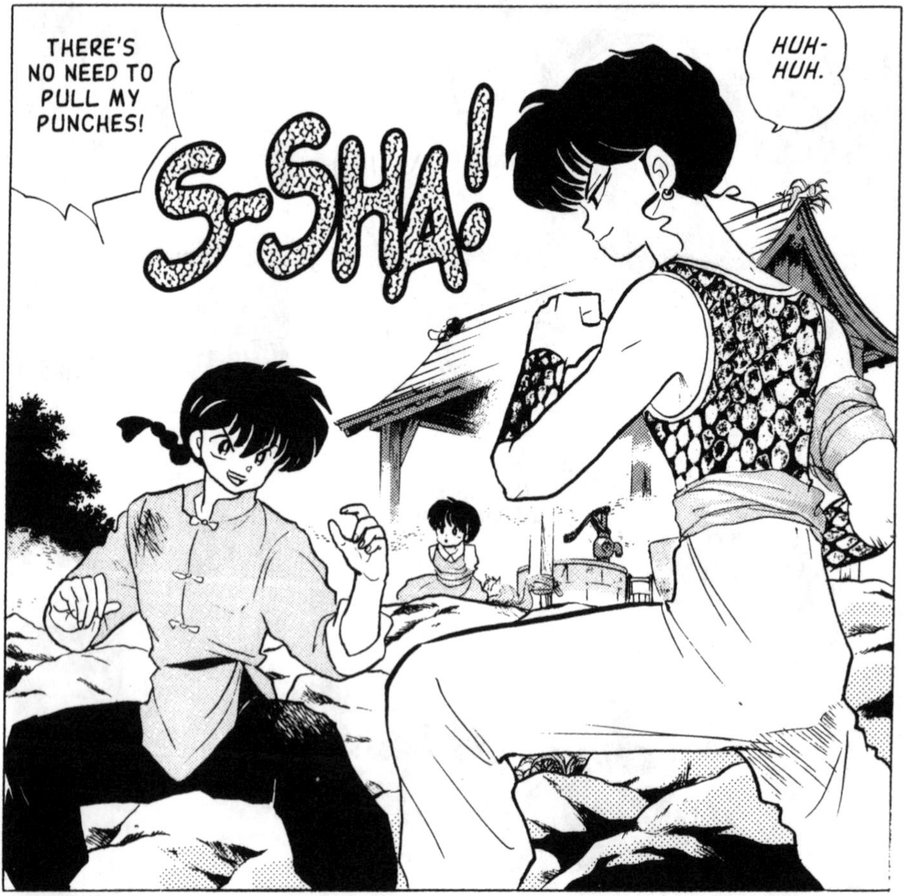
THERE'S NO NEED TO PULL MY PUNCHES!
S-SHA!
HUH-HUH.

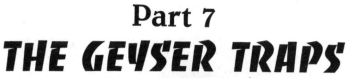

Part 7
THE GEYSER TRAPS

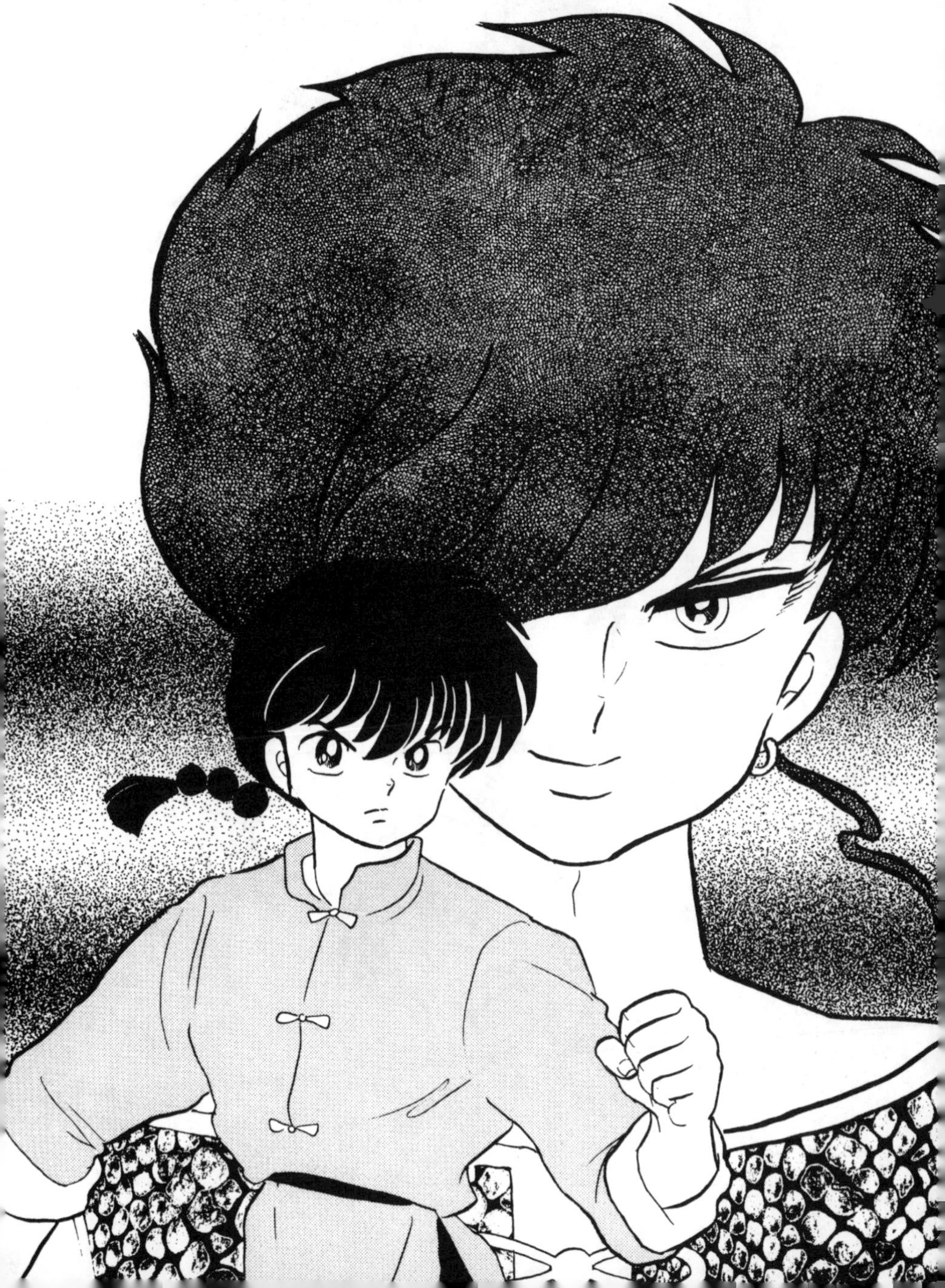

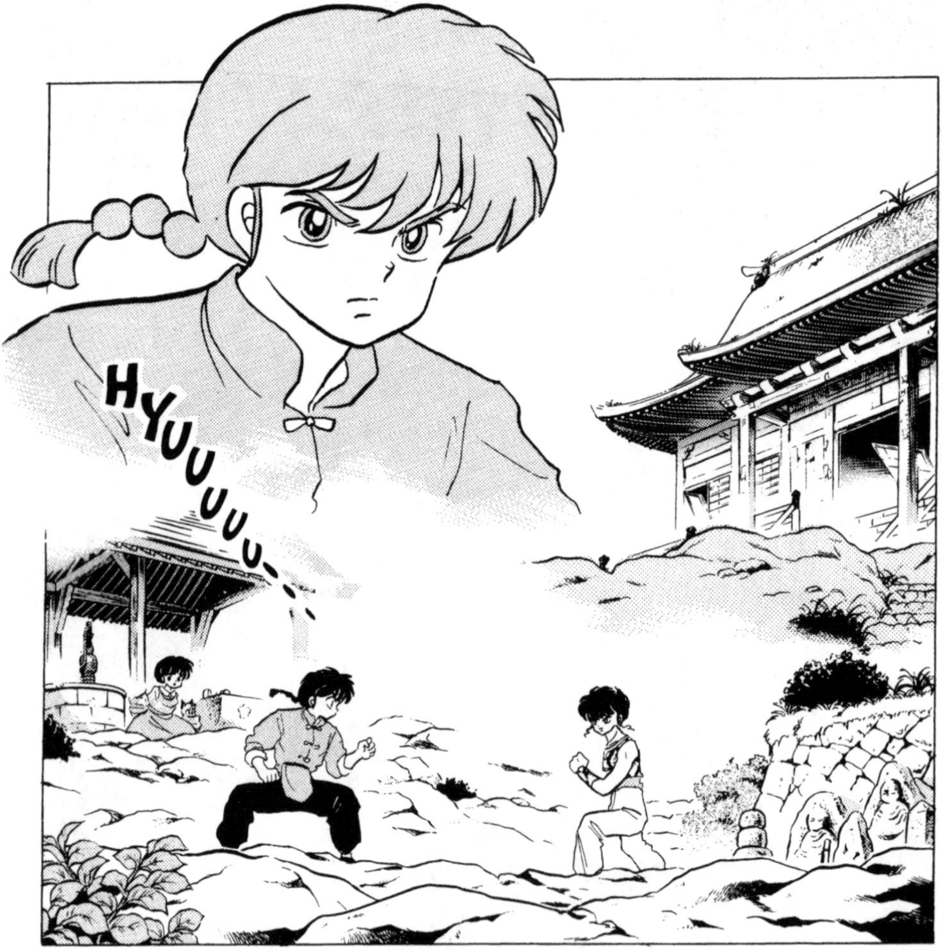
HYUUUUUU...

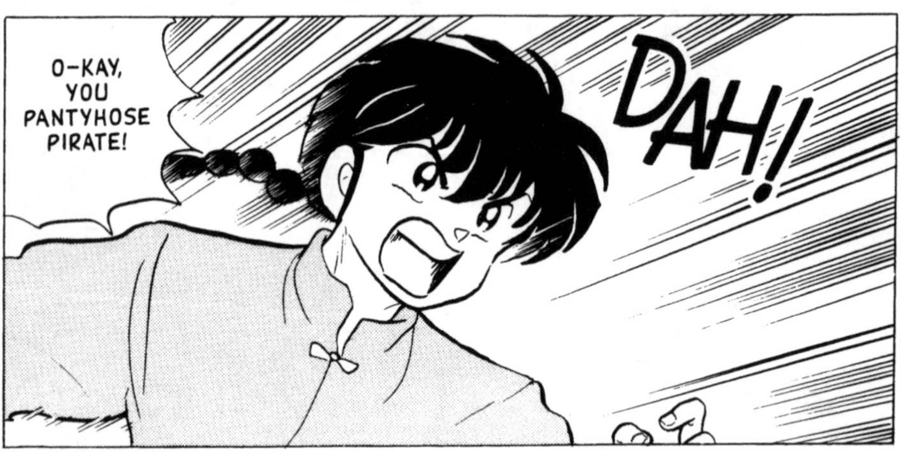
O-KAY, YOU PANTYHOSE PIRATE!
DAH!

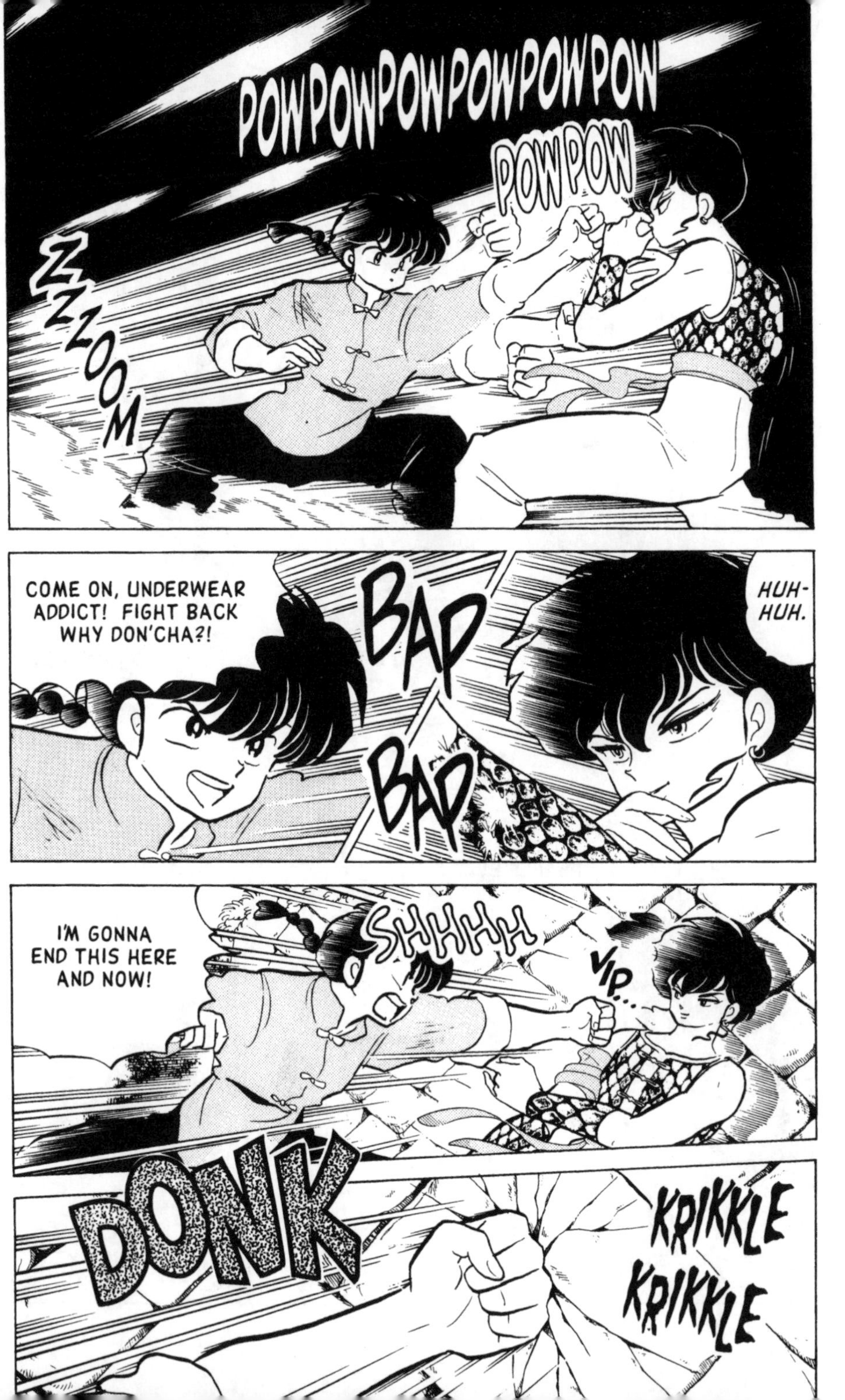
POW POW POW POW POW POW POW
POW POW
ZZZOOOM
COME ON, UNDERWEAR ADDICT! FIGHT BACK WHY DON'CHA?!
BAP
BAP
HUH-HUH.
I'M GONNA END THIS HERE AND NOW!
SHHHHH
VIP...
DONK
KRIKKLE KRIKKLE

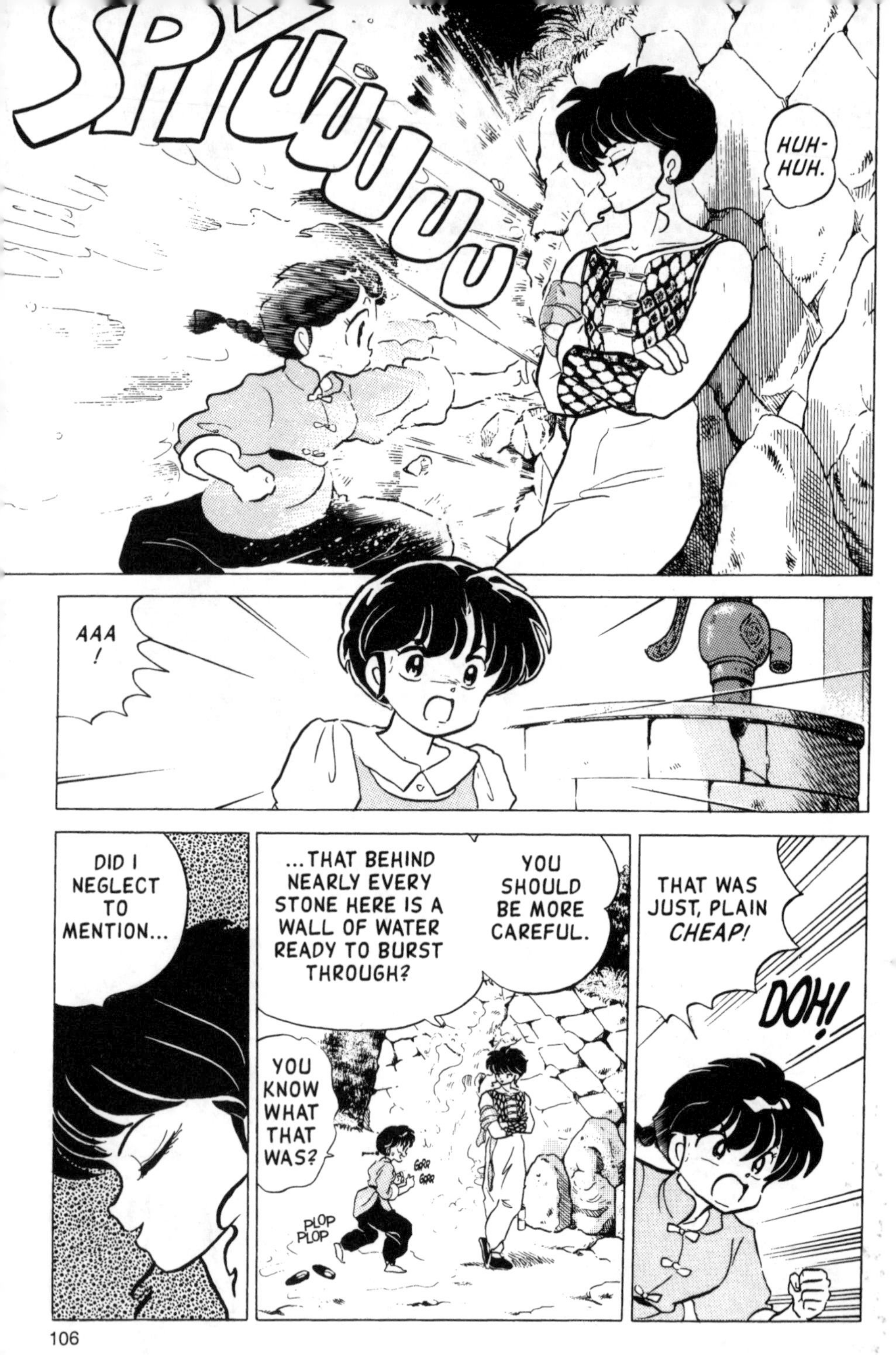
SPIUUUUUU
HUH-HUH.
AAA!
DID I NEGLECT TO MENTION...
...THAT BEHIND NEARLY EVERY STONE HERE IS A WALL OF WATER READY TO BURST THROUGH?
YOU SHOULD BE MORE CAREFUL.
YOU KNOW WHAT THAT WAS?
GRR GRR
PLOP PLOP
THAT WAS JUST, PLAIN *CHEAP!*
DOH!

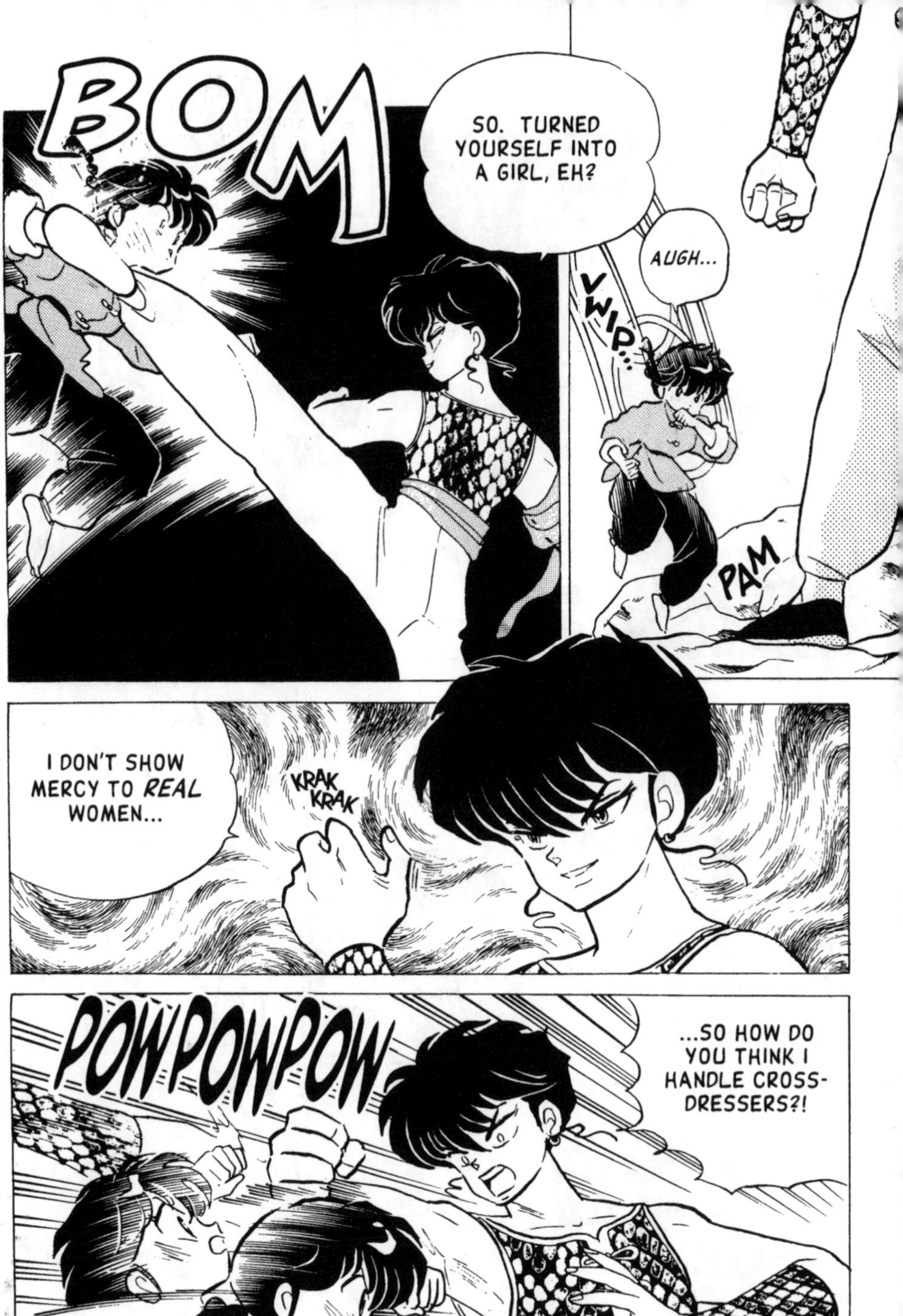
BOM
SO. TURNED YOURSELF INTO A GIRL, EH?
AUGH...
VWIP...
PAM
I DON'T SHOW MERCY TO *REAL* WOMEN...
KRAK KRAK
POW POW POW
...SO HOW DO YOU THINK I HANDLE CROSS-DRESSERS?!

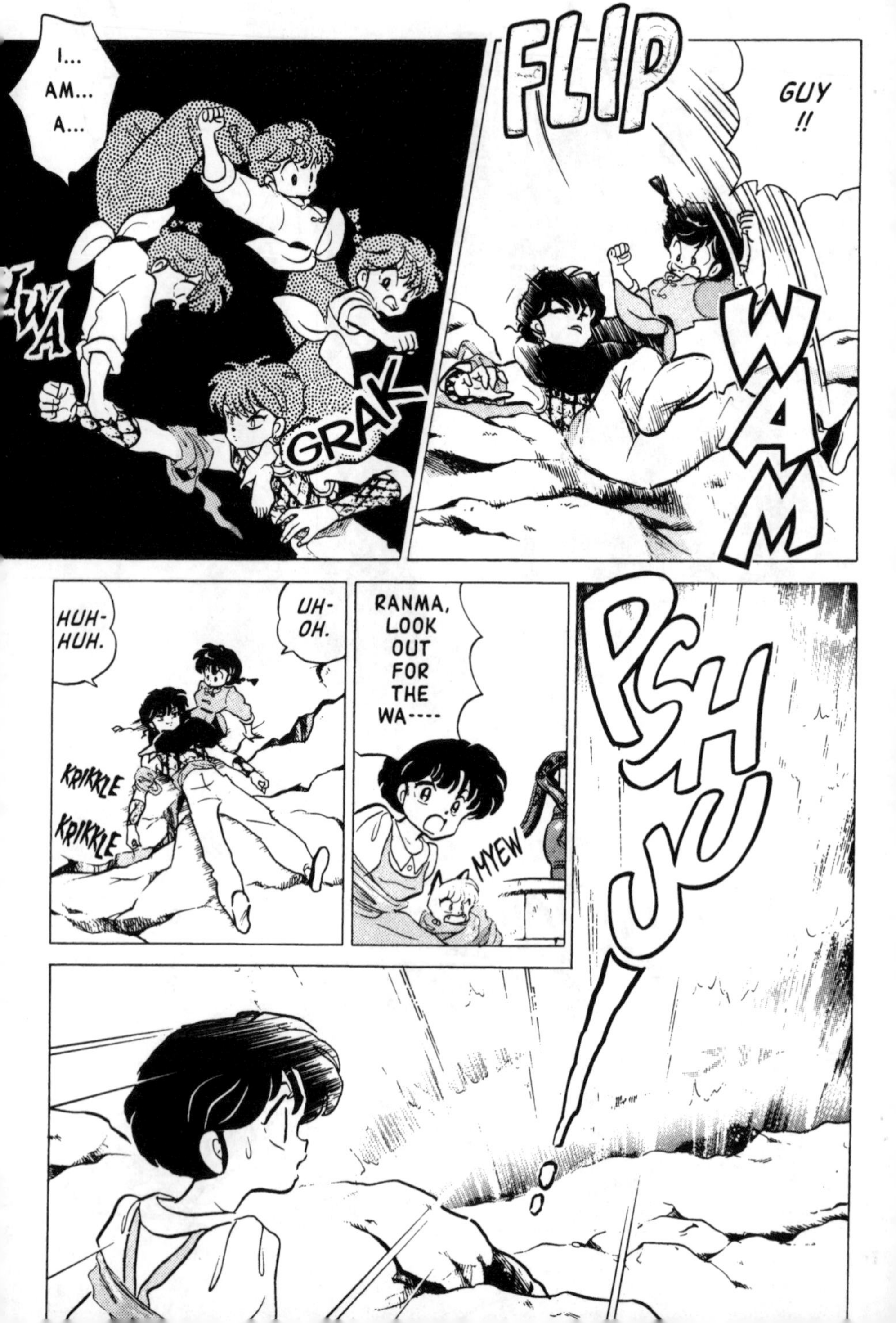
I... AM... A...
WA
GRAK
FLIP
GUY !!
WAM
HUH-HUH.
UH-OH.
KRIKKLE
KRIKKLE
RANMA, LOOK OUT FOR THE WA----
MYEW
PSHUU

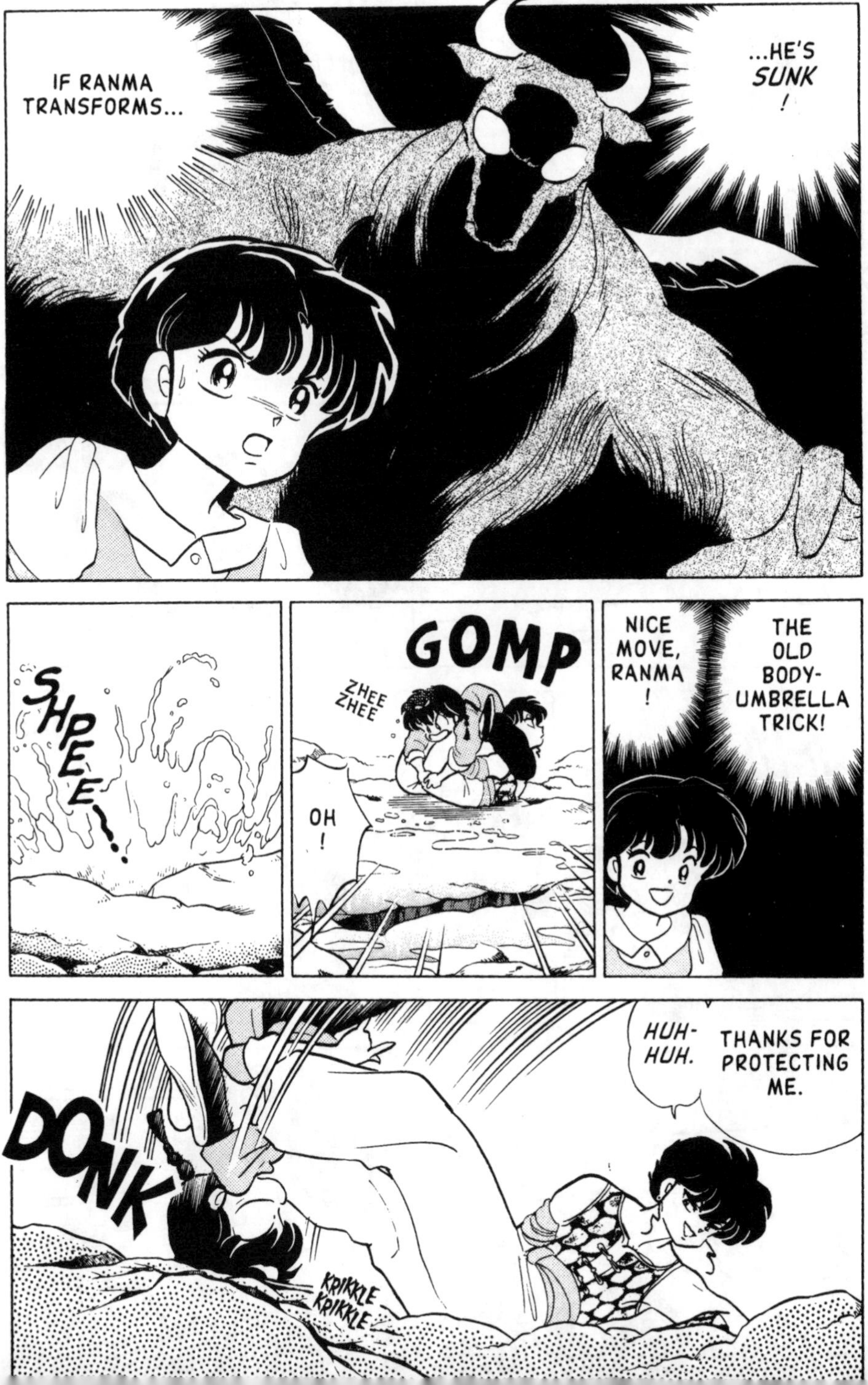
IF RANMA TRANSFORMS...
...HE'S SUNK!
SHPEEE...!
GOMP
ZHEE ZHEE
OH!
NICE MOVE, RANMA!
THE OLD BODY-UMBRELLA TRICK!
DONK
KRIKKLE KRIKKLE
HUH-HUH.
THANKS FOR PROTECTING ME.

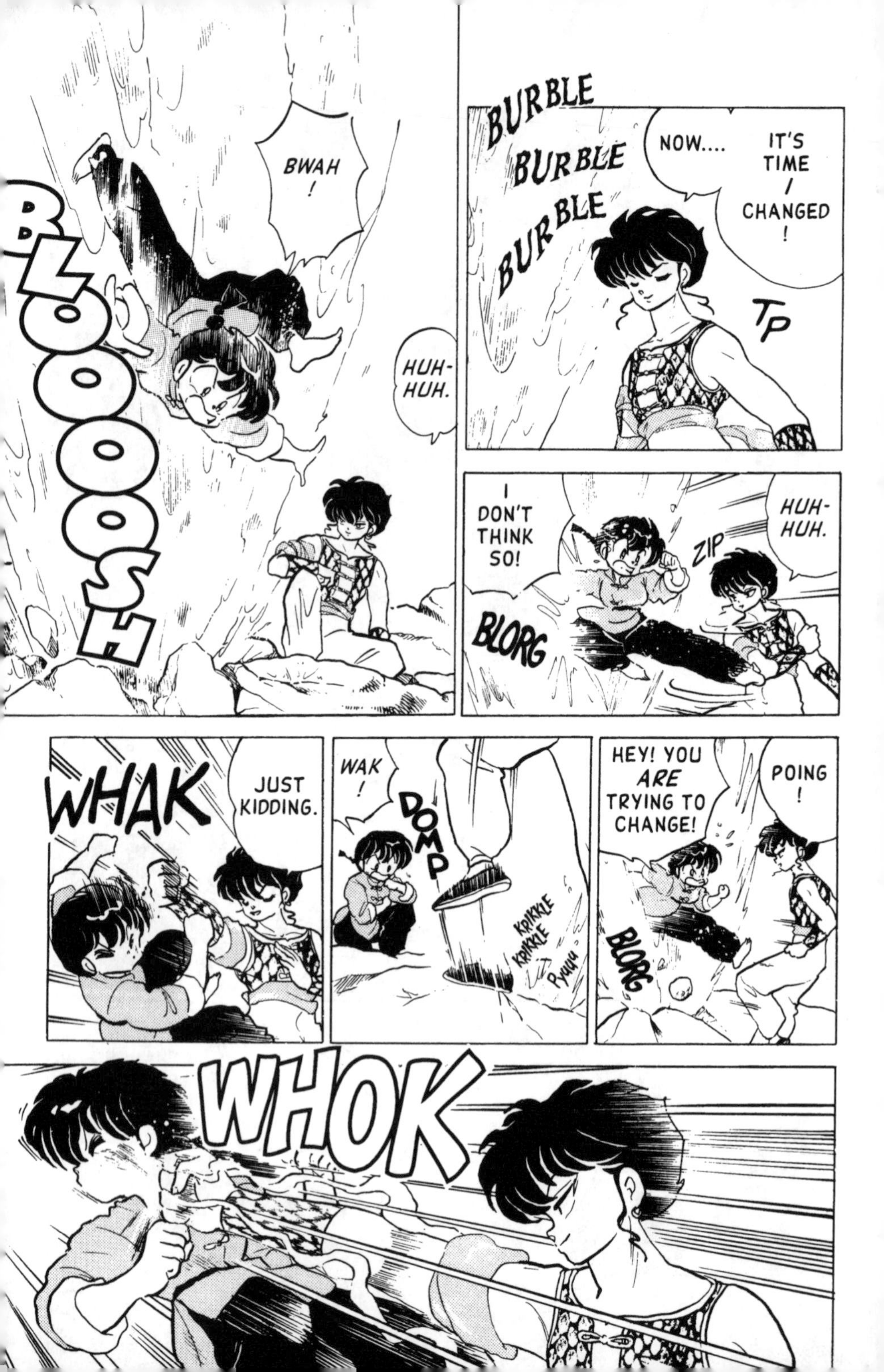
BLOOOOSH
BWAH!
HUH-HUH.
BURBLE BURBLE BURBLE
NOW....
IT'S TIME I CHANGED!
TP
I DON'T THINK SO!
ZIP
HUH-HUH.
BLORG
WHAK
JUST KIDDING.
WAK!
DOMP
KRIKKLE KRIKKLE
Pyuyu
HEY! YOU ARE TRYING TO CHANGE!
POING!
BLORG
WHOK

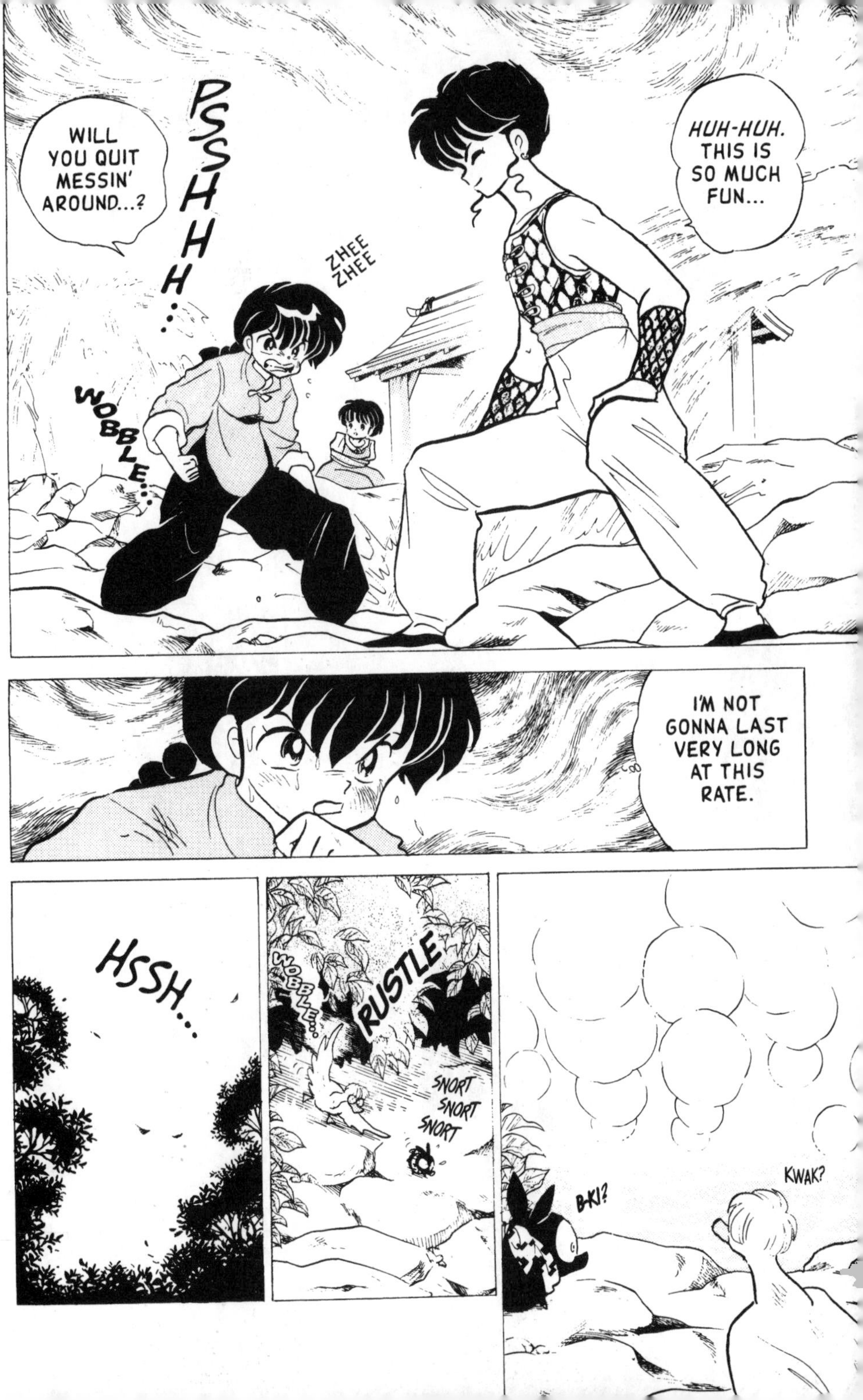
WILL YOU QUIT MESSIN' AROUND...?
PSSHHH...
ZHEE ZHEE
WOBBLE...
HUH-HUH. THIS IS SO MUCH FUN...
I'M NOT GONNA LAST VERY LONG AT THIS RATE.
HSSH...
WOBBLE...
RUSTLE
SNORT SNORT SNORT
B-KI?
KWAK?

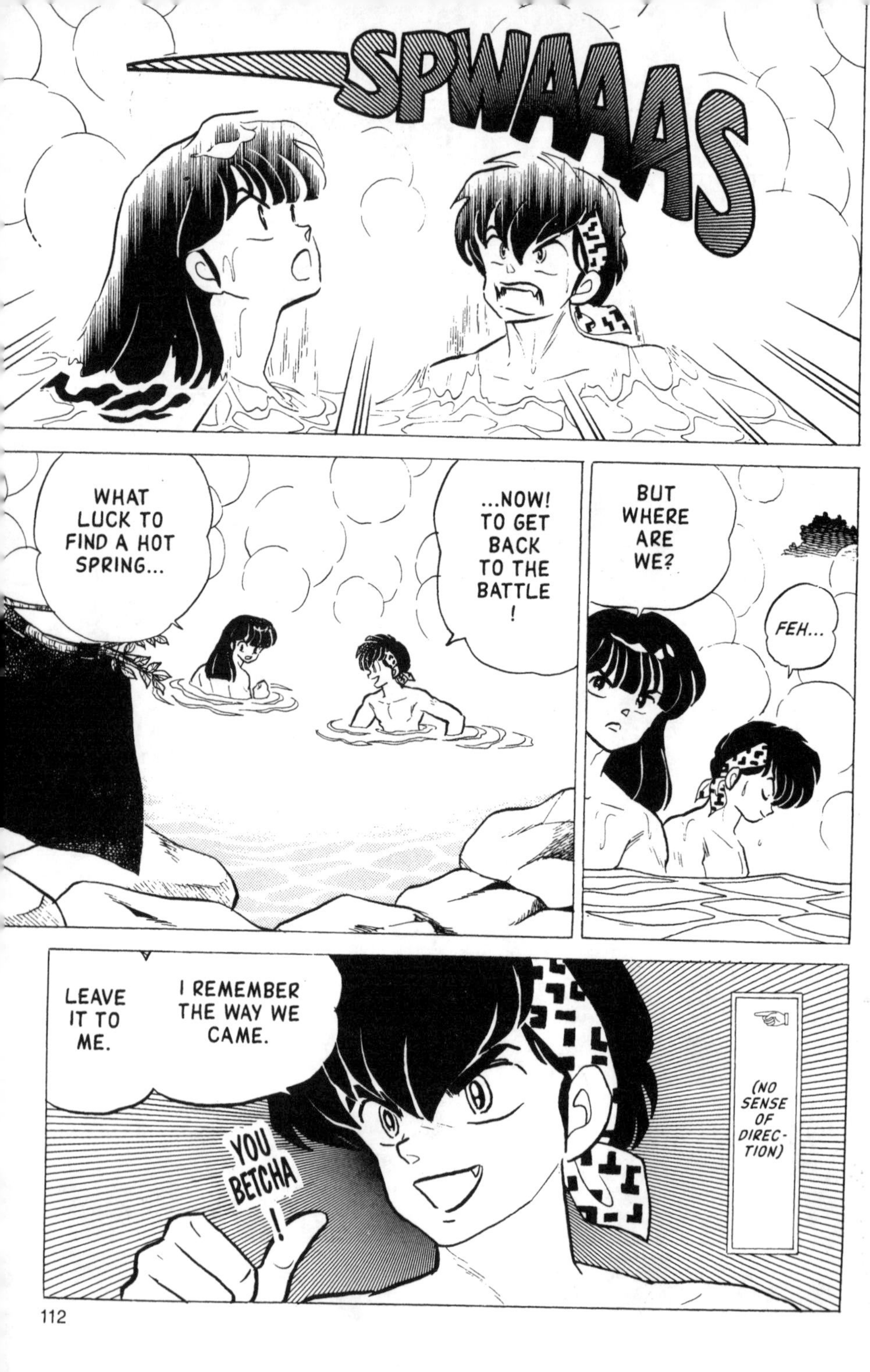
SPWAAAS
WHAT LUCK TO FIND A HOT SPRING...
...NOW! TO GET BACK TO THE BATTLE!
BUT WHERE ARE WE?
FEH...
LEAVE IT TO ME.
I REMEMBER THE WAY WE CAME.
YOU BETCHA!
(NO SENSE OF DIREC-TION)

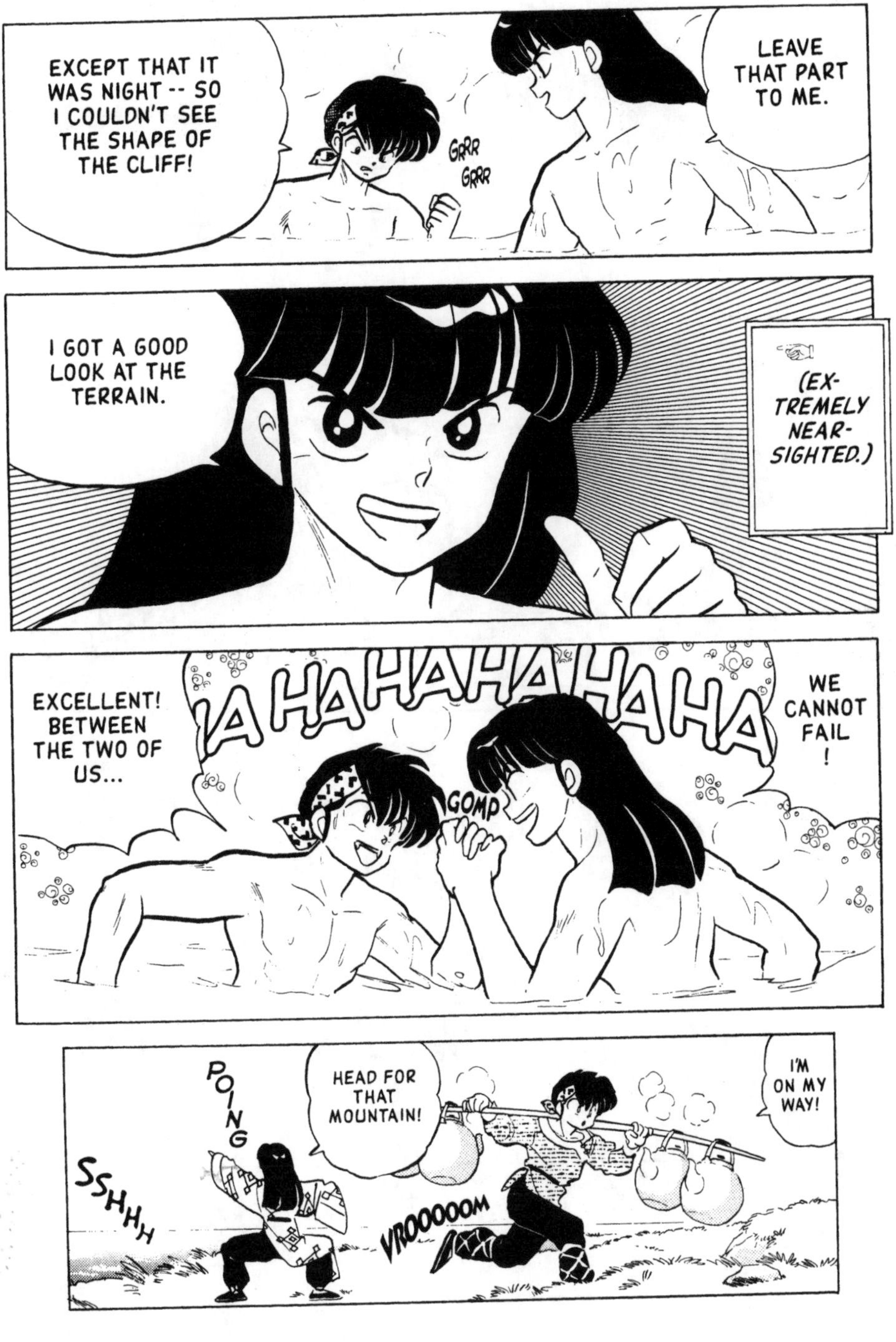
EXCEPT THAT IT WAS NIGHT -- SO I COULDN'T SEE THE SHAPE OF THE CLIFF!
GRRR GRRR
LEAVE THAT PART TO ME.
I GOT A GOOD LOOK AT THE TERRAIN.
(EX-TREMELY NEAR-SIGHTED.)
EXCELLENT! BETWEEN THE TWO OF US...
HA HA HA HA HA HA HA
GOMP
WE CANNOT FAIL!
POING
SSHHH
HEAD FOR THAT MOUNTAIN!
VROOOOOM
I'M ON MY WAY!

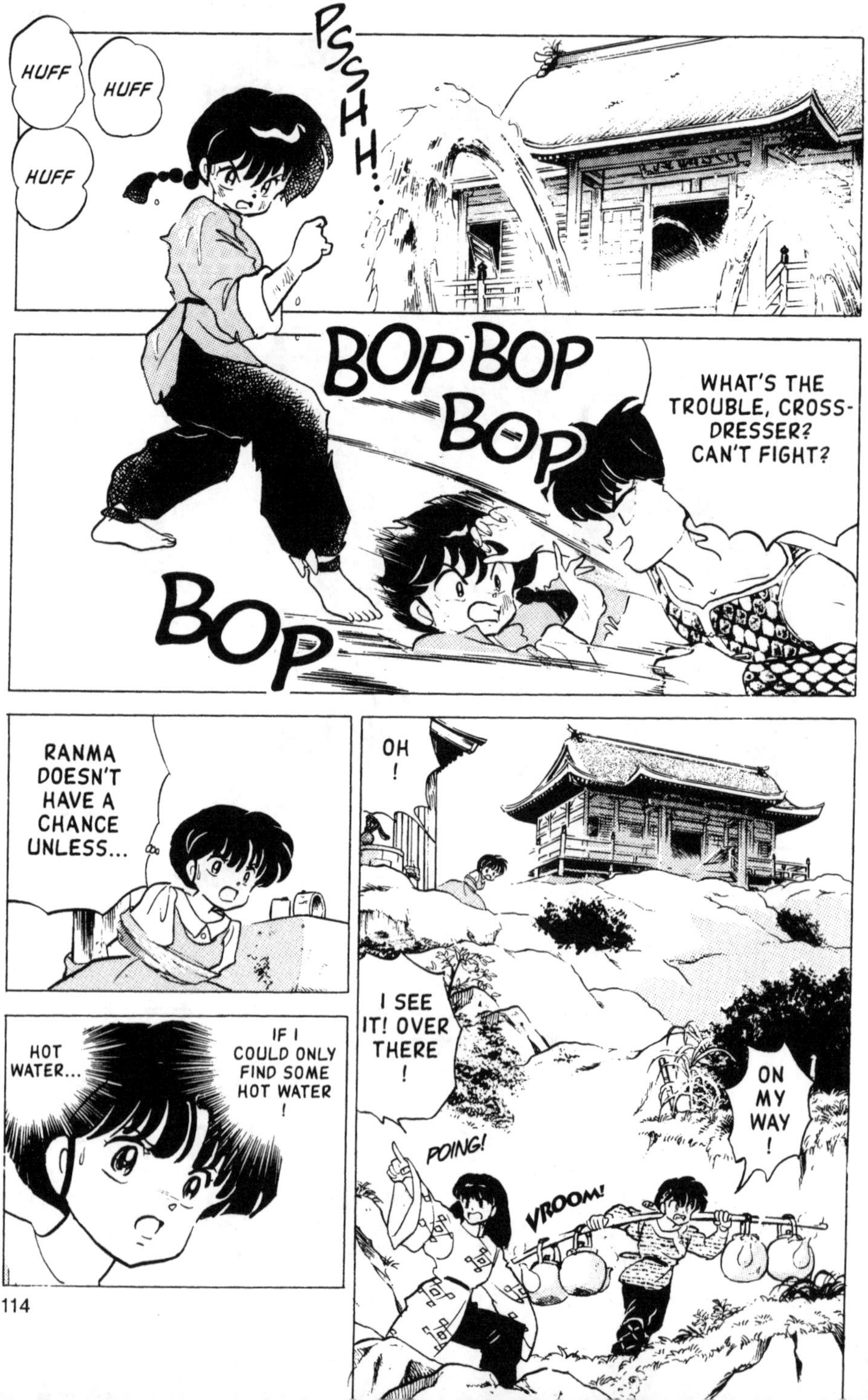
HUFF
HUFF
HUFF
PSSHH...
BOPBOP
BOP
WHAT'S THE TROUBLE, CROSS-DRESSER? CAN'T FIGHT?
BOP
RANMA DOESN'T HAVE A CHANCE UNLESS...
HOT WATER...
IF I COULD ONLY FIND SOME HOT WATER!
OH!
I SEE IT! OVER THERE!
ON MY WAY!
POING!
VROOM!

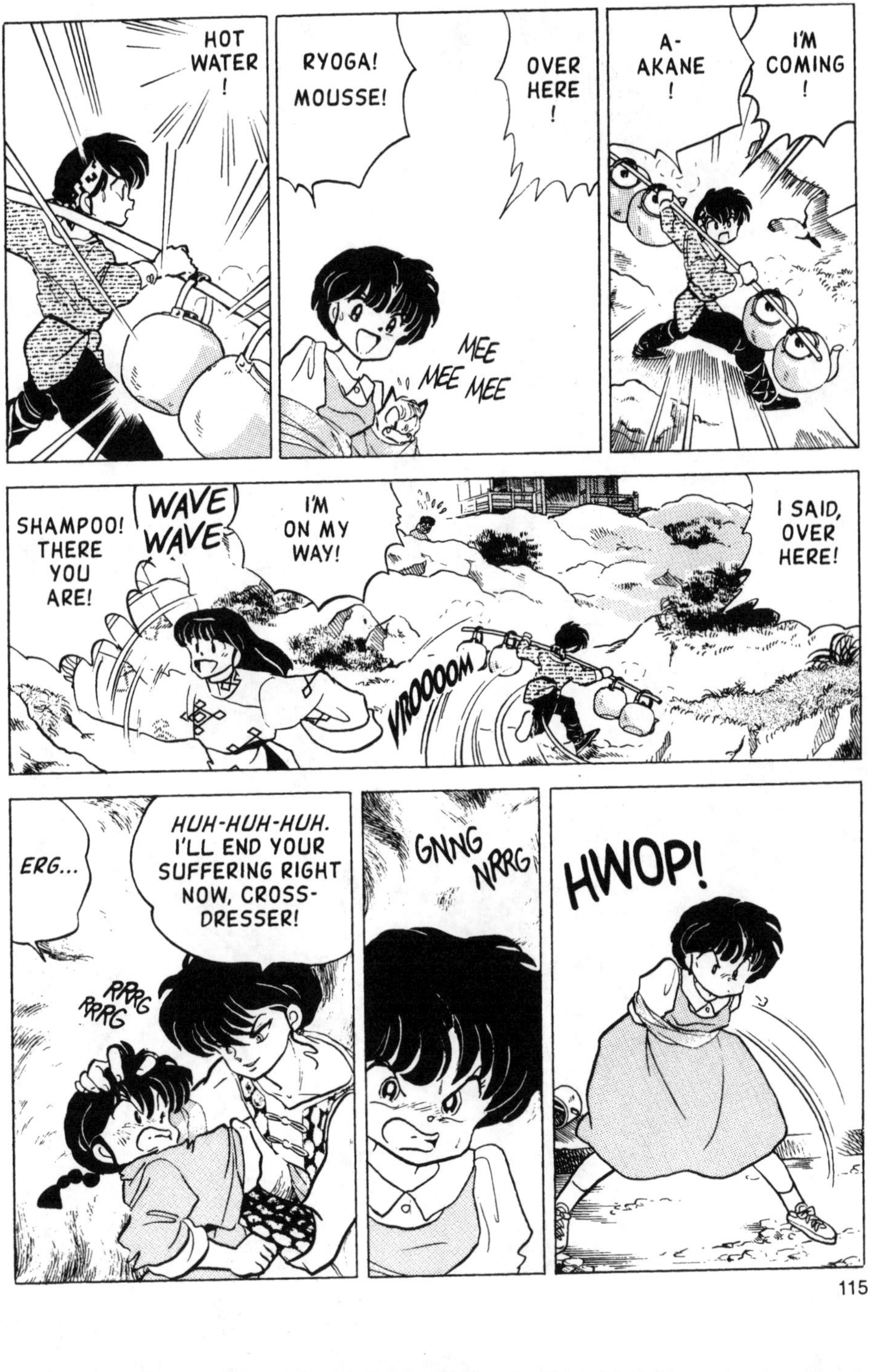
HOT WATER!
RYOGA! MOUSSE!
OVER HERE!
MEE MEE MEE
A- AKANE!
I'M COMING!
SHAMPOO! THERE YOU ARE!
WAVE WAVE
I'M ON MY WAY!
I SAID, OVER HERE!
VROOOOOM
ERG...
HUH-HUH-HUH. I'LL END YOUR SUFFERING RIGHT NOW, CROSS-DRESSER!
RRRG RRRG
GNNG NRRG
HWOP!

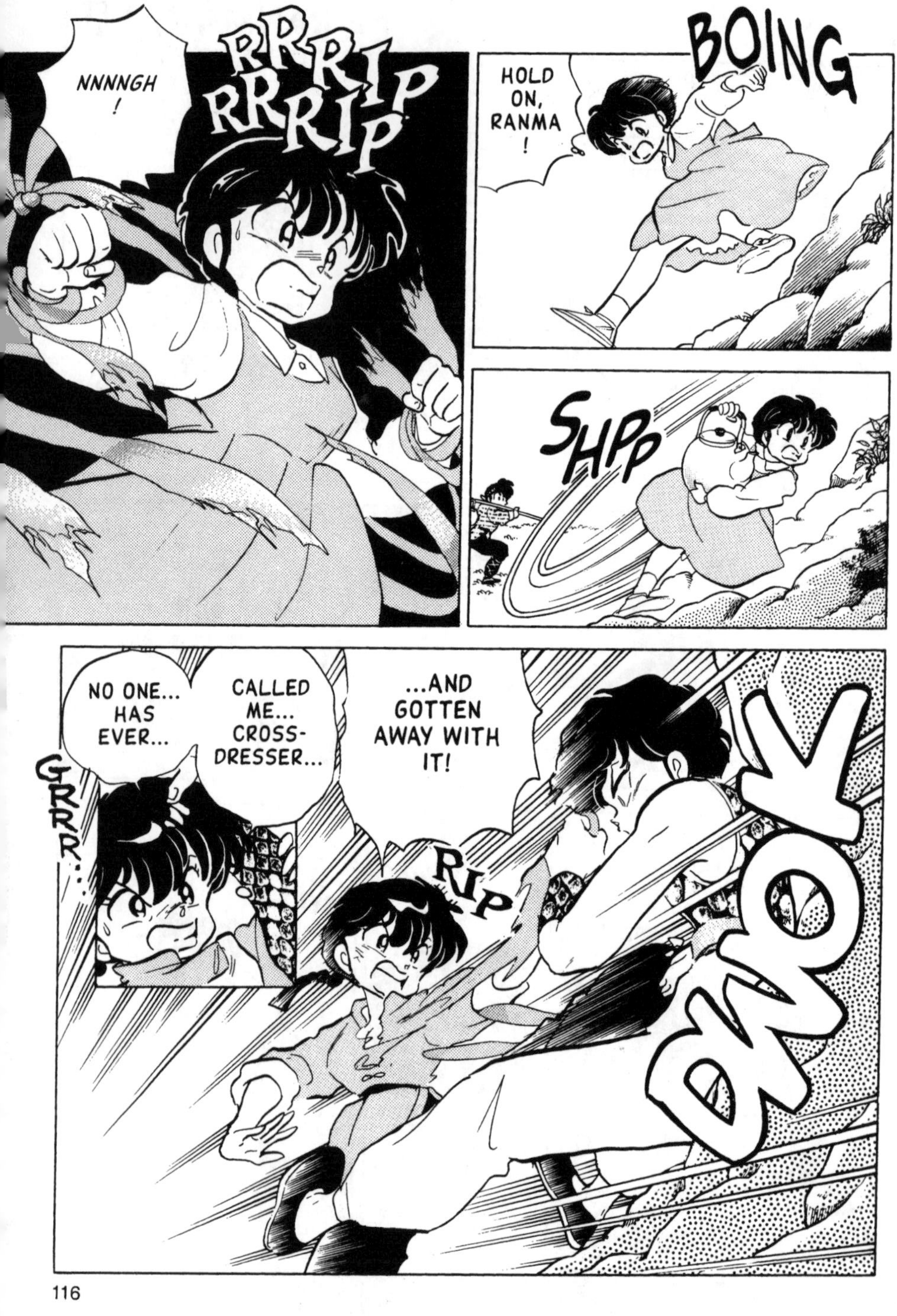
NNNNGH!
RRRIP RRRIP
HOLD ON, RANMA!
BOING
SHPP
GRRRR...
NO ONE... HAS EVER...
CALLED ME... CROSS-DRESSER...
...AND GOTTEN AWAY WITH IT!
RIP
BWOK

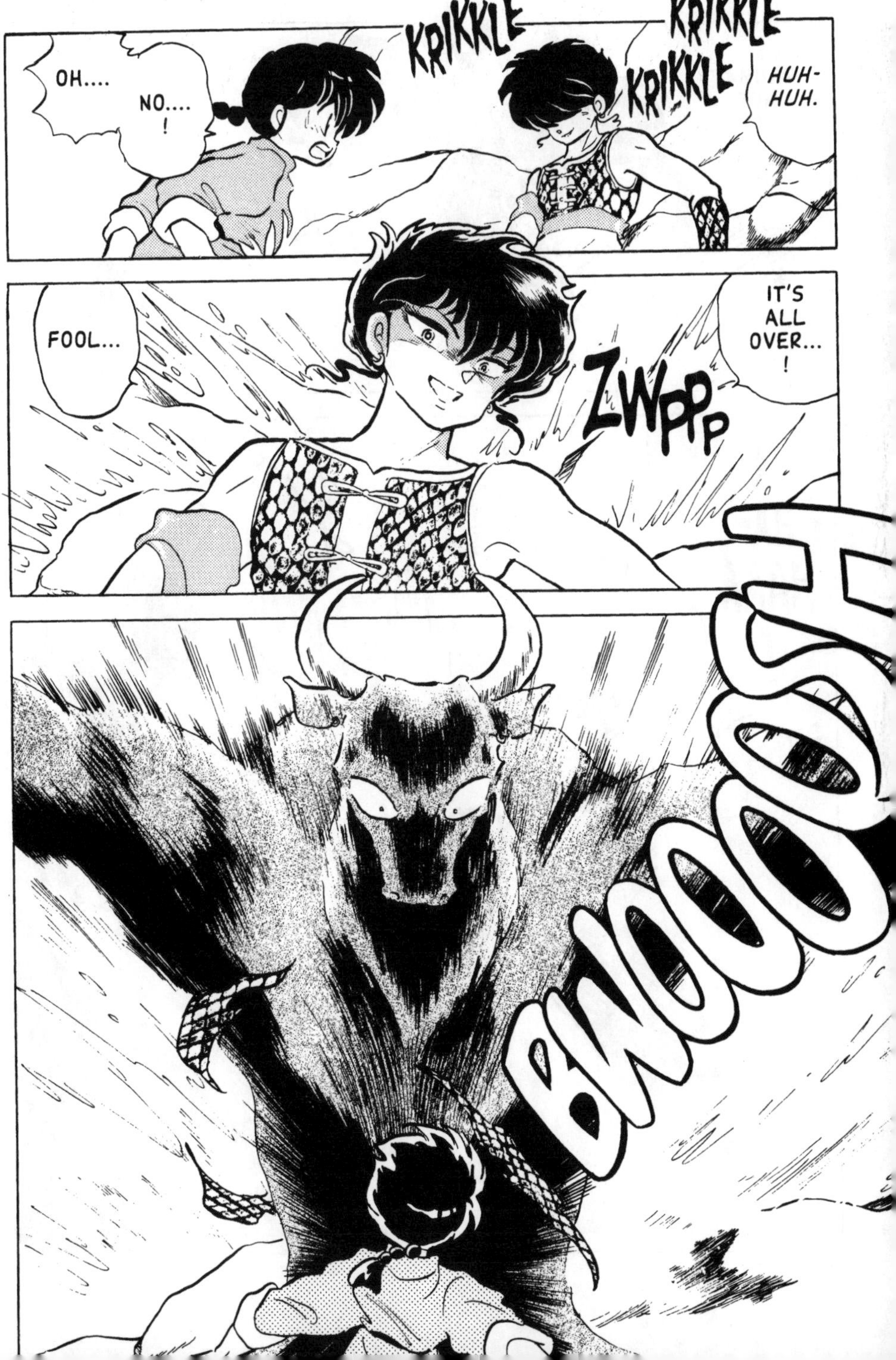
OH.... NO.... !
KRIKKLE
KRIKKLE KRIKKLE
HUH-HUH.
FOOL...
ZWPPP
IT'S ALL OVER... !
BWOOOOSH

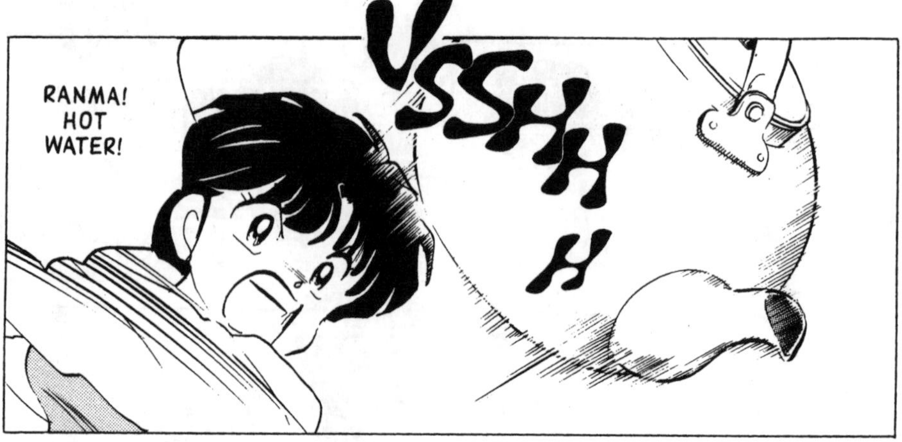
RANMA! HOT WATER!
VSSHHH

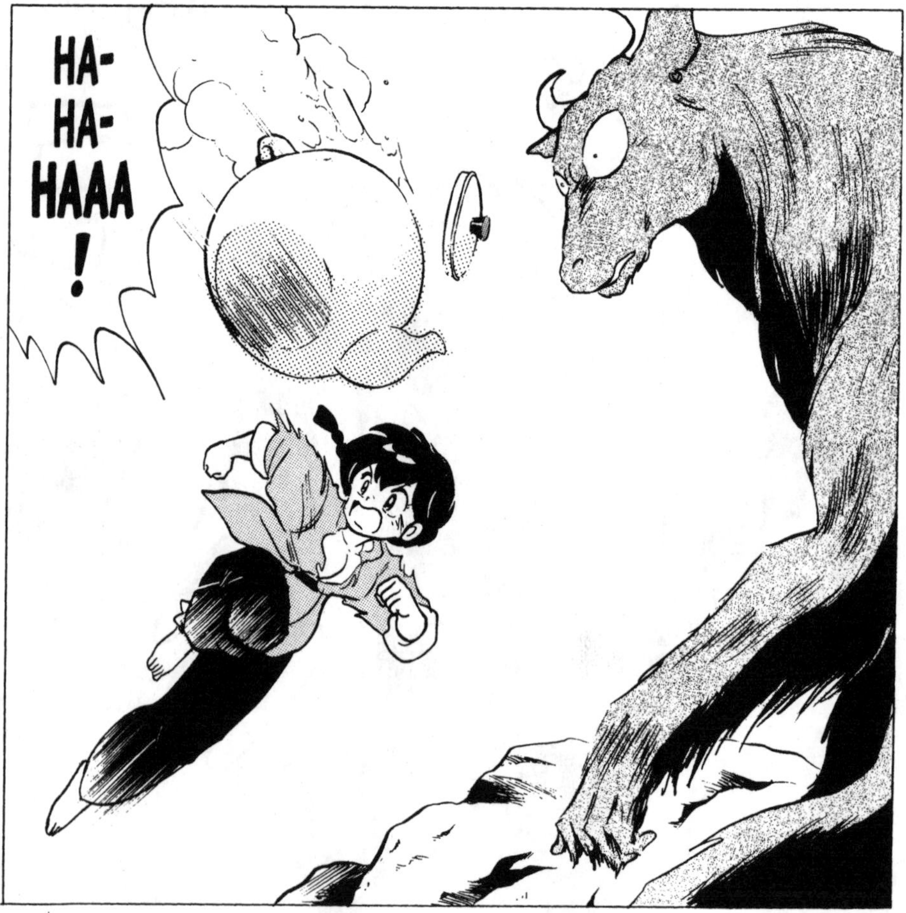
HA-HA-HAAA!

Part 8
BOILING RETALIATION

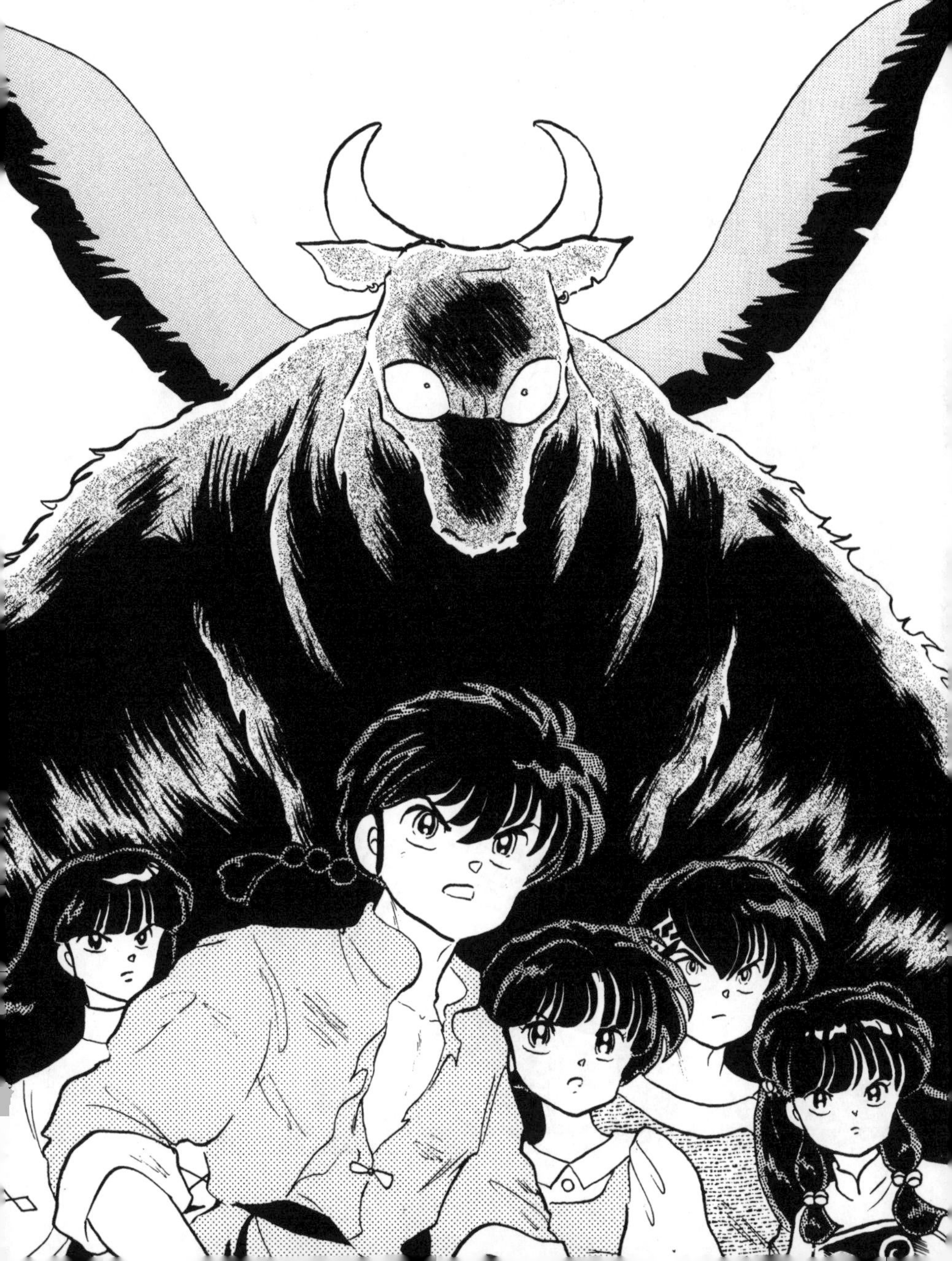

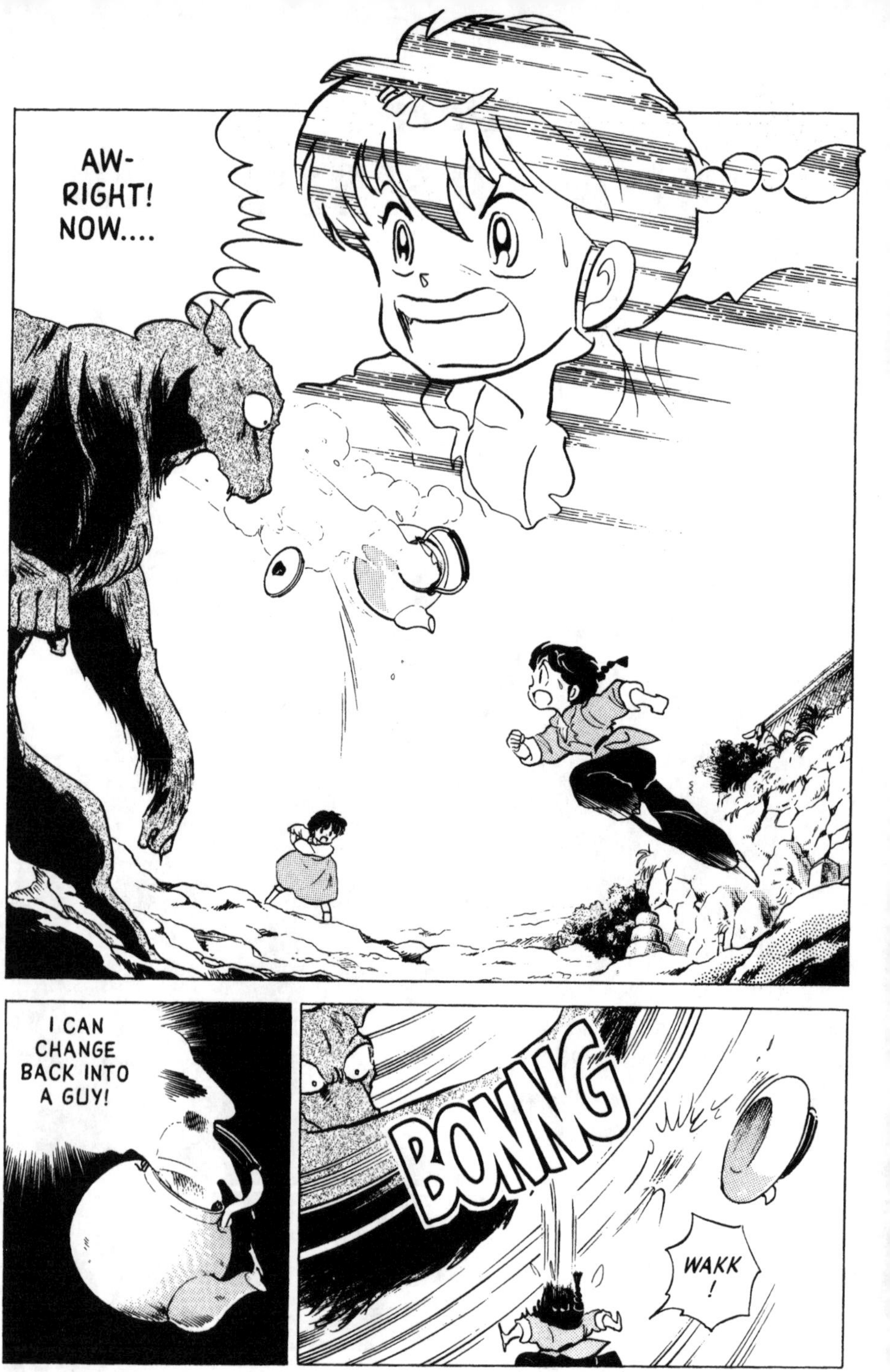

AW-RIGHT! NOW....
I CAN CHANGE BACK INTO A GUY!
BONNG
WAKK!

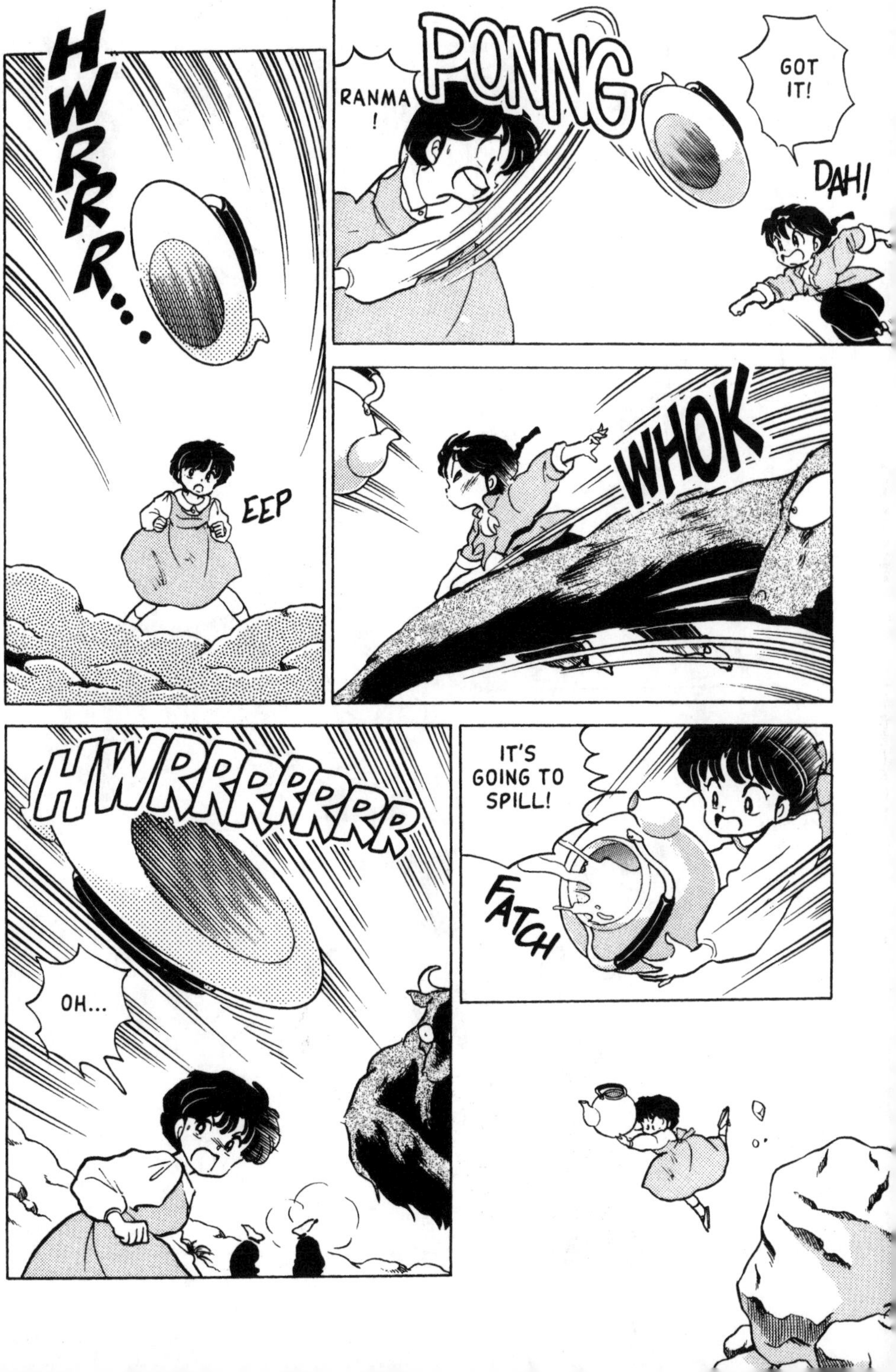
HWRRR...
EEP
RANMA!
PONNG
GOT IT!
DAH!
WHOK
HWRRRRRRRR
OH...
IT'S GOING TO SPILL!
FATCH

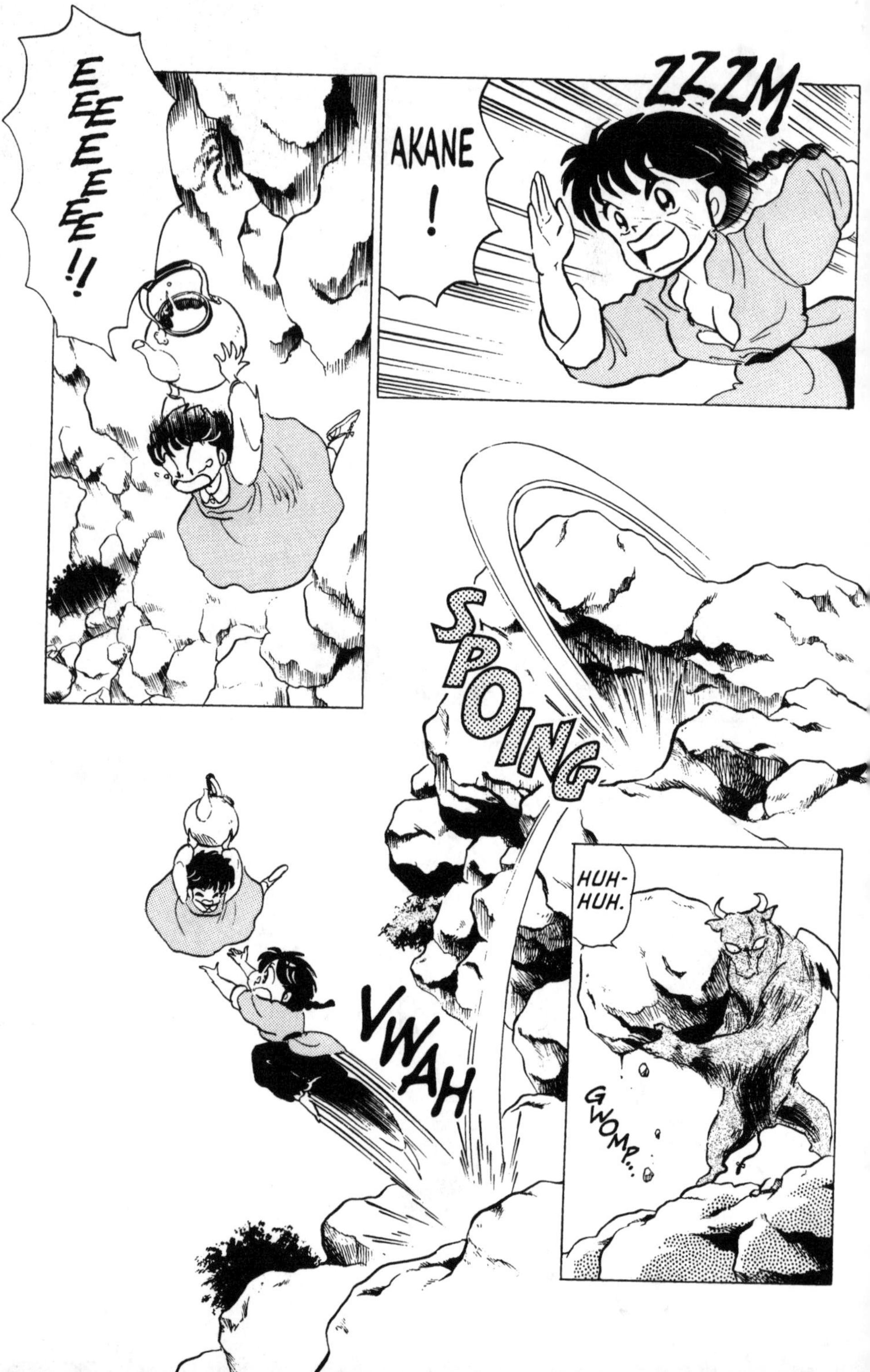
EEEEEEE!!
ZZZM
AKANE!
SPOING
VWAH
HUH-HUH.
GWOMP...

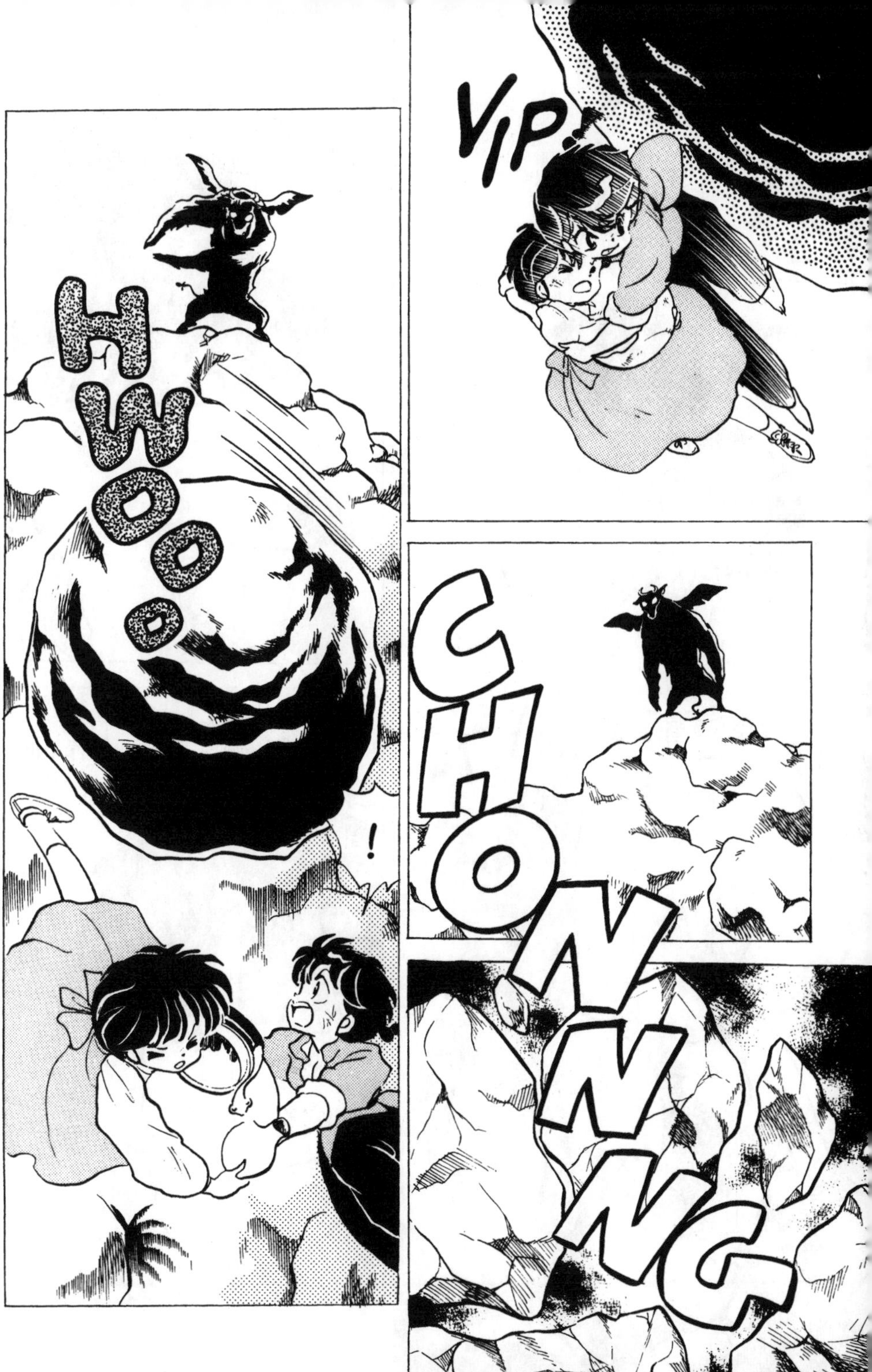
HWOOO
!
YIP!
CHONNNNG

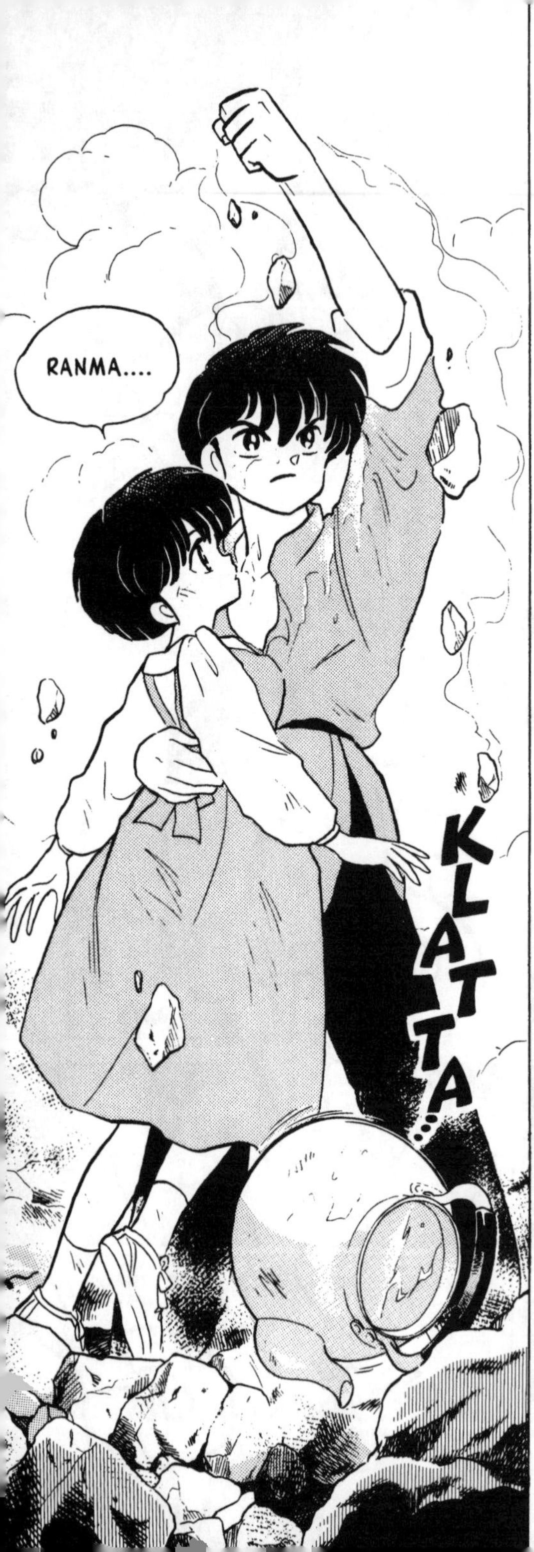
RANMA....
KLATTA...
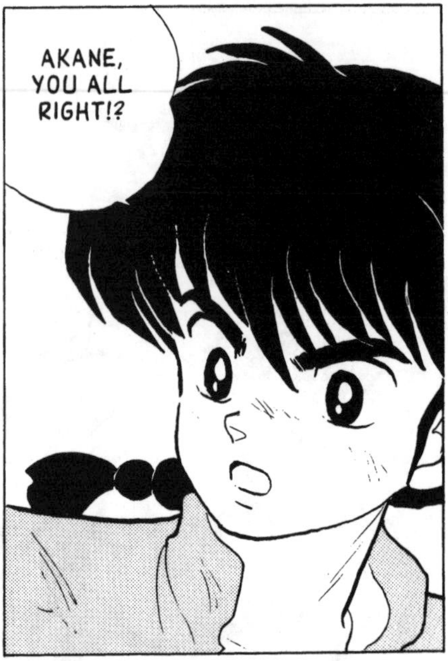
AKANE, YOU ALL RIGHT!?
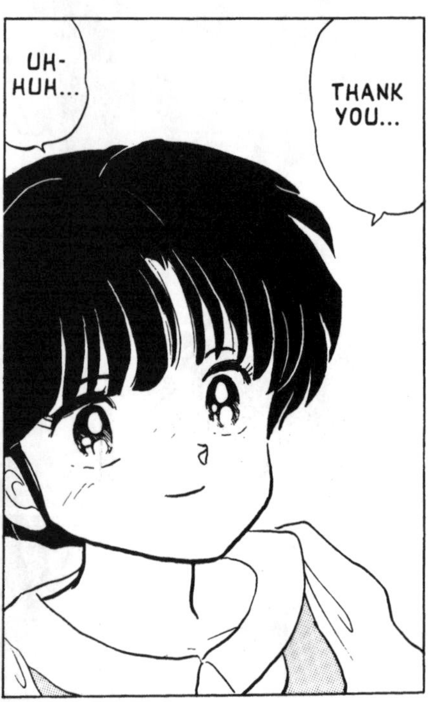
UH-HUH...
THANK YOU...

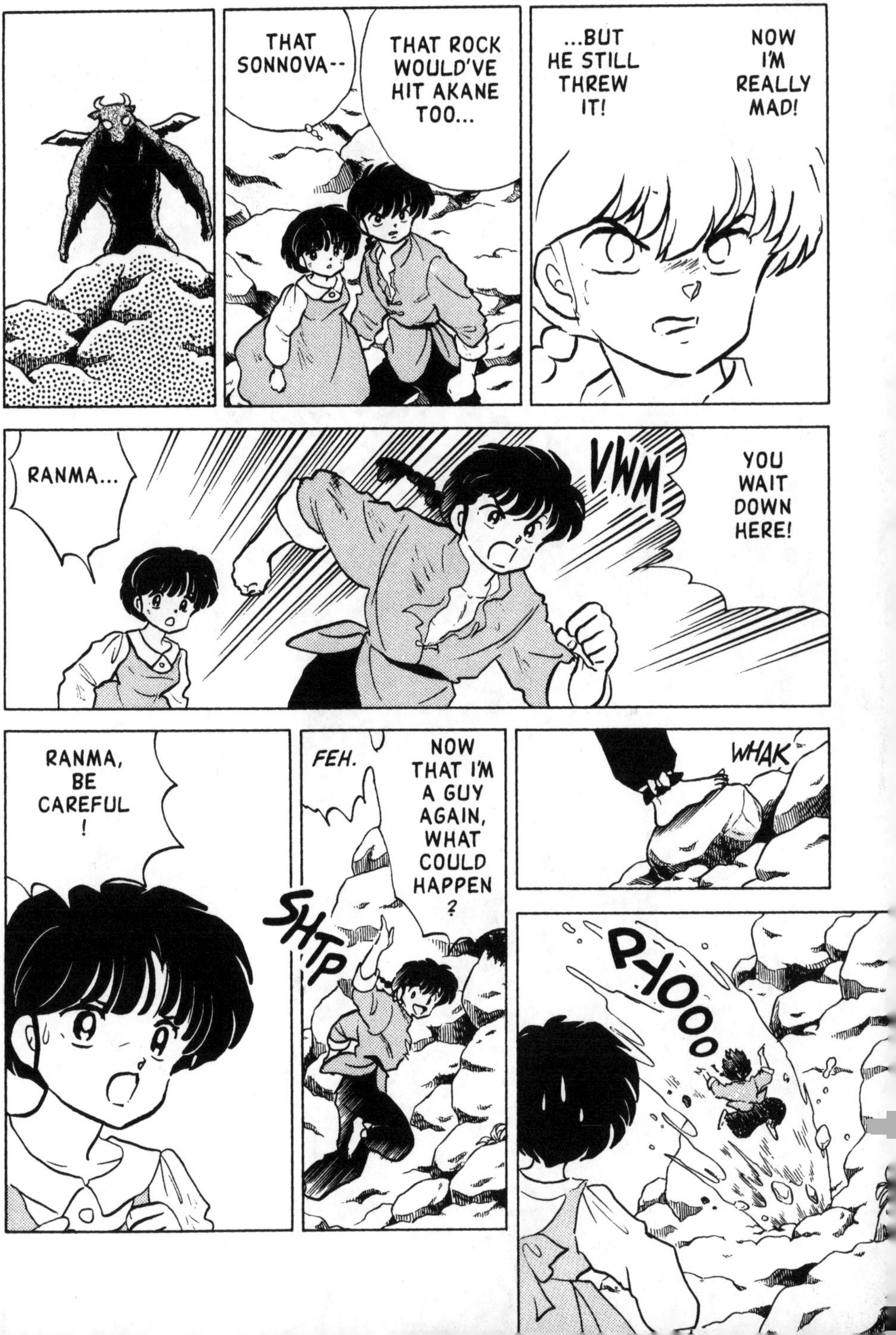
THAT SONNOVA--
THAT ROCK WOULD'VE HIT AKANE TOO...
...BUT HE STILL THREW IT!
NOW I'M REALLY MAD!
RANMA...
VWM
YOU WAIT DOWN HERE!
RANMA, BE CAREFUL!
FEH.
NOW THAT I'M A GUY AGAIN, WHAT COULD HAPPEN?
SHTP
WHAK
P-YOOOO

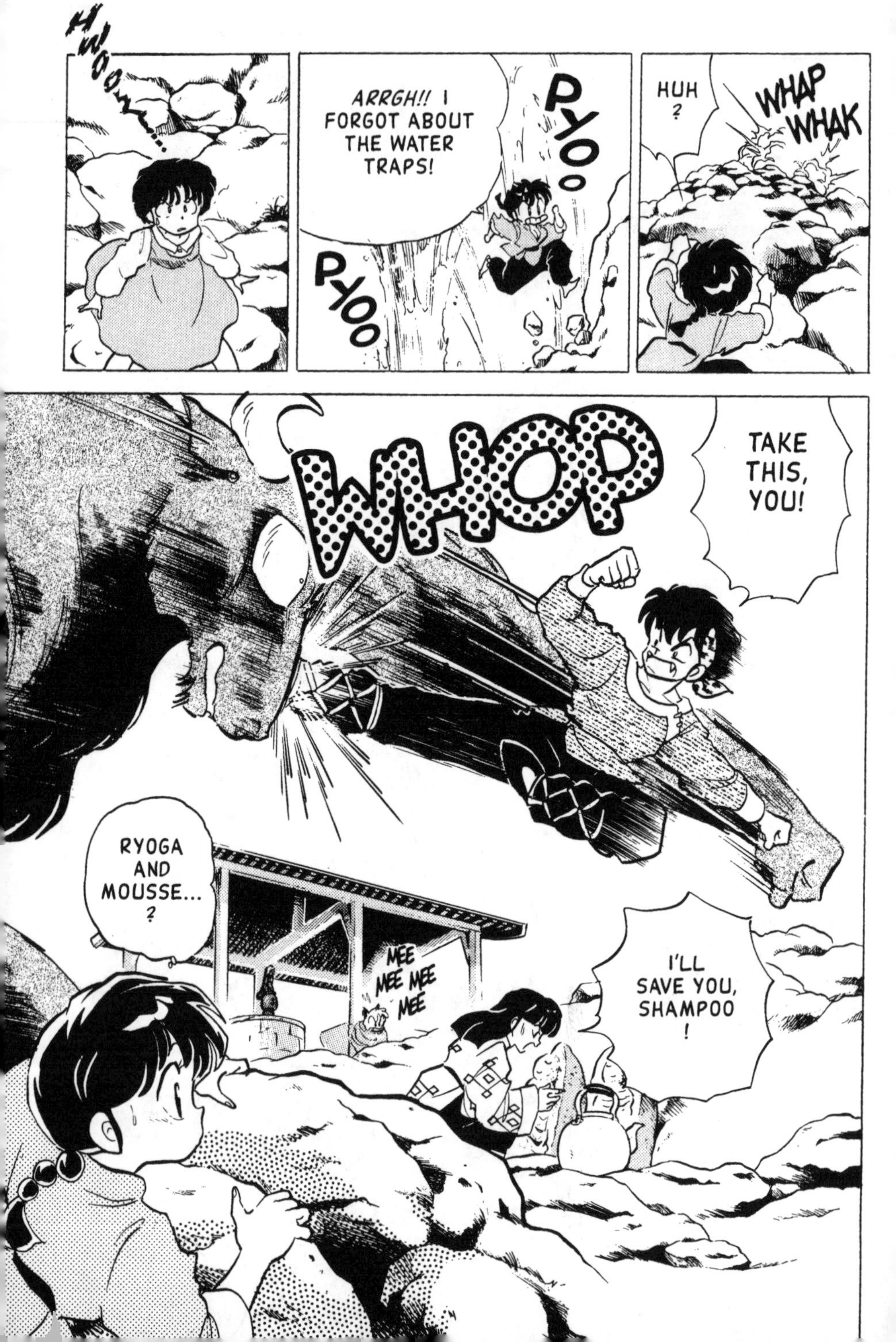
HWOOM.....
ARRGH!! I FORGOT ABOUT THE WATER TRAPS!
PYOO
PYOO
HUH?
WHAP WHAK
WHOP
TAKE THIS, YOU!
RYOGA AND MOUSSE...?
MEE MEE MEE MEE
I'LL SAVE YOU, SHAMPOO!

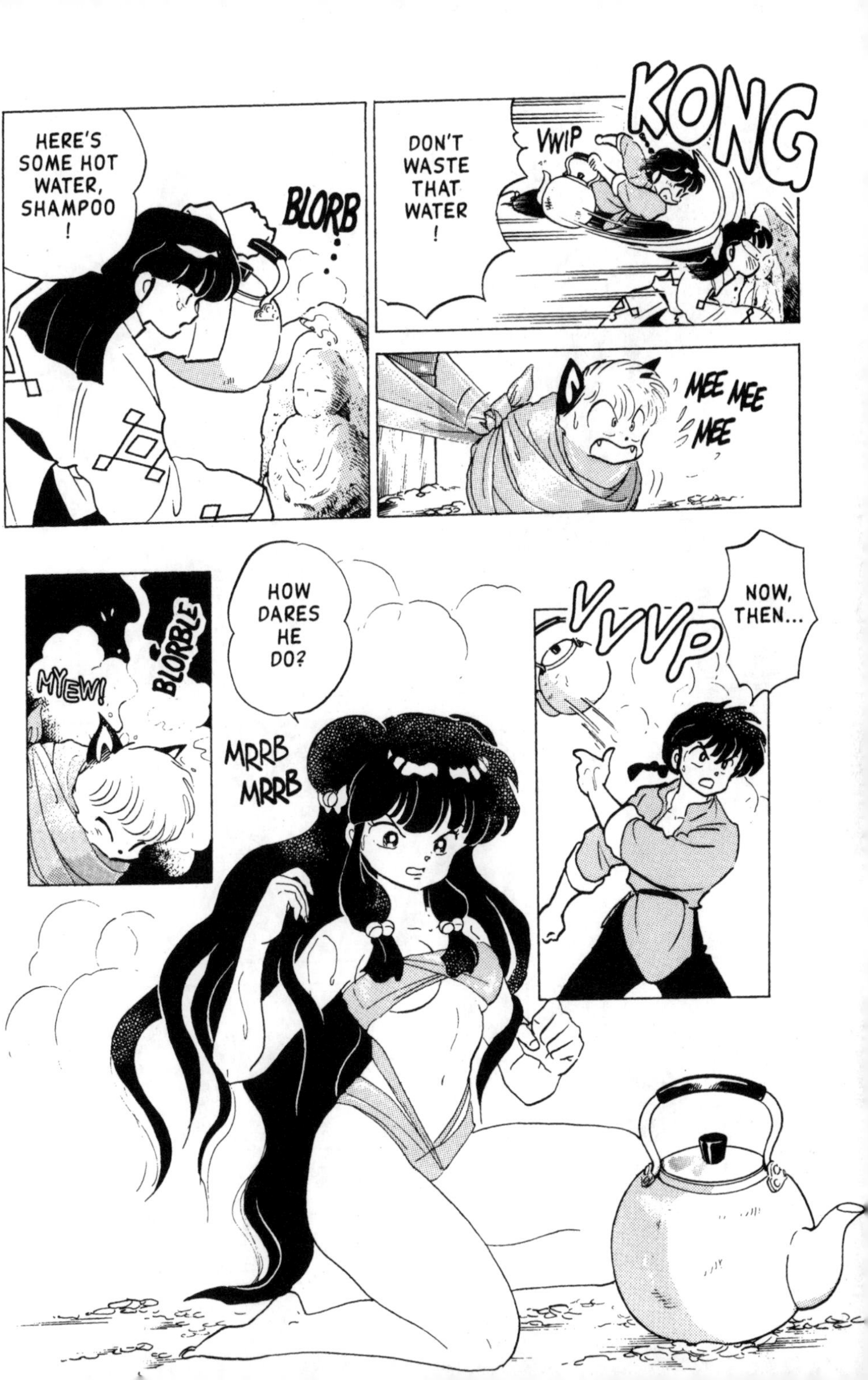
HERE'S SOME HOT WATER, SHAMPOO !
BLORB
KONG
DON'T WASTE THAT WATER !
VWIP
MEE MEE MEE
MYEW!
BLORBLE
HOW DARES HE DO?
MRRB MRRB
VVVP
NOW, THEN...

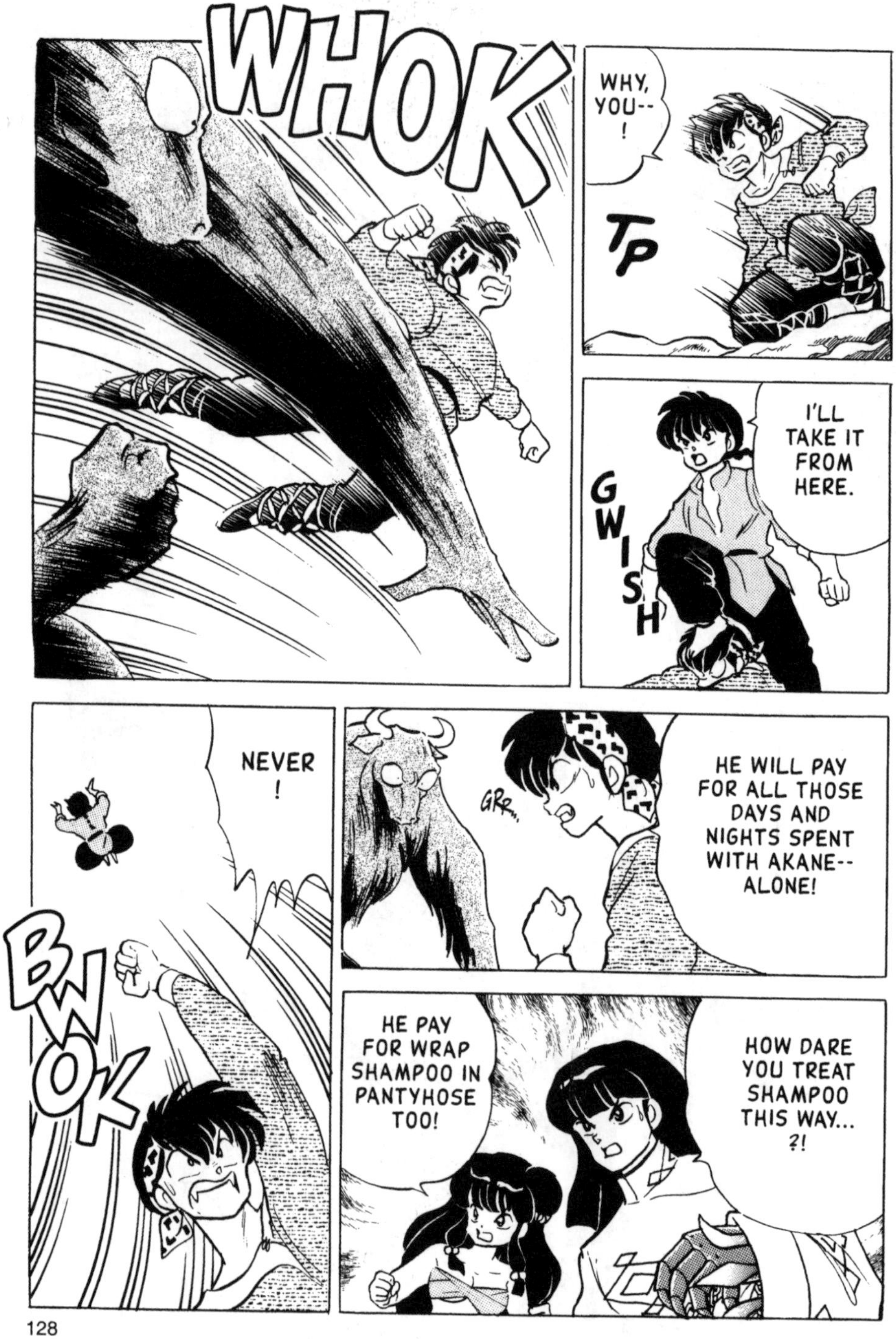
WHOK
WHY, YOU-- !
TP
I'LL TAKE IT FROM HERE.
GWISH
NEVER !
BWOK
GRR...
HE WILL PAY FOR ALL THOSE DAYS AND NIGHTS SPENT WITH AKANE-- ALONE!
HE PAY FOR WRAP SHAMPOO IN PANTYHOSE TOO!
HOW DARE YOU TREAT SHAMPOO THIS WAY... ?!

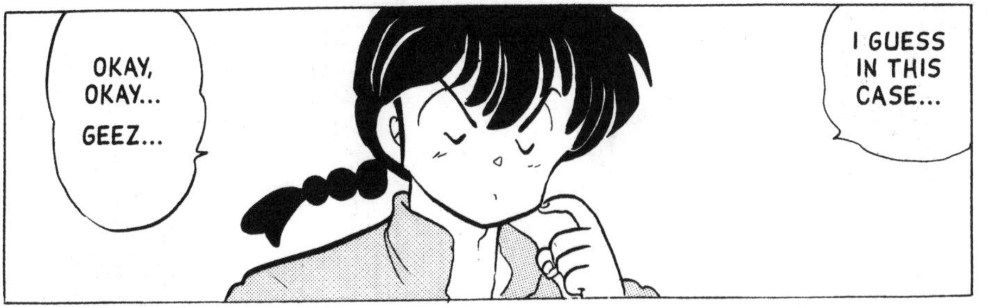
OKAY, OKAY... GEEZ...
I GUESS IN THIS CASE...

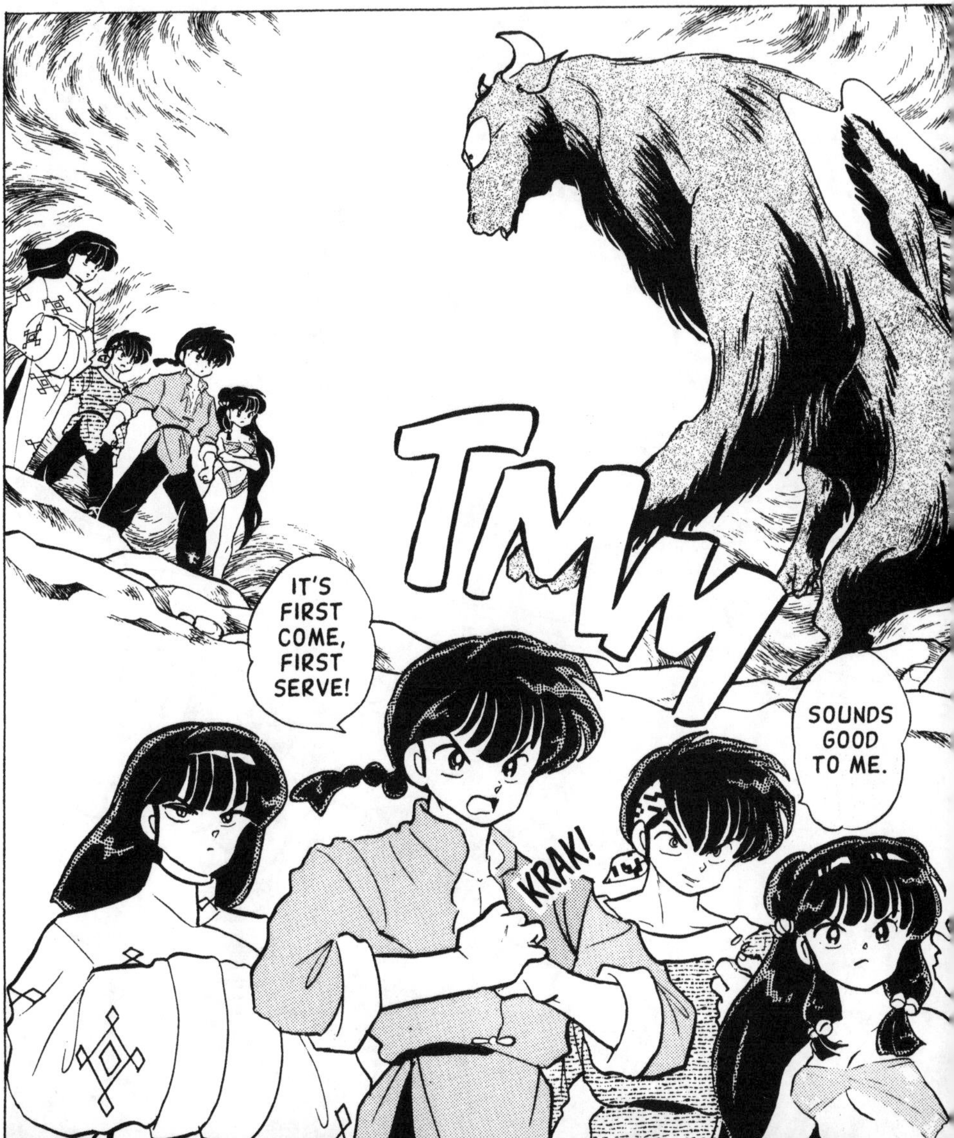
TMM
IT'S FIRST COME, FIRST SERVE!
SOUNDS GOOD TO ME.
KRAK!

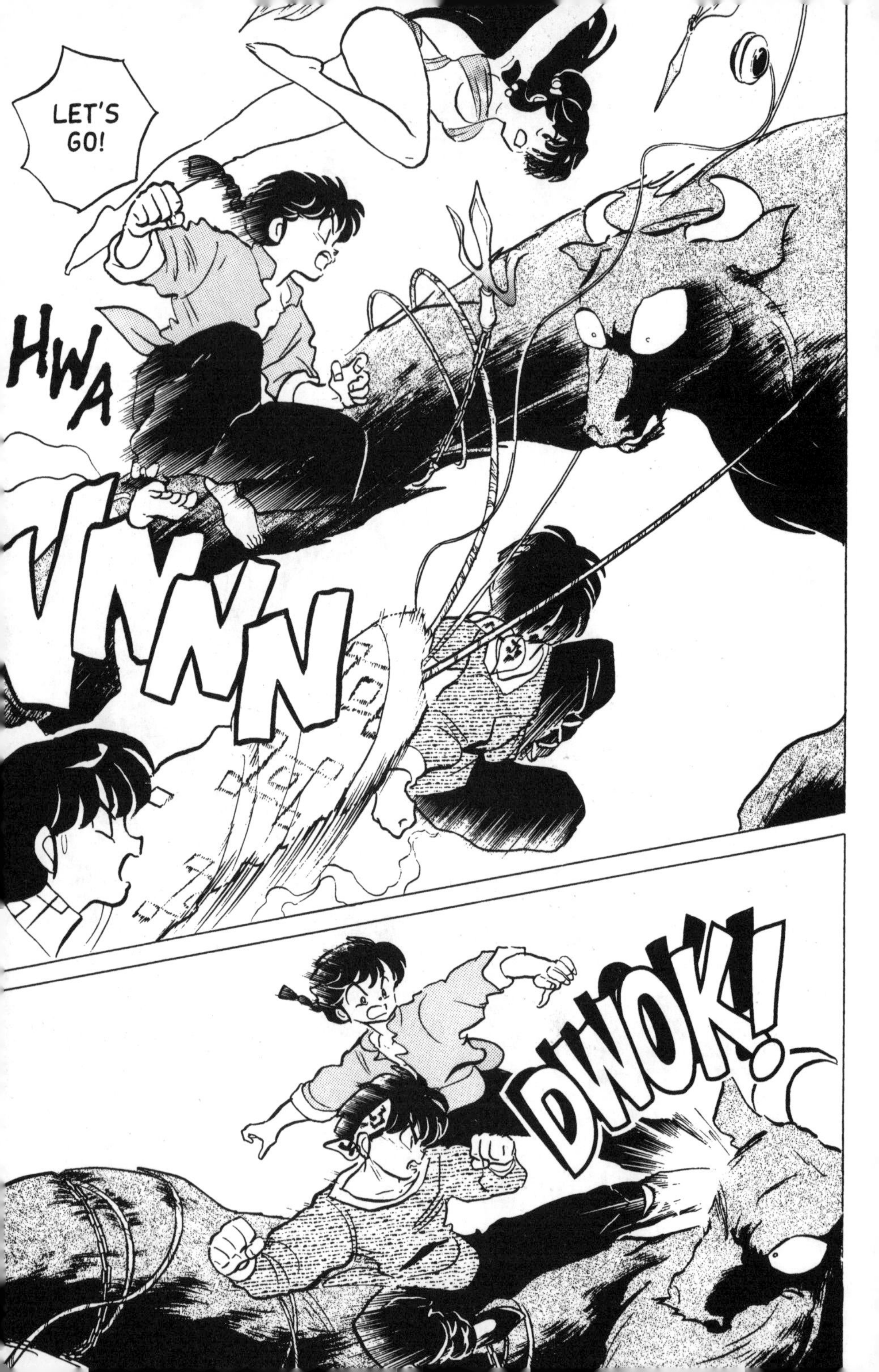
LET'S GO!
HWA
VNNN
DWOK!

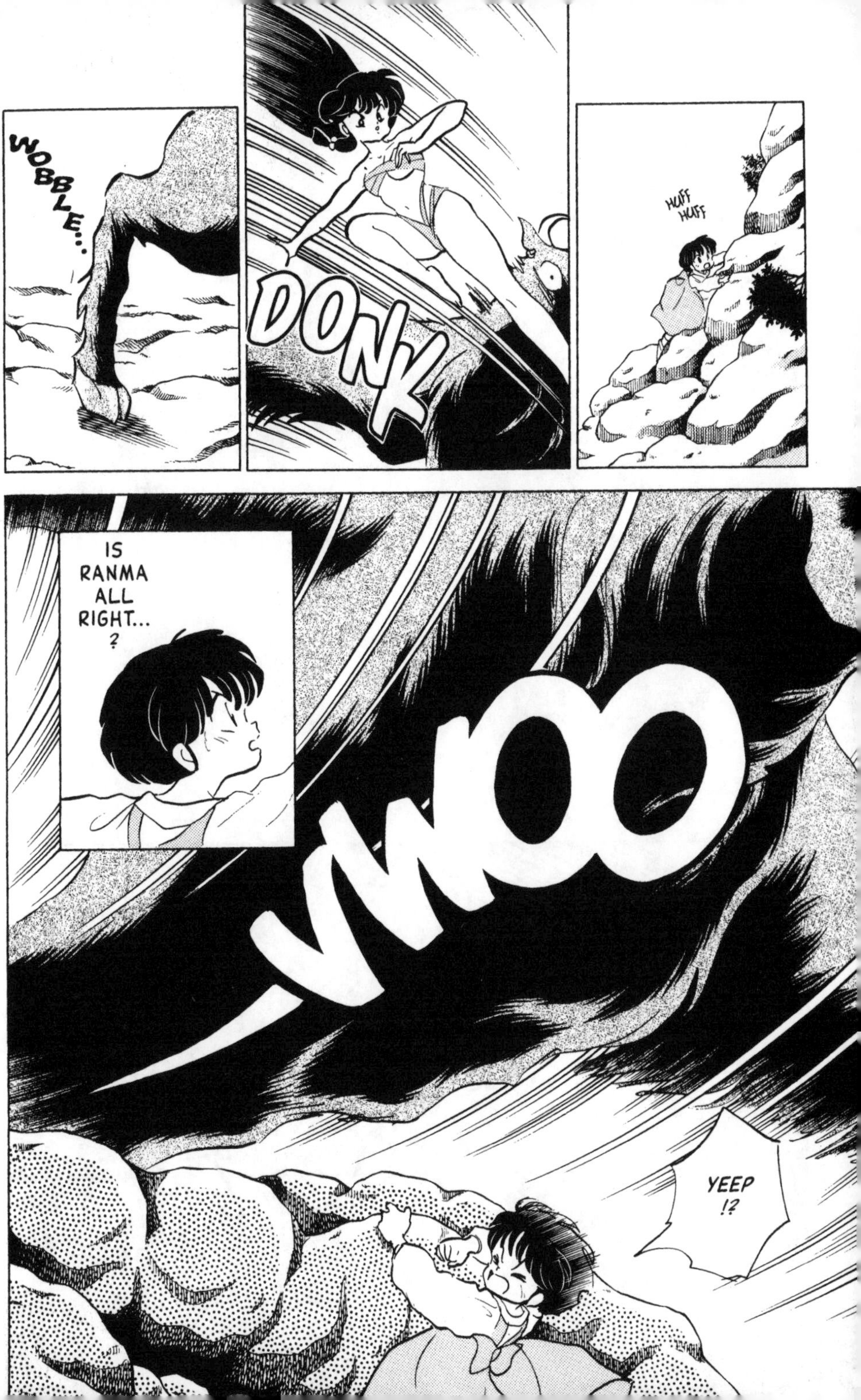
WOBBLE...
DONK
HUFF HUFF
IS RANMA ALL RIGHT...?
VWOO
YEEP!?

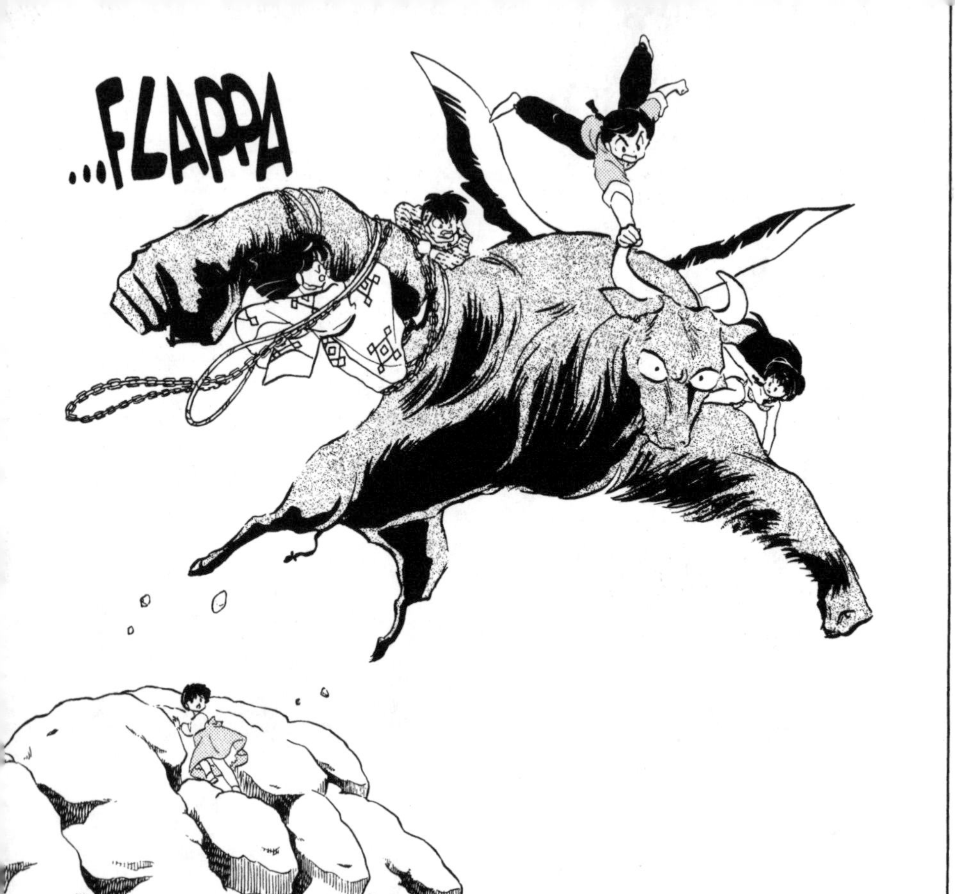
...FLAPPA

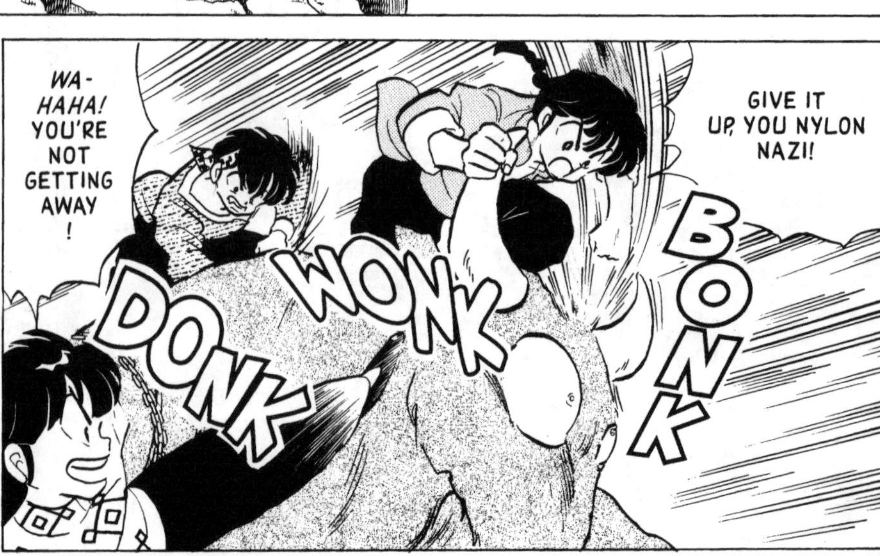
WA-HAHA! YOU'RE NOT GETTING AWAY!
DONK
WONK
GIVE IT UP, YOU NYLON NAZI!
BONK

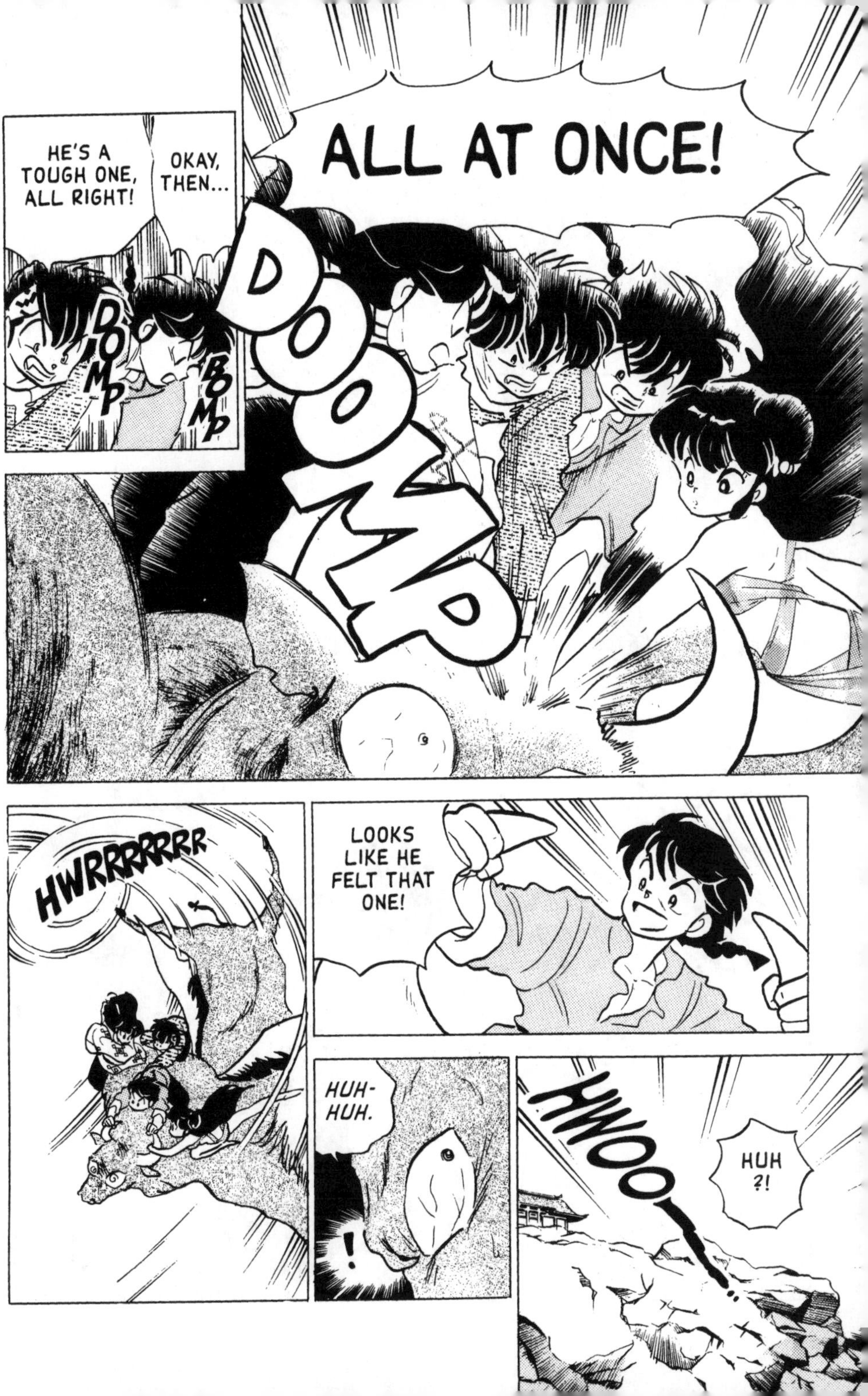
HE'S A TOUGH ONE, ALL RIGHT!
DOMP
OKAY, THEN...
BOMP
ALL AT ONCE!
DOOOMP
HWRRRRRRR
LOOKS LIKE HE FELT THAT ONE!
HUH-HUH.
!
HWOO--...
HUH ?!

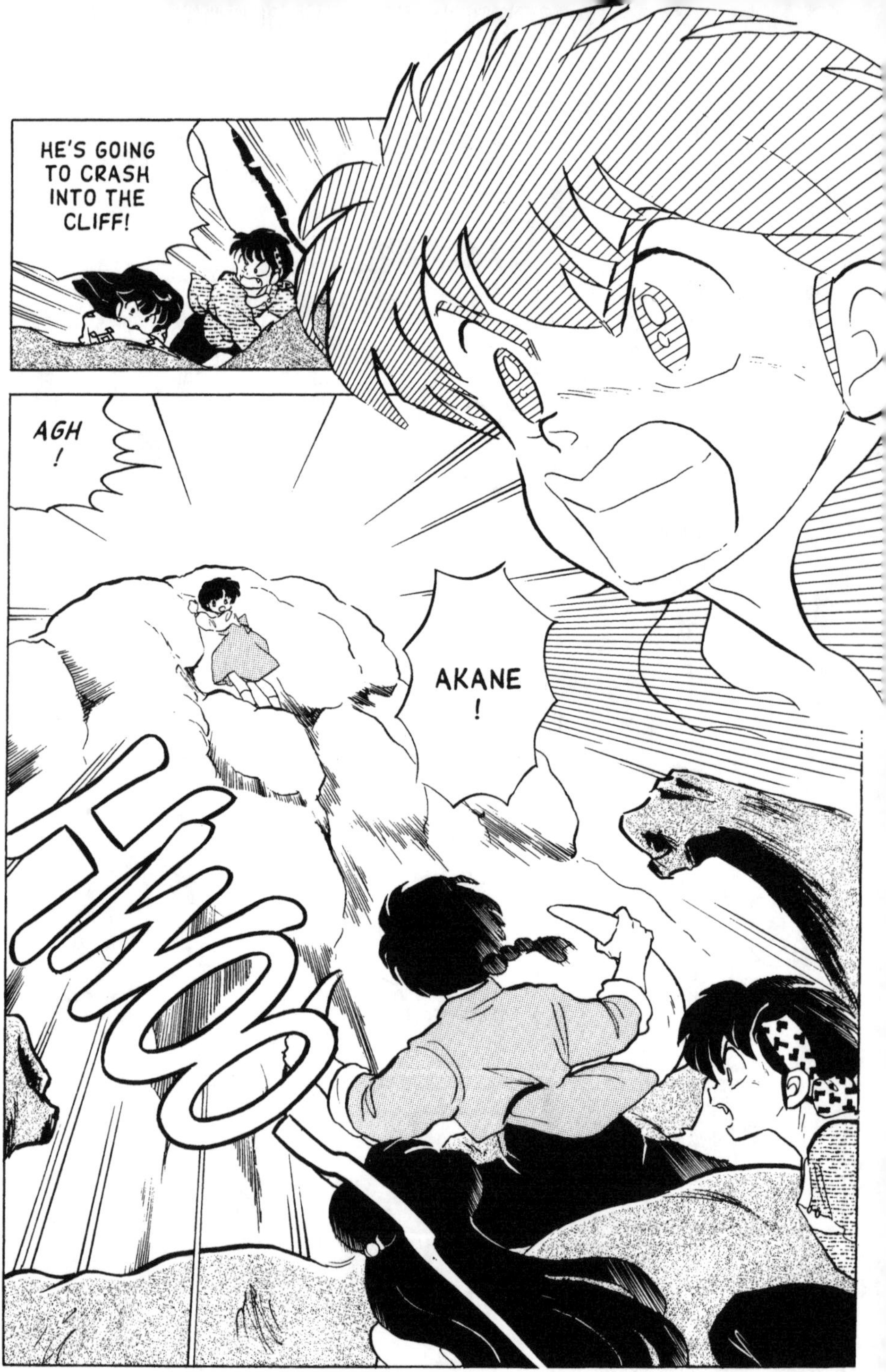
HE'S GOING TO CRASH INTO THE CLIFF!
AGH!
AKANE!

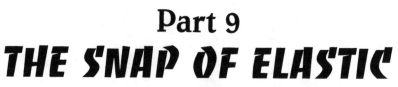

Part 9
THE SNAP OF ELASTIC

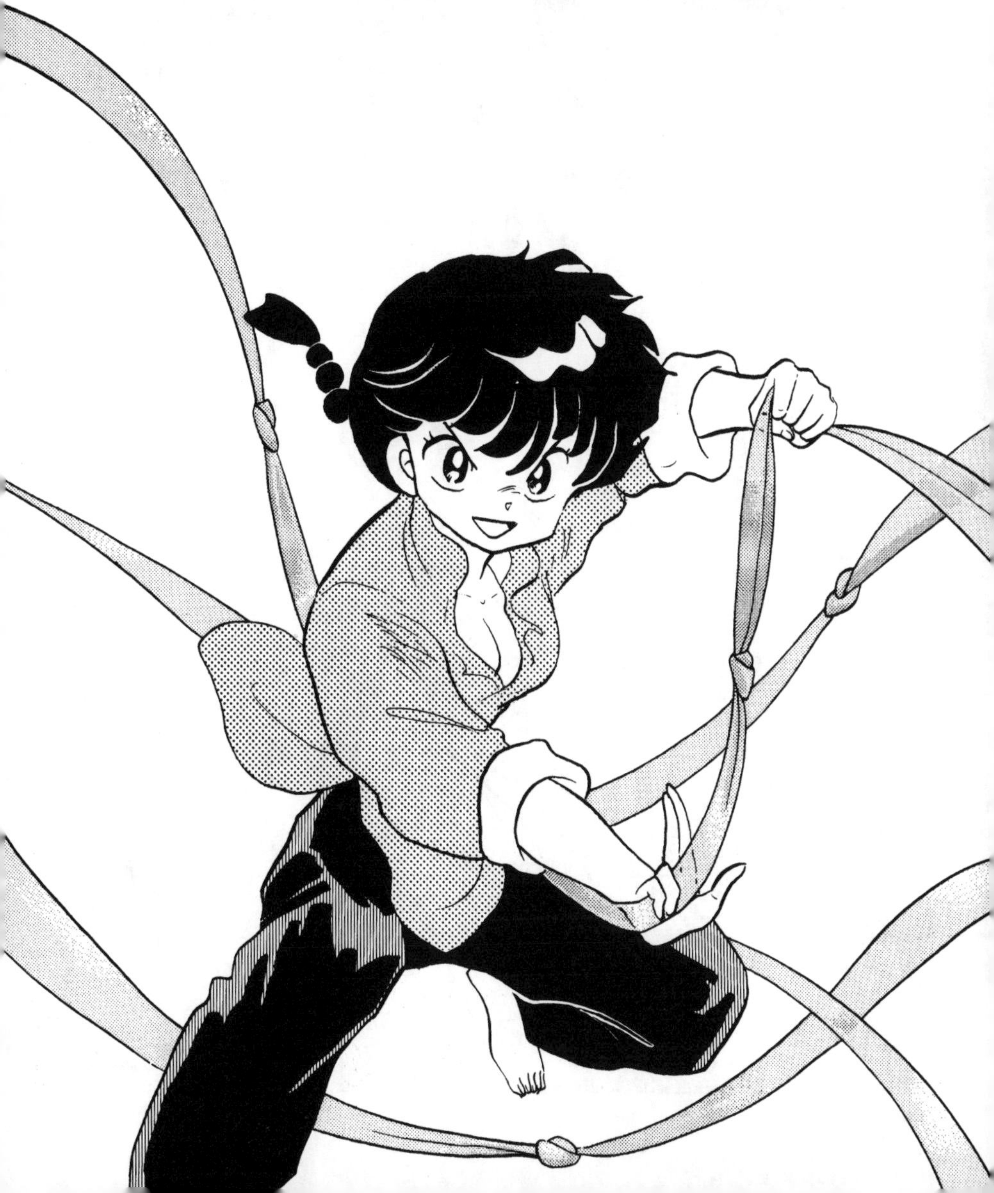

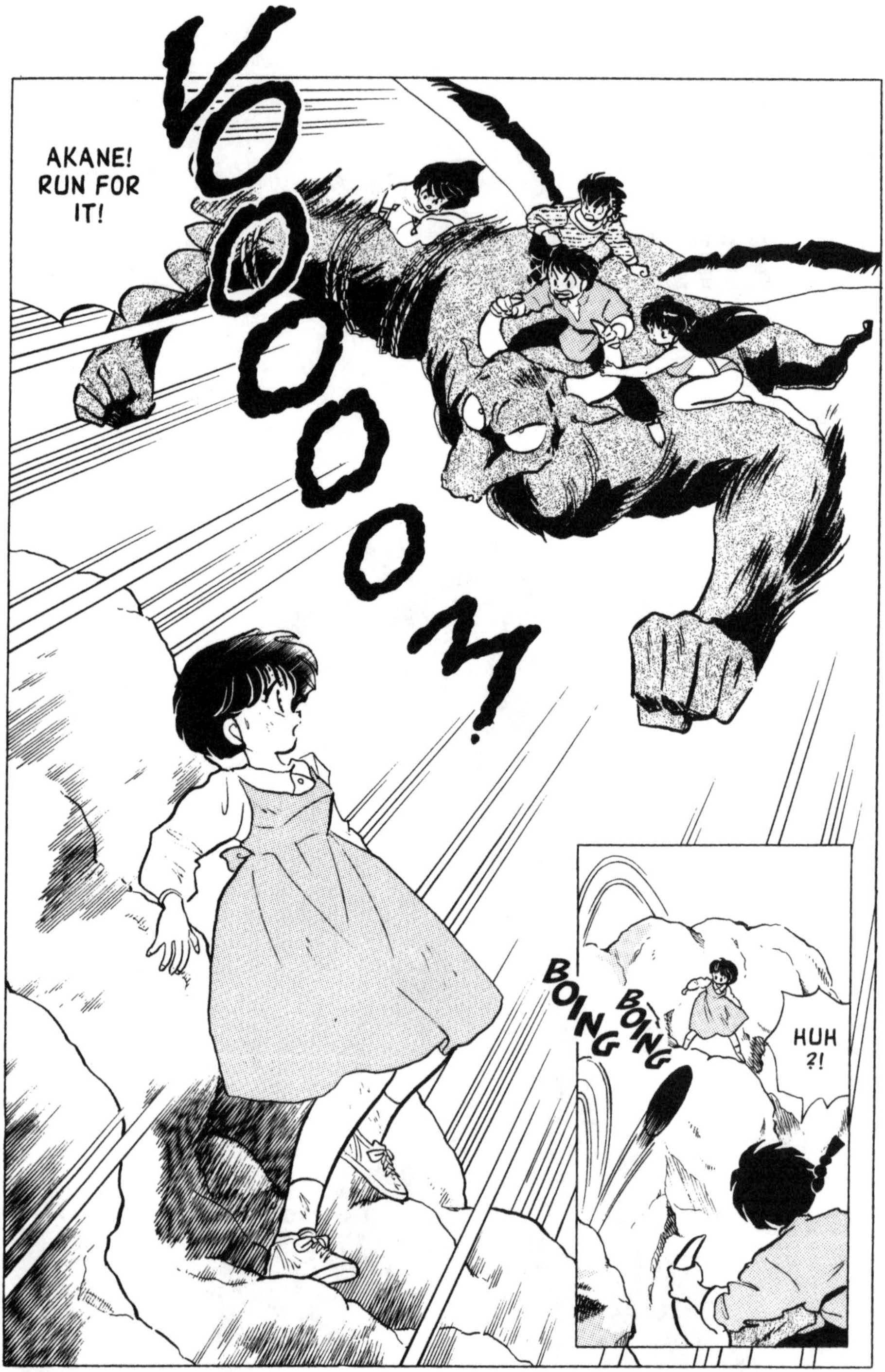
AKANE! RUN FOR IT!
VOOOOOM!
BOING
BOING
HUH ?!

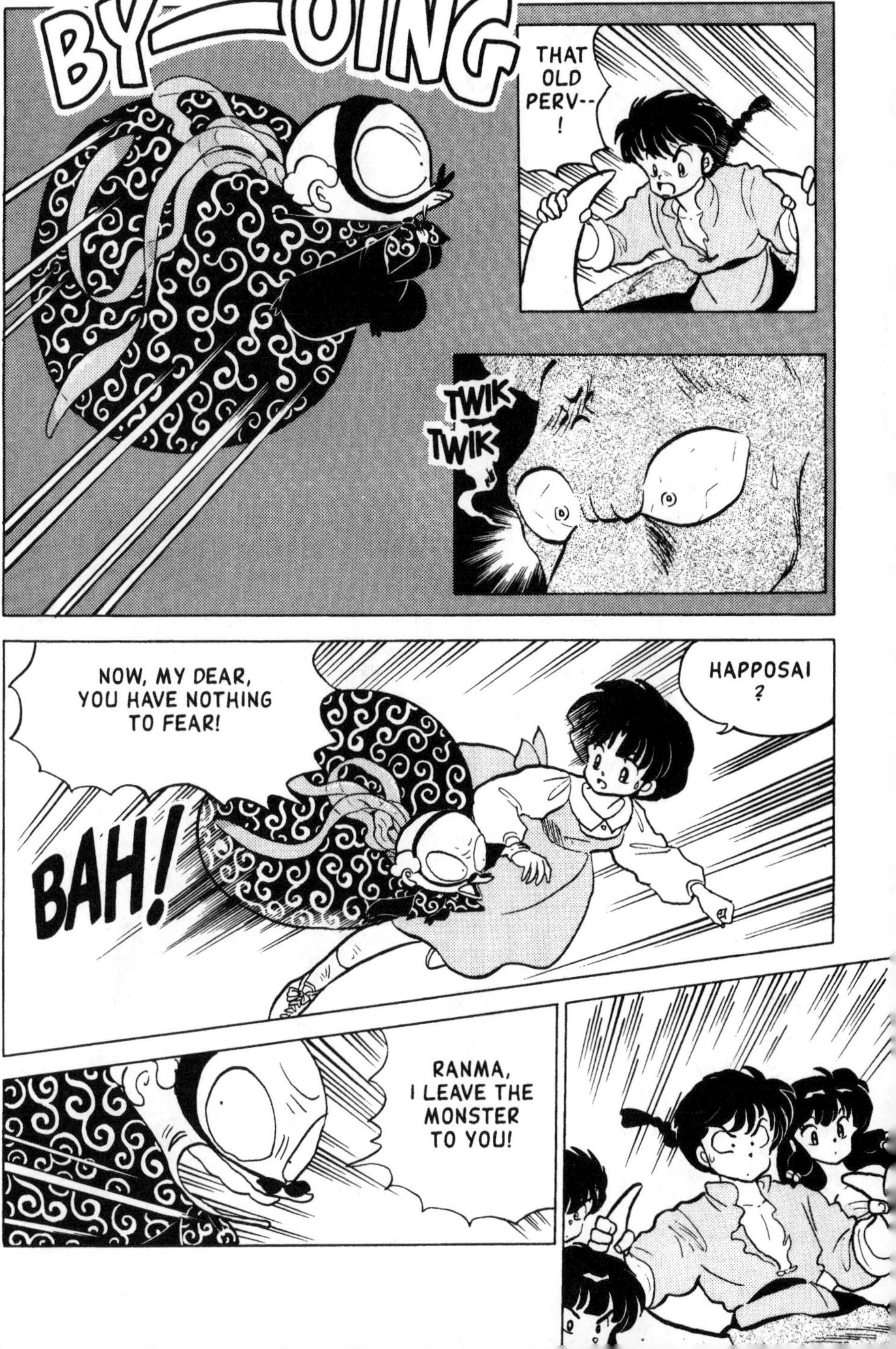
BY—OING
THAT OLD PERV-- !
TWIK TWIK
NOW, MY DEAR, YOU HAVE NOTHING TO FEAR!
HAPPOSAI ?
BAH!
RANMA, I LEAVE THE MONSTER TO YOU!

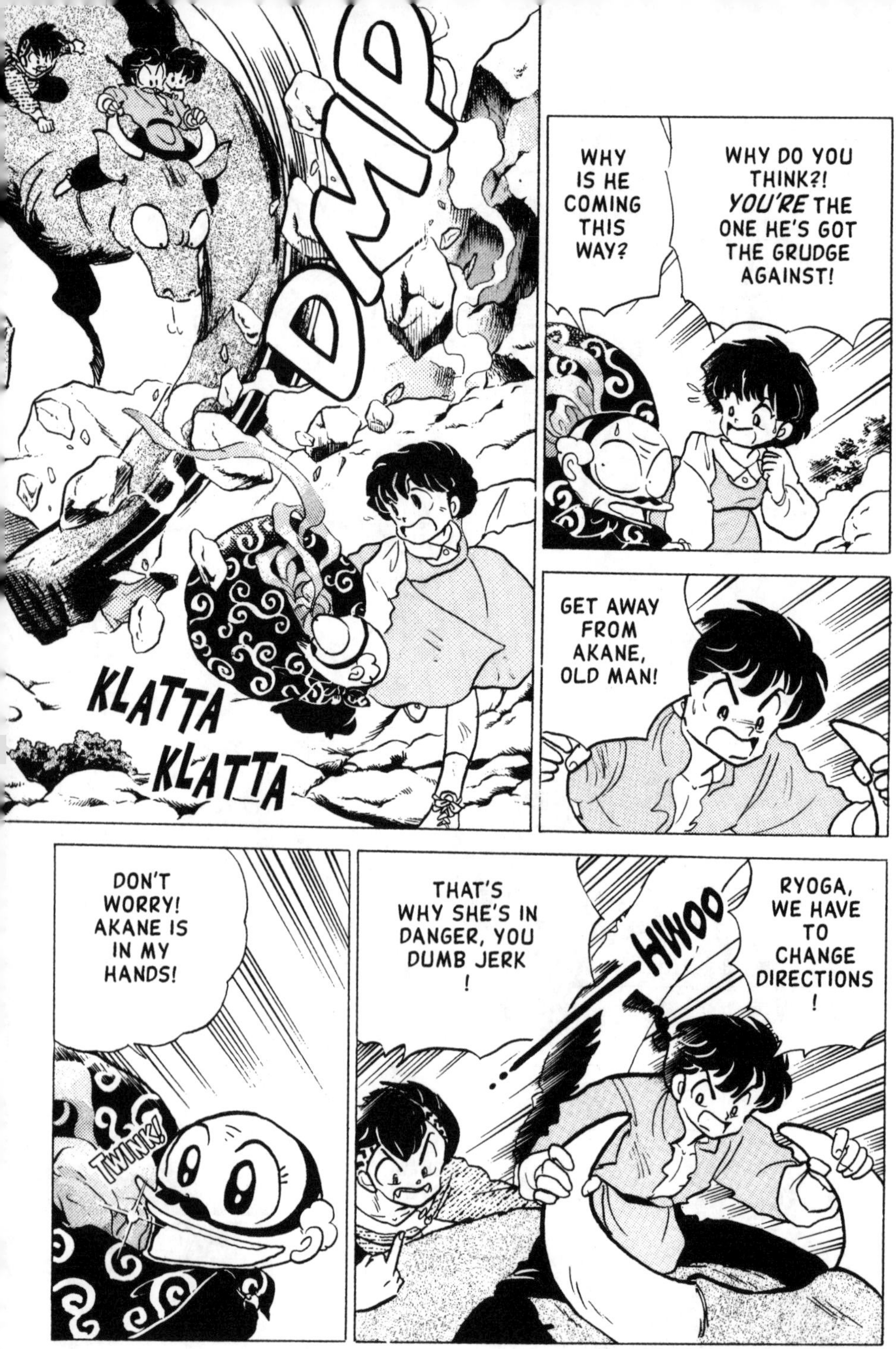
DOMP
KLATTA KLATTA
WHY IS HE COMING THIS WAY?
WHY DO YOU THINK?! *YOU'RE* THE ONE HE'S GOT THE GRUDGE AGAINST!
GET AWAY FROM AKANE, OLD MAN!
DON'T WORRY! AKANE IS IN MY HANDS!
TWINK!
THAT'S WHY SHE'S IN DANGER, YOU DUMB JERK!
HWOO
RYOGA, WE HAVE TO CHANGE DIRECTIONS!

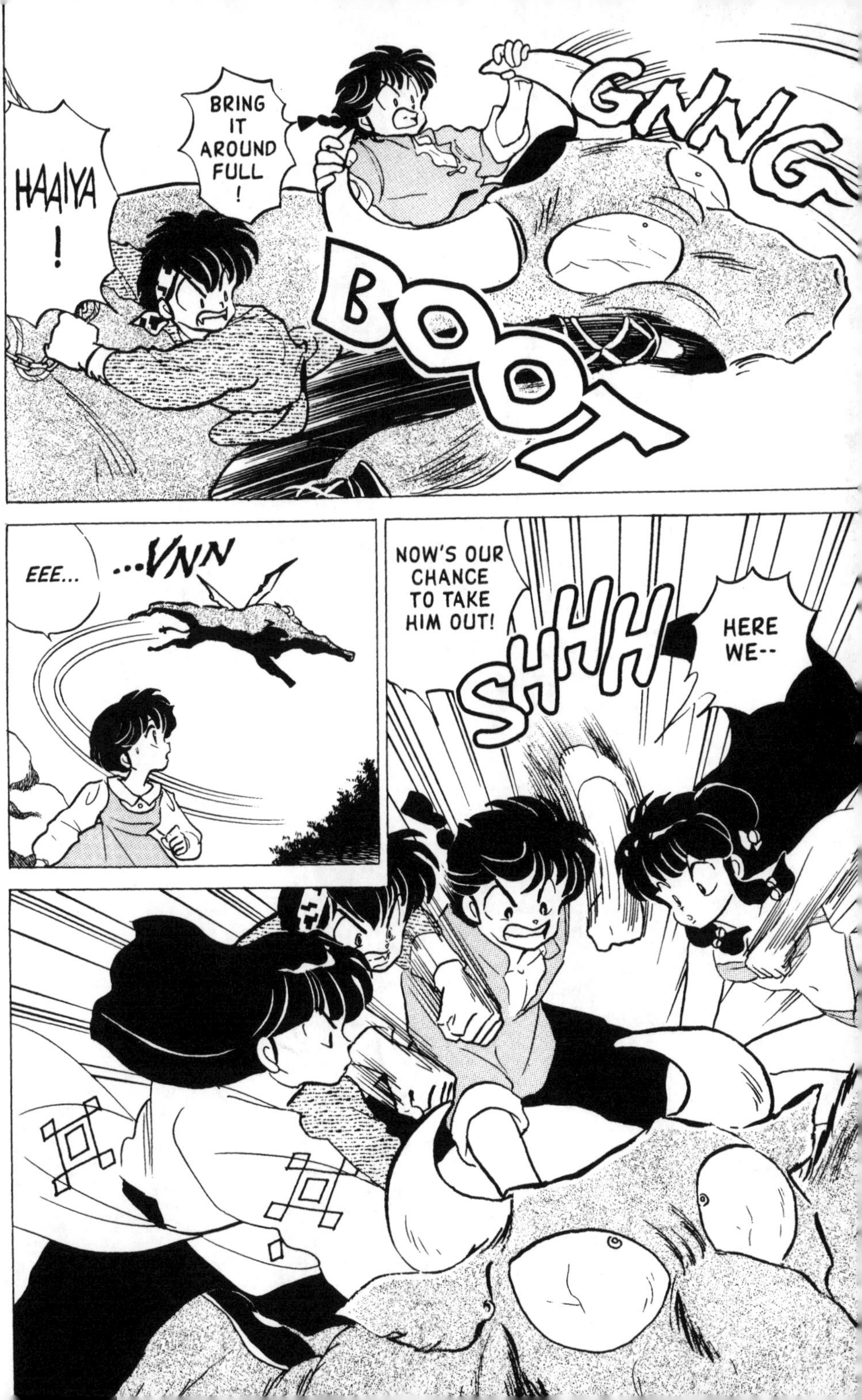
HAAIYA !
BRING IT AROUND FULL !
GNNG
BOOOT
EEE...
...VNN
NOW'S OUR CHANCE TO TAKE HIM OUT!
SHHH
HERE WE--

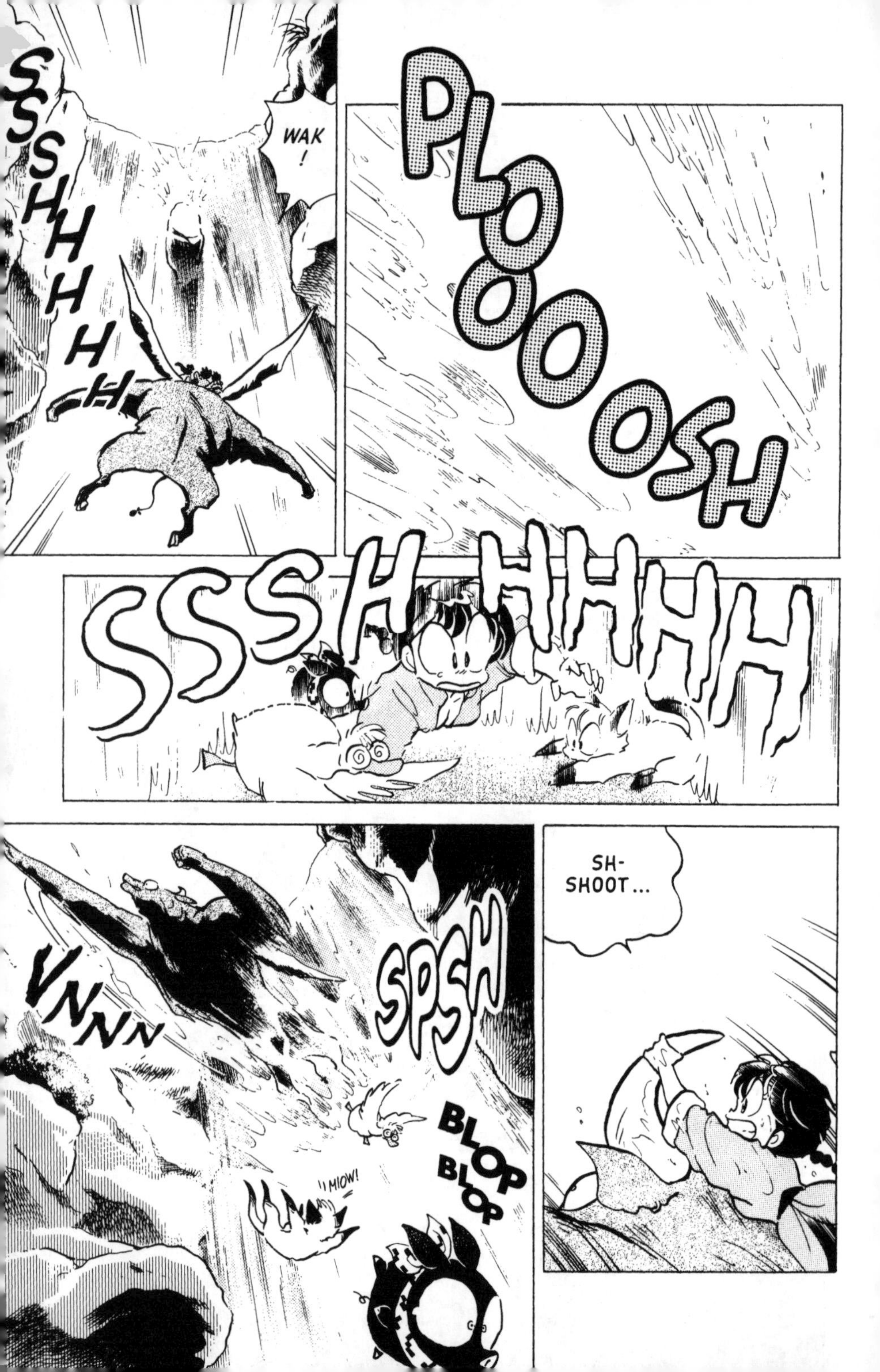
SSSHHHHHH
WAK!
PLOOOOOSH
SSSHHHHHH
VNNNN
SPSH
MIOW!
BLOP
BLOP
SH-
SHOOT...

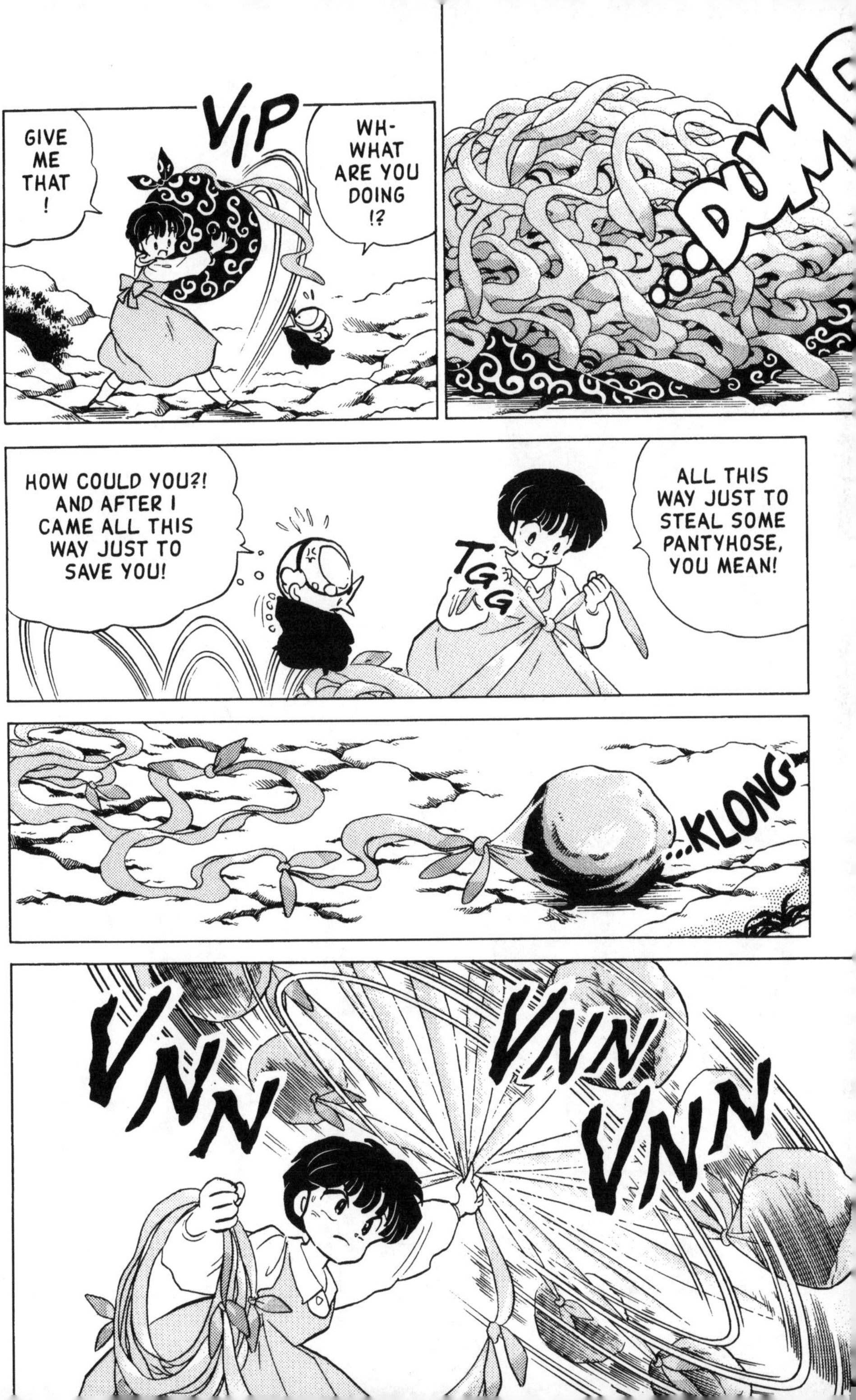
GIVE ME THAT!
VIP
WH- WHAT ARE YOU DOING!?
...DUMP
HOW COULD YOU?! AND AFTER I CAME ALL THIS WAY JUST TO SAVE YOU!
TGG
ALL THIS WAY JUST TO STEAL SOME PANTYHOSE, YOU MEAN!
...KLONG
VNN
VNN
VNN

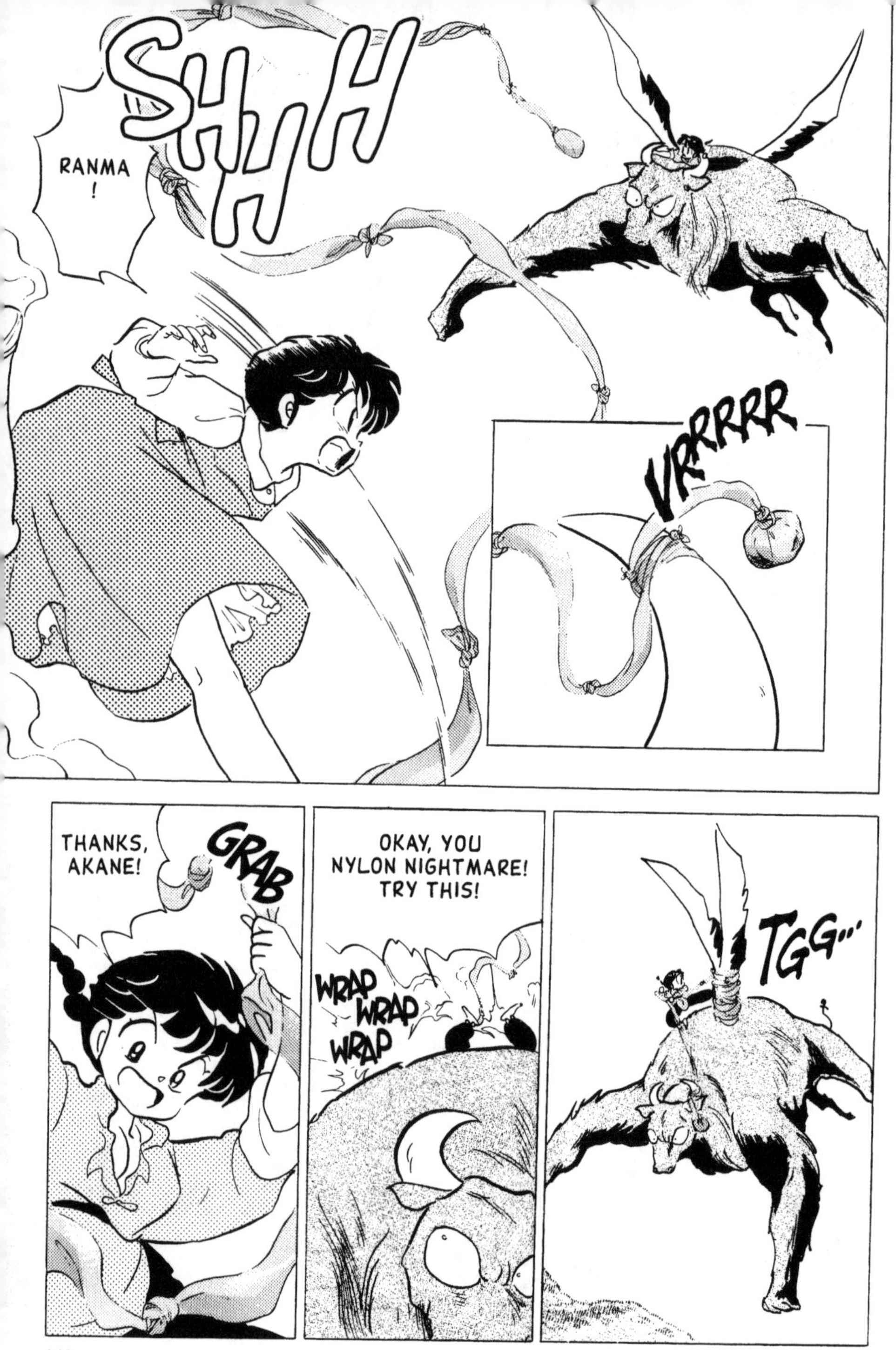
SHHH
RANMA!
VRRRRR
THANKS, AKANE!
GRAB
OKAY, YOU NYLON NIGHTMARE! TRY THIS!
WRAP WRAP WRAP
TGG...

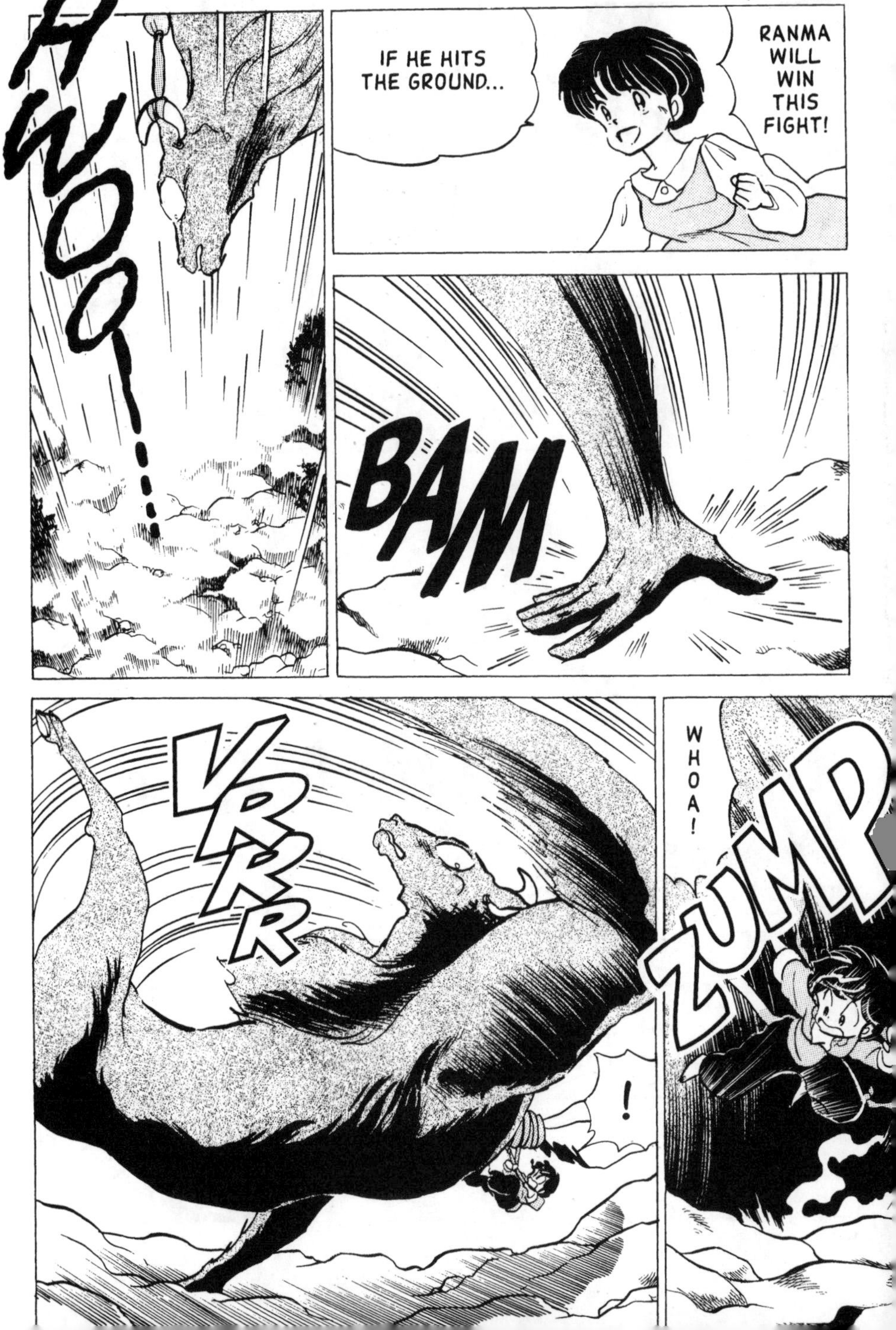
HWOOO...
IF HE HITS THE GROUND...
RANMA WILL WIN THIS FIGHT!
BAM
VRRR
WHOA!
ZUMP
!

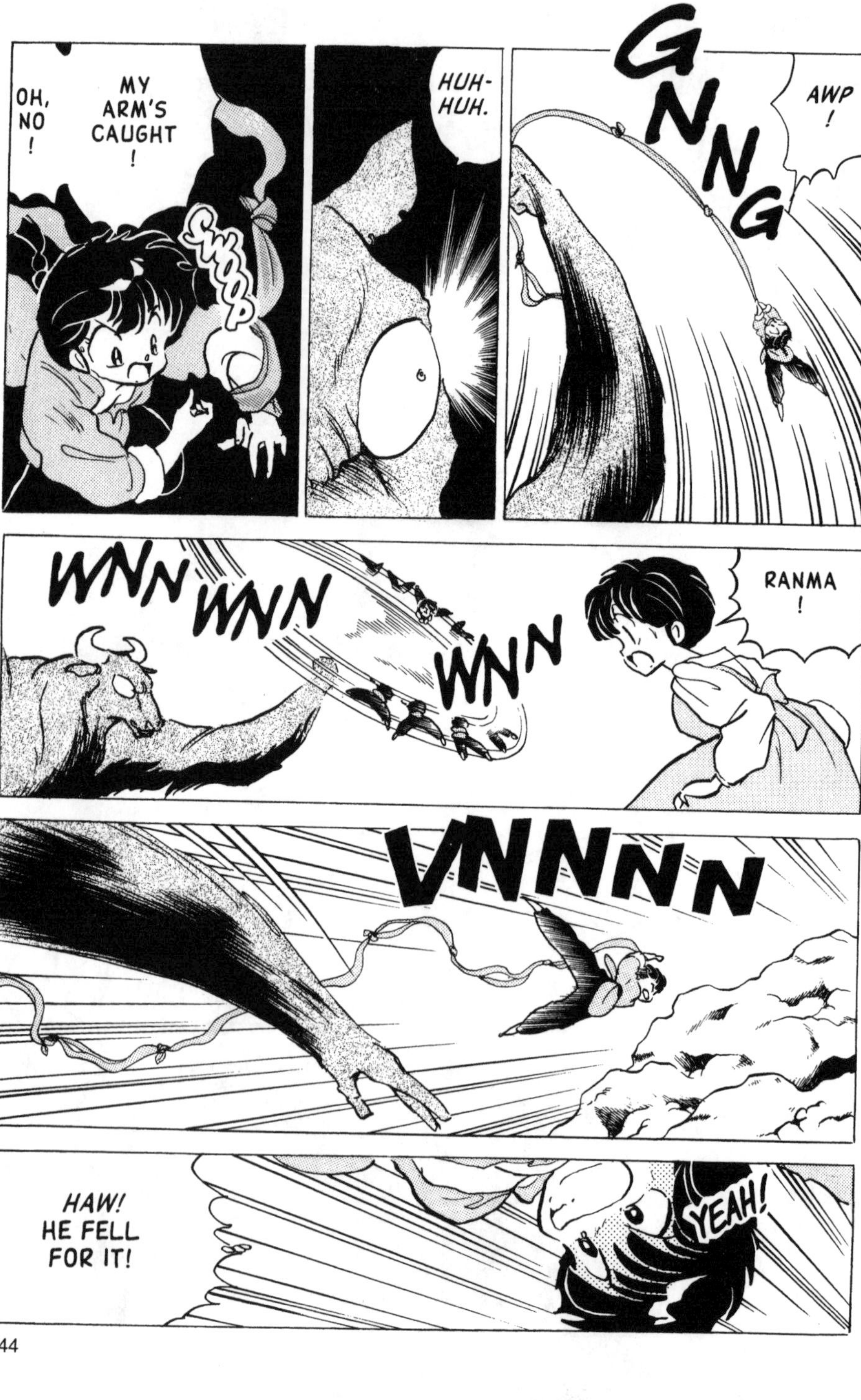
OH, NO!
MY ARM'S CAUGHT!
SWOOP
HUH-HUH.
GNNG
AWP!
WNN WNN
WNN
RANMA!
VNNNN
HAW! HE FELL FOR IT!
YEAH!

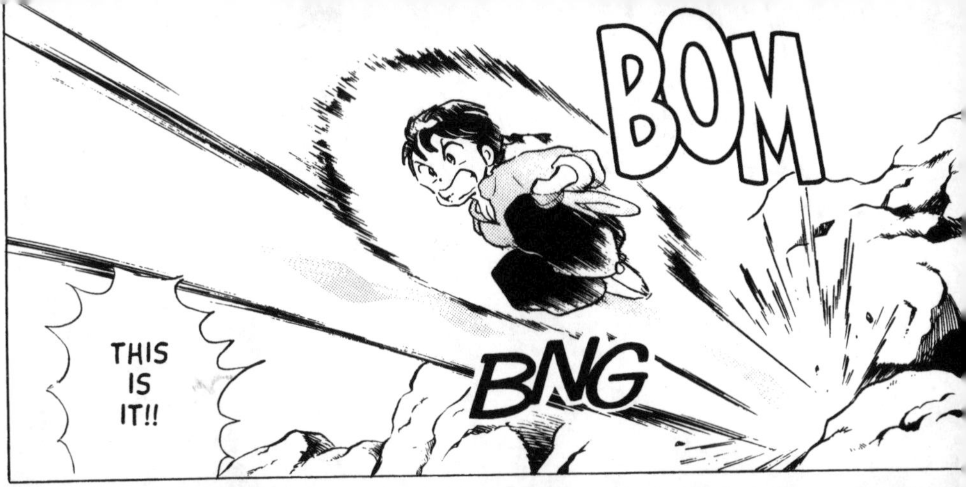
BOM
THIS IS IT!!
BNG

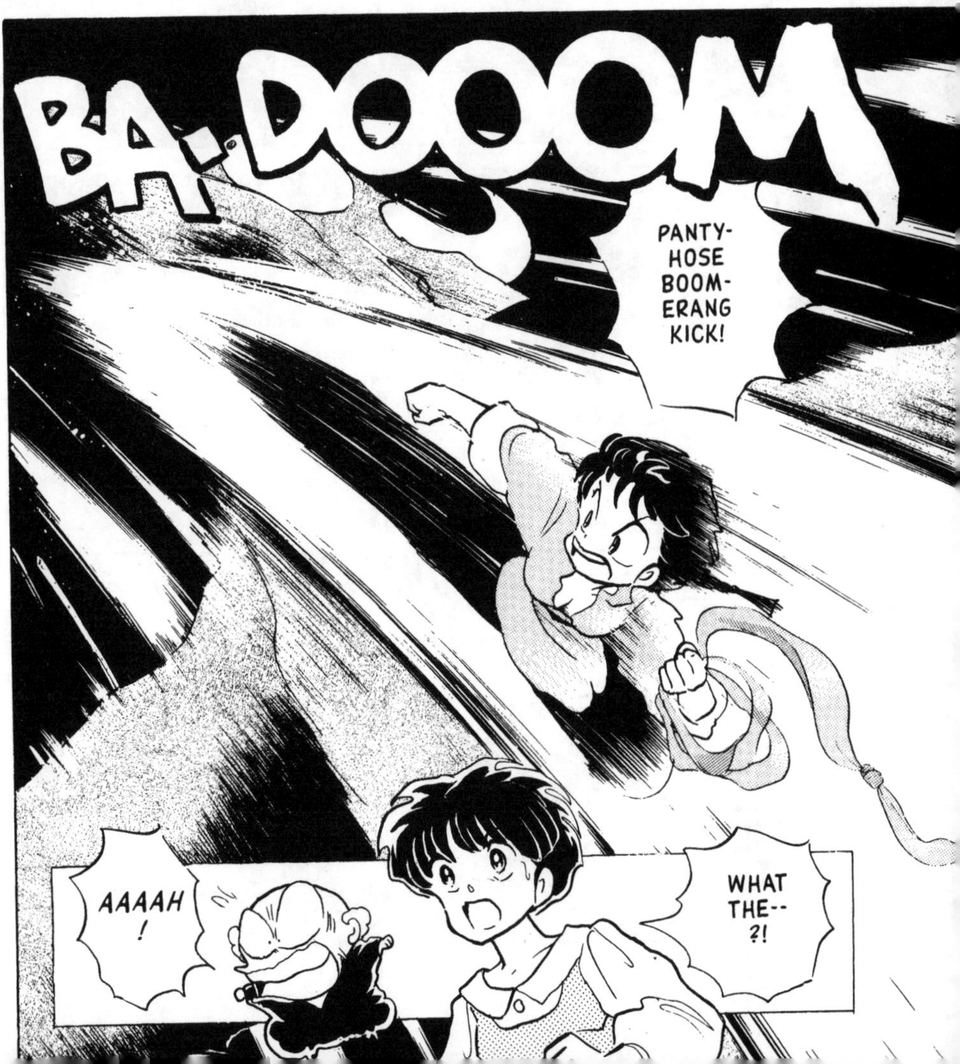
BA-DOOOM
PANTY-HOSE BOOM-ERANG KICK!
AAAAH!
WHAT THE--?!

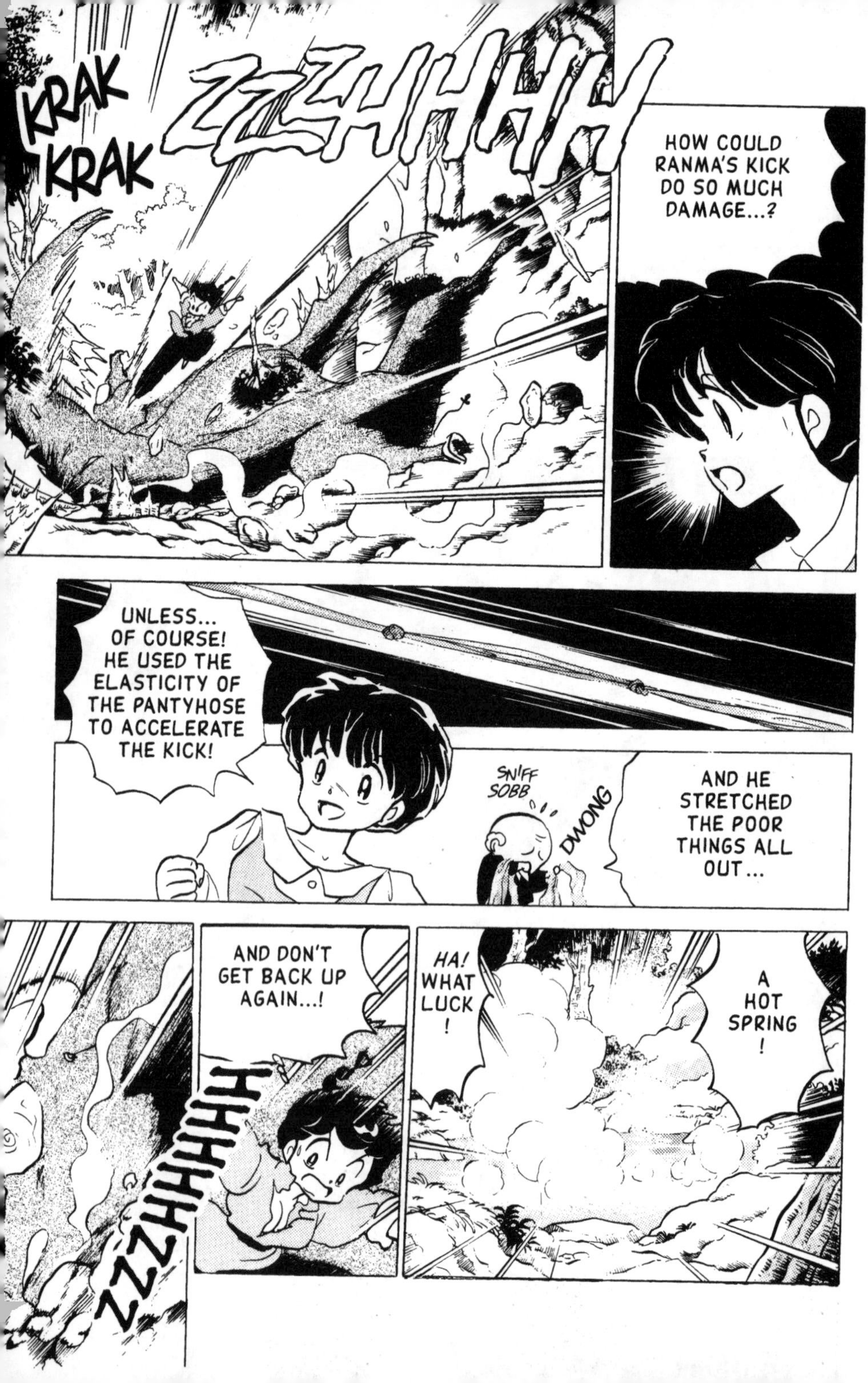
KRAK
KRAK
ZZZHHHHH
HOW COULD RANMA'S KICK DO SO MUCH DAMAGE...?
UNLESS... OF COURSE! HE USED THE ELASTICITY OF THE PANTYHOSE TO ACCELERATE THE KICK!
SNIFF SOBB
DWONG
AND HE STRETCHED THE POOR THINGS ALL OUT...
AND DON'T GET BACK UP AGAIN...!
ZZZHHHHHH
HA! WHAT LUCK!
A HOT SPRING!

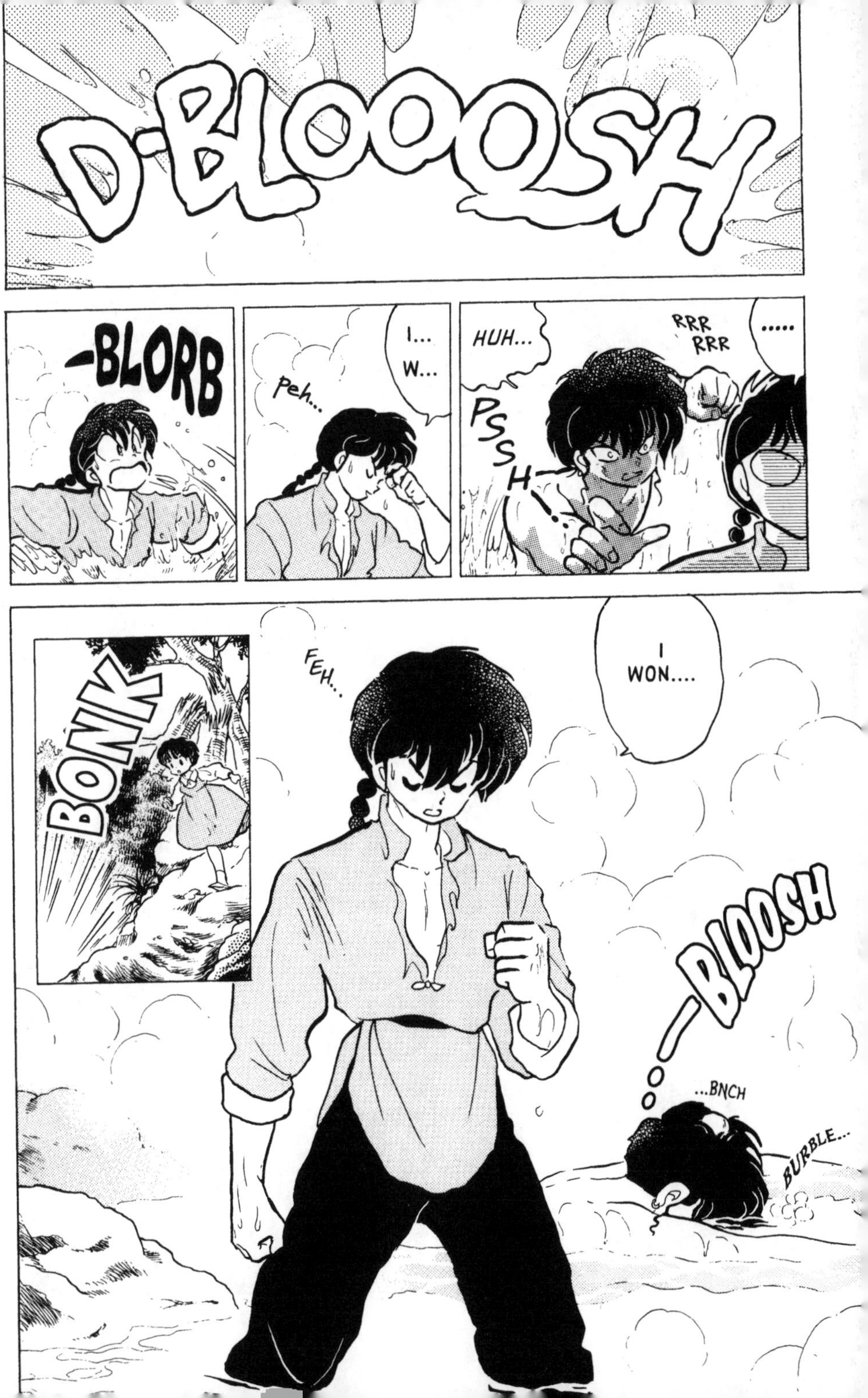
D-BLOOOSH
-BLORB
Peh...
I... W...
HUH...
PSSH
RRR RRR
.....
BONK
FEH...
I WON....
-BLOOSH
...BNCH
BURBLE...

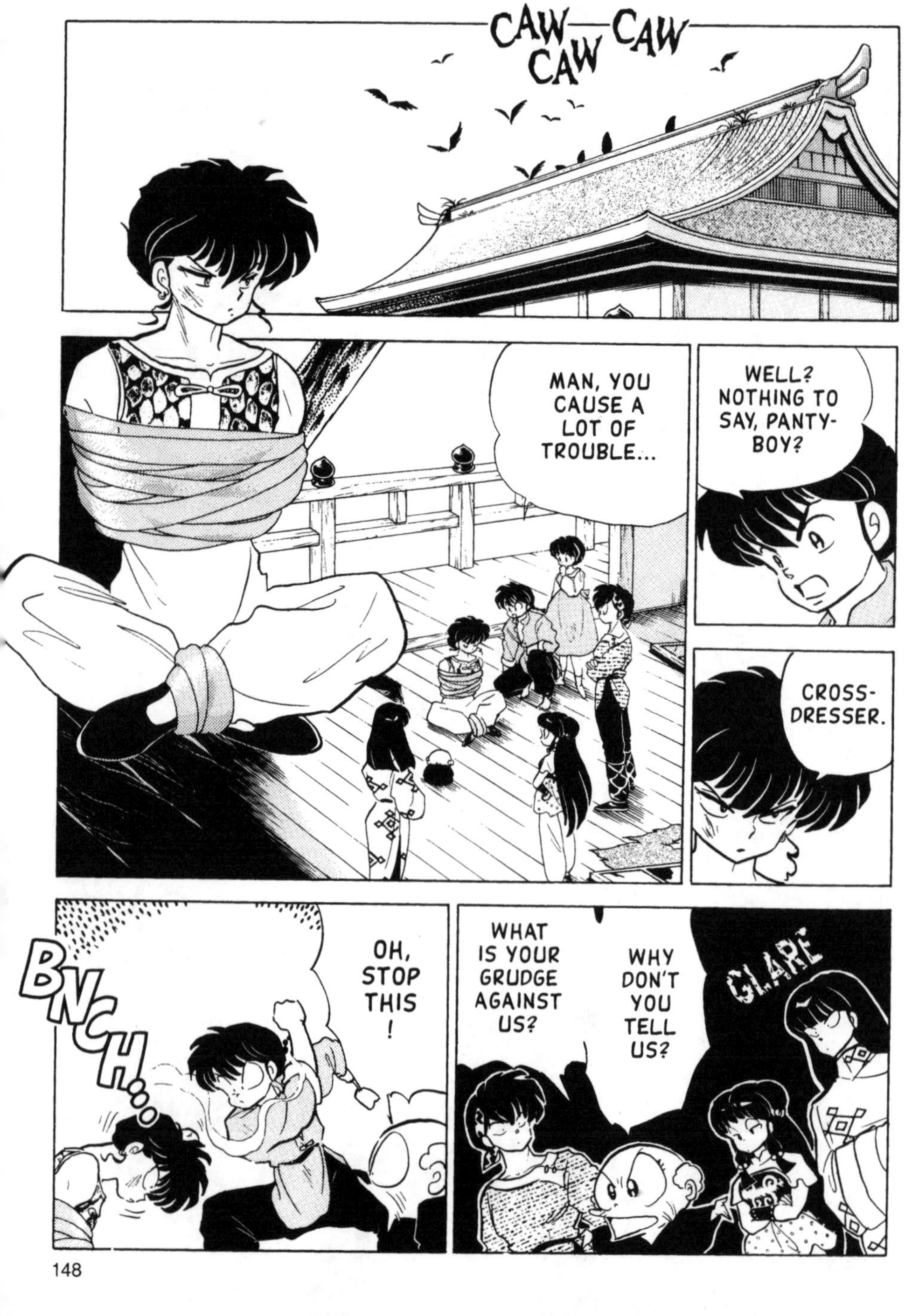
CAW CAW CAW
MAN, YOU CAUSE A LOT OF TROUBLE...
WELL? NOTHING TO SAY, PANTY-BOY?
CROSS-DRESSER.
BNCH...
OH, STOP THIS!
WHAT IS YOUR GRUDGE AGAINST US?
WHY DON'T YOU TELL US?
GLARE

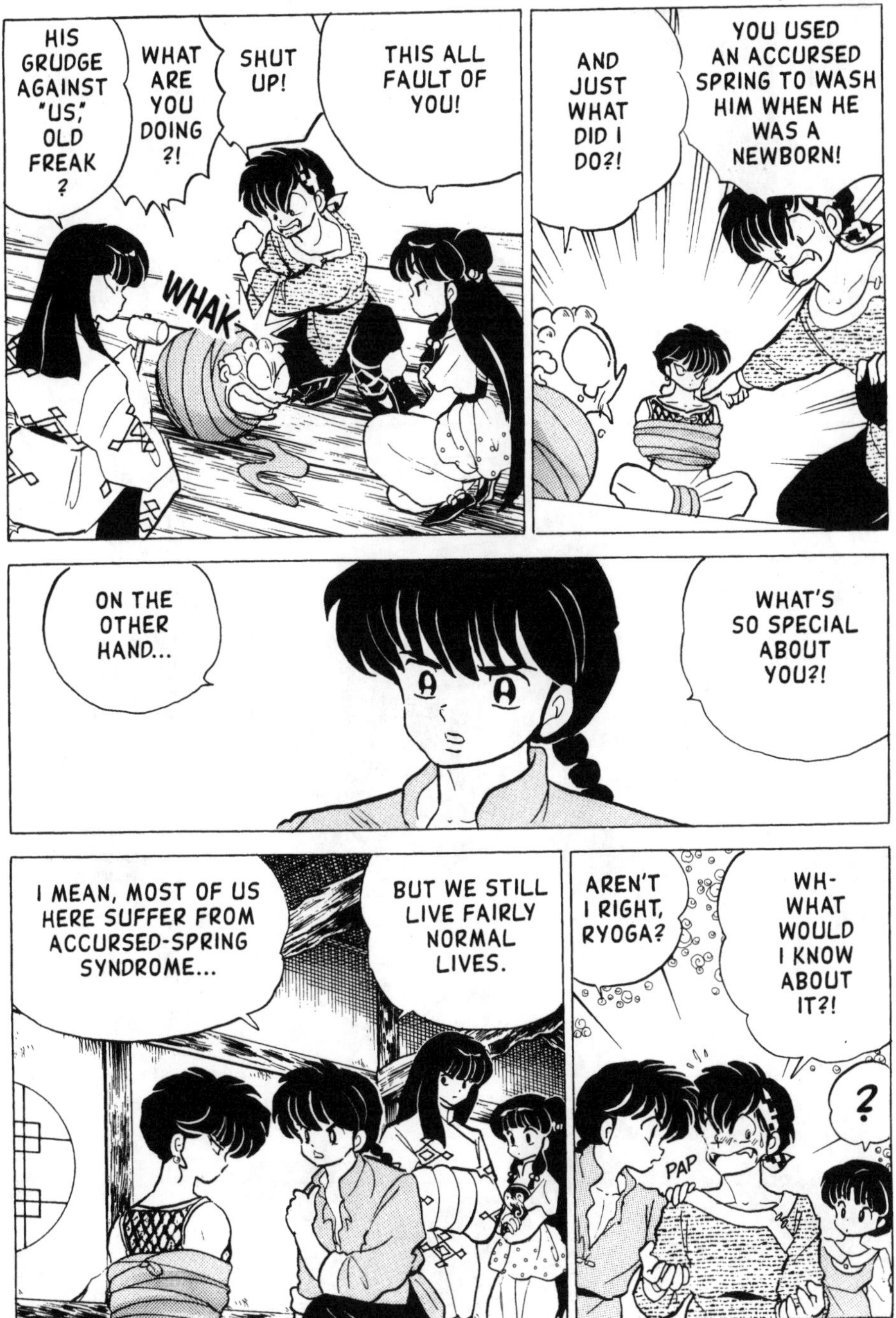
HIS GRUDGE AGAINST "US," OLD FREAK?
WHAT ARE YOU DOING?!
SHUT UP!
THIS ALL FAULT OF YOU!
WHAK
AND JUST WHAT DID I DO?!
YOU USED AN ACCURSED SPRING TO WASH HIM WHEN HE WAS A NEWBORN!
ON THE OTHER HAND...
WHAT'S SO SPECIAL ABOUT YOU?!
I MEAN, MOST OF US HERE SUFFER FROM ACCURSED-SPRING SYNDROME...
BUT WE STILL LIVE FAIRLY NORMAL LIVES.
AREN'T I RIGHT, RYOGA?
WH- WHAT WOULD I KNOW ABOUT IT?!
PAP
?

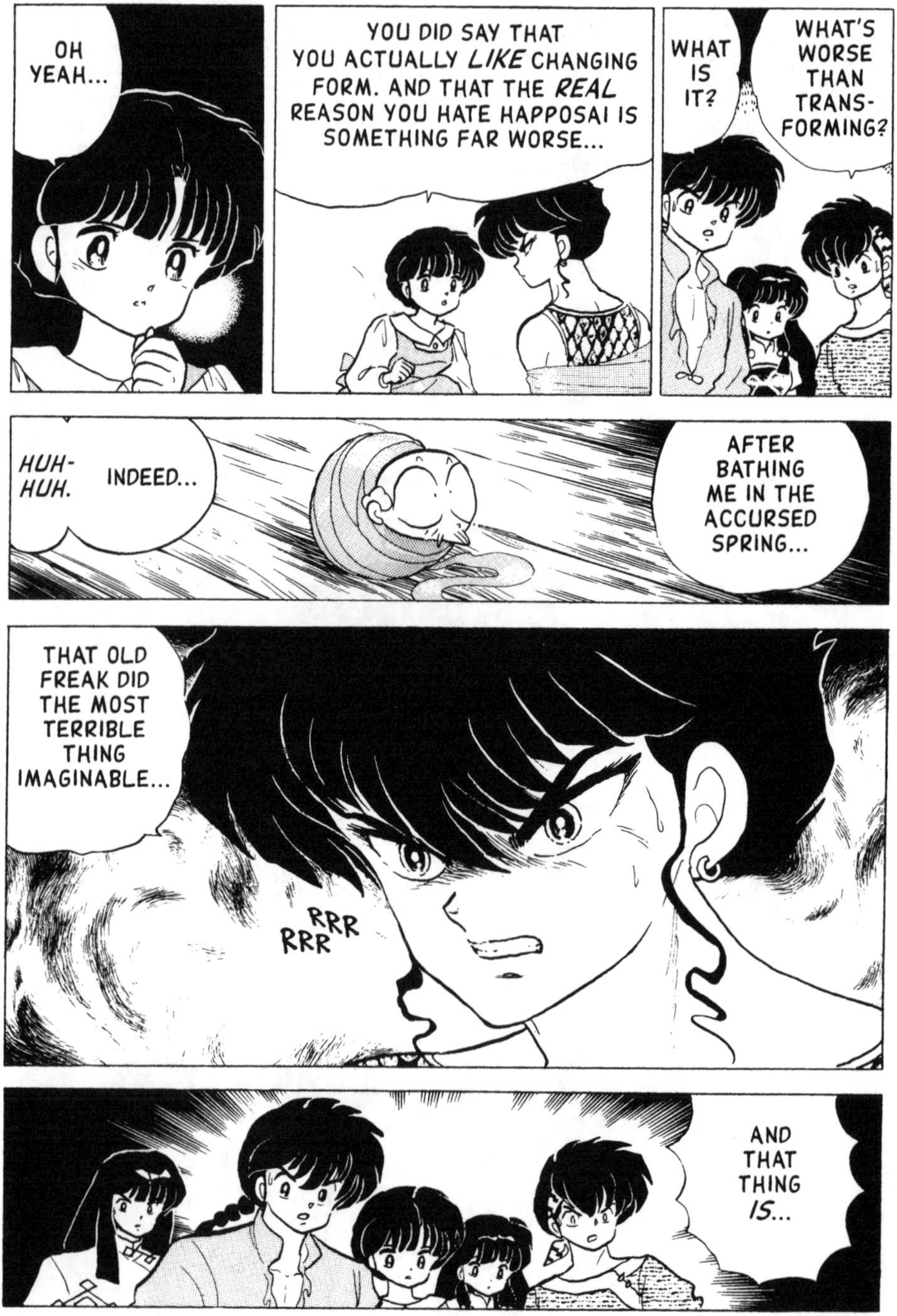
OH YEAH...
YOU DID SAY THAT YOU ACTUALLY *LIKE* CHANGING FORM. AND THAT THE *REAL* REASON YOU HATE HAPPOSAI IS SOMETHING FAR WORSE...
WHAT IS IT?
WHAT'S WORSE THAN TRANS-FORMING?
HUH-HUH.
INDEED...
AFTER BATHING ME IN THE ACCURSED SPRING...
THAT OLD FREAK DID THE MOST TERRIBLE THING IMAGINABLE...
RRR RRR
AND THAT THING *IS*...

Part 10
WHAT'S IN A NAME?

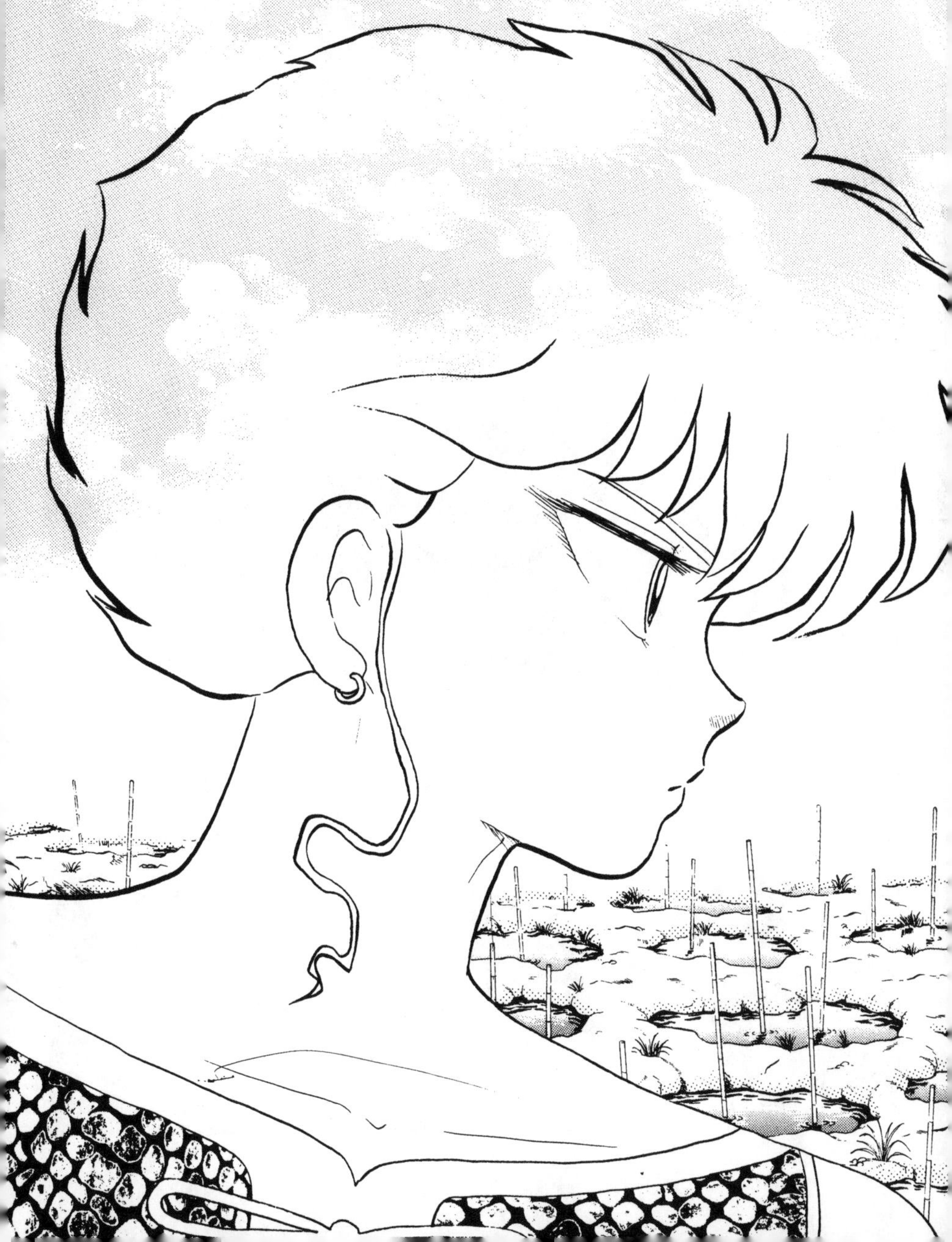

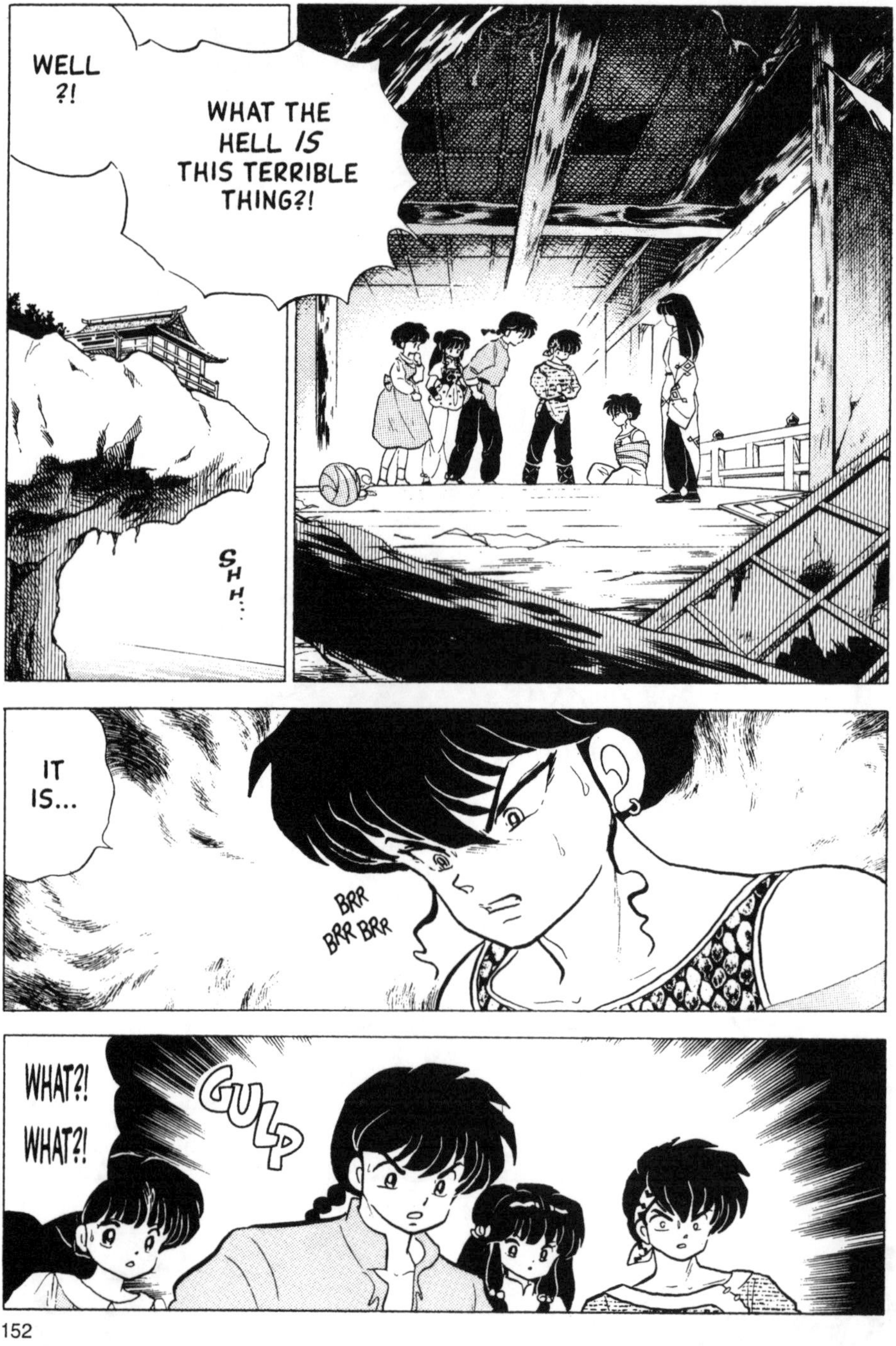
WELL ?!
WHAT THE HELL IS THIS TERRIBLE THING?!
SHH...
IT IS...
BRR BRR BRR
WHAT?! WHAT?!
GULP

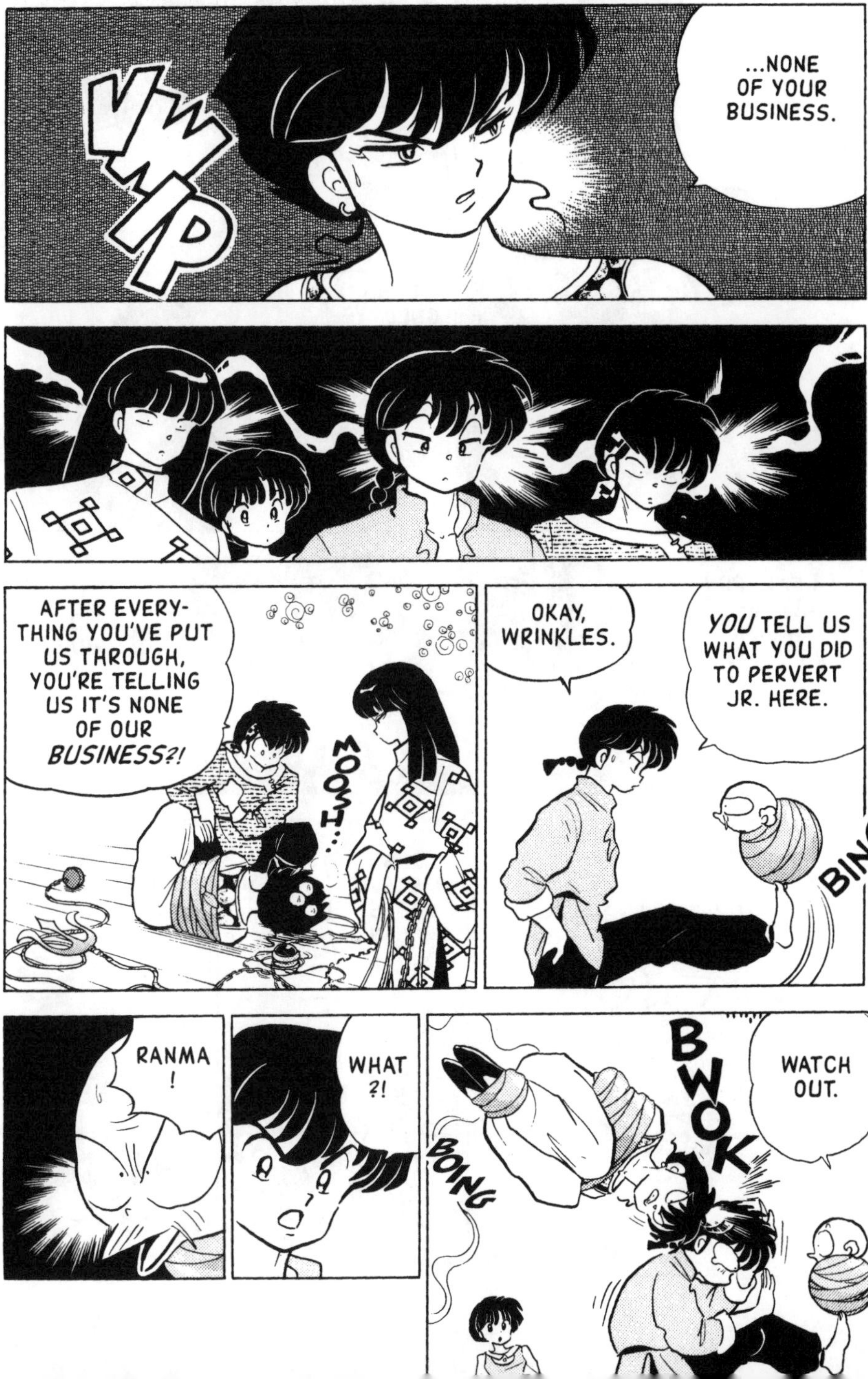
VWIP
...NONE OF YOUR BUSINESS.
AFTER EVERY-THING YOU'VE PUT US THROUGH, YOU'RE TELLING US IT'S NONE OF OUR *BUSINESS?!*
WOOSH...
OKAY, WRINKLES.
YOU TELL US WHAT YOU DID TO PERVERT JR. HERE.
BING
RANMA!
WHAT?!
BOING
BWOK
WATCH OUT.

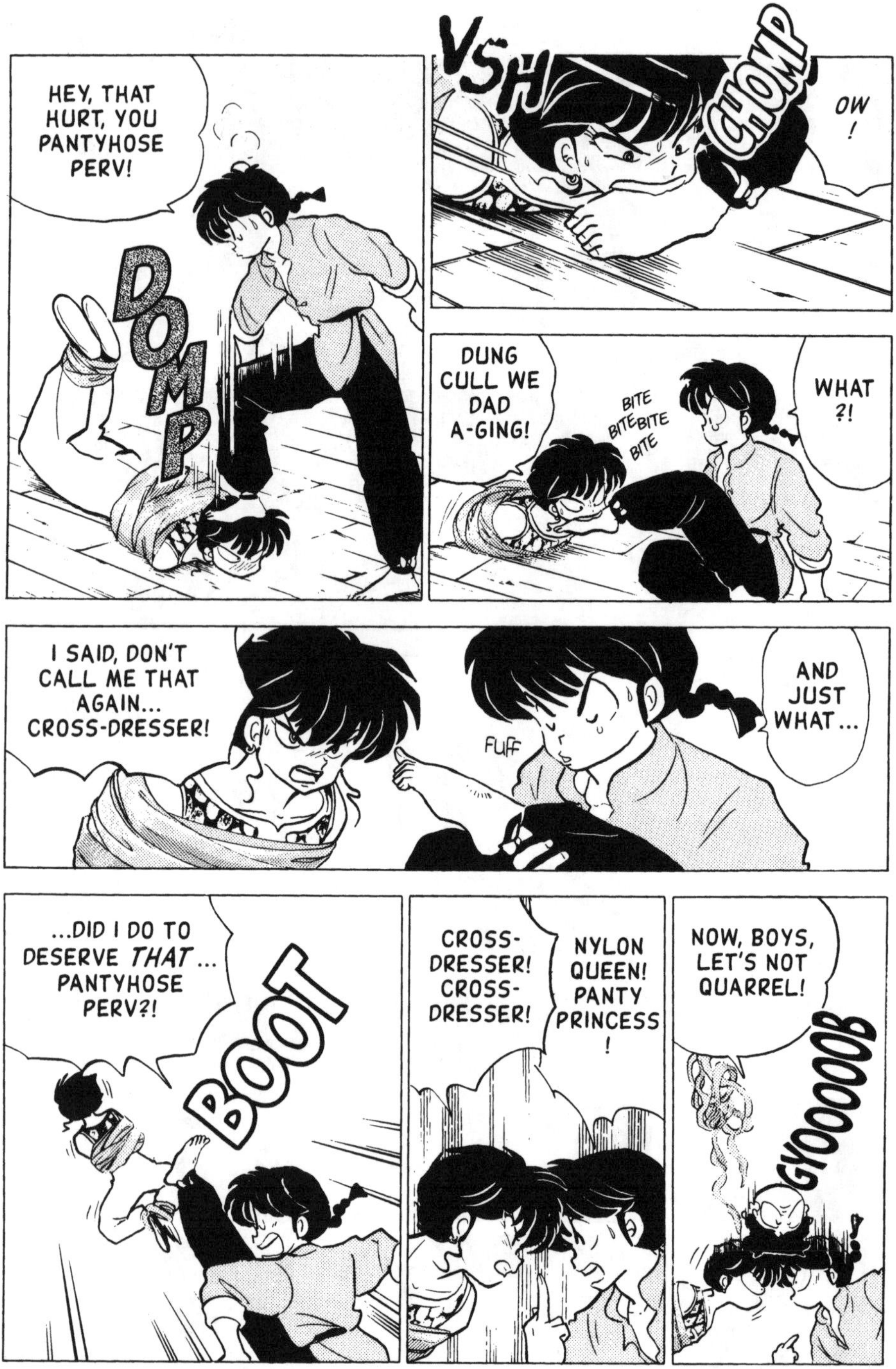
HEY, THAT HURT, YOU PANTYHOSE PERV!
DOMP
VSH
CHOMP
OW!
DUNG CULL WE DAD A-GING!
BITE BITE BITE BITE
WHAT?!
I SAID, DON'T CALL ME THAT AGAIN... CROSS-DRESSER!
FUFF
AND JUST WHAT...
...DID I DO TO DESERVE *THAT*... PANTYHOSE PERV?!
BOOT
CROSS-DRESSER! CROSS-DRESSER!
NYLON QUEEN! PANTY PRINCESS!
NOW, BOYS, LET'S NOT QUARREL!
GYOOOOOB

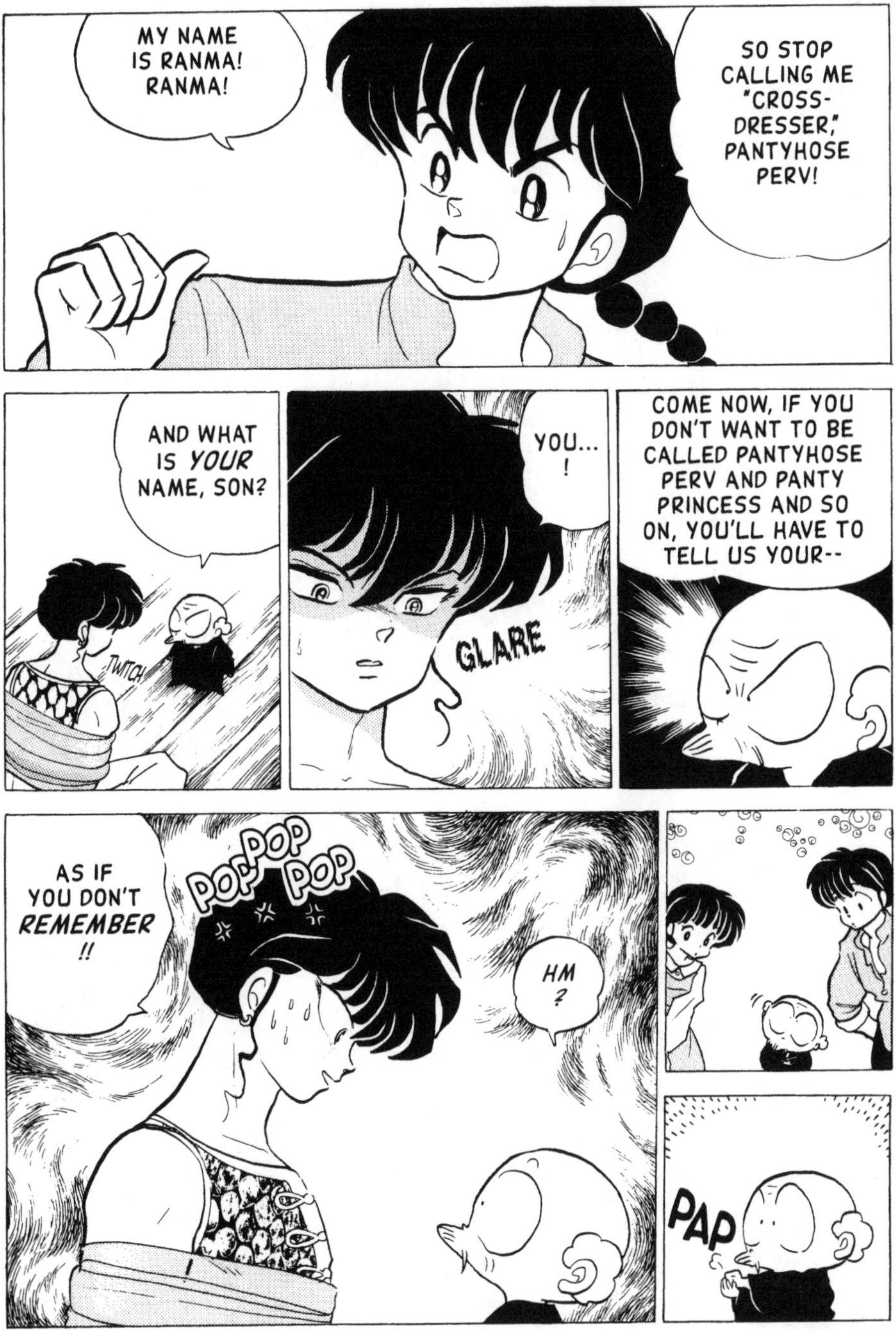
MY NAME IS RANMA! RANMA!
SO STOP CALLING ME "CROSS-DRESSER," PANTYHOSE PERV!
AND WHAT IS *YOUR* NAME, SON?
TWITCH
YOU... !
GLARE
COME NOW, IF YOU DON'T WANT TO BE CALLED PANTYHOSE PERV AND PANTY PRINCESS AND SO ON, YOU'LL HAVE TO TELL US YOUR--
AS IF YOU DON'T *REMEMBER* !!
POP POP POP
HM ?
PAP

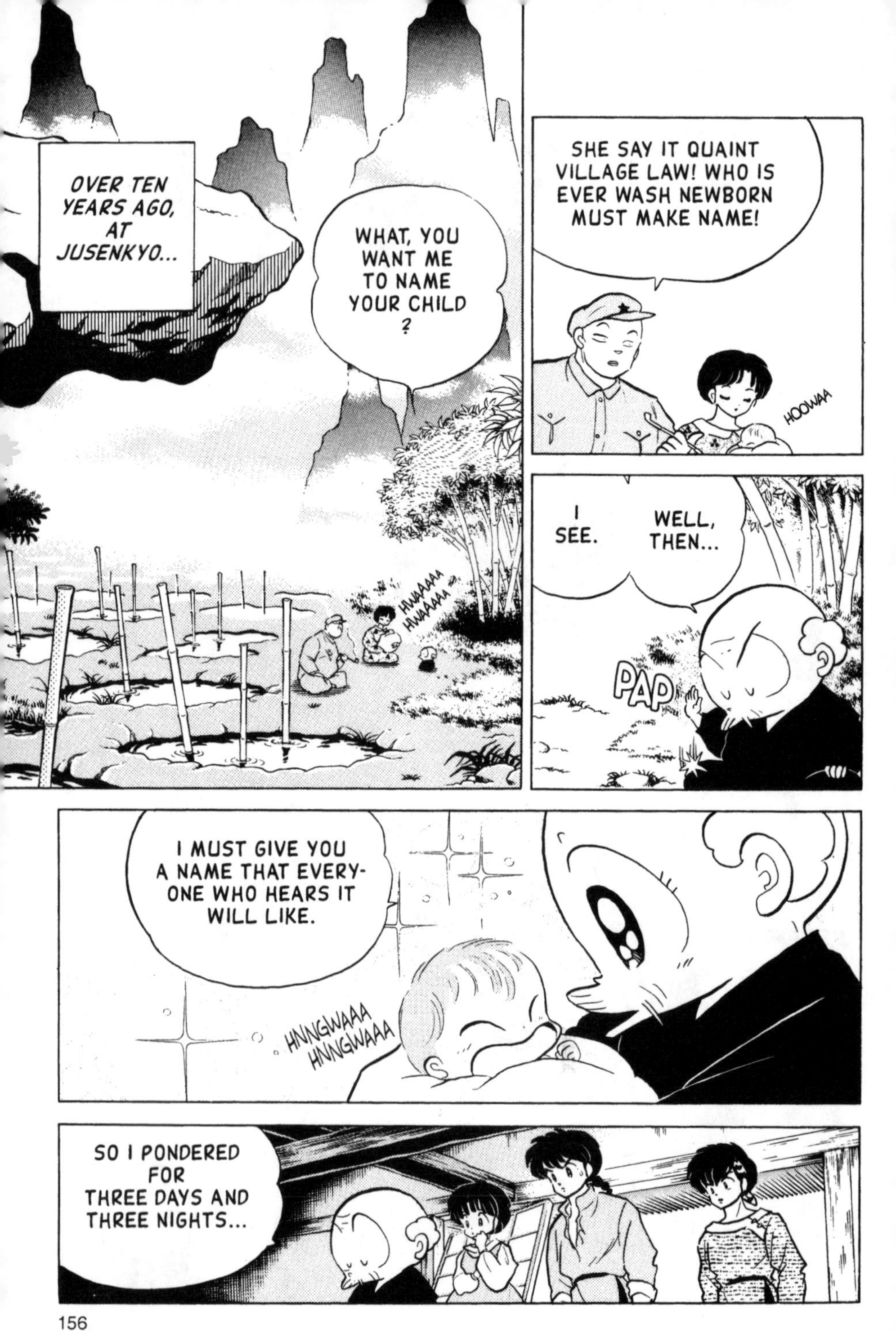

OVER TEN YEARS AGO, AT JUSENKYO...
WHAT, YOU WANT ME TO NAME YOUR CHILD?
HWAAAAA HWAAAAA
SHE SAY IT QUAINT VILLAGE LAW! WHO IS EVER WASH NEWBORN MUST MAKE NAME!
HOOWAA
I SEE.
WELL, THEN...
PAP
I MUST GIVE YOU A NAME THAT EVERY-ONE WHO HEARS IT WILL LIKE.
HNNGWAAA HNNGWAAA
SO I PONDERED FOR THREE DAYS AND THREE NIGHTS...

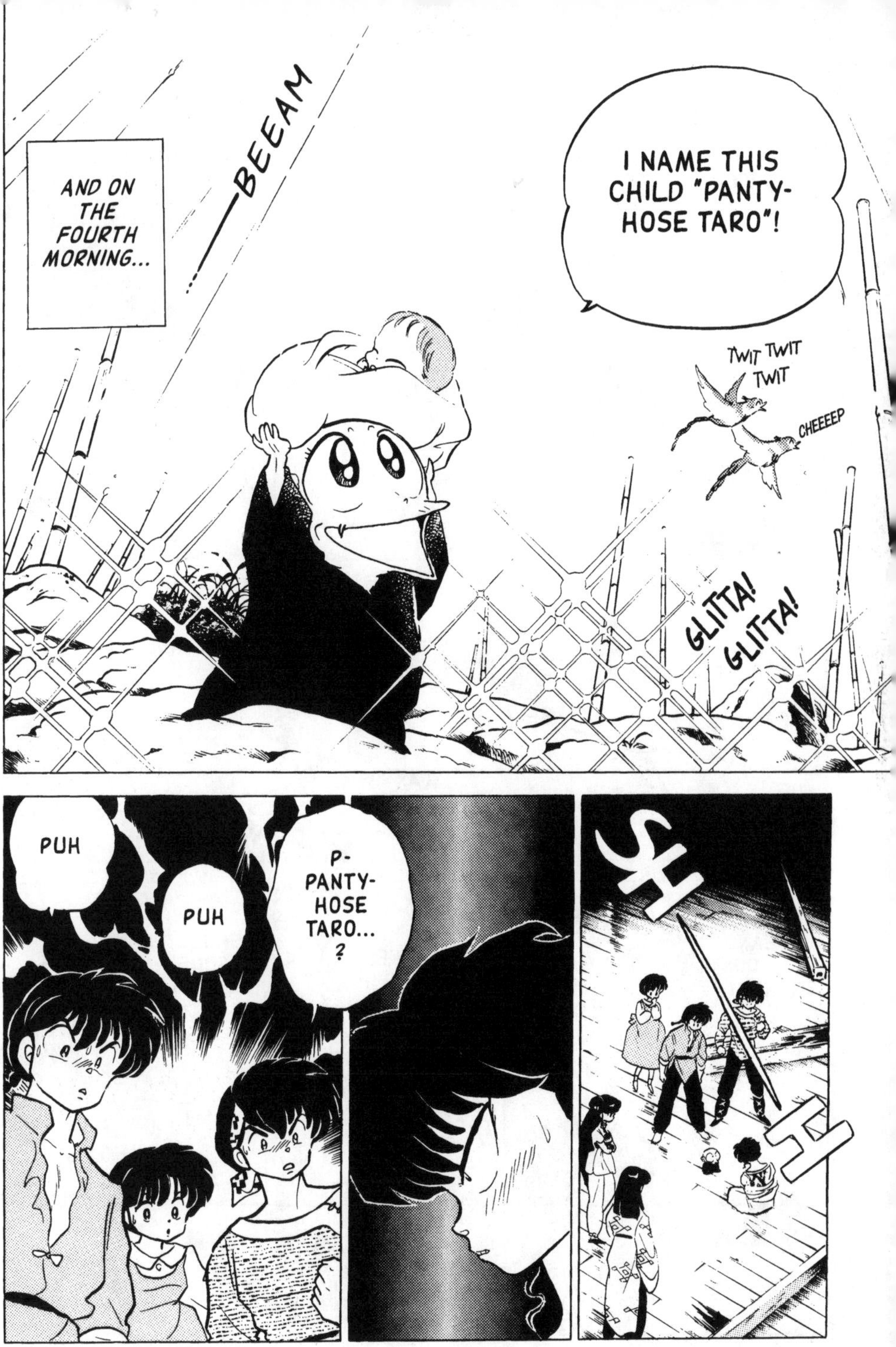
AND ON THE FOURTH MORNING...
BEEAM
I NAME THIS CHILD "PANTY-HOSE TARO"!
TWIT TWIT TWIT
CHEEEEP
GLITTA! GLITTA!
PUH
PUH
P-PANTY-HOSE TARO...?
SH
H

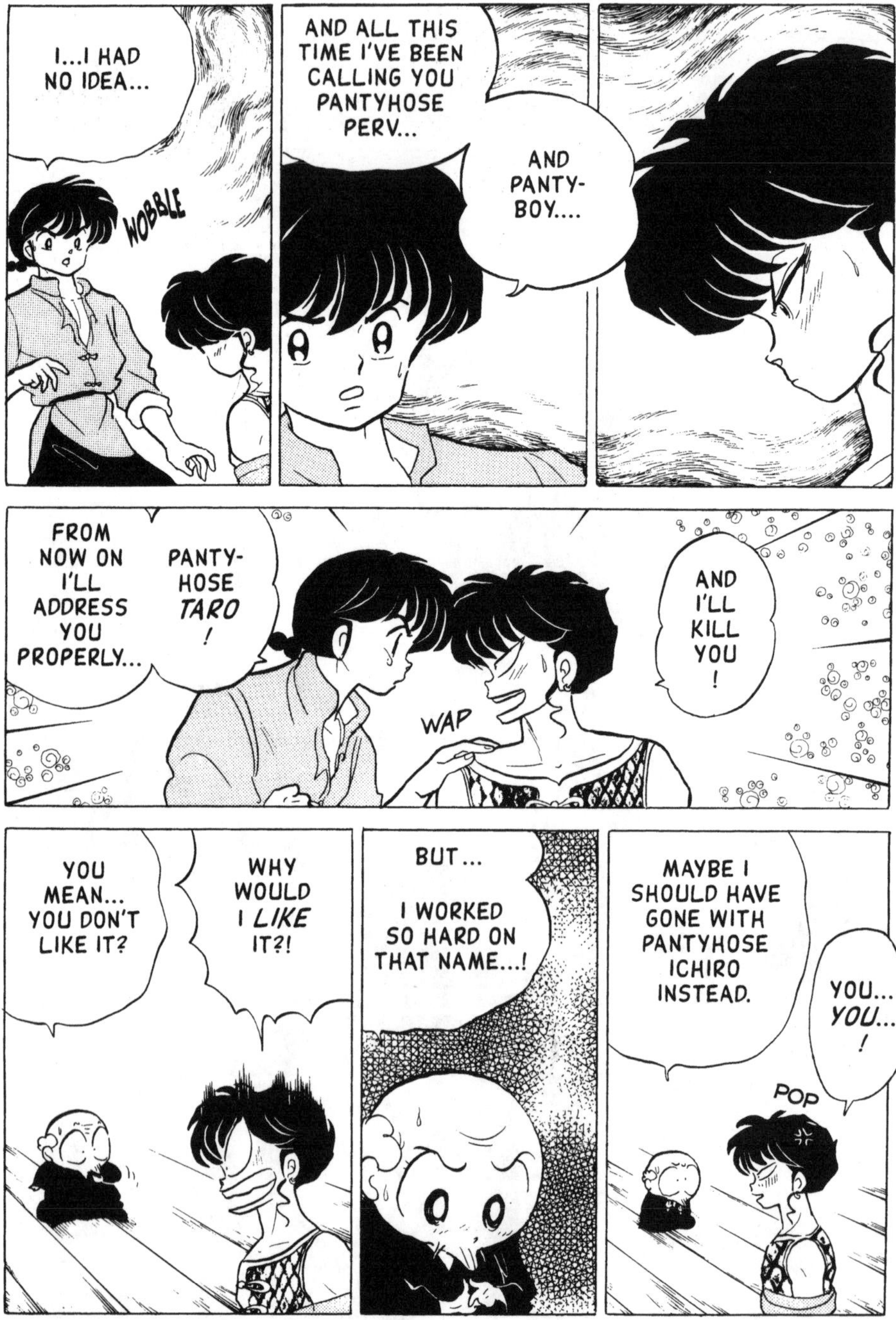
I...I HAD NO IDEA...
WOBBLE
AND ALL THIS TIME I'VE BEEN CALLING YOU PANTYHOSE PERV...
AND PANTY-BOY....
FROM NOW ON I'LL ADDRESS YOU PROPERLY...
PANTY-HOSE *TARO* !
WAP
AND I'LL KILL YOU !
YOU MEAN... YOU DON'T LIKE IT?
WHY WOULD I *LIKE* IT?!
BUT...
I WORKED SO HARD ON THAT NAME...!
MAYBE I SHOULD HAVE GONE WITH PANTYHOSE ICHIRO INSTEAD.
YOU... *YOU*... !
POP

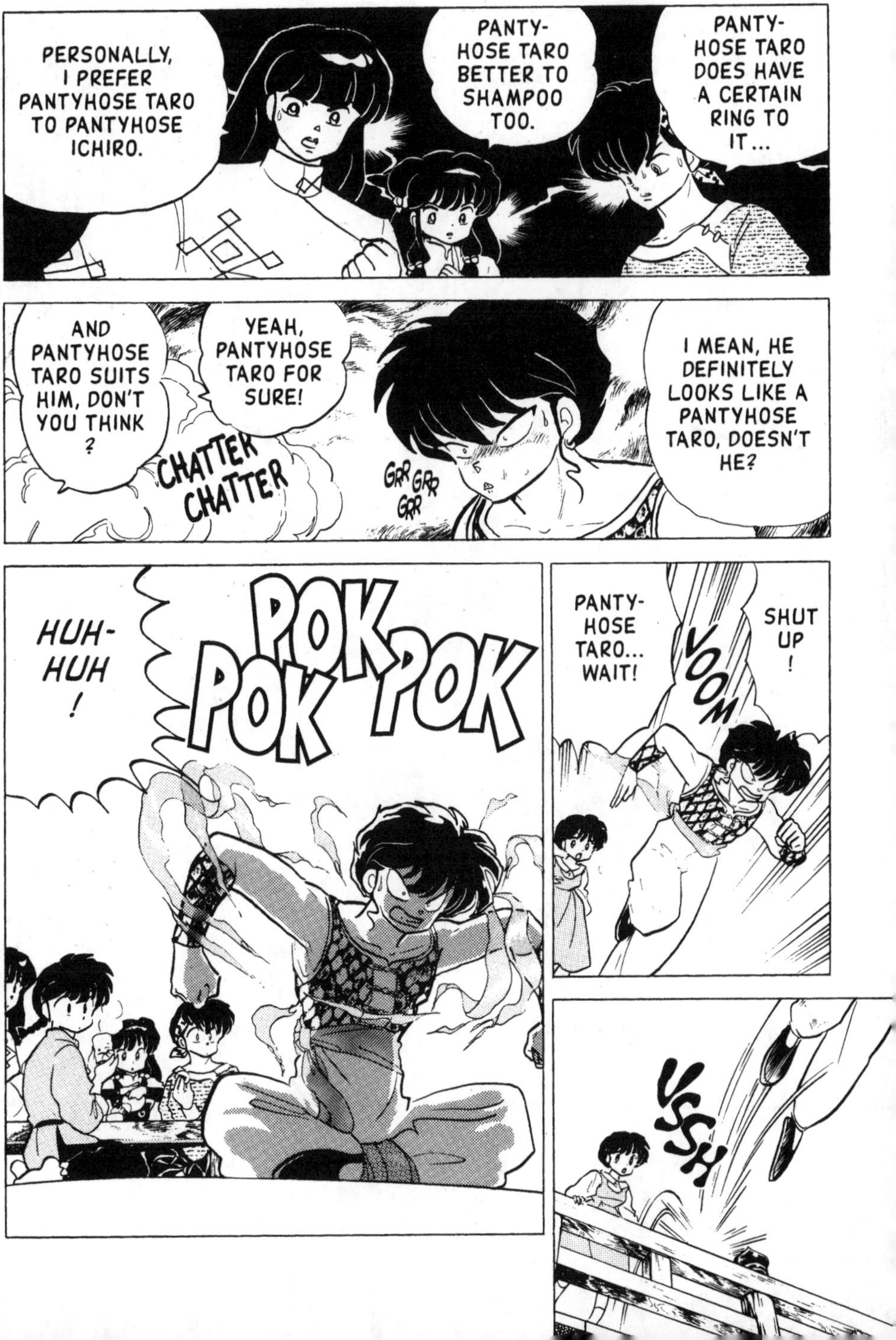
PERSONALLY, I PREFER PANTYHOSE TARO TO PANTYHOSE ICHIRO.
PANTY-HOSE TARO BETTER TO SHAMPOO TOO.
PANTY-HOSE TARO DOES HAVE A CERTAIN RING TO IT...
AND PANTYHOSE TARO SUITS HIM, DON'T YOU THINK?
YEAH, PANTYHOSE TARO FOR SURE!
CHATTER CHATTER
GRR GRR GRR
I MEAN, HE DEFINITELY LOOKS LIKE A PANTYHOSE TARO, DOESN'T HE?
HUH-HUH!
POK POK POK POK
PANTY-HOSE TARO... WAIT!
VOOM
SHUT UP!
VSSH

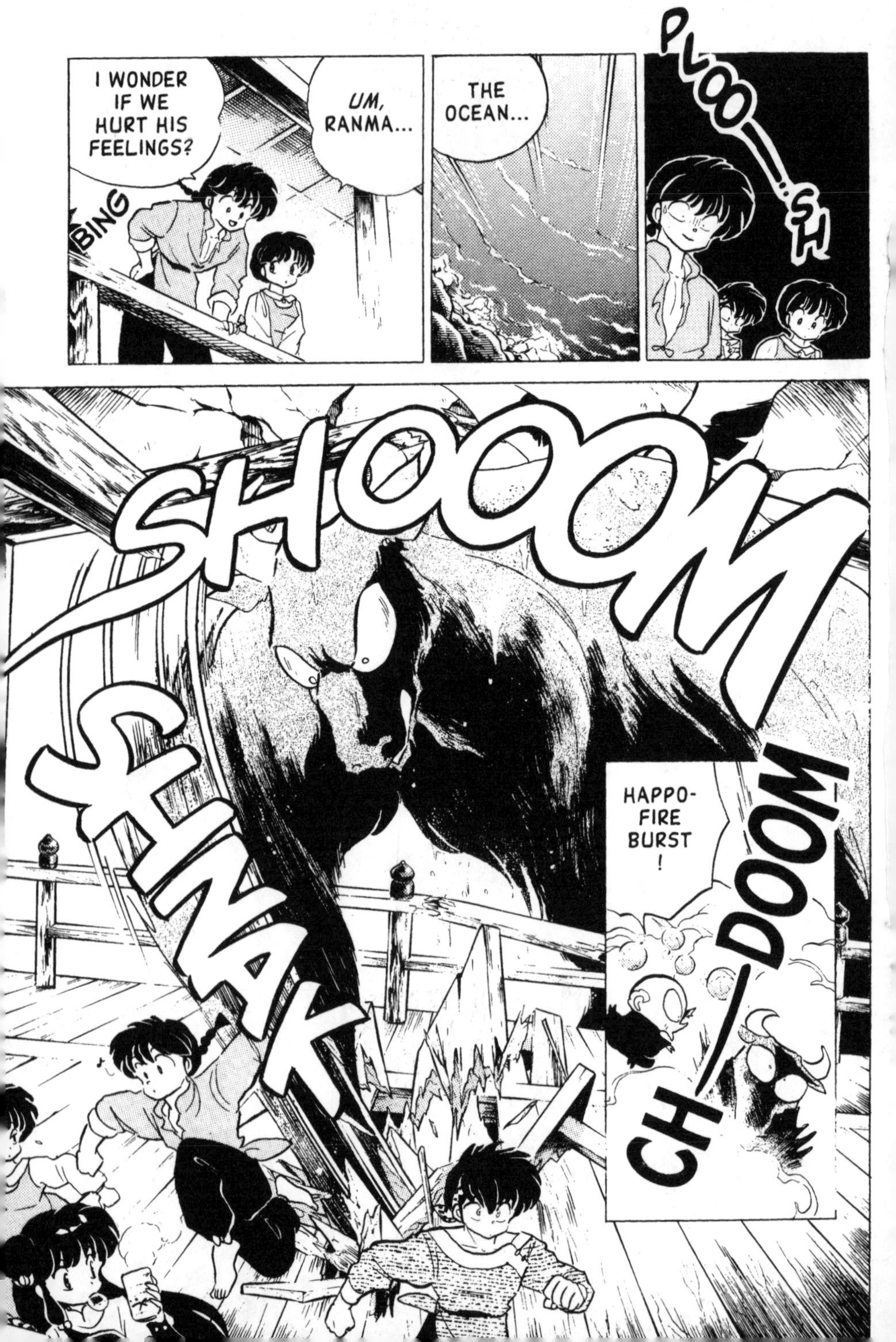
I WONDER IF WE HURT HIS FEELINGS?
BING
UM, RANMA...
THE OCEAN...
PLOO—SH
SHOOOM
SHNAK
HAPPO-FIRE BURST!
CH—DOOM

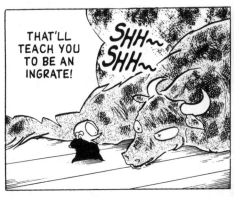

THAT'LL TEACH YOU TO BE AN INGRATE!

SHH~ SHH~

KRAK

KRAK

WE WANT YOU TO KNOW THAT WE SYMPATHIZE.

SO FEEL FREE TO CREAM THE OLD PERVERT, PANTYHOSE TARO.

HEY!

DON'T CALL ME THAT!

OLD MAN.

I COMMAND YOU...

...TO CHANGE MY NAME RIGHT HERE AND NOW!

GNG

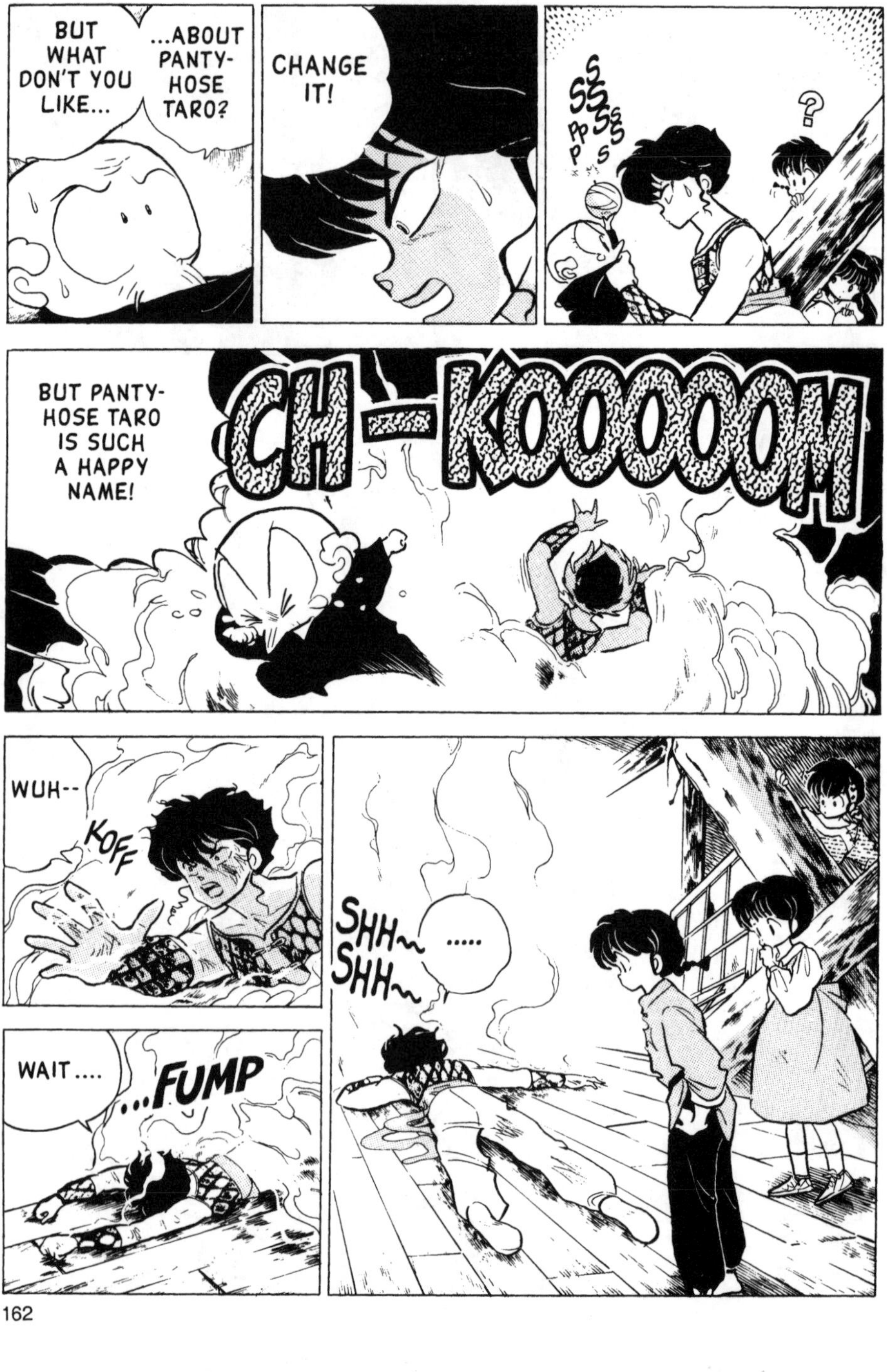
BUT WHAT DON'T YOU LIKE...
...ABOUT PANTY-HOSE TARO?
CHANGE IT!
?
BUT PANTY-HOSE TARO IS SUCH A HAPPY NAME!
CH-KOOOOOM
WUH--
KOFF
WAIT....
...FUMP
SHH~ SHH~
.....

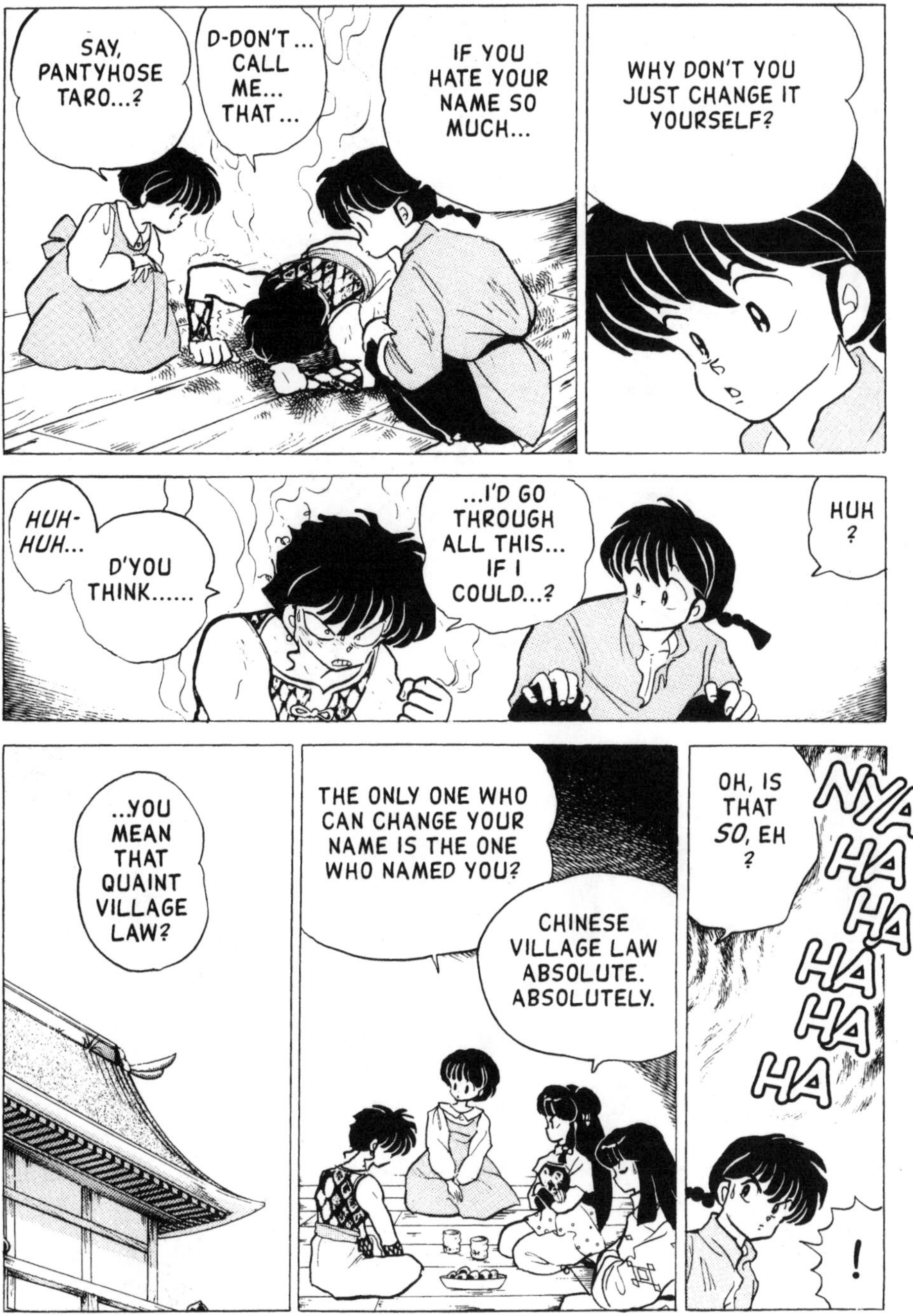
SAY, PANTYHOSE TARO...?
D-DON'T... CALL ME... THAT...
IF YOU HATE YOUR NAME SO MUCH...
WHY DON'T YOU JUST CHANGE IT YOURSELF?
HUH-HUH...
D'YOU THINK......
...I'D GO THROUGH ALL THIS... IF I COULD...?
HUH?
...YOU MEAN THAT QUAINT VILLAGE LAW?
THE ONLY ONE WHO CAN CHANGE YOUR NAME IS THE ONE WHO NAMED YOU?
CHINESE VILLAGE LAW ABSOLUTE. ABSOLUTELY.
OH, IS THAT *SO*, EH?
NYA HA HA HA HA HA
!

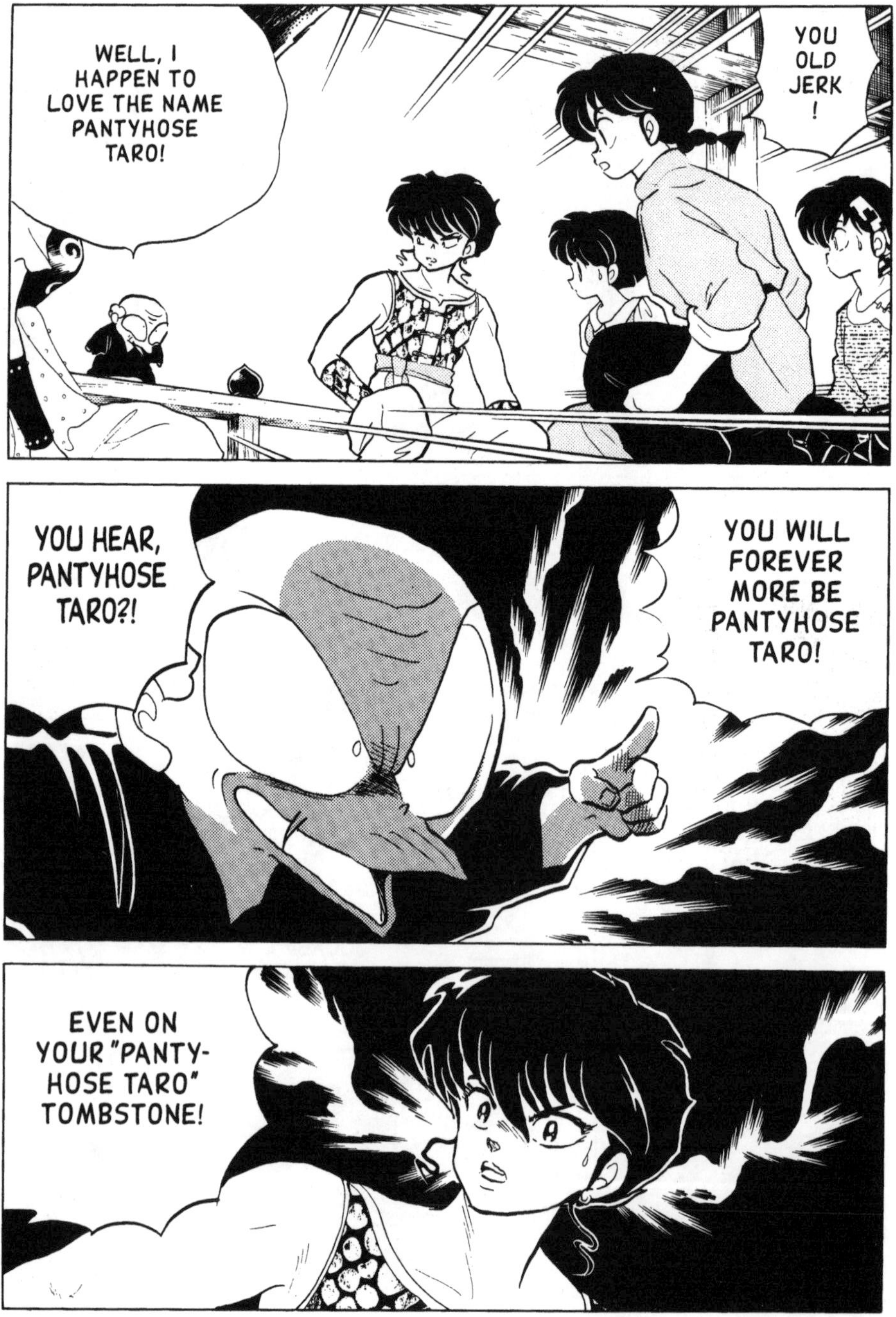
WELL, I HAPPEN TO LOVE THE NAME PANTYHOSE TARO!
YOU OLD JERK !
YOU HEAR, PANTYHOSE TARO?!
YOU WILL FOREVER MORE BE PANTYHOSE TARO!
EVEN ON YOUR "PANTY-HOSE TARO" TOMBSTONE!

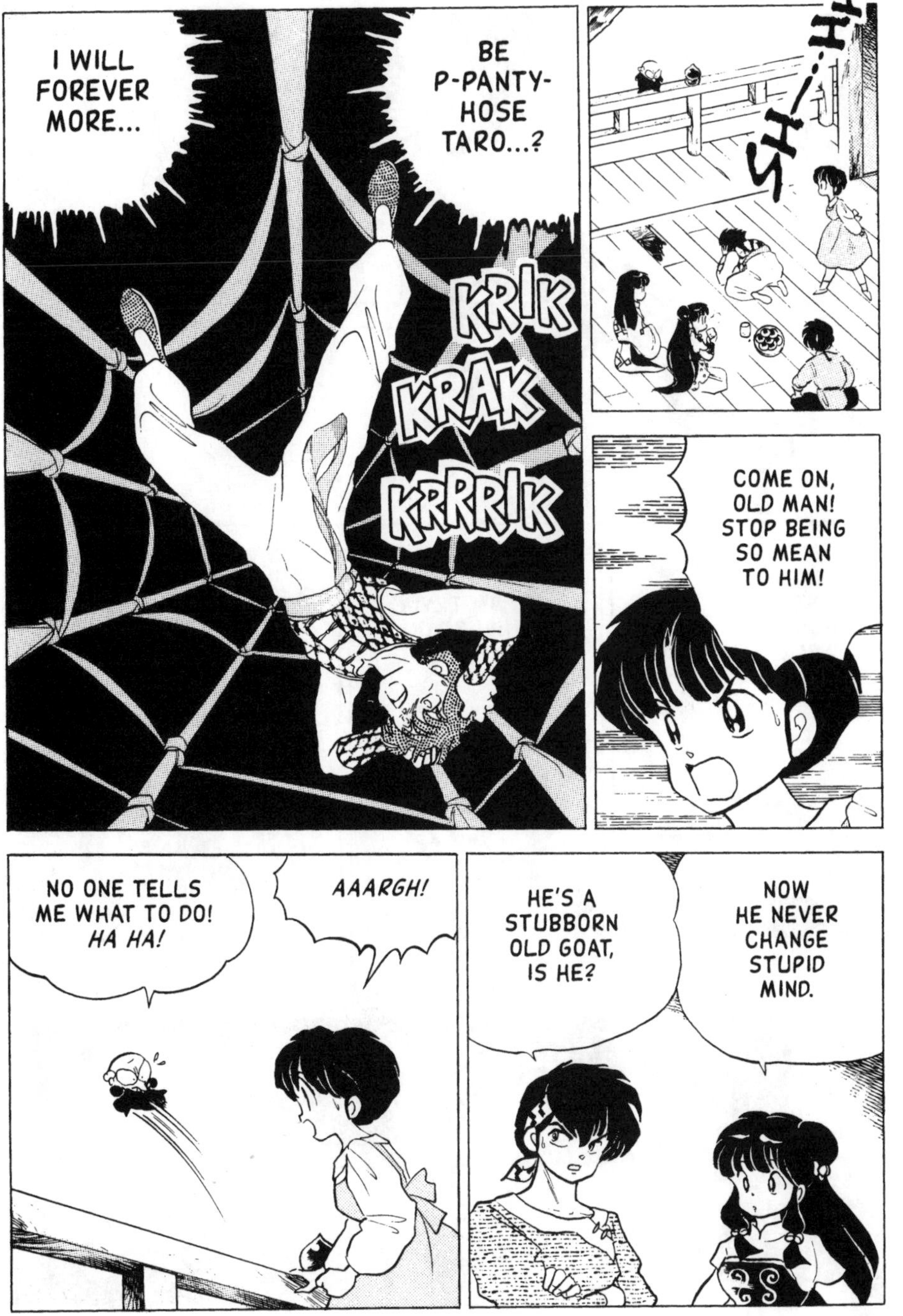
I WILL FOREVER MORE...
BE P-PANTY-HOSE TARO...?
KRIK
KRAK
KRRRIK
COME ON, OLD MAN! STOP BEING SO MEAN TO HIM!
NO ONE TELLS ME WHAT TO DO! *HA HA!*
AAARGH!
HE'S A STUBBORN OLD GOAT, IS HE?
NOW HE NEVER CHANGE STUPID MIND.

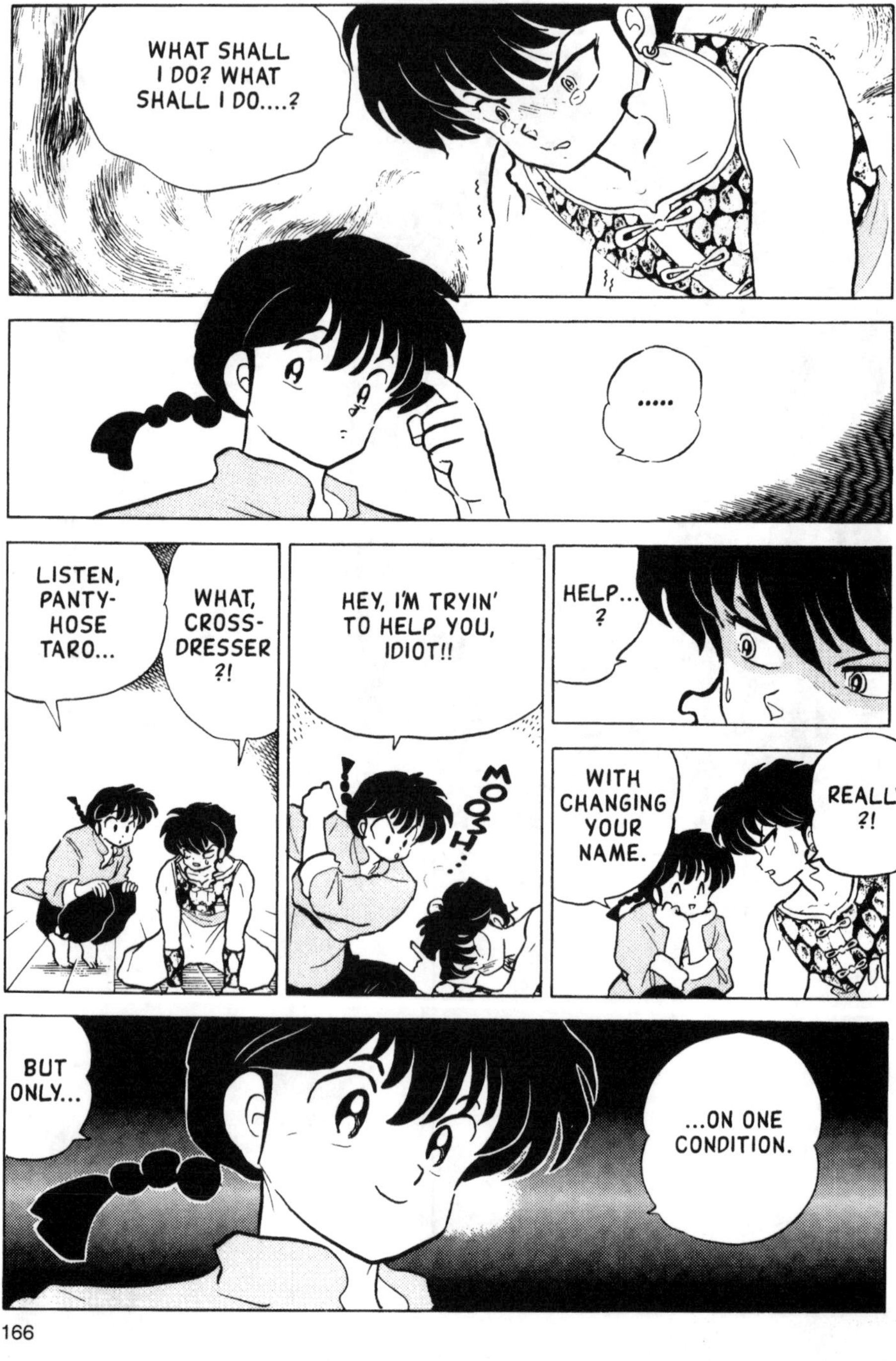
WHAT SHALL I DO? WHAT SHALL I DO....?
.....
LISTEN, PANTY-HOSE TARO...
WHAT, CROSS-DRESSER ?!
HEY, I'M TRYIN' TO HELP YOU, IDIOT!!
!
WHOOSH...
HELP...?
WITH CHANGING YOUR NAME.
REALLY ?!
BUT ONLY...
...ON ONE CONDITION.

Part 11
BACK TO THE FREAK-TURE!

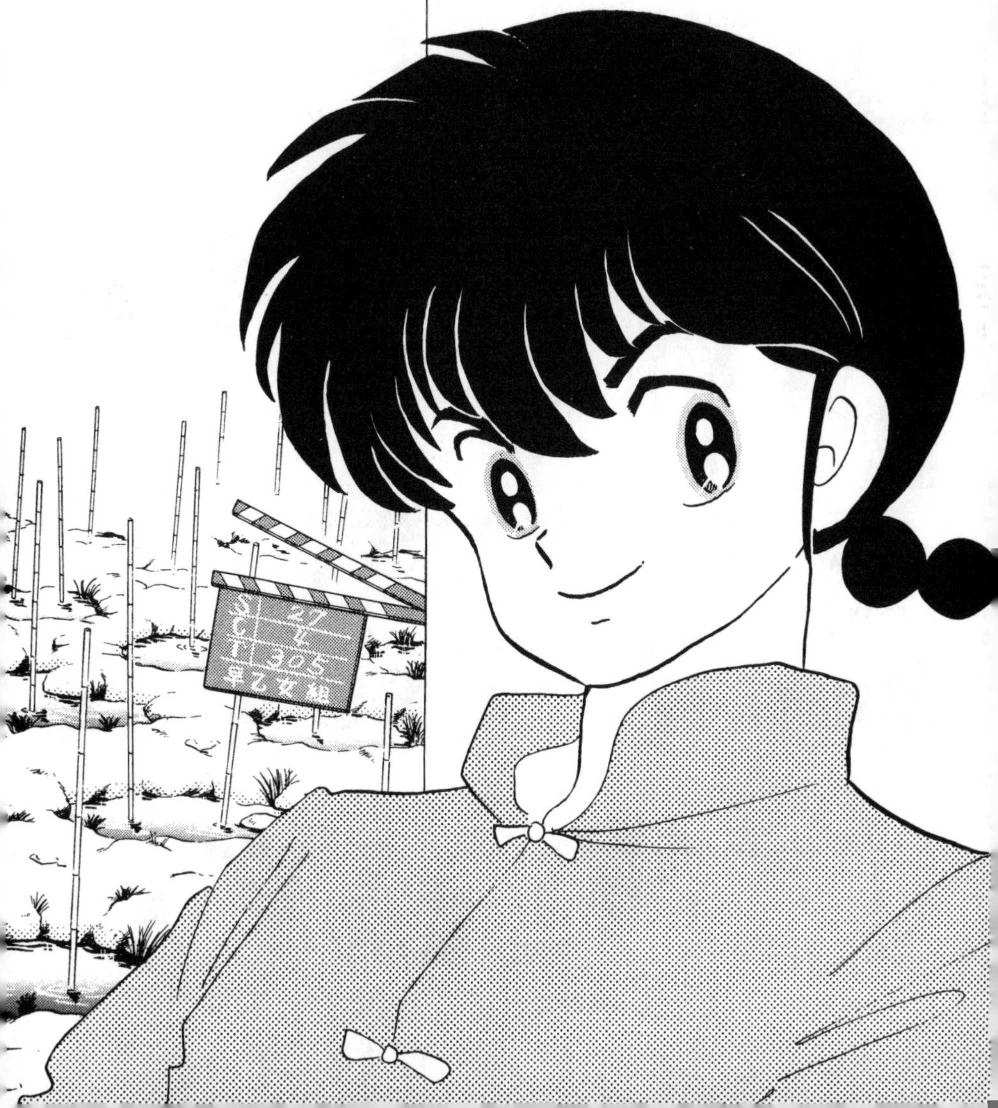
S 27
T 305
早乙女組

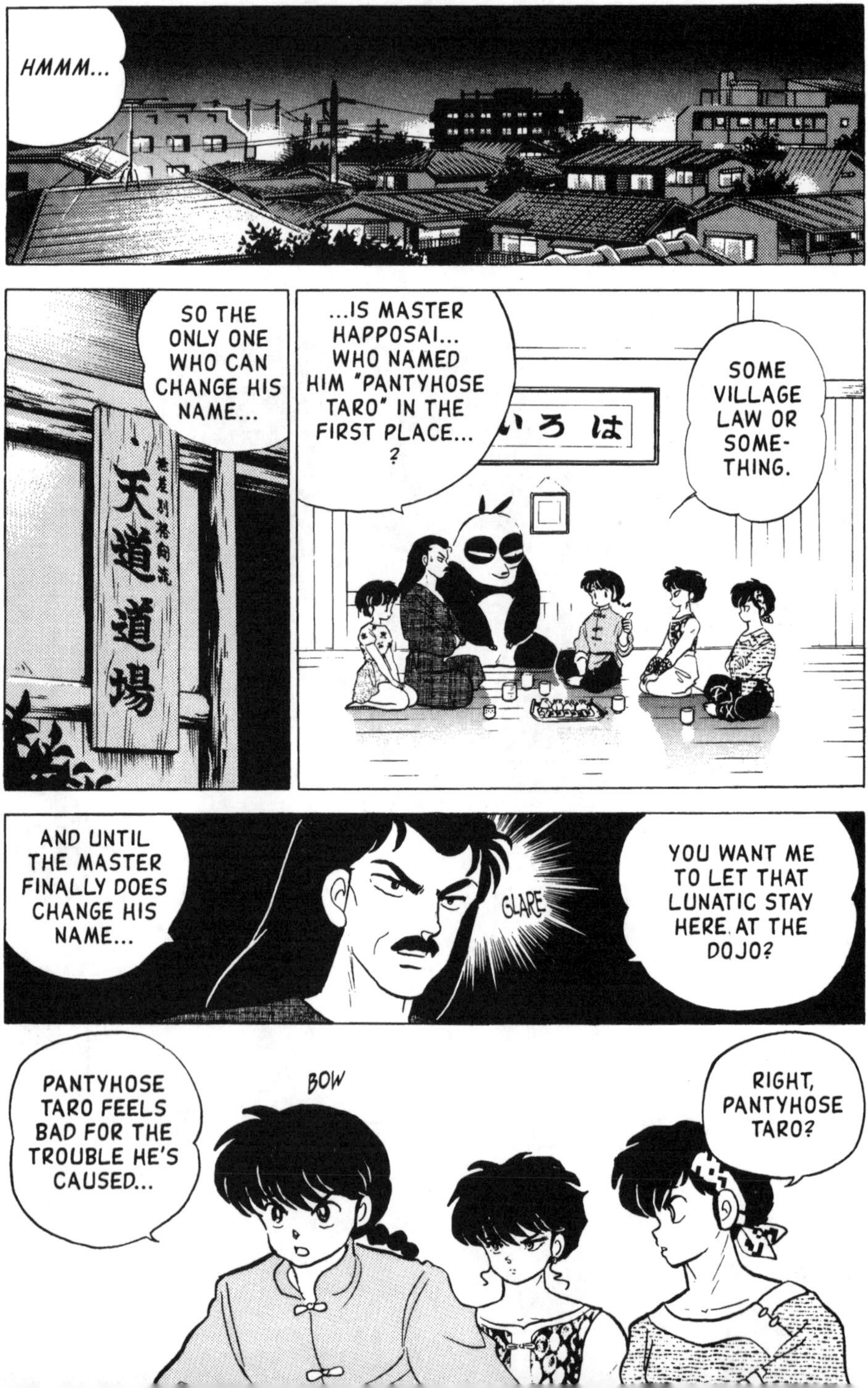
HMMM...
SO THE ONLY ONE WHO CAN CHANGE HIS NAME...
...IS MASTER HAPPOSAI... WHO NAMED HIM "PANTYHOSE TARO" IN THE FIRST PLACE...?
SOME VILLAGE LAW OR SOME-THING.
天道道場
いろは
AND UNTIL THE MASTER FINALLY DOES CHANGE HIS NAME...
GLARE
YOU WANT ME TO LET THAT LUNATIC STAY HERE AT THE DOJO?
PANTYHOSE TARO FEELS BAD FOR THE TROUBLE HE'S CAUSED...
BOW
RIGHT, PANTYHOSE TARO?

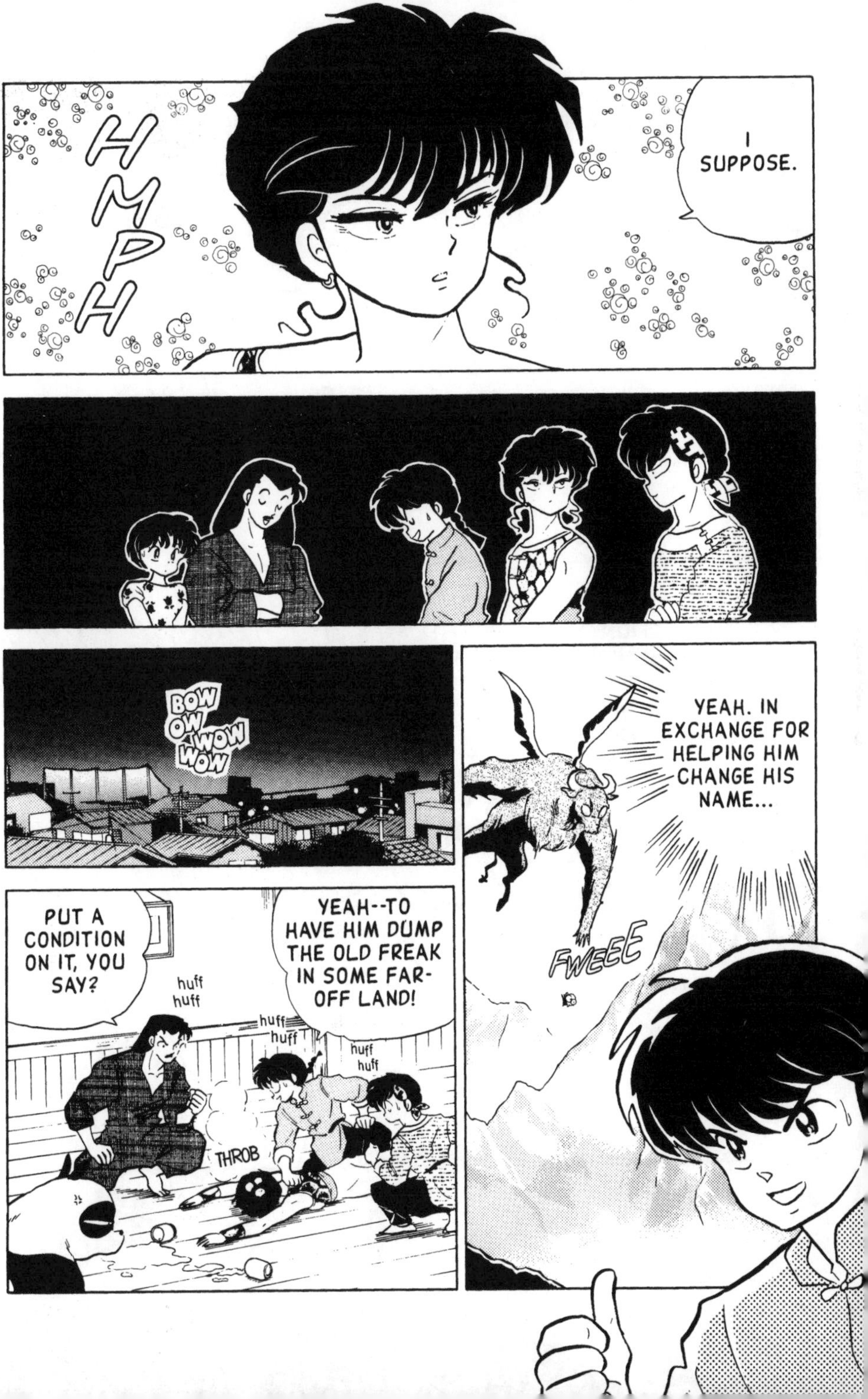
HMPH
I SUPPOSE.
BOW OW WOW WOW
YEAH. IN EXCHANGE FOR HELPING HIM CHANGE HIS NAME...
FWEEEE
PUT A CONDITION ON IT, YOU SAY?
huff huff
YEAH--TO HAVE HIM DUMP THE OLD FREAK IN SOME FAR-OFF LAND!
huff huff
huff huff
THROB

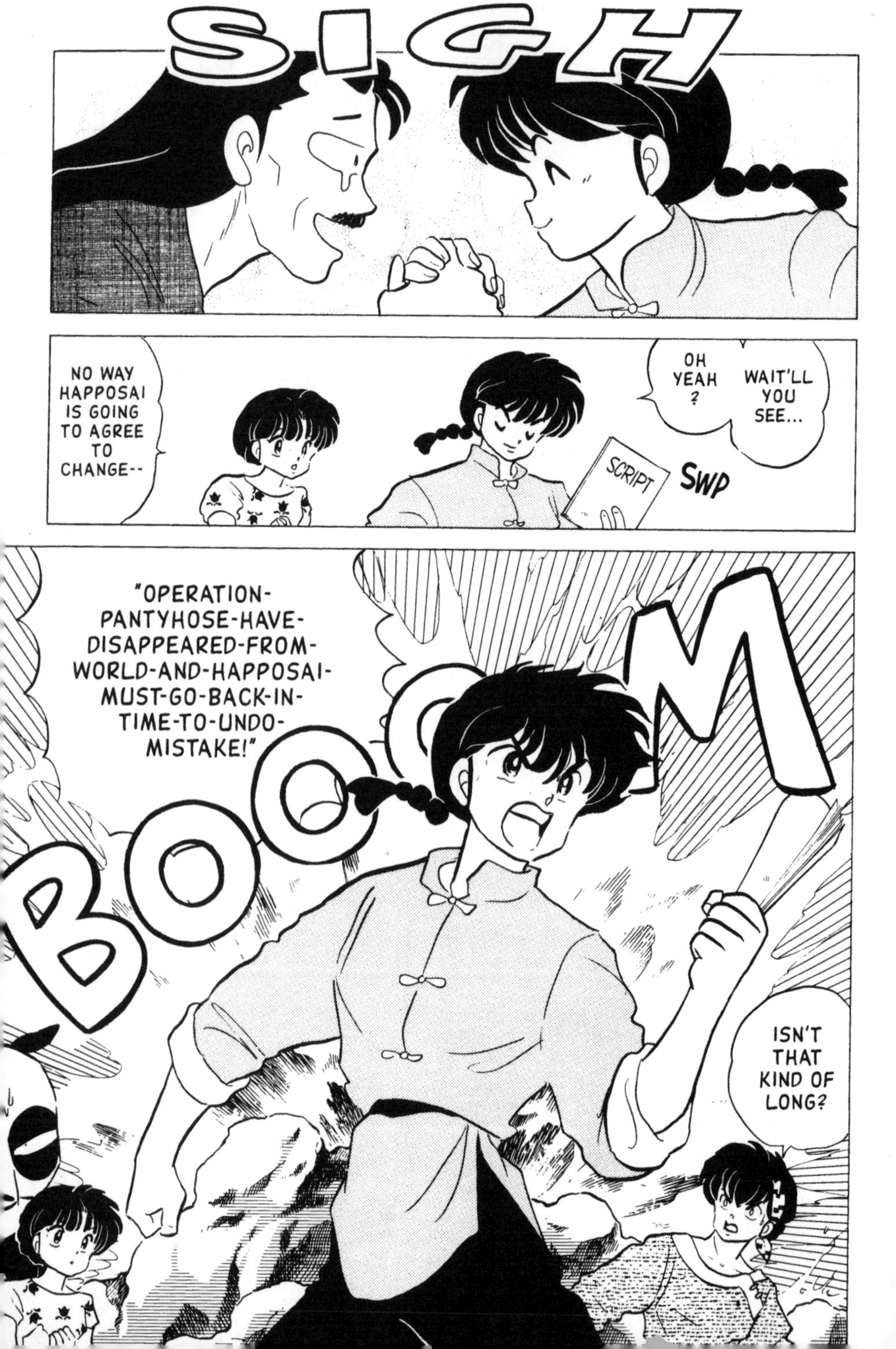
SIGH
NO WAY HAPPOSAI IS GOING TO AGREE TO CHANGE--
OH YEAH?
WAIT'LL YOU SEE...
SCRIPT
SWP
"OPERATION-PANTYHOSE-HAVE-DISAPPEARED-FROM-WORLD-AND-HAPPOSAI-MUST-GO-BACK-IN-TIME-TO-UNDO-MISTAKE!"
BOOOM
ISN'T THAT KIND OF LONG?

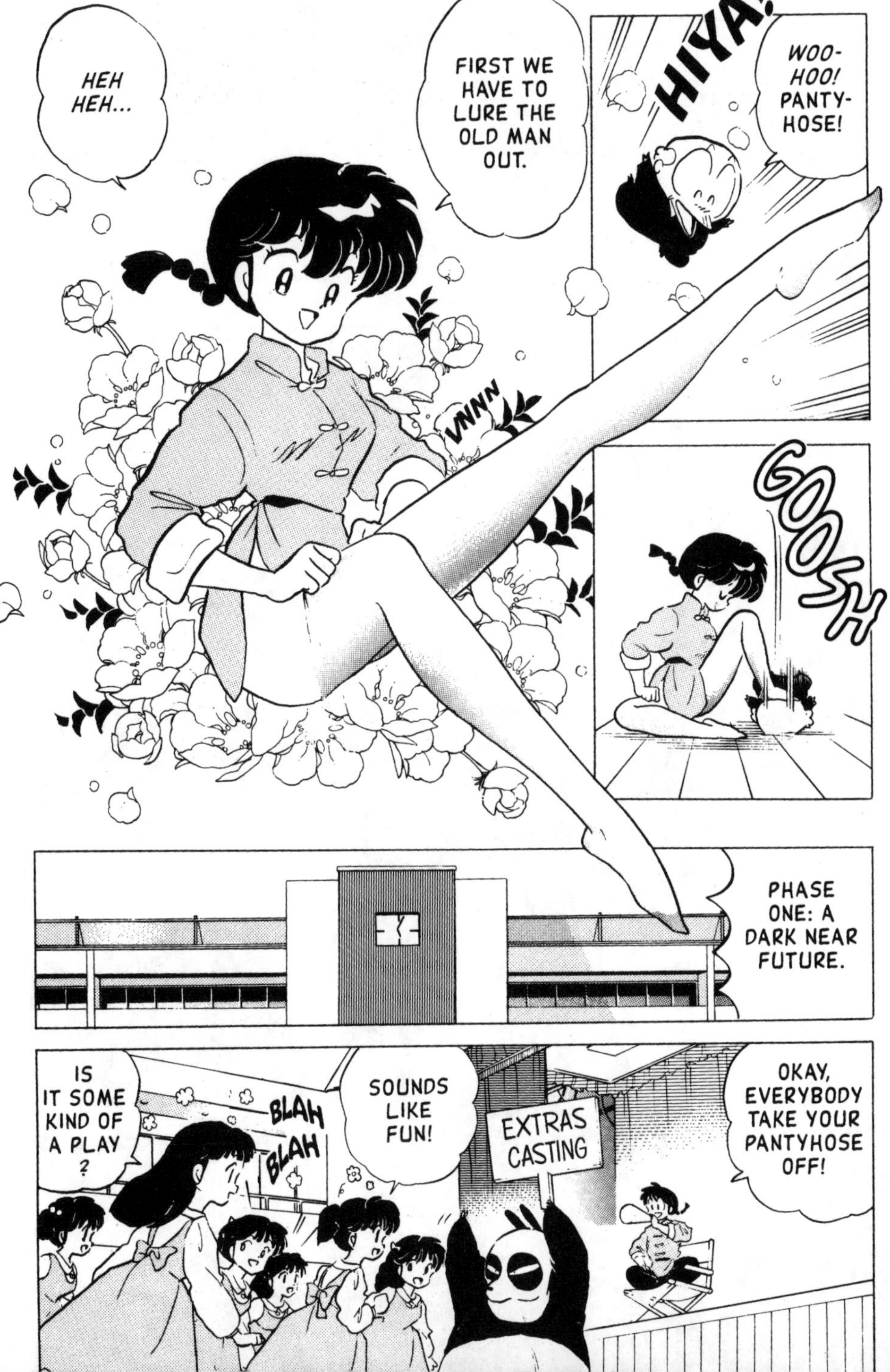
HEH HEH...
FIRST WE HAVE TO LURE THE OLD MAN OUT.
VNNN
HIYA!
WOO-HOO! PANTY-HOSE!
GOOSH
PHASE ONE: A DARK NEAR FUTURE.
IS IT SOME KIND OF A PLAY ?
BLAH BLAH
SOUNDS LIKE FUN!
EXTRAS CASTING
OKAY, EVERYBODY TAKE YOUR PANTYHOSE OFF!

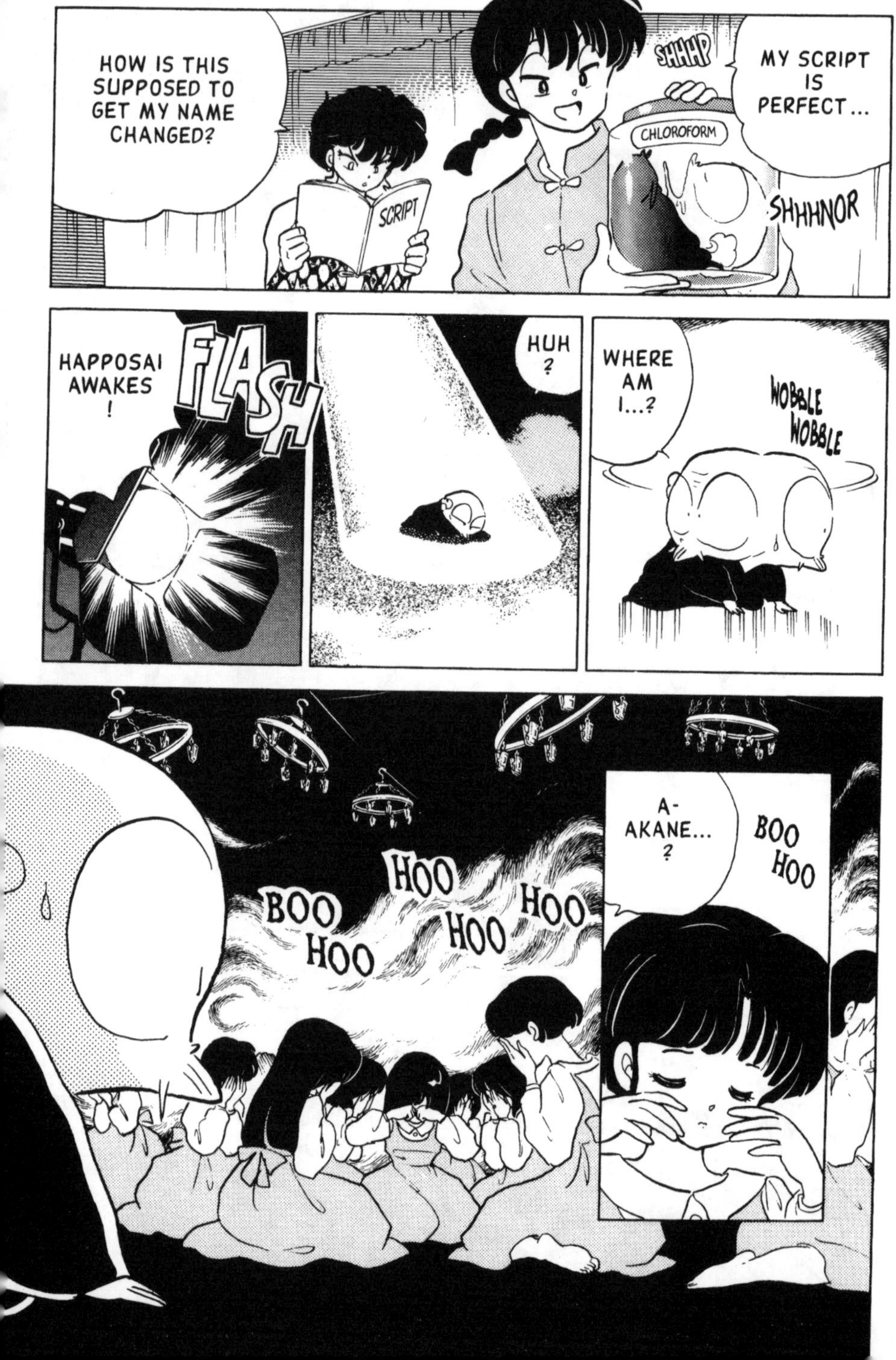
HOW IS THIS SUPPOSED TO GET MY NAME CHANGED?
SCRIPT
SHHHP
MY SCRIPT IS PERFECT...
CHLOROFORM
SHHHNOR
HAPPOSAI AWAKES!
FLASH
HUH?
WHERE AM I...?
WOBBLE WOBBLE
BOO HOO
HOO
HOO
HOO
A-AKANE...?
BOO HOO

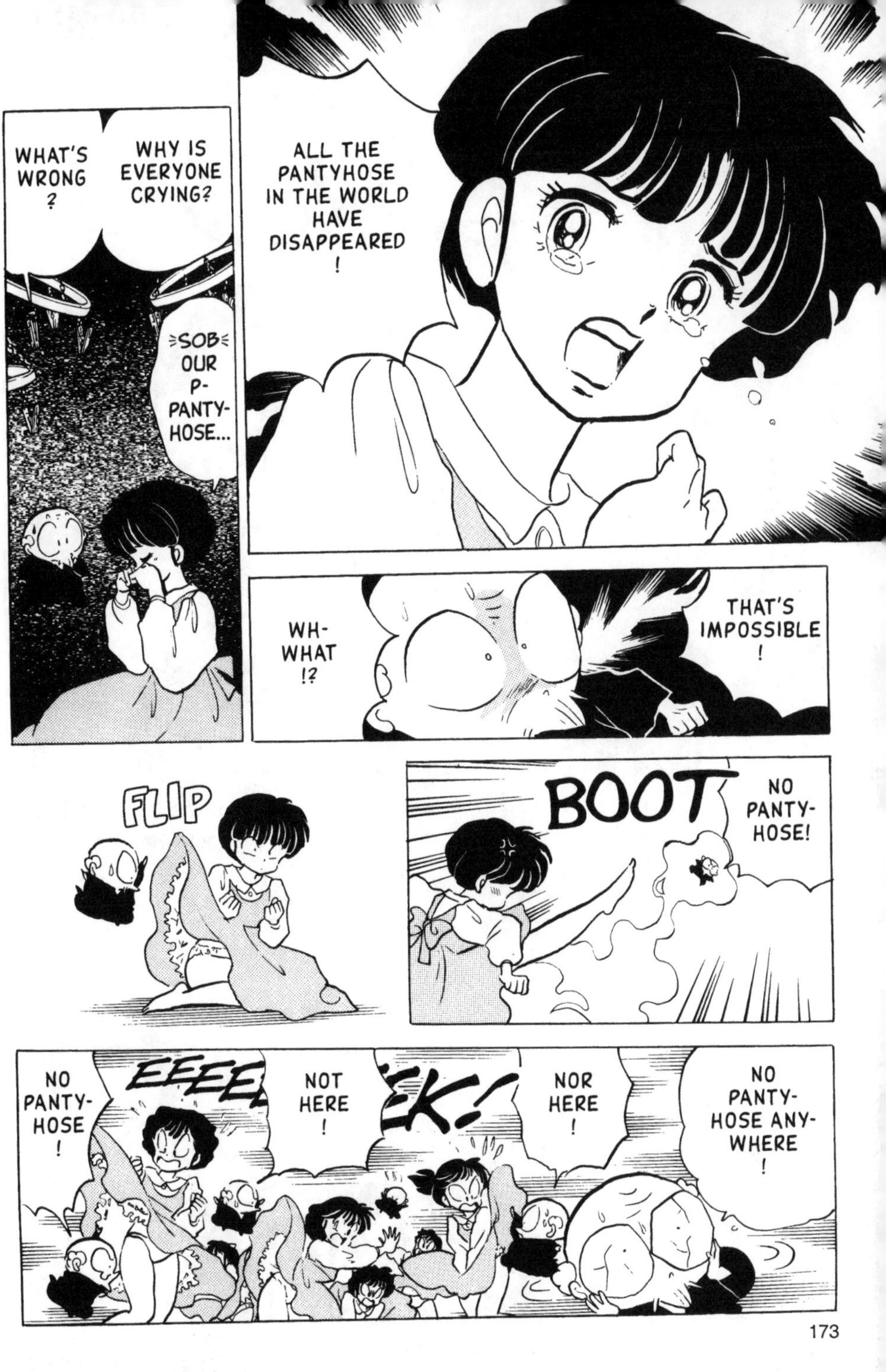
WHAT'S WRONG?
WHY IS EVERYONE CRYING?
SOB OUR P-PANTYHOSE...
ALL THE PANTYHOSE IN THE WORLD HAVE DISAPPEARED!
WH-WHAT!?
THAT'S IMPOSSIBLE!
FLIP
BOOT
NO PANTYHOSE!
NO PANTYHOSE!
EEEEEEK!
NOT HERE!
NOR HERE!
NO PANTYHOSE ANYWHERE!

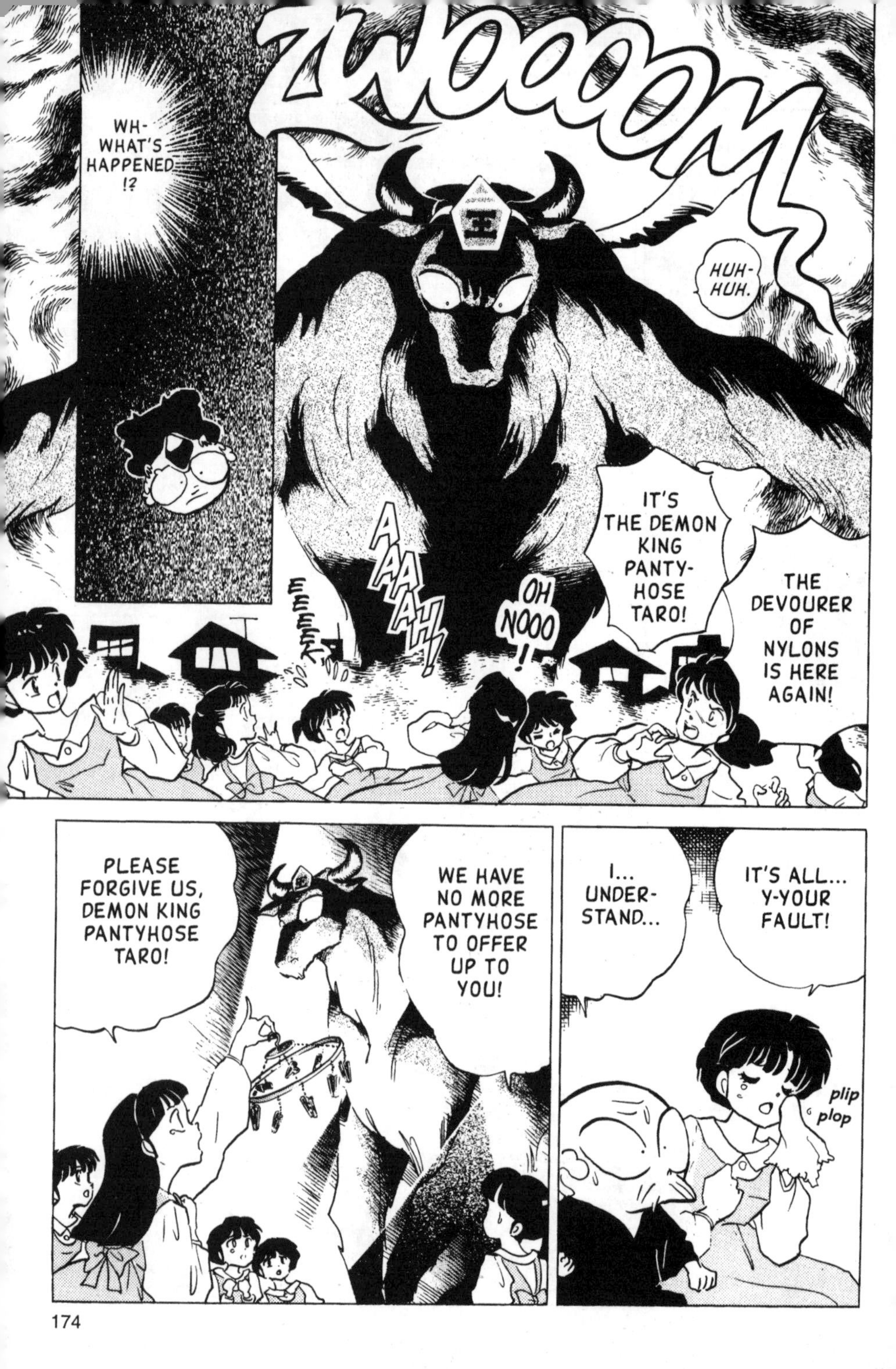
ZWOOOOM
WH-WHAT'S HAPPENED!?
HUH-HUH.
EEEEK
AAAAH!
OH NOOO!
IT'S THE DEMON KING PANTY-HOSE TARO!
THE DEVOURER OF NYLONS IS HERE AGAIN!
PLEASE FORGIVE US, DEMON KING PANTYHOSE TARO!
WE HAVE NO MORE PANTYHOSE TO OFFER UP TO YOU!
I... UNDER-STAND...
IT'S ALL... Y-YOUR FAULT!
plip plop

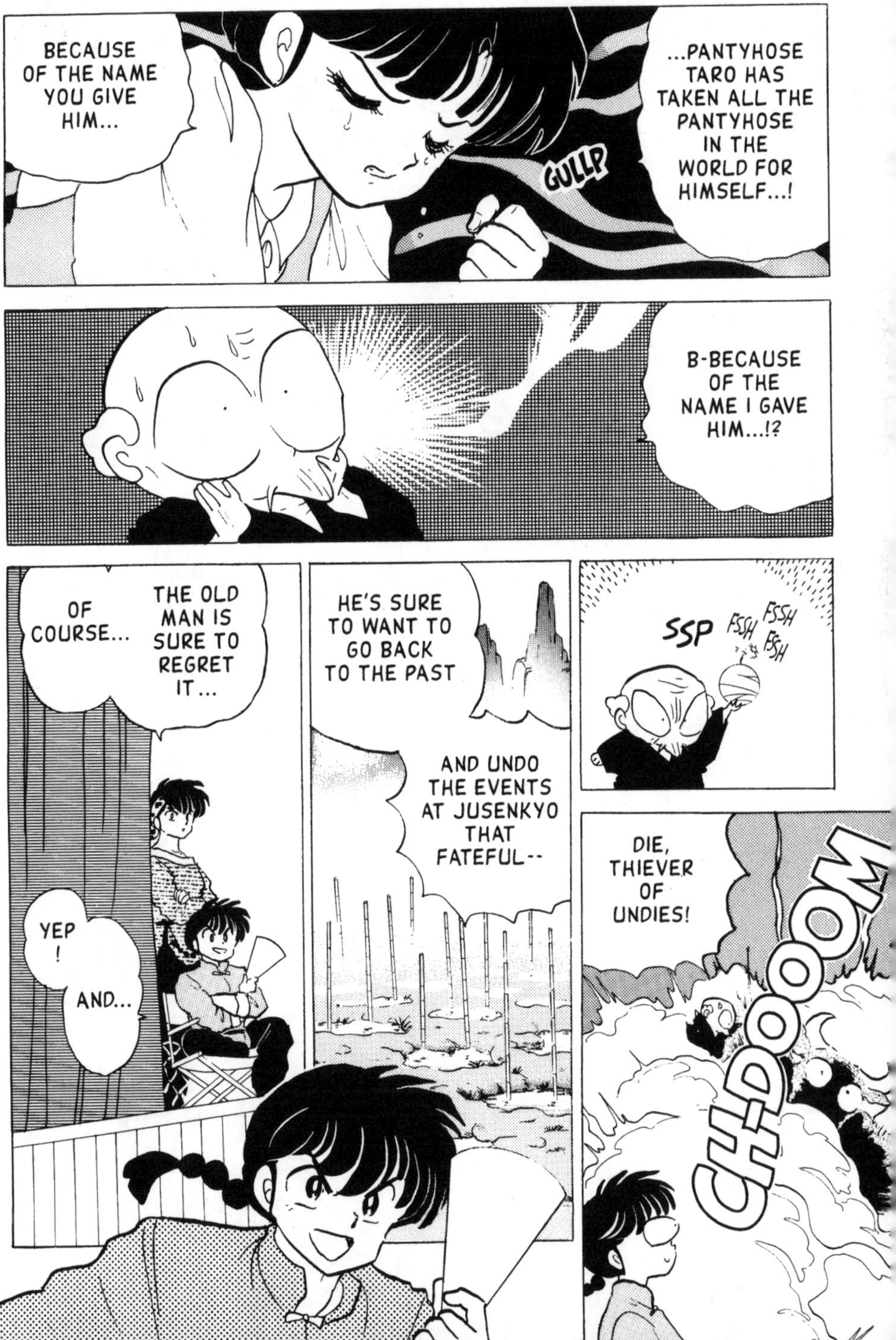
BECAUSE OF THE NAME YOU GIVE HIM...
GULLP
...PANTYHOSE TARO HAS TAKEN ALL THE PANTYHOSE IN THE WORLD FOR HIMSELF...!
B-BECAUSE OF THE NAME I GAVE HIM...!?
OF COURSE...
THE OLD MAN IS SURE TO REGRET IT...
YEP!
AND...
HE'S SURE TO WANT TO GO BACK TO THE PAST
AND UNDO THE EVENTS AT JUSENKYO THAT FATEFUL--
SSP
FSSH
FSSH
FSSH
DIE, THIEVER OF UNDIES!
CH-DOOOOM

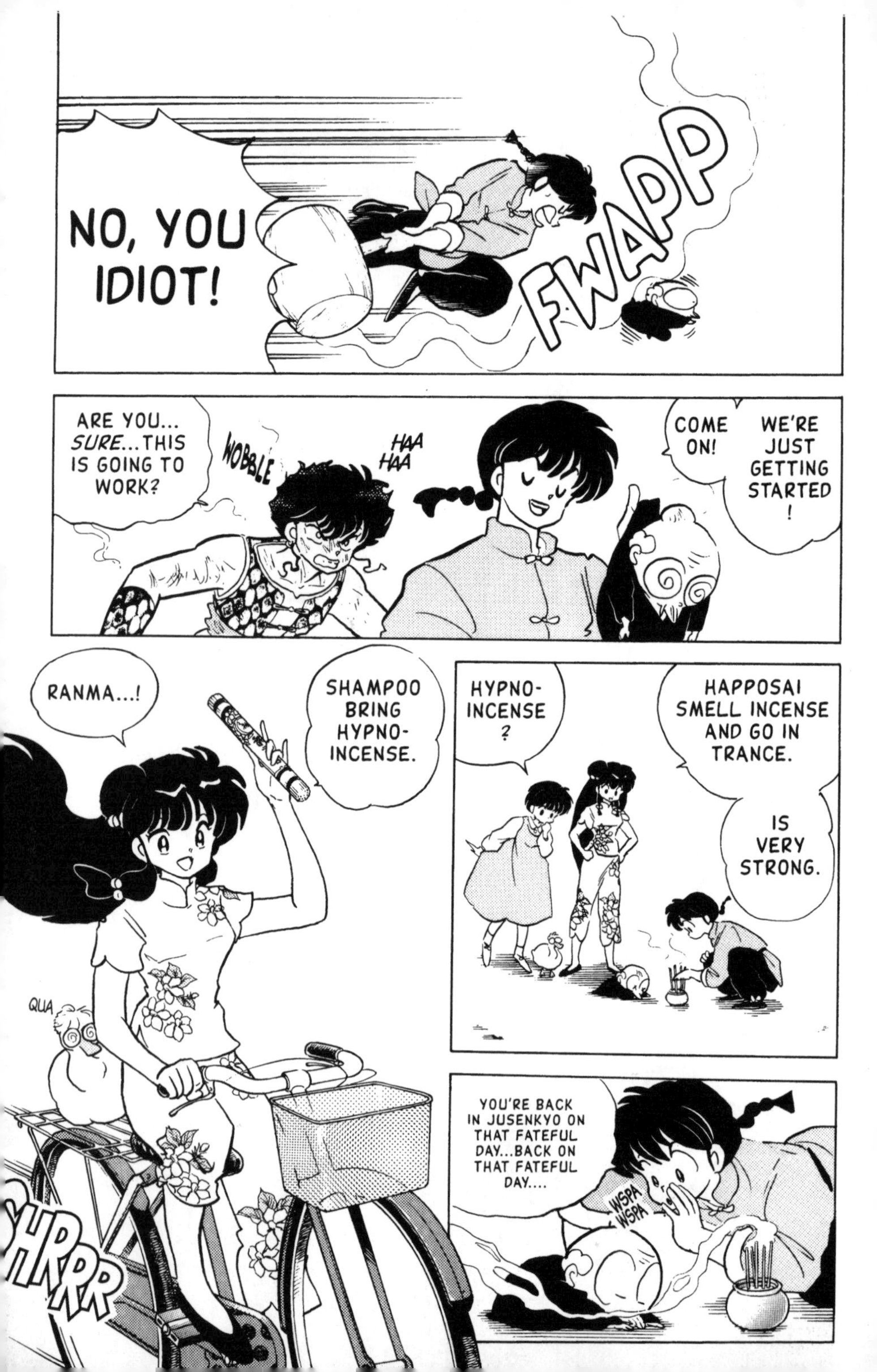
NO, YOU IDIOT!
FWAPP
ARE YOU... SURE...THIS IS GOING TO WORK?
WOBBLE
HAA HAA
COME ON!
WE'RE JUST GETTING STARTED!
RANMA...!
SHAMPOO BRING HYPNO-INCENSE.
QUA
SHRRR
HYPNO-INCENSE?
HAPPOSAI SMELL INCENSE AND GO IN TRANCE.
IS VERY STRONG.
YOU'RE BACK IN JUSENKYO ON THAT FATEFUL DAY...BACK ON THAT FATEFUL DAY....
WSPA WSPA

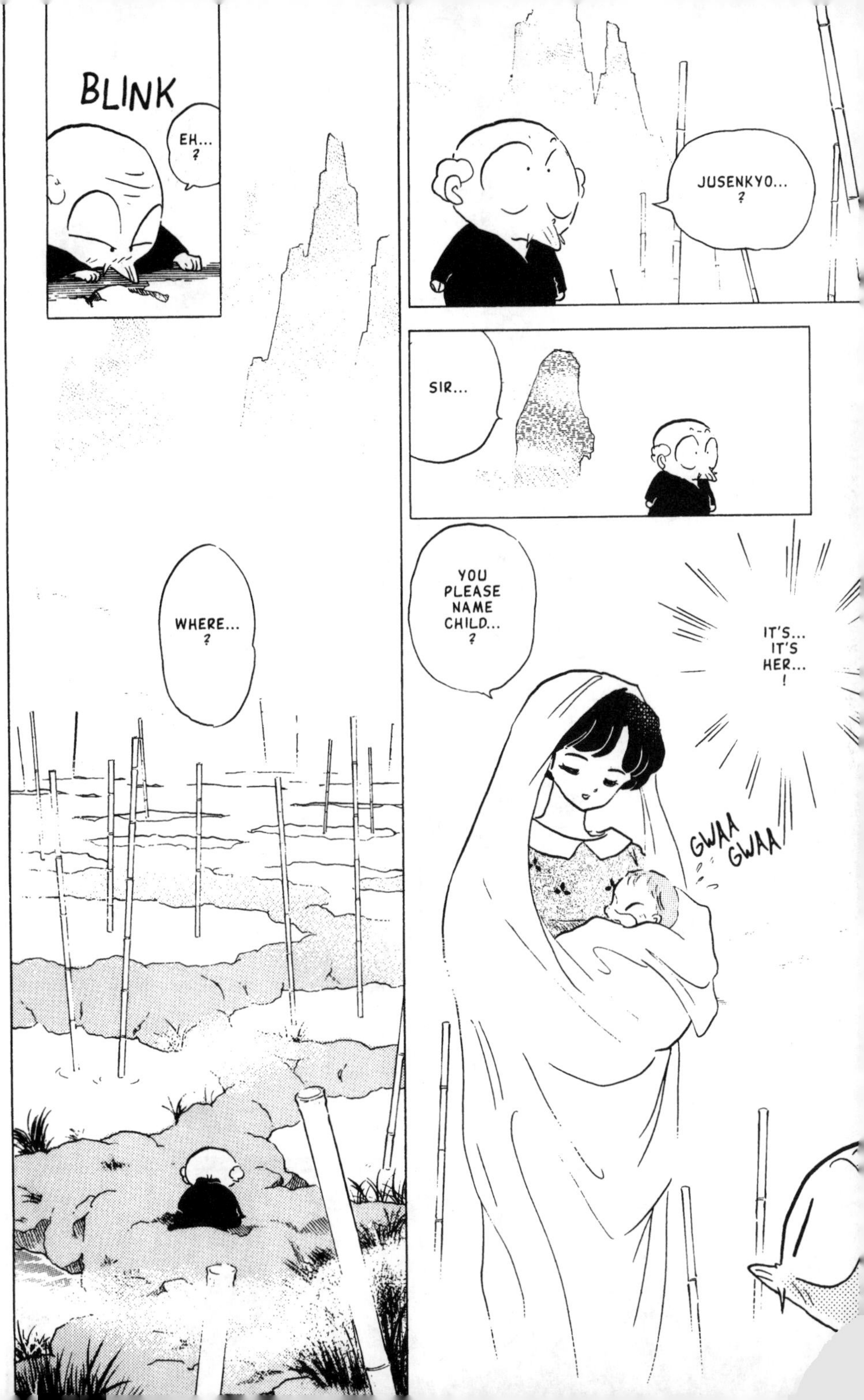
BLINK
EH...?
WHERE...?
JUSENKYO...?
SIR...
YOU PLEASE NAME CHILD...?
IT'S... IT'S HER...!
GWAA GWAA

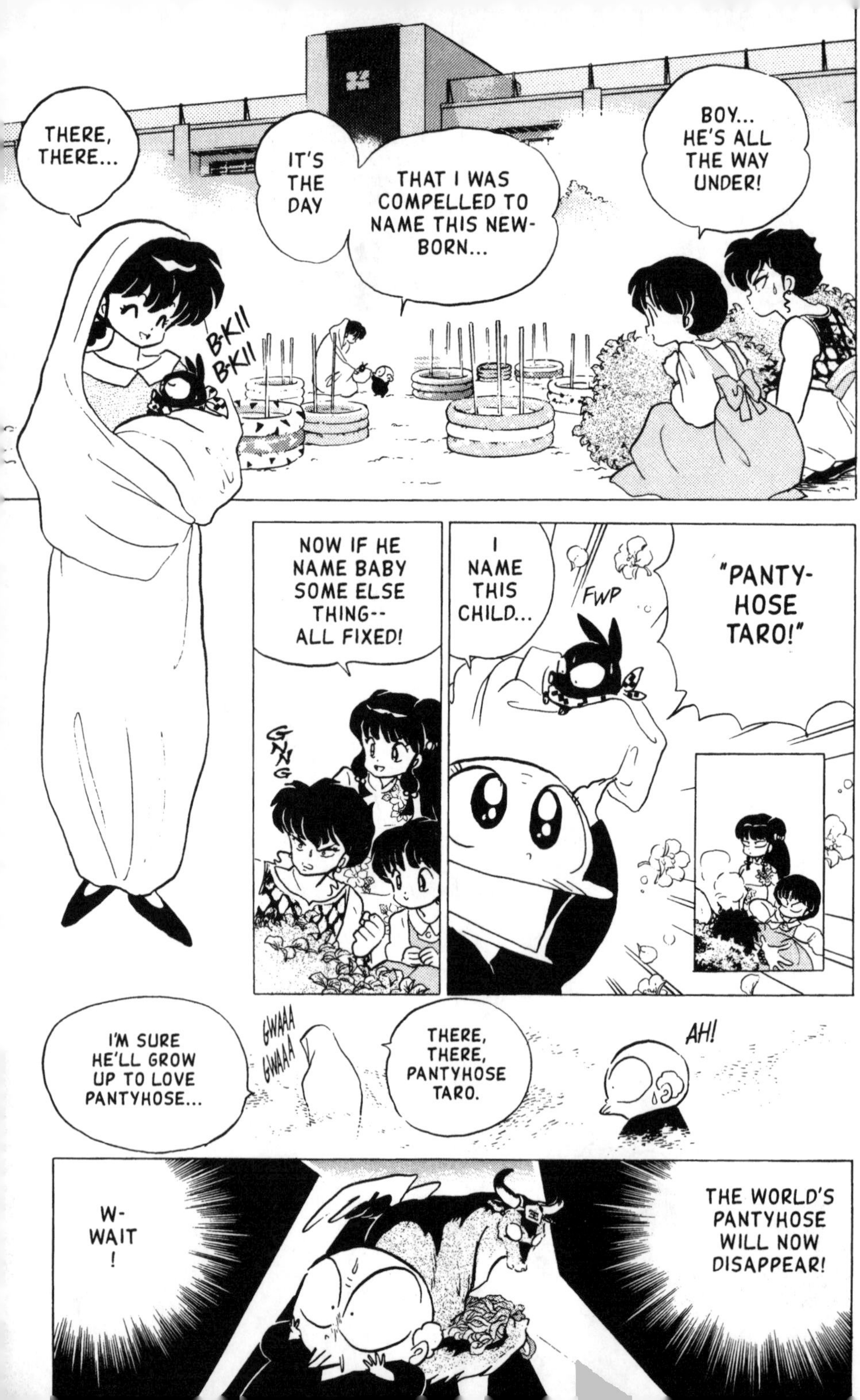
THERE, THERE...
B-KII B-KII
IT'S THE DAY
THAT I WAS COMPELLED TO NAME THIS NEW-BORN...
BOY... HE'S ALL THE WAY UNDER!
NOW IF HE NAME BABY SOME ELSE THING-- ALL FIXED!
GNNG
I NAME THIS CHILD...
FWP
"PANTY-HOSE TARO!"
I'M SURE HE'LL GROW UP TO LOVE PANTYHOSE...
GWAAA GWAAA
THERE, THERE, PANTYHOSE TARO.
AH!
W-WAIT!
THE WORLD'S PANTYHOSE WILL NOW DISAPPEAR!

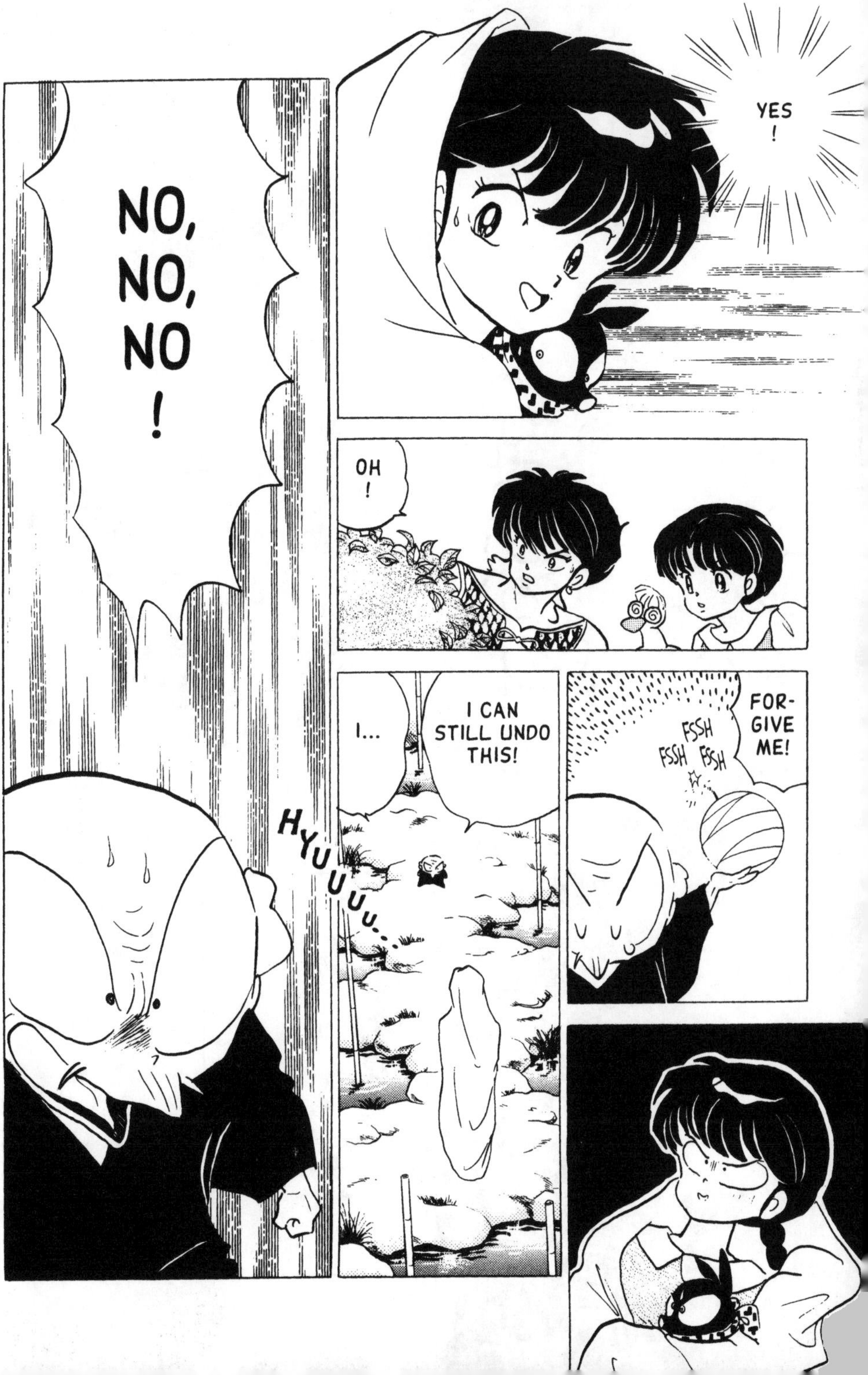
NO, NO, NO!
YES!
OH!
I...
I CAN STILL UNDO THIS!
HYUUUUU...
FORGIVE ME!
FSSH FSSH FSSH

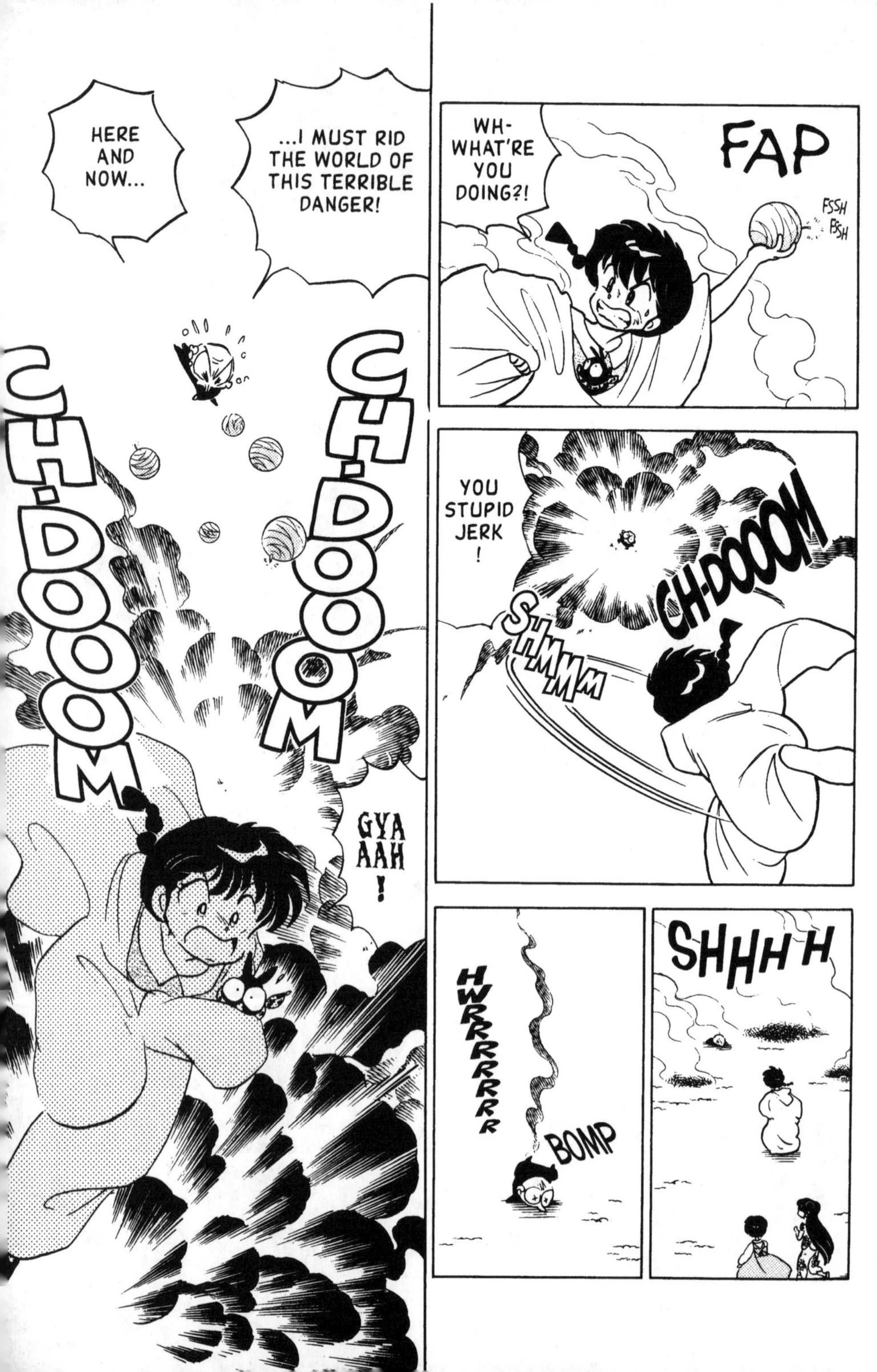
HERE AND NOW...
...I MUST RID THE WORLD OF THIS TERRIBLE DANGER!
CH-DOOOOM
CH-DOOOM
GYAAAH!
WH-WHAT'RE YOU DOING?!
FAP
FSSH FSSH
YOU STUPID JERK!
CH-DOOOOM
SHMMMM
HWRRRRRRRR
BOMP
SHHHH

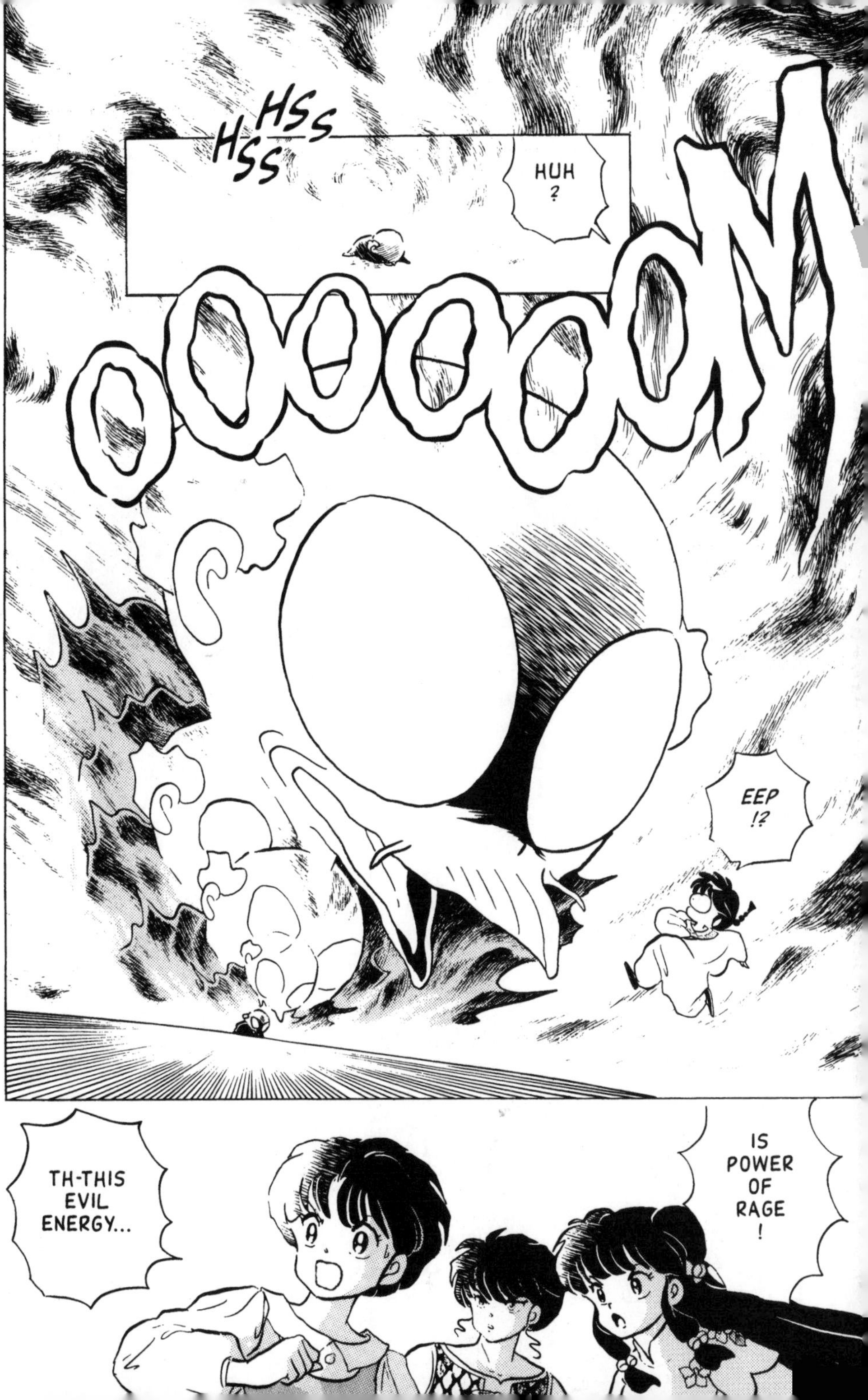
HSSS
HSSS
HUH ?
OOOOOOM
EEP !?
TH-THIS EVIL ENERGY...
IS POWER OF RAGE !

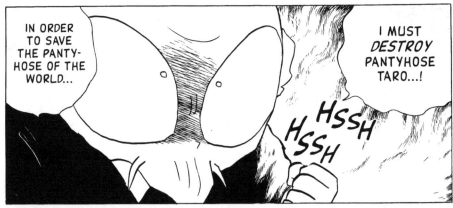

IN ORDER TO SAVE THE PANTYHOSE OF THE WORLD...

I MUST *DESTROY* PANTYHOSE TARO...!

HSSH HSSH

WHERE HAS HE GONE...!?

BOOM BOOM

AIEEE!

SSSSS

WELL?

MAYBE WE NEED TO REVISE THE SCRIPT A BIT...

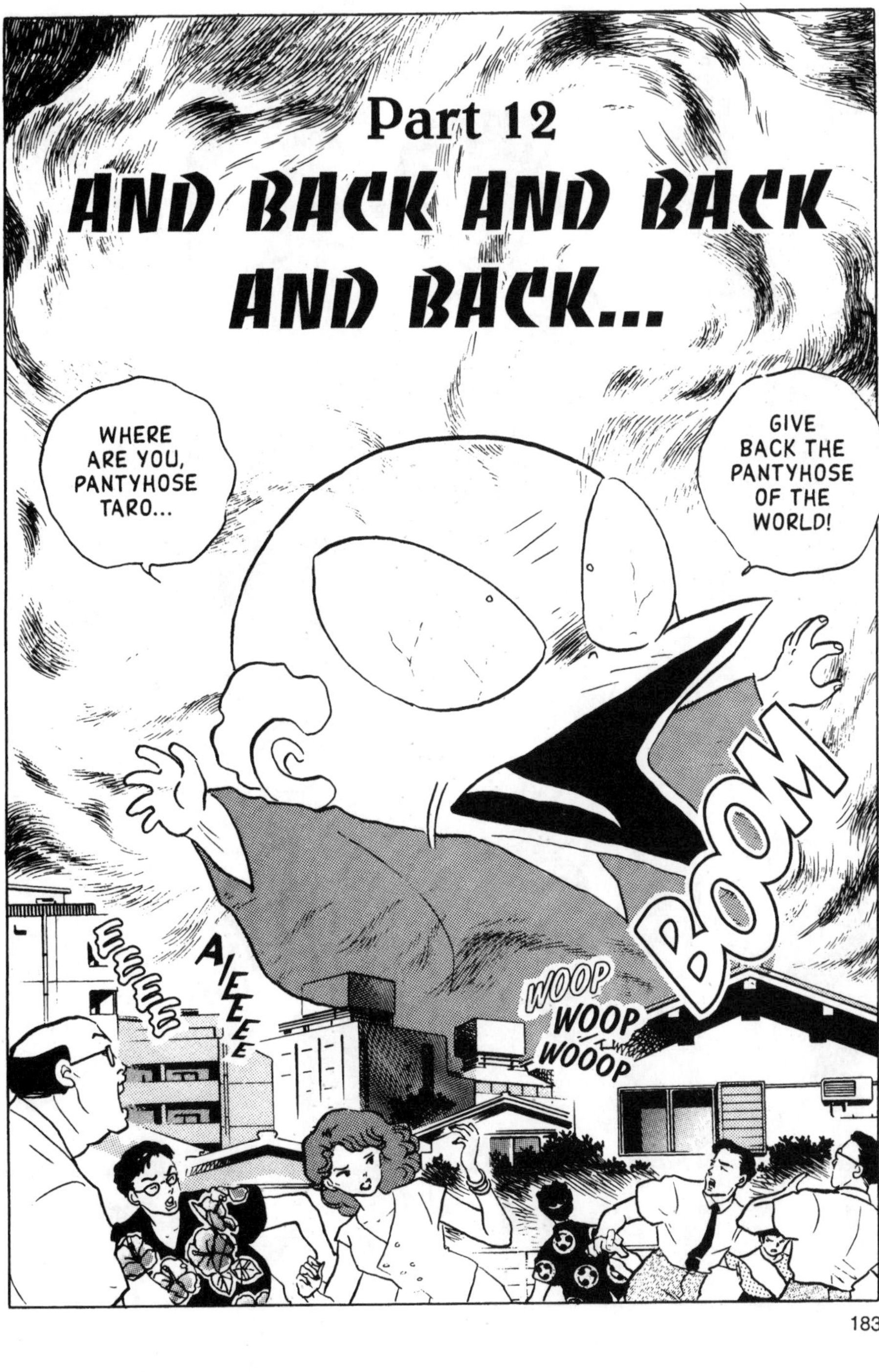
Part 12
AND BACK AND BACK AND BACK...
WHERE ARE YOU, PANTYHOSE TARO...
GIVE BACK THE PANTYHOSE OF THE WORLD!
BOOM
AIEEEEE
WOOP
WOOP
WOOOP

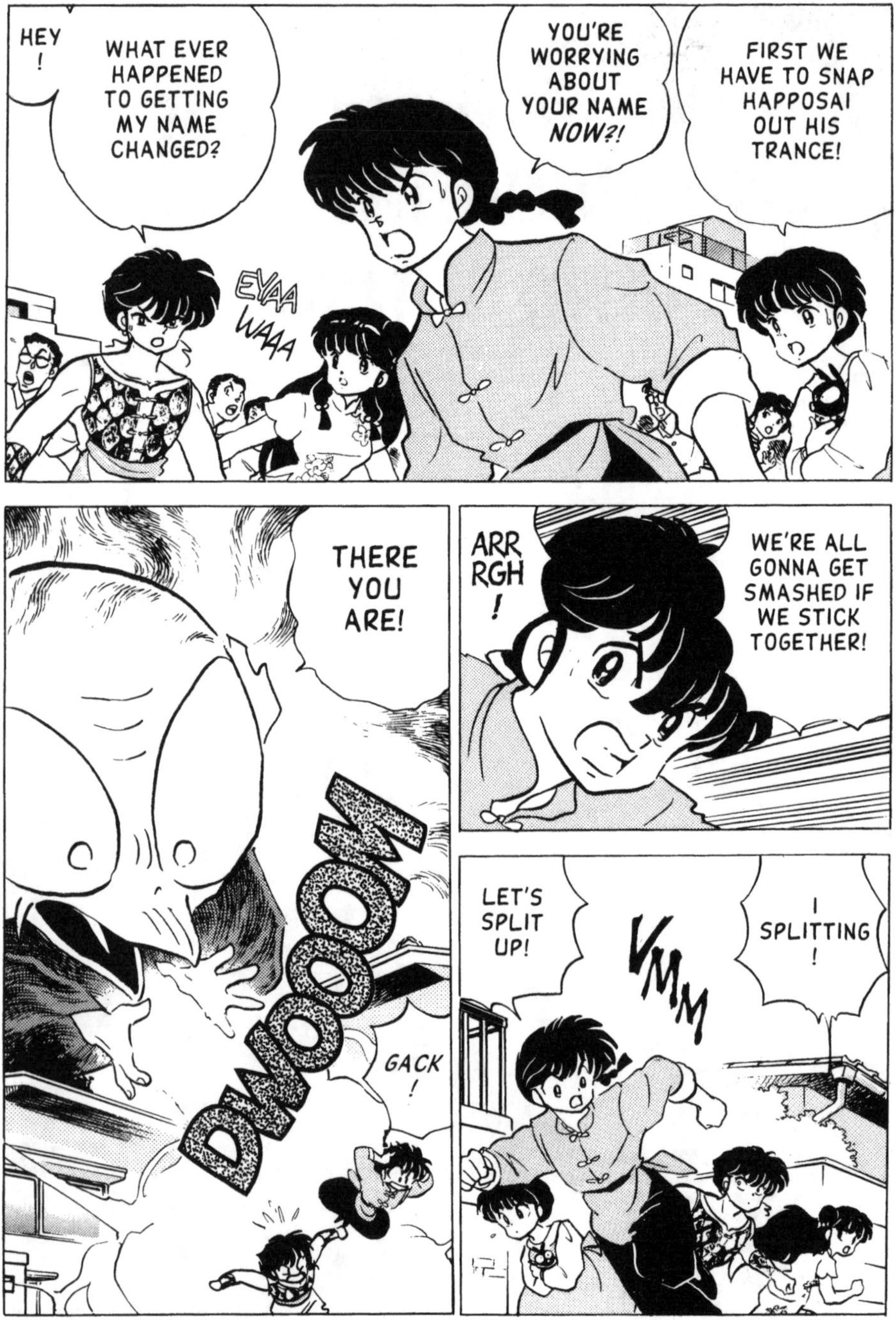
HEY!
WHAT EVER HAPPENED TO GETTING MY NAME CHANGED?
EYAA WAAA
YOU'RE WORRYING ABOUT YOUR NAME *NOW?!*
FIRST WE HAVE TO SNAP HAPPOSAI OUT HIS TRANCE!
THERE YOU ARE!
DWOOOM
GACK!
ARR RGH!
WE'RE ALL GONNA GET SMASHED IF WE STICK TOGETHER!
LET'S SPLIT UP!
VMM
I SPLITTING!

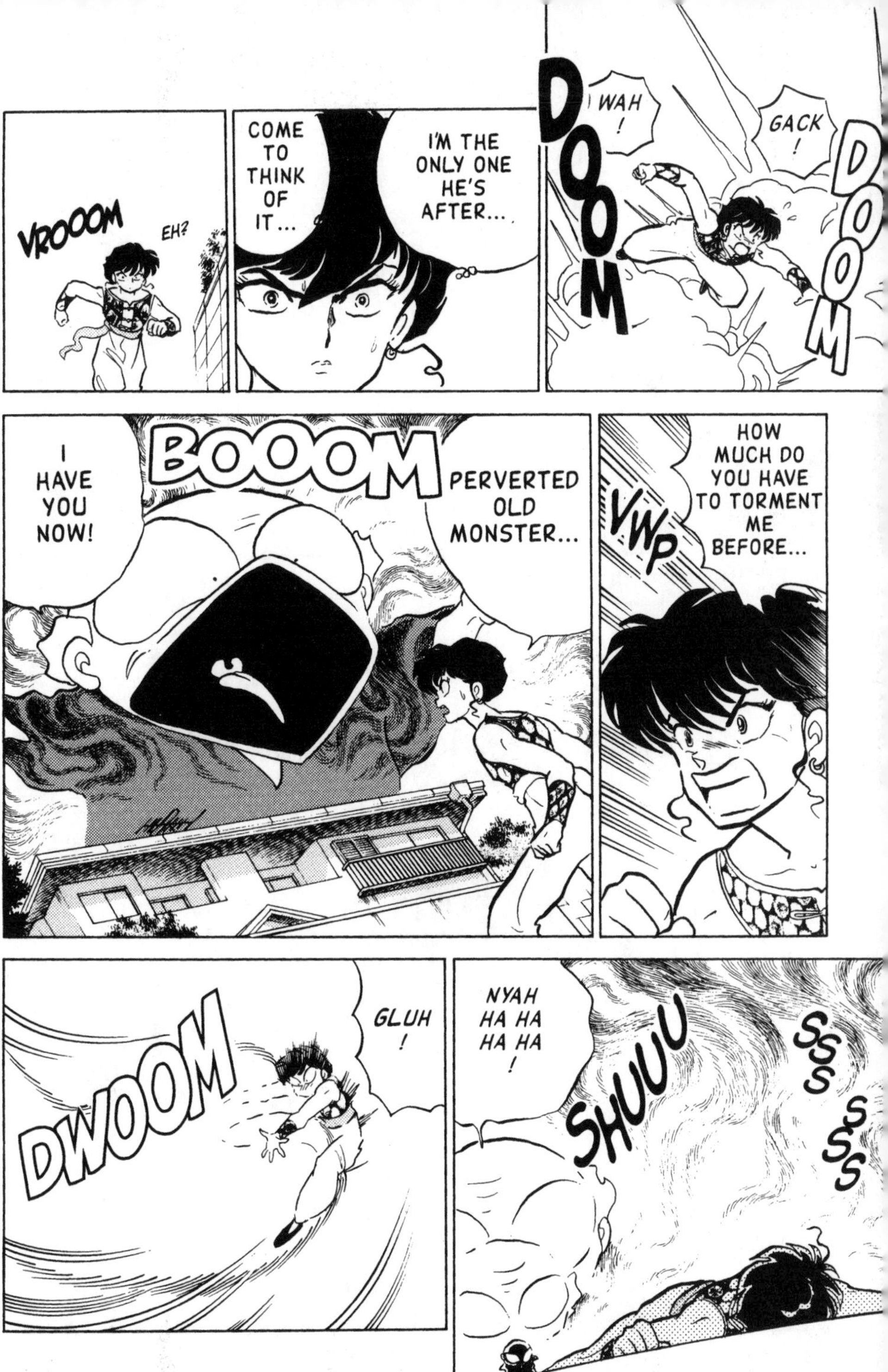
VROOOM
EH?
COME TO THINK OF IT...
I'M THE ONLY ONE HE'S AFTER...
DOOM
WAH!
GACK!
DOOM
I HAVE YOU NOW!
BOOOM
PERVERTED OLD MONSTER...
VWP
HOW MUCH DO YOU HAVE TO TORMENT ME BEFORE...
DWOOM
GLUH!
NYAH HA HA HA HA!
SHUUU
SSS
SSS

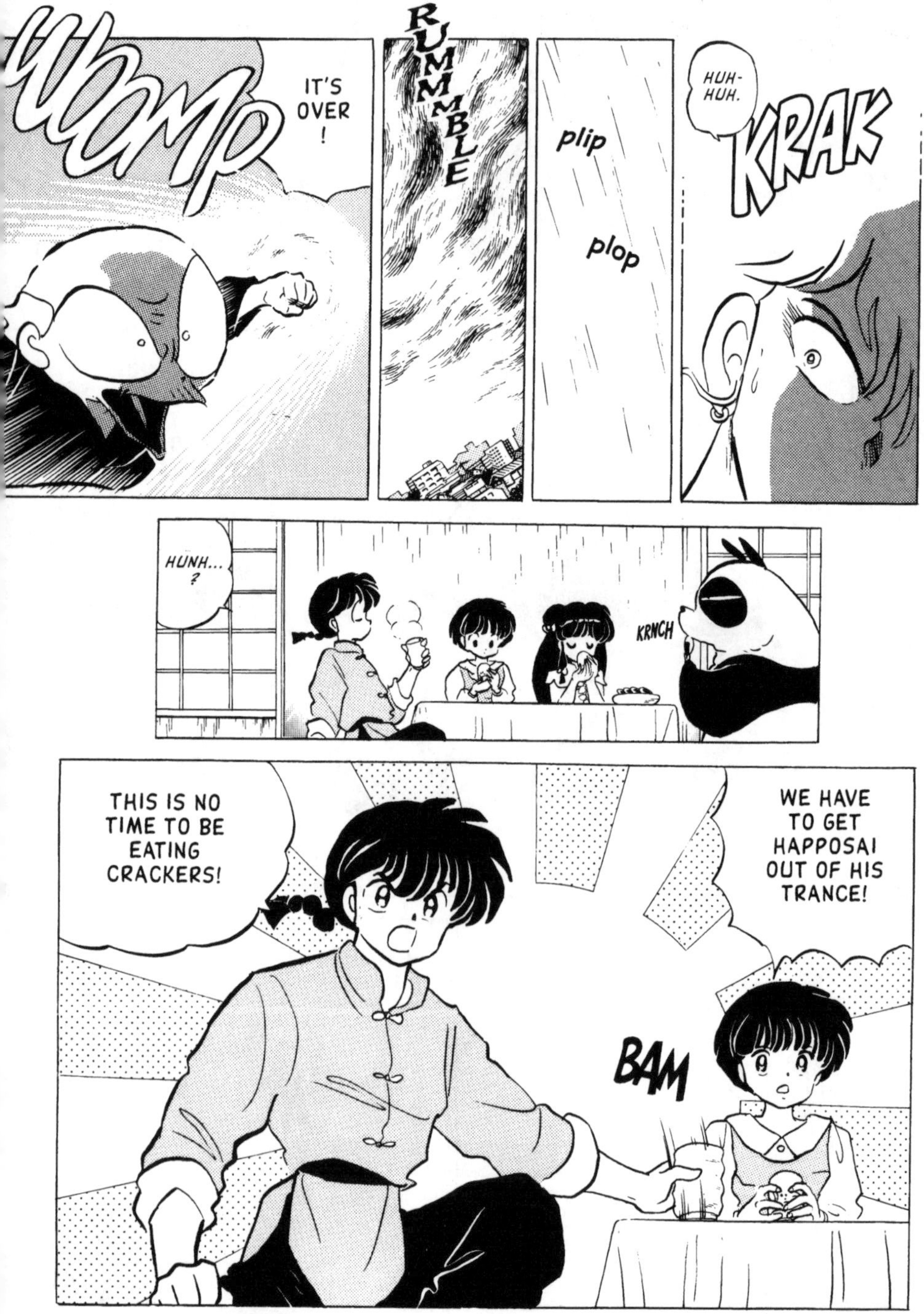

WOMP
IT'S OVER !
RUMMMBLE
plip
plop
HUH-HUH.
KRAK
HUNH... ?
KRNCH
THIS IS NO TIME TO BE EATING CRACKERS!
WE HAVE TO GET HAPPOSAI OUT OF HIS TRANCE!
BAM

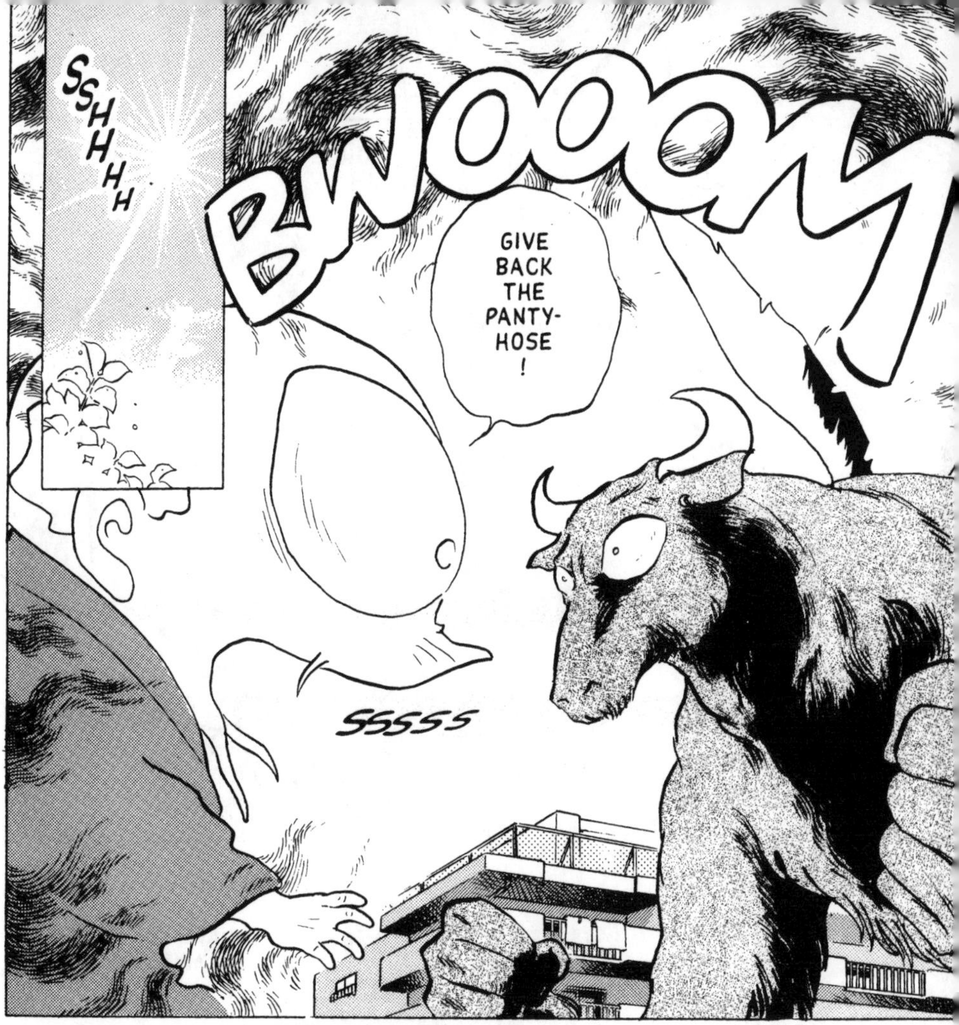
SSHHHH
BWOOOM
GIVE BACK THE PANTY-HOSE!
SSSSS
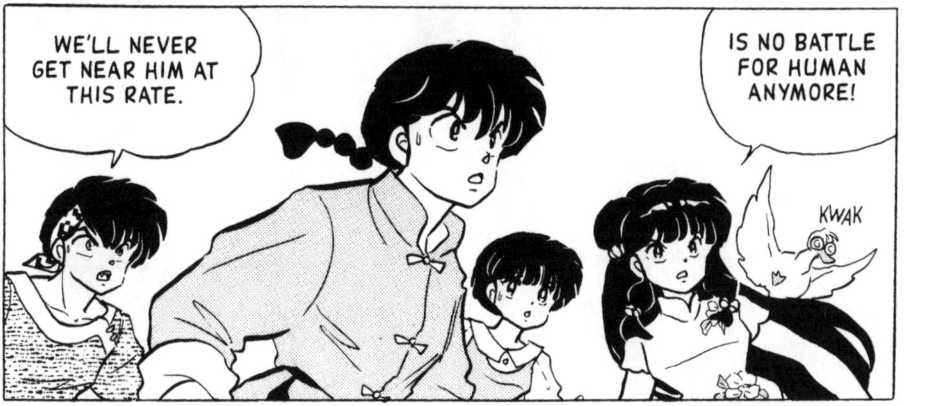
WE'LL NEVER GET NEAR HIM AT THIS RATE.
IS NO BATTLE FOR HUMAN ANYMORE!
KWAK

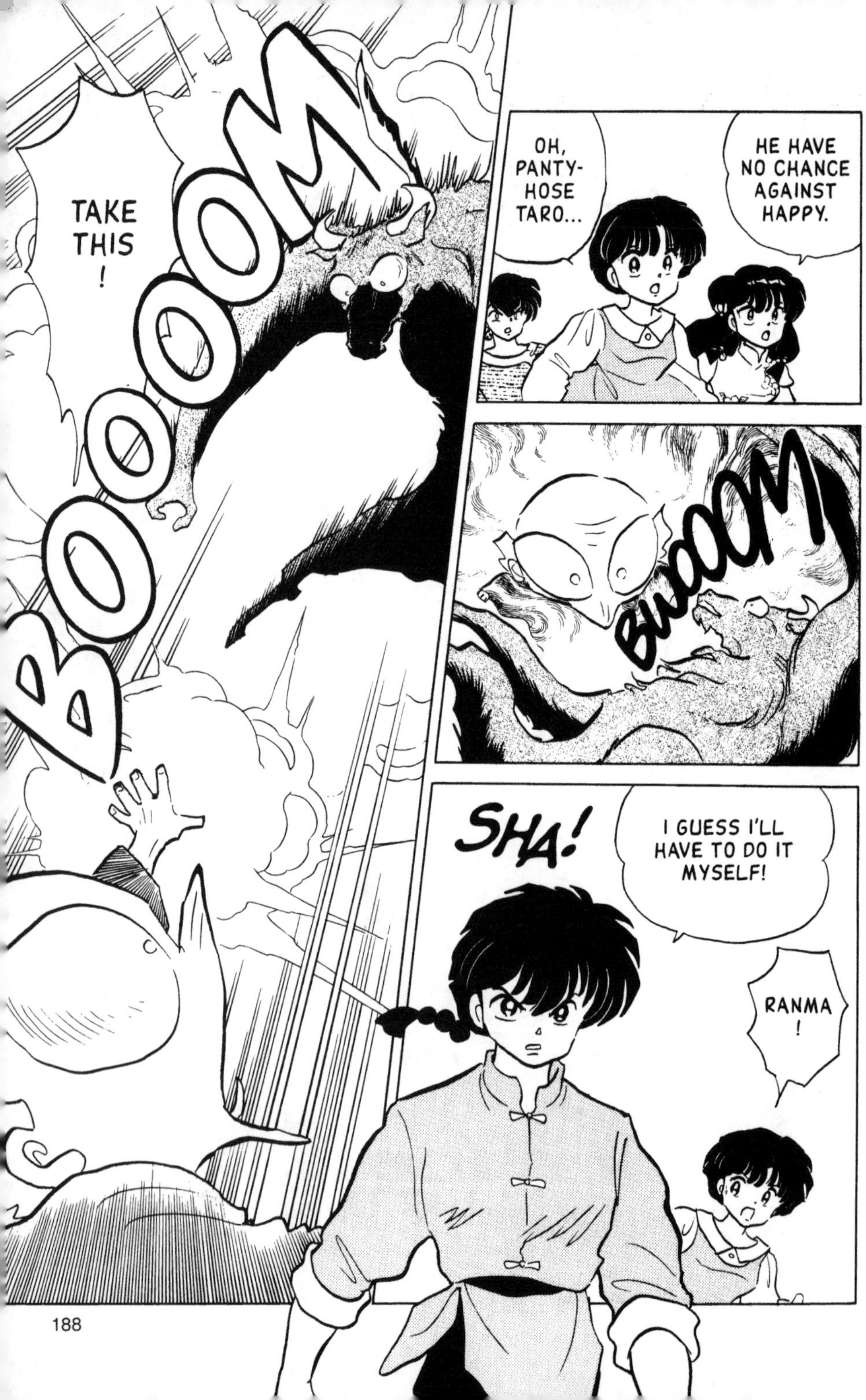
TAKE THIS !
BOOOOOOM
OH, PANTY-HOSE TARO...
HE HAVE NO CHANCE AGAINST HAPPY.
BUOOOM
SHA!
I GUESS I'LL HAVE TO DO IT MYSELF!
RANMA !

HERE
I COME,
OLD
FREAK!

SHHHHH

VM

HERE.

FzZz

SHUUU

PANTY-
HOSE!

GWONNNG

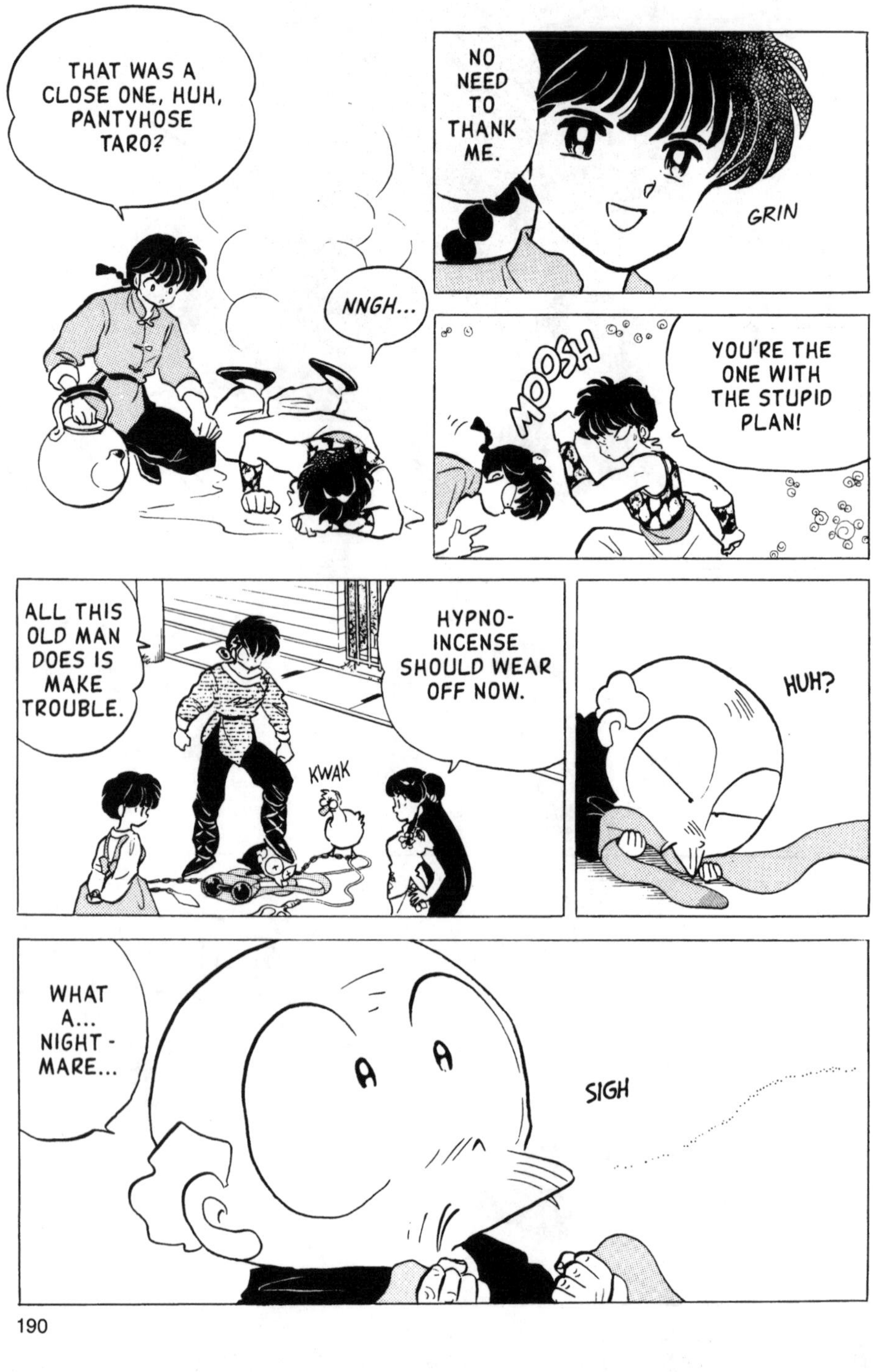

THAT WAS A CLOSE ONE, HUH, PANTYHOSE TARO?
NNGH...
NO NEED TO THANK ME.
GRIN
MOOSH
YOU'RE THE ONE WITH THE STUPID PLAN!
ALL THIS OLD MAN DOES IS MAKE TROUBLE.
KWAK
HYPNO-INCENSE SHOULD WEAR OFF NOW.
HUH?
WHAT A... NIGHT-MARE...
SIGH

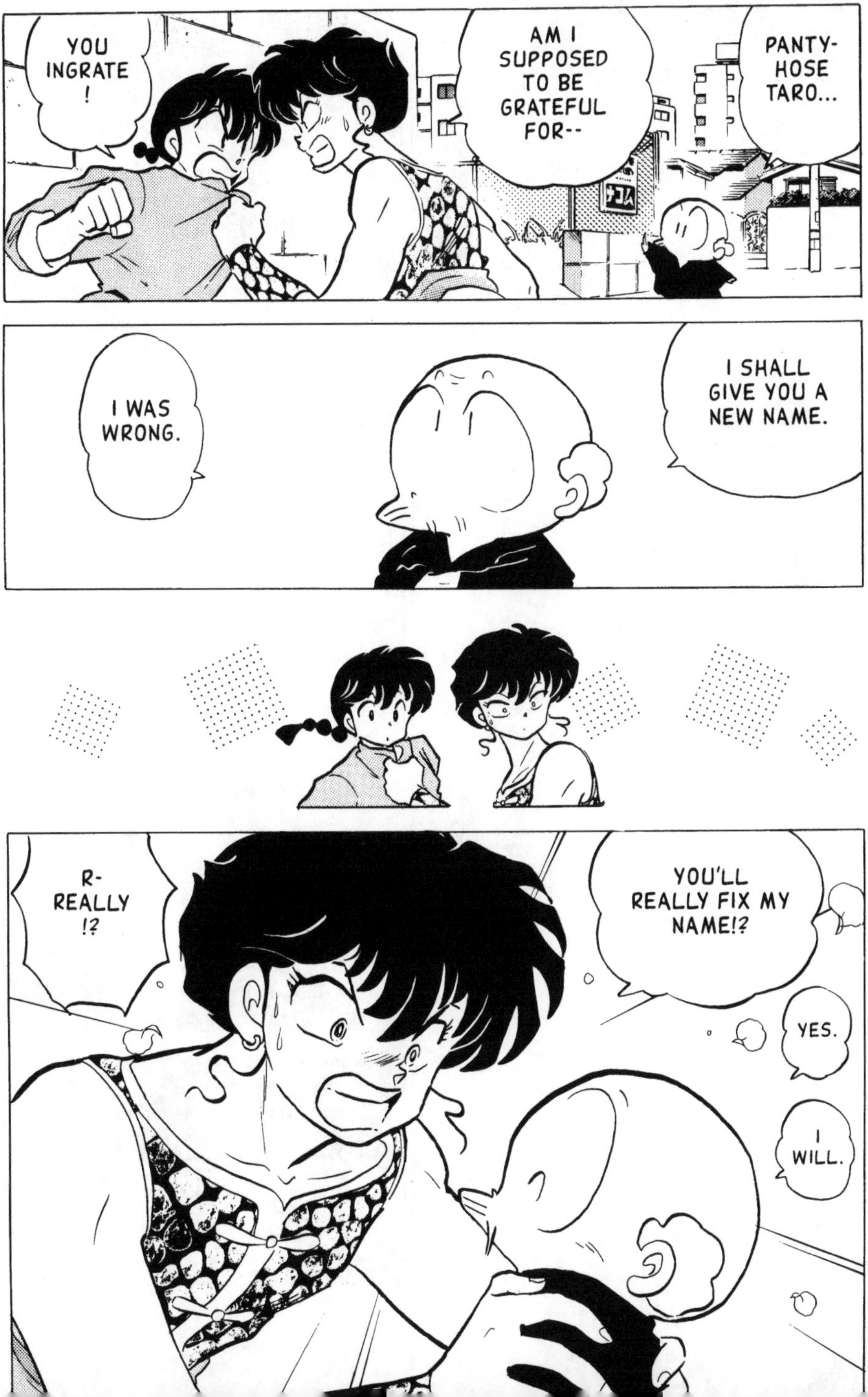
YOU INGRATE !
AM I SUPPOSED TO BE GRATEFUL FOR--
PANTY-HOSE TARO...
I WAS WRONG.
I SHALL GIVE YOU A NEW NAME.
R-REALLY !?
YOU'LL REALLY FIX MY NAME!?
YES.
I WILL.

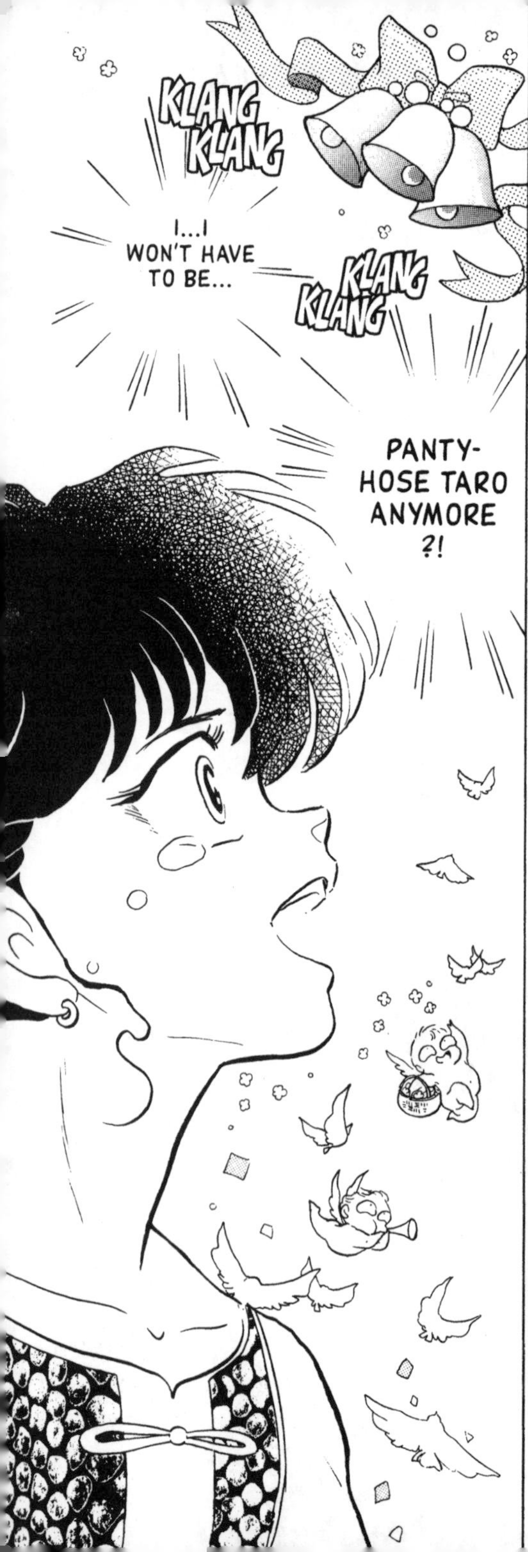
KLANG KLANG
I...I WON'T HAVE TO BE...
KLANG KLANG
PANTY-HOSE TARO ANYMORE ?!

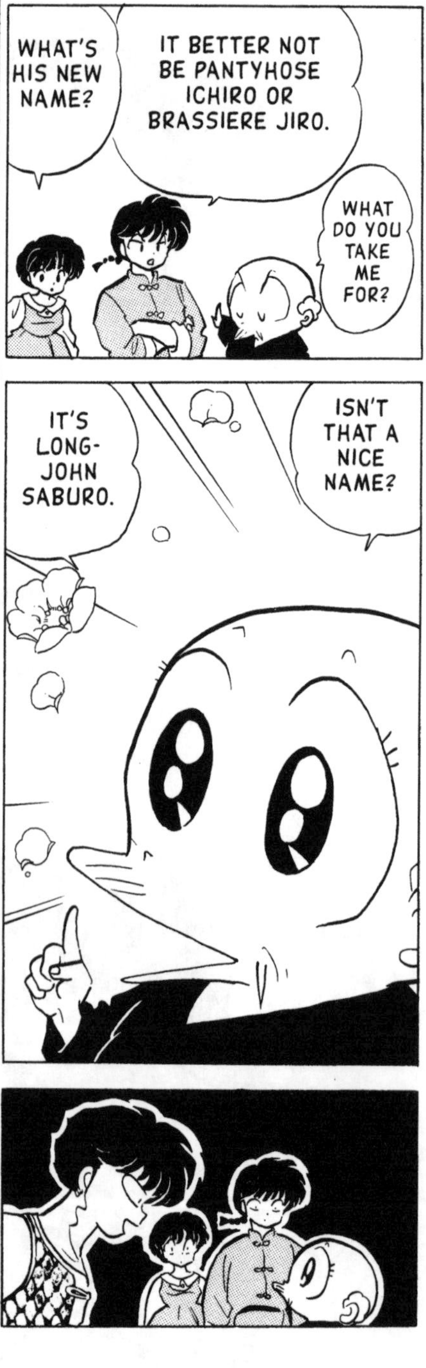
WHAT'S HIS NEW NAME?
IT BETTER NOT BE PANTYHOSE ICHIRO OR BRASSIERE JIRO.
WHAT DO YOU TAKE ME FOR?
IT'S LONG-JOHN SABURO.
ISN'T THAT A NICE NAME?

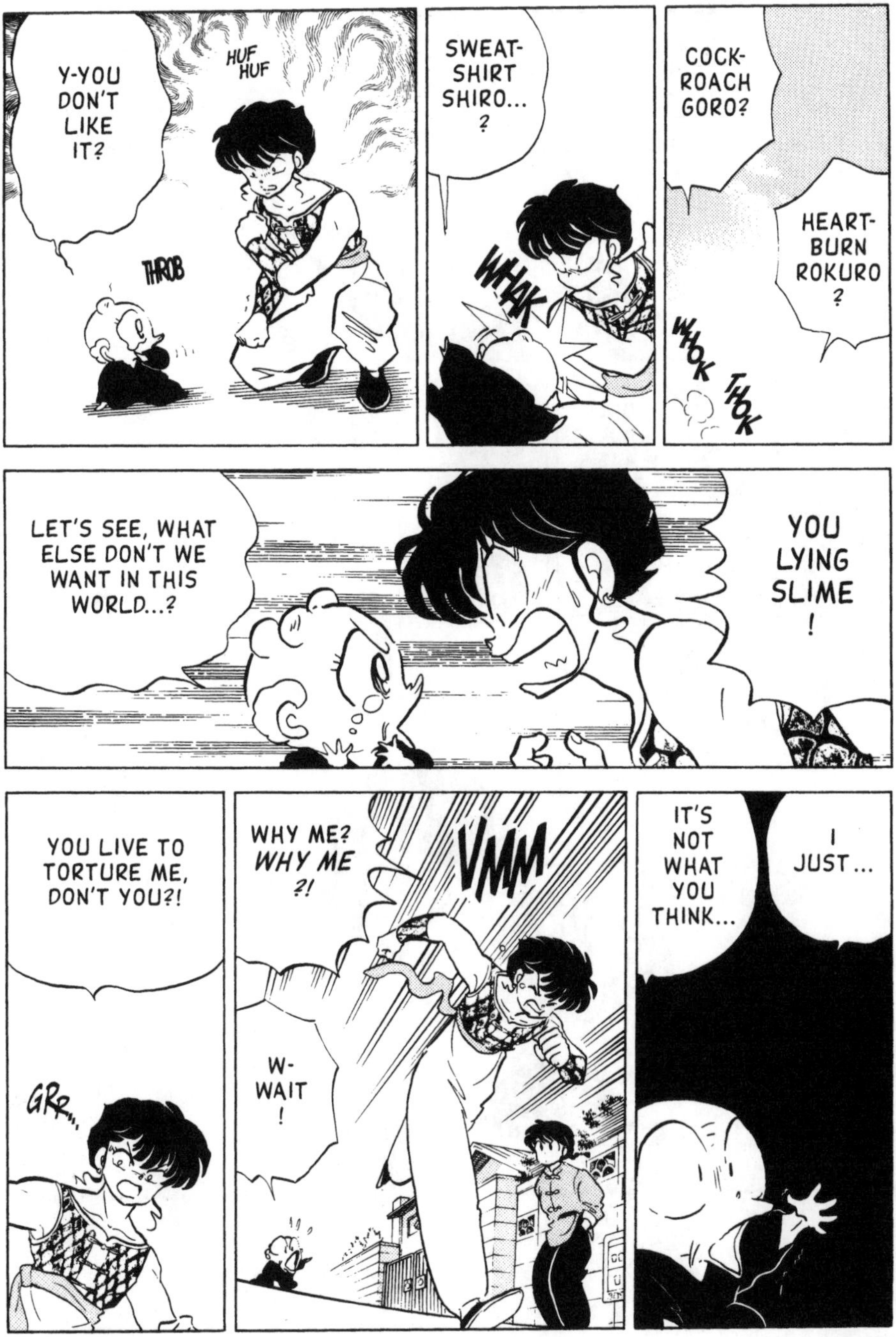
Y-YOU DON'T LIKE IT?
HUF HUF
THROB
SWEAT-SHIRT SHIRO...?
WHAK
COCK-ROACH GORO?
HEART-BURN ROKURO?
WHOK THOK
LET'S SEE, WHAT ELSE DON'T WE WANT IN THIS WORLD...?
YOU LYING SLIME!
YOU LIVE TO TORTURE ME, DON'T YOU?!
GRR...
WHY ME? *WHY ME* ?!
VMM
W-WAIT!
IT'S NOT WHAT YOU THINK...
I JUST...

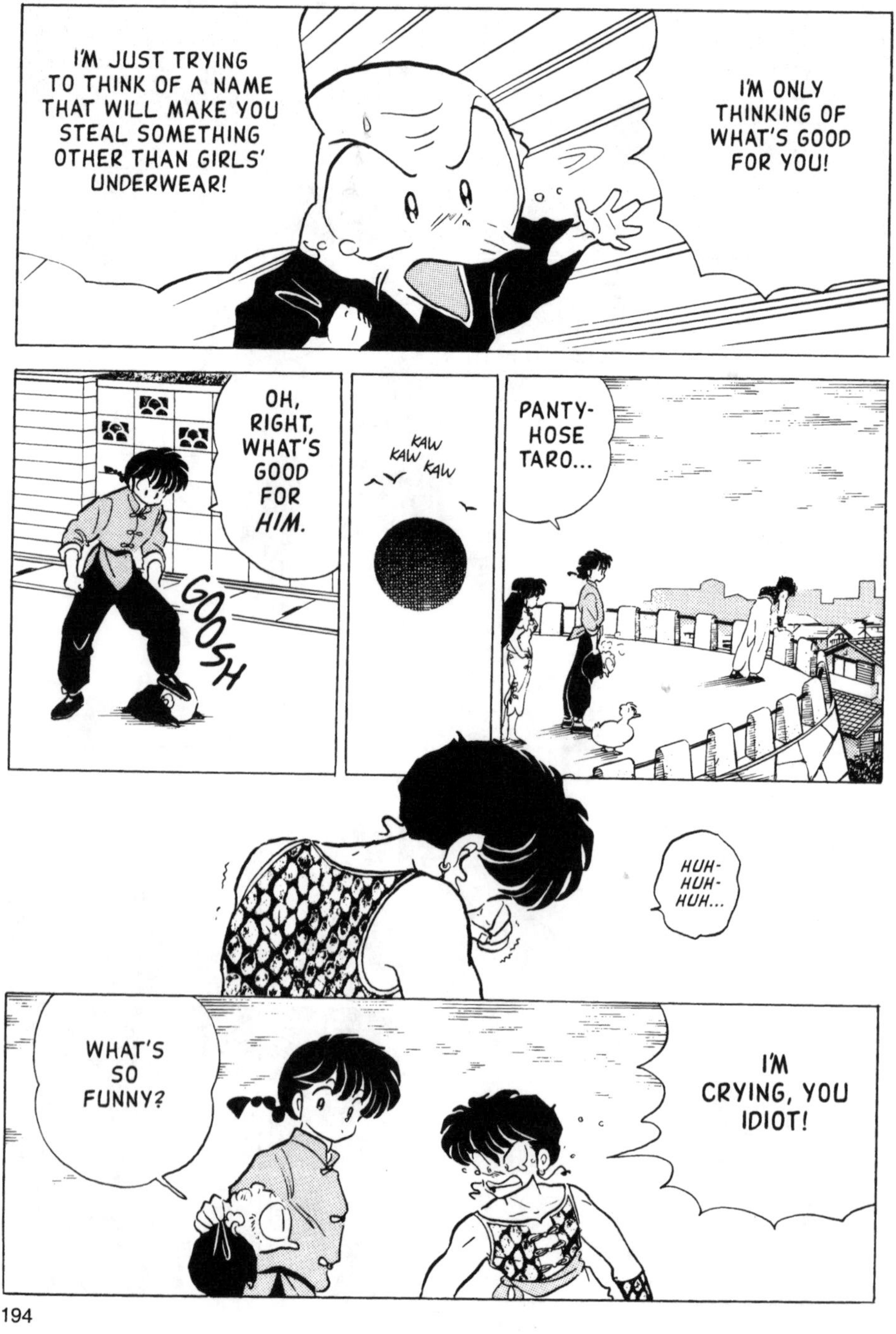
I'M JUST TRYING TO THINK OF A NAME THAT WILL MAKE YOU STEAL SOMETHING OTHER THAN GIRLS' UNDERWEAR!
I'M ONLY THINKING OF WHAT'S GOOD FOR YOU!
OH, RIGHT, WHAT'S GOOD FOR HIM.
GOOSH
KAW KAW KAW
PANTY-HOSE TARO...
HUH-HUH-HUH...
WHAT'S SO FUNNY?
I'M CRYING, YOU IDIOT!

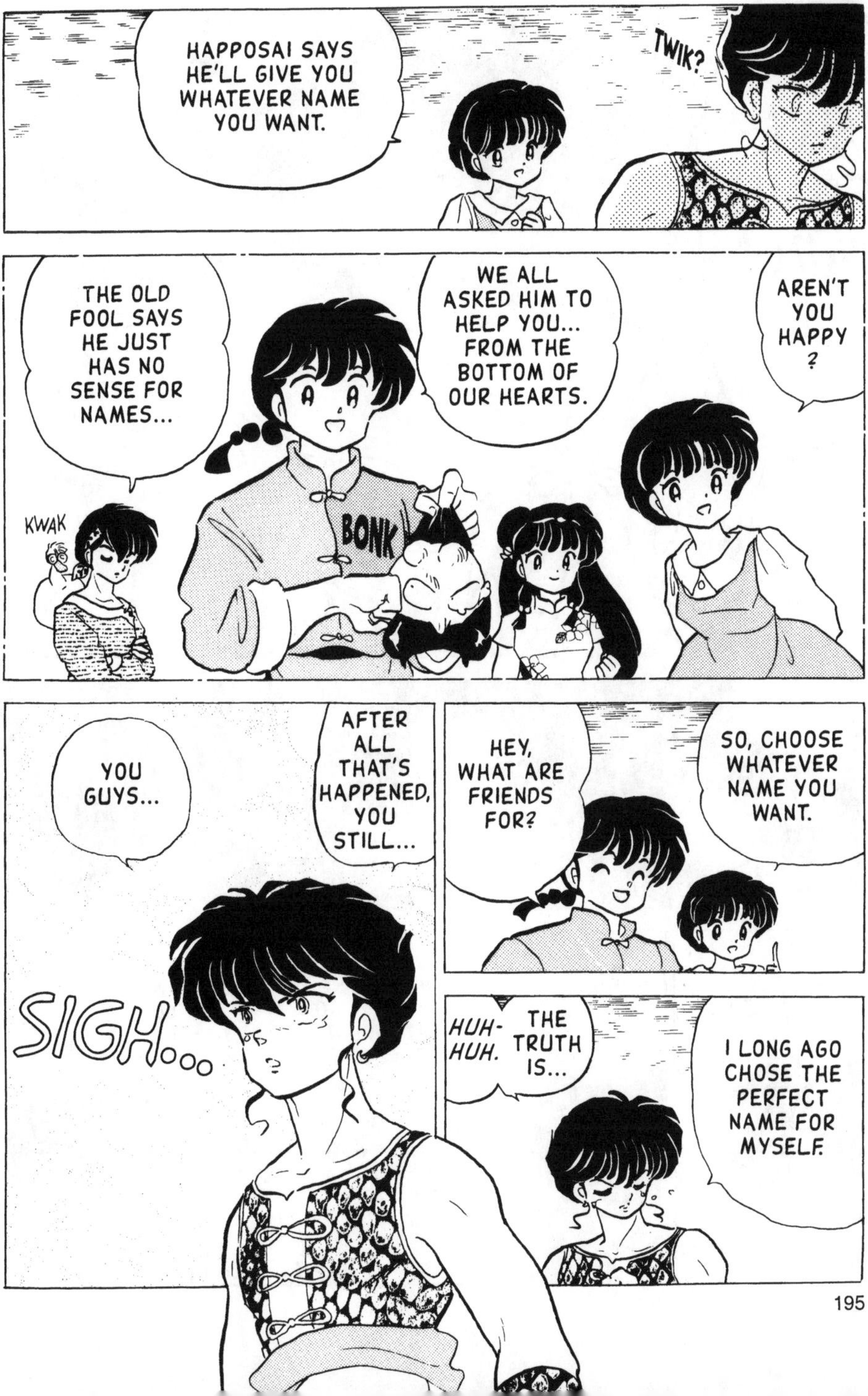
HAPPOSAI SAYS HE'LL GIVE YOU WHATEVER NAME YOU WANT.
TWIK?
THE OLD FOOL SAYS HE JUST HAS NO SENSE FOR NAMES...
KWAK
BONK
WE ALL ASKED HIM TO HELP YOU... FROM THE BOTTOM OF OUR HEARTS.
AREN'T YOU HAPPY?
YOU GUYS...
AFTER ALL THAT'S HAPPENED, YOU STILL...
SIGH...
HEY, WHAT ARE FRIENDS FOR?
SO, CHOOSE WHATEVER NAME YOU WANT.
HUH-HUH.
THE TRUTH IS...
I LONG AGO CHOSE THE PERFECT NAME FOR MYSELF.

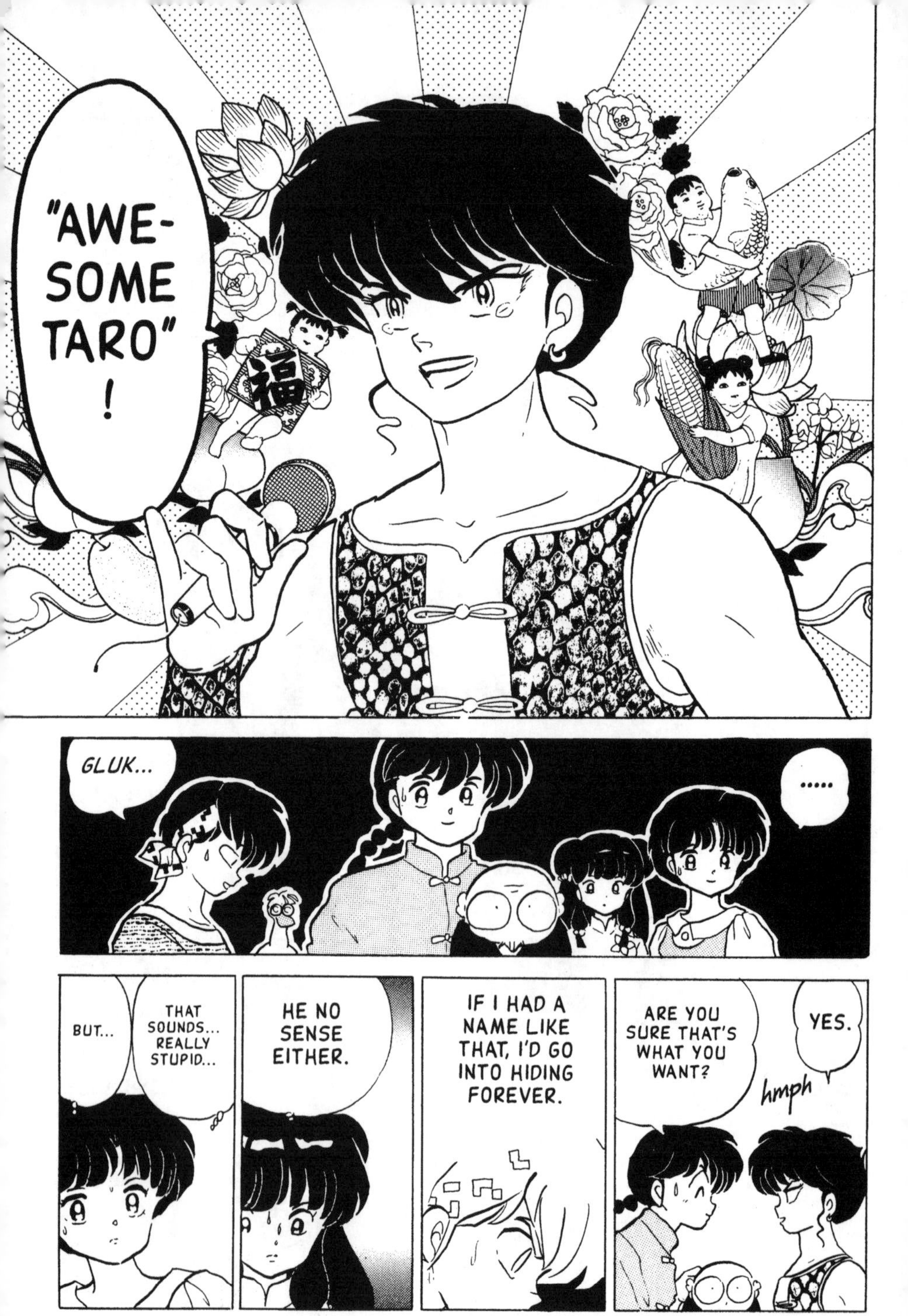
"AWE-SOME TARO"!
GLUK...
......
BUT...
THAT SOUNDS... REALLY STUPID...
HE NO SENSE EITHER.
IF I HAD A NAME LIKE THAT, I'D GO INTO HIDING FOREVER.
ARE YOU SURE THAT'S WHAT YOU WANT?
YES.
hmph

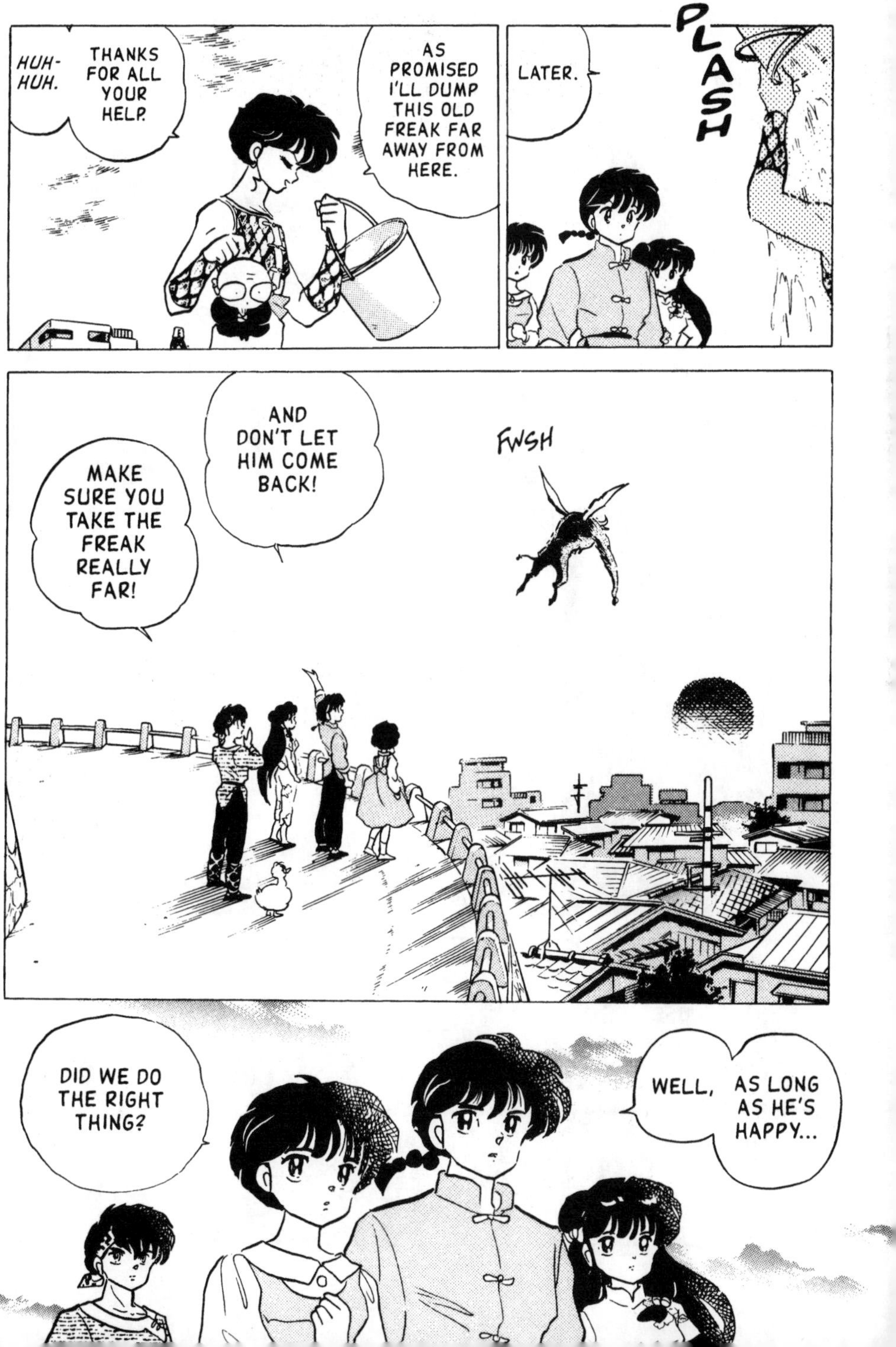
HUH-HUH.
THANKS FOR ALL YOUR HELP.
AS PROMISED I'LL DUMP THIS OLD FREAK FAR AWAY FROM HERE.
LATER.
PLASH
MAKE SURE YOU TAKE THE FREAK REALLY FAR!
AND DON'T LET HIM COME BACK!
FWSH
DID WE DO THE RIGHT THING?
WELL, AS LONG AS HE'S HAPPY...

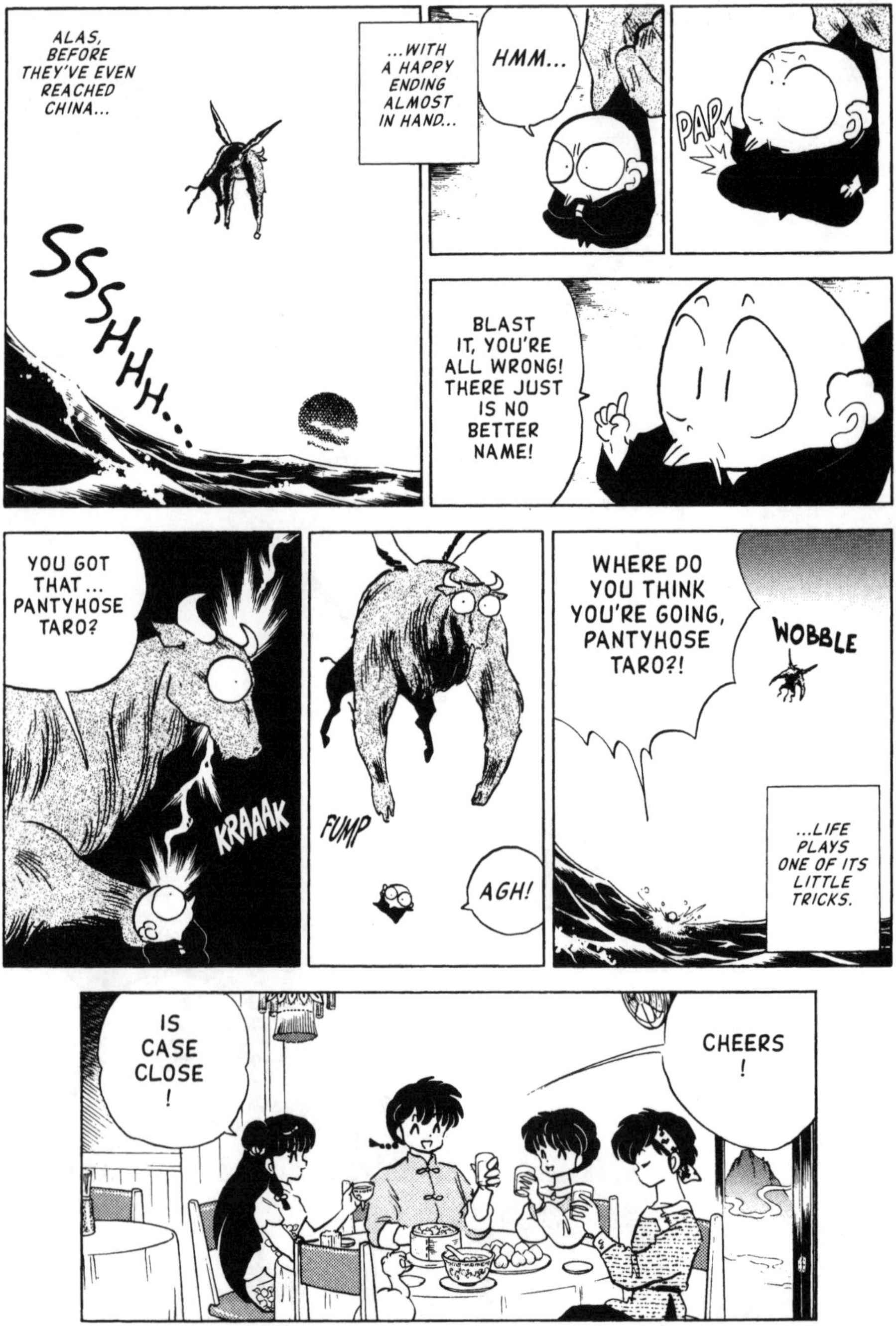
ALAS, BEFORE THEY'VE EVEN REACHED CHINA...
SSSHHH...
...WITH A HAPPY ENDING ALMOST IN HAND...
HMM...
PAP
BLAST IT, YOU'RE ALL WRONG! THERE JUST IS NO BETTER NAME!
YOU GOT THAT... PANTYHOSE TARO?
KRAAAK
FUMP
AGH!
WHERE DO YOU THINK YOU'RE GOING, PANTYHOSE TARO?!
WOBBLE
...LIFE PLAYS ONE OF ITS LITTLE TRICKS.
IS CASE CLOSE !
CHEERS !